The Arizona Saga

NATIVE BORN

NATIVE BORN

J.P.S. Brown

A Double D Western
DOUBLEDAY
New York London Toronto Sydney Auckland

A Double D Western
PUBLISHED BY DOUBLEDAY
a division of Bantam Doubleday Dell Publishing Group, Inc.
1540 Broadway, New York, New York 10036

Double D Western, Doubleday,
and the portrayal of the letters DD
are trademarks of Doubleday, a division of
Bantam Doubleday Dell Publishing Group, Inc.

Library of Congress Cataloging-in-Publication Data

Brown, J. P. S.
    Native born/J.P.S. Brown.—1st ed.
        p.   cm.— (A Double D western)
    I. Title
PS3552 .R6856 N38   1993
813'.54—dc20   92-43614
CIP

ISBN 0-385-47038-X
Copyright © 1993 by J.P.S. Brown
All Rights Reserved
Printed in the United States of America
August 1993
First Edition

10   9   8   7   6   5   4   3   2   1

For my cousin Emily Parker Gray,
estimada maestra of young Arizonans

NATIVE BORN

One

ON NEW YEAR'S MORNING, 1886, Les Cowden went to shave off his whiskers for his brother's wedding and for the first time noticed his cauliflower ear. His face had healed since a fist fight with Jack Odoms before Christmas, but it sure was changed.

He had not looked at his ear while it was puffed up and healing. He only dabbed it with wet cloths to keep it clean. Now he examined his face to see if it looked good for the fiesta of his brother Ben's wedding, and it looked awful.

His left ear was a lump. After the fight it had swelled three times its normal size and stayed sore. His right ear had been pummeled as much as the left, but it split open and bled, so it was scarred, but not lumpy. His left eyebrow was parted by a red scar and it drooped so much he could see it. He realized he'd waited too long to have it sewn back together.

The sight of his cauliflower ear made him feel bad, so he did not look at it again. He was sad, anyway, because his brother Ben's marriage to Maudy Jane Pendleton was about to happen. An awful sense of doom had settled on him during the past week's preparation for the wedding.

He dressed in his best three-piece suit, took a large swallow of mescal from the jug he kept under his bed, and went out to the front room where the ceremony would be held. Ben and Maudy were already standing by the fireplace with Judge Dunn. Every single person who could fit in the room had squeezed in and seemed happy about it. Everybody was talking, but the atmosphere was subdued and wary. After all, the Cowdens were still in a range war and people were being killed.

Les made his way along the wall to a corner and stood so his cauliflower ear would not be noticed. He could not see why anybody should be happy about this wedding. The Cowden family's captain was about to head out on a honeymoon. Every friendly neighbor of the Cowdens was present and one stick of dynamite tossed in the middle of this room would finish the war once and for all. Duncan Vincent, owner of the VO ranch on the San Rafael Valley and representative of an eastern syndicate that was trying to eliminate the Cowden family, was the only cattleman of the region who was not there.

Les figured the Cowdens must be the most forgiving people in Arizona. He counted several people at the wedding who should not have been allowed to cross the battle line to accept the Cowden hospitality.

1

Doris Vincent was in attendance. She was Duncan Vincent's wife. State Senator Royal Vincent was there, and he was Duncan's brother and as much an enemy as Duncan. Doris was always welcome at El Durazno, the Cowden ranch, and would have been missed at the wedding, but Les wondered why she could not have found somebody better than Royal to drive her there.

The Campana brothers and Billy Stiles were standing out under a walnut tree in the front yard drinking whiskey out of ceramic cups. Antonio Campana had been in on three attempts by Duncan Vincent's hoodlums to shoot the Cowden brothers. The other brother, Ernesto, had just been released from prison. The Campanas had come to the wedding with their three sisters, who were friends of the Cowden brothers.

The Campana sisters ran a *casa de cita*, a bawdy boarding house in Santa Cruz, Sonora, where they entertained guests from both sides of the war. They had been friends of the Cowden brothers since childhood.

After a recent fight in the Nogales, Sonora, cowpens, Ben, Les, and Mark Cowden had left Billy Stiles, Antonio Campana, and a cowboy named Smiley for dead. Stiles and Campana, badly wounded, played possum and survived, but Les had shot Smiley dead after he raised up and shot Ben in the back. A week ago Stiles had shown up at Uncle Vince Farley's saloon while Ben and his brothers were enjoying Christmas drinks and apologized for having fought for Vincent. Ben forgave him on the spot and invited him to his wedding.

Les thought that was carrying hospitality too far and allowing Royal Vincent in their house could be insurance against the VO blowing it up, or it could be a careless mistake. He did not know how insane Royal really was, but he dressed in an awfully eccentric manner and people who knew him liked to tell stories about his craziness. What if he just decided to pull a gun and shoot Ben in front of his new wife and wedding guests? The VO paid desperate characters money to shoot at the Cowdens, so crazy Royal certainly had reason enough to do it.

Les, the warrior, was miserable. He felt silly that he was expected to put on his best suit, tight collar, and new boots and act happy that Ben was going on a honeymoon. Not even Mark was thinking straight. Mark was the youngest of the three brothers, the only other person at the wedding Les could count on for help in a fight, and was acting as smiley sweet and careless as a preacher at a ladies' garden party.

The ceremony began and Mark stood up front as Ben's best man. Proud as he acted, he might as well have been the one getting married. Ben had asked Les to be his best man, but Les had gone off on a high lonesome a few days before the wedding. That meant he'd corraled himself with a lady friend and a jug and could not be counted on as a best man. He'd known his responsibility, was aware of it all during the binge, had come in with plenty of time to spare, but his family had worried he would not show and had given the honor to Mark. Well, Mark ought to be best man. He wanted Ben to be married.

Les would not have minded for Ben and Maudy to be married someday, but not while the Cowdens were in a fight. He did not want his family to be snuck up on and eliminated while their captain was marrying, or off honeymooning. His sisters, Eileen, Betty, and Paula Mary, were standing up front with their faces rapt and happy. When Ben and Maudy kissed at the end of the ceremony, the sisters held their breath and puckered their lips as though they were the ones getting kissed. Well, it was done and Ben would soon be gone.

While the people dispersed to the other rooms, the porches, and the yard outside, Les went back to his bedroom and took another shot of mescal. Mark came in and Les handed him the jug. "I better not," Mark said. "I'm fixing to drink a lot of that French champagne and it might not mix good."

"Chase this with that," Les said and pressed the jug on his brother. "Good mescal mixes good with everything."

"All right." Mark lifted the jug, sipped the hard stuff, and rinsed his mouth with it before he swallowed it, then took another swallow.

"I never could figure how you do that," Les said.

"Come on, brother," Mark said. "There's ladies and music out there waiting for us."

Les followed Mark to the front room where the Cowden sisters were pouring champagne. Mrs. Hopkins, who was said to have been a spy for the Confederacy in her young girlhood, came in with two of the Soto brothers carrying bushel baskets full of fried chicken. Joe Coyle, the Cowdens' blacksmith, was outside unearthing a whole beef that had cooked in the ground on mesquite coals.

A.B., their father, offered Les and Mark an open box of cigars. When they only took one apiece, he stuffed their shirt pockets with more. The color was high on his cheeks and his blue eyes shone. His mustache bristled with good humor. "Come with me, sons," he said, and he led them to a twenty-gallon barrel of his J. P. S. Brown Tennessee bourbon whiskey on the back porch with the lid off. A dipper hung on the brim. A.B. handed his sons ceramic cups. Les looked inside his empty cup and A.B. pulled it over the top of the barrel and filled it with whiskey. A.B. seldom invited these two sons to drink whiskey with him. Ben was the one who most shared his thoughts, cigars, and whiskey.

A.B. filled Mark's cup, filled one for himself, and held it up in salute. "Sons, this marriage brings us a new treasure, and it's the nicest addition to this family since your little dead brother Freddie Lee was born. To Maudy Jane Cowden."

The boys drank to Maudy. They loved the girl as much as they loved their sisters. Freddie Lee had been dragged to death by a burro a few

3

months before. Life at El Durazno had been sad and full of violence for the past year. A.B. had always been high on Maudy Jane, so it was no wonder he felt good that day.

"Now, boys, you know where the whiskey is. This day it's yours to drink, as it is for all our guests. I don't want to see any whiskey in the bottom of this barrel when everyone goes home." He pointed to three more barrels under the table. "When you've emptied this one, open another." He patted his sons on their shoulders and went inside.

Les looked down into the amber depths of the spirits. "I didn't feel so good about this wedding until now," he said. "To hell with my caulifower ear."

"What cauliflower ear?" Mark asked.

Les turned so his brother could see the lump on the side of his head.

"By God, I hadn't noticed. You look like the great Paddy Ryan. By gosh, brother, it's a great and handsome flowering you've sprouted there."

"Yeah, it looks like hell, don't it?"

"No, it looks good. Come on, now. My girlfriend Garbie wants you to dance with her."

The front room was cleared for dancing and an orchestra of seven mariachis were tuning their instruments. Les felt his drinks now and his humor changed. His breast was full of good spirit. Big muscles glowed inside his three-piece suit. He stopped being critical of himself. He noticed his brother Mark's hair was trimmed above the collar showing a strip of untanned neck. Mark's brow was rosy clear above the tan of his face. The lower half of his face was sunburned reddish brown below the eyes. Mark was a bull. His neck was thick as Les's and Les was twenty and Mark would not be eighteen until March. Ben had turned twenty-two in August. The Cowden brothers were grownups now and they all looked elegant except Les, but he didn't care much now that his father had given him whiskey.

Les was still growing. His big hands hung down on the ends of his long arms showing three inches of thick, bare wrist outside his coat sleeves. He was not awkward, he was just growing big. What the hell, now was no time to lose his spirit. He might as well take hold of the celebration, have a good time, and leave the worrying to the ladies and the old fellers.

Garbie Burr was pretty and blonde. Her smile showed great heart. She and her sister had come to Arizona as mail-order brides, found their suitors too strange to marry, rejected them, and stayed anyway.

Garbie's sister had been murdered in the war and Garbie would probably be the next one to join the Cowden family, because she and Mark were best friends. She would be a definite reinforcement. Upon declaring war, Ben Cowden and Duncan Vincent agreed that the women would not be excluded. Ben had meant that Vincent could

4

always expect animosity from the Cowden women, but the Cowdens had respected Vincent's women. Vincent had not respected the women on the Cowden side. Ten days ago Margarita Elias had been shot and killed by Duncan Vincent's regulator, Jack Odoms. Margarita and her father, Don Juan Pedro Elias, were members of the Cowden faction and she and Ben had been the best of friends. Gabriel Kosterlinsky, the chief of the Mexican Rural Police, took Odoms away to jail and since then he had not been seen.

Les went over to dance with Garbie. She was pretty, bright, and shapely. Garbie was shiny. Her eyes were green as jade and she was almost as tall as Mark. Her bosom was full and her waist was tiny. Her grip was sure when she shook Les's hand and she did not look at his cauliflower ear or droopy brow.

Mariachi musicians from Santa Cruz in Sonora began playing *"Dos Arbolitos,"* the song about the two little trees who lived their lives side by side with their roots and branches entwined. Ben and Maudy walked out to dance. Les and Garbie danced on the polished oak floor. Garbie did not dance very well, but she was not self-conscious about it and she talked to him in a soft, husky voice. Les did not listen to a word she said, but the sound and touch of her with music made him happy.

When they finished dancing the set, Garbie said, "Do you drink a lot, or are you just drinking because your brother got married?"

"I don't drink much, why?"

"I just wondered. It's a sin to drink too much, isn't it?"

"It's not against *my* religion."

"Will you do me a favor and arrange it so I can talk to your father before Mark comes back?"

"Sure. Don't you want to dance anymore?"

"As you can plainly see, Les Cowden, I'm not much of a dancer, but I'll dance with you again if you'll ask your father to give me a few minutes while Mark isn't looking. I don't want Mark to butt in."

Les led the girl across the floor to A.B. and Viney. Viney was Les's mother, a tiny woman with jet-black hair and blue eyes that could light a fire or lay a frost. Mark and Garbie had been keeping company for several months and Viney liked the girl.

"Mr. Cowden," Garbie said. "I want to stop the traffic of Chinese singsong girls who are being smuggled into Arizona."

"Well, young lady, that's commendable," A.B. said.

My Lord, Les thought. Garbie's turned out to be a damned do-gooder. He did not leave her side, though.

"Mr. Cowden, I know this is not a good time to talk about it, but I need to talk to you now. Can I just have a few minutes with you and Mrs. Cowden?"

A.B. said, "Of course."

Viney said, "Young lady, you just come with us." She wheeled A.B.

5

about and headed out the door. Les followed with Garbie. Viney led them out to a cold corner of the Arizona room where she did her sewing in the summer. A.B. opened the screen door and threw out his cigar. Les stayed by the door.

"My father, Terence Burr, was a doctor missionary and spent fifteen years in China when he was young. I happen to know that little girls are being sold in China and brought here and resold, sometimes three or four times, the same as livestock. You know I work for Frank Wong in his restaurant. There's a little girl there who was brought here illegally. She's lucky she landed with Frank."

"How can we help, young lady?" Viney said.

"A certain Mr. Lee comes often to Harshaw to meet with Royal Vincent. I think he is responsible for trafficking Chinese singsong girls through this part of the territory. I thought Sheriff Cowden should do something about it."

"Is Frank working with that man?" A.B. asked.

"I don't think so. Frank has little to do with him."

"Frank's a good man. I've already talked to him about this. He contracted to have the girl brought here, but he has nothing to do with the smuggling."

"What can be done? May, the girl at Frank's, said twenty other girls were brought into the territory with her."

"I'm aware of this smuggling and I won't talk about what is being done. This is a big country, but word of mouth travels as fast as the telegraph and reaches corners a telegram would never reach. We have to be secretive about any plan to stop this kind of trouble."

"You can tell me, Sheriff Cowden. I won't blab."

"I can't and won't. I doubt you can be much help."

"Why, sir?"

"You won't be included in any action I take against the kind of people who would traffic in slavery."

"Pardon me, but you are too smug, Sheriff Cowden. Your son Mark may be the best friend I have in the world, but it seems to me the Cowdens have their own way too much. I can help you. I think my place of work is right in the dead center of this traffic."

Les had never seen his father sit and listen to anybody confront him with his shortcomings, especially a woman. He was embarrassed for A.B. and offended that anyone should have the effrontery to brace his father this way. A.B. was a gentleman and Les knew he would be patient with this girl, but Les did not want to watch. He slipped out the door and went back to the party. If he had looked back in the next instant, he would have been surprised to see his father and mother smile at Garbie Burr and then laugh with her.

Paula Mary was teaching Jimmy Coyle how to dance the Varsoviana, the "Put Your Little Foot." She had just turned thirteen and was the youngest of the Cowden sisters. Ben looked around for Chris Wilson, Paula Mary's former favorite dancing partner. Chris drove an ore wagon hitched to eighteen or twenty mules on a regular haul from the Harshaw mine to the railroad in Patagonia. He was a tall, burly man. One of his shoes weighed almost as much as Paula Mary. Chris was on the edge of the dance floor, smiling at being replaced.

Les saw Dick Martin, the Harshaw constable, drive a horse and buggy into the barnyard and help his passenger to the ground. Les went outside to see if he would have to head them off. The passenger was Lorrie Briggs. Les enjoyed the sight of her, but he was not glad to see her at this celebration. She hated Ben Cowden. Once she even shot off his little toe. Her two older brothers had been killed during the war between the Cowdens and the VO and she blamed Ben. Apaches had killed Hoozy and Whitey Briggs with big arrows and lances, but Lorrie still blamed Ben. Les was positive she had come to El Durazno to cause trouble, but the rules of ranch hospitality prevented him from turning her away.

Les shook Dick Martin's hand and turned to Lorrie. "You're in luck. The dancing's started and you look lighter on your feet than ever."

Lorrie was agile as a cougar, supple, sensual, and plainly, by god, not pregnant. Three months ago she'd lured Ben to her house with the complaint that Duncan Vincent had made her pregnant.

Lorrie gave Les a dirty look and Dick Martin stepped between them. "I'm not here on a social call, Les. I need to see A.B. and all three Cowden brothers for a few minutes."

"This is not a good day for anybody to try to do business with us. We're having a good time today."

"I know. Lorrie wanted to come out and congratulate Ben and Maudy. I hope you don't mind."

"They'll be glad to see you. Come on and finish your business quick so you can have some fun."

Les helped Dick unhitch his buggy and put the horse in a stall with half a gallon of grain. Dick's horse was always about to drop dead of starvation.

He let Dick and Lorrie go out of the barn ahead of him so he could go into A.B.'s office for a drink of whiskey. That jug under his father's desk was his favorite. When he moved it, he caught a glimpse of something that did not belong under the desk. He brought out a bundle wrapped in an oily rag, removed the rag, and uncovered twelve fused sticks of dynamite tied in a bundle.

The Cowdens never kept dynamite near the house and barn. They kept blasting materials three miles away in a sealed and hidden cave. With all the whiskey being poured up at the house, somebody had figured no one would go near A.B.'s office jug that day. Somebody had

7

used imagination. Twelve sticks of dynamite would have doused A.B.'s whiskey all over everybody from El Durazno to Harshaw.

He put the dynamite in a bucket, turned the bucket over, and sank it in a water trough inside the barn, then went out and led Dick and Lorrie to the Arizona room. He was surprised to see A.B., Viney, and Garbie coming out the door laughing. Viney laughed a lot, but A.B. almost never did.

A.B. said, "Son, this girl's another one who'll do to ride the river with. She'll be staying with us a while. She's going to fit right in with our family."

Garbie stared at Lorrie. Lorrie's brother Hoozy had murdered her sister.

"Don't look at me," Lorrie said, and gave Garbie the deadeye. "I'm no Cowden."

Garbie said innocently, "Oh? Well, you're probably somebody I'd like to get to know better, anyway."

"Not if you're expecting another Cowden."

Les walked Viney, Garbie, and Lorrie to the dance, found his brothers, and took them back to the Arizona room. Addressing only Ben, Dick Martin told the Cowdens that the woodcutter Tomás Gil had found Jack Odoms's dead body in Sycamore Canyon that morning.

"What happened to him?" Les asked. He was almost sure he knew what had happened to the son of a bitch. On their way home the night Odoms killed Margarita Elias, Ben had sent his brothers ahead and ridden by himself into Sycamore Canyon. How Ben knew Jack Odoms would show up there was a mystery, because Odoms was supposed to have been taken to Kosterlinsky's jail that evening. Now Les was sure Ben had gone into Sycamore Canyon to kill Jack Odoms. Somehow he'd worked it out for Kosterlinsky to let Odoms go. Somehow Odoms had been directed to Sycamore Canyon and Ben simply waited there and killed him.

"It's nice of you to tell us our enemy is dead," Ben said. "Thank you, Dick." His face was stone.

"I thought you'd want to know. He's been murdered and the Cowdens will undoubtedly be named as suspects," Dick said.

"We know it, but don't look so sad about doing your duty. Odoms was a cold-blooded son of a bitch and somebody made him pay for murdering Margarita. Any one of a thousand Mexicans would have been glad to do it, not only the Cowdens."

"I'm sad for your sake, that's all."

"Don't be sad," Ben said. "This is my wedding day." He did not smile.

"I just hope I won't be handed another warrant for your arrest, Ben. I don't know if I can go through another year of this war and all the killing."

"Why tell me about it? I'm not waging war."

8

"Ben, who else should I tell? I care what happens to the Cowdens. I believe you're being handed a bad deal by the Pima County government and the Live Stock Association."

"Young man, don't concern yourself about the Pima County government, except to draw your paycheck," A.B. said. "Don't concern yourself about warrants for my sons. You've done your duty, and we appreciate it."

"You don't need to worry about me anymore either, Dick," Ben said. "I'm out of it. Maudy and I are going on a short vacation and then settling down on the Vaca ranch. No more war. With Odoms dead, Vincent's back is broken. I think he lost his stomach for war when his cutthroat killed Margarita Elias right in front of him at La Acequia."

Les watched his brother. Ben was a passionate man, but lately he showed no feeling at all. Margarita's killing had turned him cold. Before that he had passionately, earnestly led the fight against the VO. Since Margarita's death he had become detached, almost as cold-blooded as Vincent's hired men.

Just when Les was sure Ben was about go into a killing rage against his enemies and finish them while he had them on the run, he had checked himself and announced that he was marrying Maudy and moving to the Vaca ranch. He did not even show true satisfaction for the death of Odoms. Every black hair on his head was in place, every whisker shaved, every bristle of his mustache evenly trimmed. His eye was as frosty as A.B.'s, but he was distant to everyone, even his family. His attire was spotless and expensive and Les did not know when or where he could have acquired it. Before the change Les would have bet he even knew when his elder brother said his prayers and could have given the details of the prayers. Now he did not think Ben Cowden prayed at all, might not feel he even needed to pray.

"Well . . ." Dick Martin looked around, as though to find a way to make a graceful exit. ". . . I just wanted to let you know. . . ."

"Thank you, Dick," Ben said. "We appreciate it. Come on with me now and have a drink and dinner. Hell, have a bunch of drinks." Ben led Martin out to the party, but the constable only congratulated Maudy and left.

Maudy brought Ben a plate of hot beef barbecue, mashed potatoes and gravy, red beans swimming in broth, fried chicken, and a great mug of foaming beer. That would warm him up if anything could. He seemed relaxed, was the handsomest devil at his party, but he was not at peace, anymore than an Apache or any other predator could be at peace when he was feeding. He looked at people as though sizing them up to bring them down. He might even have discovered he liked to do that.

Les went to find a glass of champagne and when he returned to Ben and Maudy, Billy Stiles was standing directly over their heads, drunker than hell and bragging about how much he admired Ben Cowden. *He* had always known Duncan Vincent was in the wrong. *He* had helped Ben Cowden escape from the Rillito jail where Vincent's henchman, Frank Marshall, had subjected Ben to several days of beating and starvation. *He* was the one who had sneaked water to Ben when he was dying of thirst.

Ben and Maudy tried to ignore Stiles and watch the dancers, but this last statement was delivered so loudly that they were buffeted by the wind of his breath. Les thought, oh, oh, that's it for Stiles. He's unstoppered my brother. Stiles had been put in the cell across from Ben in that jail to spy on him. Nobody gave him any water except Dick Martin and one of the Irish jailers. Wedding or no wedding, Ben would never sit and listen to a son of a bitch yell lies at him that both he and the son of a bitch knew were lies.

Ben looked straight at Stiles a moment, but instead of jumping him for being a sneak, enemy, and liar, he reached up and gently moved him out of the way, stood up and told him to hurry and eat dinner before it was all gone. "Have you had a drink, yet, Billy?" he asked.

"Oh hell yes."

"I want you to feel at home now. We have plenty to eat and drink. This celebration marks the end of all the trouble: yours, mine, and Duncan Vincent's." He led Maudy out to the dance floor.

That pulled Les's stopper. As Stiles swaggered by the front door, Les encircled his waist with an arm, lifted him off the floor, and carried him outside.

"You big . . ." Stiles said. Then he saw who was carrying him. Les dropped him. He'd been so intent on getting Stiles outside without a scene that he found he was holding his breath.

Stiles was angry, but knew he was not man enough to do anything about it. He could talk a fight, though. "What's the idea, Cowden? You might be a great big bastard, but don't get the idea I'll let you manhandle me."

"Hell, Stiles, you haven't been manhandled." Les took him by the thick hair on the back of his neck, shook him, and pushed him around the corner of the house to the orchard. He shook him again until he slobbered, jerked him hard, and sent him stumbling against a tree. "*Now* you've been manhandled. If you're to find peace with me, you better learn your boundaries when you're near my family. I thought you learned your lesson after the real manhandling we gave you at the Nogales cowpens."

Billy Stiles did not act drunk anymore. "You're lucky I'm not armed, you bastard."

"No, you're lucky today's my brother's wedding day, or you'd be down with your head in a spittoon where you belong, instead of enjoying the privileges of a guest. Behave yourself and stay away from my brother and his bride with your lying brags and you can stay for dinner. Keep up your damned swaggering and I won't just shake you, I'll mash you."

Ernesto Campana and another thug Les did not recognize came around the corner of the house. They separated and spread out on both sides of Stiles. They were both armed and Les knew Campana had not been carrying a weapon when he first arrived with his sisters.

Les thought, my lord, have I been set up? I was the one crying because nobody had been careful enough to keep our enemies away from here today. He noticed the long scar along Campana's jaw, the slanted black eyes.

"What'sa matta, Beely," Campana said to Stiles. "You got trawbles?"

"You don't look a thing like your sisters," Les said to Campana in Spanish. "Are you here as a guest, or did you come looking for trouble?"

"No trouble, Les. Beely is my friend."

"You should have filled your friend with beef and beans when he came here. Tell him how bad-mannered it is to brag and lie at a wedding."

"Talk English," the other thug said. "I hate it when sonsabitches talks Mexican in front of me like I wasn't even there."

The thug wore a round-brimmed hat on the back of his head. A shock of hair white as cotton covered his brow. Teddy. This was Teddy Briggs, Lorrie's younger brother. He was as stocky and towheaded as his brother Whitey. He'd taken a chain to Ben one day with four of Vincent's other thugs who jumped him. That was another time Lorrie lured Ben away to a thicket so Vincent's thugs could beat him.

"By God, *all* the rattlesnakes came to our party and me without my pistol," Les said.

"Yeah, we came and not to eat your food, drink your whiskey, or pat you on the back," Teddy Briggs said.

"What did you come for?" Les said.

"Just like you said, to poison your party."

"No, Teddy, don't do anything," Ernesto Campana said.

"Why not?"

"Aw, Teddy. *Please* don't cause trouble," a voice pleaded from behind Les. He turned and saw Mark resting his father's double-barreled shotgun against the corner of the house. "I've got old Pappy's Purdy aimed at your privates. Old Purdy's already put the run on your outfit a time or two. Please don't make her do it again."

Stiles, Campana, and Teddy Briggs gave up. "All right, we'll be good," Stiles said. "I had a little too much to drink, that's all. We'll behave from now on."

"Ernesto is the only one who has to behave," Les said. "You two gringos get the hell off the place. Don't stop for your horses, either. Leave as quick as your little feet get going."

11

Stiles and Teddy Briggs lined out toward the barn. Les and Mark followed. As they were about to walk into the barn, Les said, "Why do you think I'd let you go in our barn?"

Stiles stopped and did not turn around. Teddy hurried to get through the door. Les snatched the Purdy from Mark, cocked both hammers, and barked. "Stand fast, you son of a bitch."

Teddy stopped and turned back. "Dammit, our saddles and bridles are in there."

"You just stay out of our barn. I'll take your horses and saddles to the hotel next time I go in. You don't need anything but your feet. Get on up the road before I stick the stuff you brought to this party up your asses and blow you home."

Briggs and Stiles skirted the barn through the corrals and headed up the road without looking back.

Mark said, "Why didn't you let them catch their horses and ride home, brother? Now you'll have to go to all the trouble of taking them back."

"I didn't want them in our barn."

"Why not?"

"Didn't want 'em in our papa's whiskey."

Two

LES AND MARK went back to the party and found their twin cousins, Danny and Donny Farley, sitting by the whiskey barrel and sipping at ceramic cups. They seemed gloomy, so Les stayed with them. They had been spending a lot of time in Sonora with a bandit named Jacinto Lopez. No warrants had been issued for them, but Les suspected they were on the verge of becoming outlaws. They were usually hardworking, hard-drinking, and full of fun. They had not done a lick of work for months and today, when they ought to be having the best time of their lives, they acted gloomy and only sipped their whiskey.

"You fellers act puny," Les said. "What's bothering you?"

"We rode all night to get here," Donny said.

"Then Mama and Papa bawled us out for being wayward," Danny said.

"Yeah, Les, what's this wayward stuff?" Donny said.

"That means you don't visit your mama and papa like you're supposed to."

"Yeah, we know what it means."

"Well, it's good to see you. What's been keeping you down south, the Campana sisters?"

"Naw, we been in San Lazaro."

"What the hell's in San Lazaro?"

Both twins gave Les a blank look.

"You have girlfriends there?"

The twins gave each other identical looks out of the corners of their eyes.

"You both after the same girl?"

They blushed identically.

"Well hell, I guess that had to happen sooner or later. You either had to separate from time to time, or fall for the same girl. You can't have the same girl, can you? How in the hell could you ever expect her to choose between you, as alike as you are?"

Donny looked away out the window. He probably finally wanted to believe he was not the exact copy of his brother. The twins were so alike that not even their family could always tell them apart.

Danny said. "Every time I want to go somewhere he has to go too."

"Well, well, do you mean you might want to go somewhere without your brother? The farthest apart I've ever seen you was during a drive when one was on one side of a herd and the other clear over on the other side."

"That's got to change," Danny said. "I'm leaving Donny home next time I go south."

Donny stared at his brother. "No, you're the one who's staying home."

The young men had become rivals and seemed angry enough to fight at any moment. Les hoped they would not do that. They were both courageous and strong and did not know how to quit.

"Listen, boys, sooner or later you were bound to find something you wanted and were not willing to share. Don't fight over a woman. Draw lots, shake the dice, have a spitting contest, or see who can pee the farthest, but don't draw each other's blood over it."

Danny said, "There'll be no fight. I'm going and he's staying. That's all there is to it."

Donny laughed. "Listen, mister, I know there'll be no fight because, if you go, I go. If you stay, I go."

"Just don't fight about it," Les said. "If you do, take yourselves clear away from the house where no one can see you. Don't spoil Ben and Maudy's party."

Les stood up, shook his head, and walked away. Children from the Cowden, Farley, Porter, Salazar, Romero, Soto, De La Osa, and Heredia families and other children of at least ten other families were having their dinner together. Gallons of sweet milk, buttermilk; iced, cinnamon-flavored barley water; *tamarindo* and pineapple-flavored water were being guzzled. Gallons of vanilla ice cream had been set out for dessert.

Paula Mary could eat almost as much red beef as a working cowboy and she was indulging a good appetite. Lorrie Briggs came down the table pouring barley water. She stopped across the table from Paula Mary and smiled, then poured her glass full. Paula Mary watched her speculatively. She turned to Les to see if he also saw that Lorrie Briggs was trying to act civilized. She blinked like a baby owl.

Les thought, if Lorrie Briggs doesn't cause some terrible calamity today, if she really only stayed here to help out and be nice, the feud between the Cowdens and Briggses might finally be over.

He went on to see how Ben and Maudy were doing. He found them with Doris Vincent. Doris was a lady, but she could not hide an inordinate affection for Ben. She beamed every time she looked at him. She was handsome, tall, graceful, and good-natured. Sometimes she became a little too high on herself as a Daughter of the American Revolution, but the Cowdens liked her. She placed both gloved hands on the shoulder of her escort and moved him forward to introduce him.

"Ben and Maudy, have you met my brother-in-law, Senator Royal Vincent?"

Ben already knew Royal Vincent, but he acted as though he did not and shook his hand. Duncan's little brother was tall and slender, narrow-shouldered, narrow-waisted, with long, dainty fingers and a long, fragile nose that barely separated his round eyes. Great, long, sandy lashes fluttered on his eyes. Every single strand of the thick, sandy hair on his head had been carefully arranged into a special place and every wisp of the fuzz of his mustache and goatee was carefully snipped and trimmed. His hand barely touched Ben's. He was in such a hurry to bow over Maudy's hand and beam toothily into her face that he did not look at Ben or speak to him.

"Senator Vincent is the new attorney for the Pima County Live Stock Association," Doris announced brightly, just as though she did not know that, if the Cowdens had an enemy in the whole country, it was that association of syndicate-serving, grafting, conniving friends of Duncan Vincent.

Les stepped up to Vincent and said, "I'm Les Cowden," and caught the dainty fingers in flight as he would catch a self-confident, self-centered fly. To make the dude know he was not among friends, Les crammed the fingers satisfyingly into his palm and released them only a fraction before their bones crumpled. That made Sir Royal stop glowing at Maudy.

All the Cowdens except Les had a sort of detached way of looking at people who were not Cowdens, a kind of amused look of disregard for other people who seemed to have trouble with being anything but a Cowden. Ben must have seen the sweat break out on Sir Royal's brow and known what Les had done, but he gave no sign that he cared one way or the other.

"What do you do?" Maudy asked Royal. "I didn't understand what Mrs. Vincent said."

Les thought, or maybe, poor Maudy, you didn't believe your ears.

"I'm an attorney," Royal said. "Specifically, I've just been appointed chief counselor to the Pima County Live Stock Association."

"Oh, is that an office of the county government?" Maudy asked innocently. She knew very damned well it was not.

"No, it's an association made up of the cattlemen of Pima County."

"Oh? You mean the members want people to think their association is part of the government, so they call it the Pima County Association?"

"Not at all. I'm surprised you don't know everything about the association. Your father and husband are cattlemen, aren't they?"

"Not all the cattlemen in Pima County belong to that organization, Mr. Vincent." Maudy's pretty, open face wore a nice, polite smile.

"Well, I've not been out west very long, but I do know all the largest and more progressive companies in the ranching business belong, especially your largest neighbor, my brother. You small settlers ought to think about joining."

"Small *settlers?*" Les said. "Pardon me, but we raise more cattle with less help and ride better horses than you Vincents."

"No, no, Les," Ben said. "The man's our guest, so today he must be right. I apologize for my brother, Mr. Vincent. If you'll excuse me, the song they're playing is a favorite of mine and Maudy's and we'd like to dance."

Les seized Doris by the hand and led her out to the dance floor. He'd always wondered how she would fit inside his arms. She fit well, smelled wonderful, and was gracious enough to seem happy when they glanced at one another. Her breath was quick and fresh, a small, soft, cool pant on his cheek.

Royal was making a spectacle of himself, looking down his nose at people, and was ready with a business card for Les when the set was over. Les took the card off the end of his fingers, careful not to touch him, afraid he'd catch something. He looked at the card. "I hope this means we're gonna fight," he said and grinned at Royal.

"Count on it, fellow," Royal said.

Joe Coyle was the Cowden's blacksmith and in charge of A.B.'s horse barn. A good volume of horses and mules were bought, sold, and rented through the Cowden barn. Wagons and teams were leased and rented and A.B. owned a large, lucrative freight business. His draft, saddle, carriage, and cowhorses owned a reputation of being the best in Arizona and Sonora.

Joe Coyle liked the Cowden family. His fourteen-year-old son,

Jimmy, was treated as another Cowden and both Coyles were included in all family affairs. Any blacksmith had plenty to do, but Joe's duties increased as the war kept the Cowden brothers away from home. He was accepted by this family and depended upon. At first, he had declared that he would not enter into the fight against Duncan Vincent. He only wanted to do good work for A.B. and raise his son to be honest, but the people were so good to him that he would have had to be awfully cold-blooded not to want to take their side. Then he fell in love with Eileen and knew he would never be able to stay out of her war.

He was careful not to show how he felt. He even still called her "Miss Cowden."

Being in love with Eileen hurt and was another terrible example of his bad luck. His thirty-four years were landmarked with monuments of bad luck. Raised in an orphanage in Galveston, he had gone to work as an apprentice blacksmith when he was ten. He married at the age of sixteen. With the good recommendation of the blacksmith, he was able to enlist in the Texas Rangers. The girl was an angel and by working together they had acquired a small ranch in south Texas. Then, while he was away on a campaign against the Comanches with his troop, his wife died.

He quit the Rangers to better attend to his ranch and son. A drought hit the country and his cattle died. He was recruited by his former captain, Jack Odoms, to join a squad of livestock association rangers to stop a gang of cattle thieves for Duncan Vincent in Arizona. He found the other rangers too bloodthirsty to suit him. And the cattle thieves? The supposed cattle thieves were the Cowden brothers.

He counted the day A.B. Cowden hired him a lucky day, but loving Eileen made him miserable again. If he joined the Cowdens in their fight, he would risk leaving his son a complete orphan. Vincent's henchmen had caused the deaths of Bill Knox, the Cowdens' last blacksmith, and two of their stableboys.

Joe Coyle was sure Eileen did not have the slightest idea he loved her and, after watching her greet a certain guest that morning, he was sure he did not have a chance to win her. That morning Pancho Elias had shown up for the wedding from Sonora and, when Eileen greeted him, Joe saw she loved him.

The Eliases arrived in a carriage drawn by a team of four. Pancho was horseback with four other armed outriders, vaqueros from the Elias's Maria Macarena ranch. On board the carriage were Don Juan Pedro Elias, the father, and the four Elias girls, sisters of Margarita, the girl Jack Odoms killed.

Eileen ran to the barn to be the first to greet them. Joe saw a new, bright happiness in the girl's face when she greeted Pancho. She stood back and shook his hand, then she laughed and impulsively embraced him.

Ben walked Don Juan Pedro and the Elias girls to the house while Joe and the vaqueros put the horses away. Then Pancho and Eileen stepped behind the carriage and embraced. Joe looked under the carriage and watched their feet. They only stopped alone that way a moment, but were happy and holding hands when they came back in sight. They turned loose of one another only after they left the barn and could be seen from the house.

Joe's heart weighed like an anvil. Eileen and Pancho had probably wished he was not there, but never looked his way. He wished he had not seen them touch and smile at each other.

Joe tacked shoes on two Elias horses that lost shoes on their way to the wedding. Then he went out and dug the barbecued heifer out of the ground. She came out smoking in her jacket of cloth and wet burlap at just the right moment for her to be eaten and Joe forgot the anvil on his heart. This family let him do a lot each day that made him happy in spite of himself.

After he finished carving and serving the meat, he went back to the barn in a black gloom. The music was exactly the best kind to make him tap his feet. He had danced a lot when he was married to Kitty. He stopped when she died. If Pancho Elias had not showed up, he probably would have stayed at the house to tap his feet to the music with everybody else and even dance with Eileen and her sisters. Nobody could say he had ambitious intentions toward Eileen if he only asked her to dance one set with him. After he saw her dance with Pancho, he knew she would have been too impersonal and polite to dance with. Bad luck, that was all it was.

He decided somebody might want to leave early, so he had better feed the horses. He moved quietly out of habit. He heard a footfall outside the barn. Eileen came through the door with her head down, watching her step, carrying a large tray with a glass full of A.B.'s whiskey, a loaf of bread, a coffee pot and mugs, and a large dinner plate covered with a linen napkin. The anvil fell off Joe Coyle's heart.

She had a nice way of walking when she carried something for somebody else, careful as though she was barefooted, soft on the ground, movements pretty with her happiness. Anybody with eyes could see an absolute masterpiece of God's creation in Eileen Cowden. In the instant before she raised her eyes to his and smiled, he gave himself up to the love of her again.

Eileen said, "Joe, I thought I better look up the man who prepared the feast. Why did you leave us? You haven't eaten, or danced with me and my sisters, or swallowed any of my papa's whiskey."

"Oh, I thought I'd better feed these horses."

"Oh no. First, you have to eat meat and drink whiskey. I know you like whiskey, because I've seen you drink with my papa."

"Well, Miss Cowden, you might be surprised, but I was given my fill when I carved that heifer and smelled her and saw she had come out of the ground just right."

Eileen's dark eyes were wide. "Do you know, that's the best beef I've ever tasted. Ben and Maudy are bragging on it. How in the world have we ever put on a fiesta here without your beef? The people may never go home until it's all gone. You have to go shake hands with people."

"That's nice of you to say, Miss Cowden."

"Can I call you 'Joe'?"

"Yes, Ma'am."

"Then call me 'Eileen'."

"Yes, ma'am, thank you."

"Now, come on and have your dinner." Eileen handed Joe his whiskey, walked past him into his room, and set the dinner tray on the table.

She uncovered the plate. A smaller plate with two large pieces of the wedding cake was on top. Joe was close at her elbow and she turned toward him and brushed his belt buckle with her arm. Her face was only a foot from his, her eyes full of light and fun. "I brought myself a piece of cake, too," she said. "Can I sit and have it with you?"

Joe Coyle laughed.

When she was gone back to the house, he thought, I wish the girl was not so good to me. She can't do that every day. And what if she never does it again? Then he thought, don't be a chickenheart, get up there and dance like she asked you to.

Three

ROYAL AND DORIS were leaving the fiesta and saying good-bye to the Cowdens in the front yard. Les knew they could not have come without an escort. He watched Doris as she laughed and hugged his mother and sisters and shook hands with A.B. and Mark. She had dropped a lot of her eastern manners in the past year and the ranch people liked her better.

Doris acted as though evil did not exist in any form in southern Arizona, but not even she could have been so foolish as to travel the twenty miles across the San Rafael Valley with only Sir Royal's dainty hands to protect her. She must have brought an escort of VO cowboys, who knew enough to get her home before dark.

Royal kept looking at his watch. The VO escort had probably spent the day in the saloons, but they would be on time, not because they were afraid Duncan Vincent would be angry if they were late, but because they liked Doris. Duncan did not care about anything but accumulating land, money, and water rights for his syndicate of railroad, mining, and meat-packing industrialists. He seemed to love no one and was unloved by everyone except poor Doris. Once he had sent a shipment of gold coin to Santa Cruz, Sonora, on a coach with Doris without telling her, even though stage robbery was commonplace. Almost everybody in southern Arizona except Doris knew he had made a target of her by sending her home with a fortune in gold. Not another man in Arizona would have put his wife in that kind of peril.

On the slope of a hill across the road from the barn, Les saw a man sitting beside a *bellota*, a black oak tree. He was an Apache, but Les could not identify him. He had been there since before the wedding ceremony. He could not be seen from the house, but was in full view of the barn.

Five VO hands rode in sight from Harshaw. They rode in a close pack down the middle of the road and were plenty loose with the whiskey they carried. Their hats were pulled down and they were all talking at once, typical of the green hands recruited by the VO. Bunched, they were good targets for an enemy and would never have been able to shoot past each other to protect themselves. When a rider talked, he could not listen. He could not hear his enemy, but his enemy could hear him coming and hide before he came in sight. Being in a loud, close pack was a perfect way for travelers to get themselves killed on a ride down the Apache war trail in southern Arizona that year, 1886. Les wished the VO would take Royal home with them, but leave Doris at El Durazno.

The VO bunch stopped in front of the Cowden barn. The Indian had disappeared. Les walked through the barn, stopped in the front door behind the VO and waited for them to become aware of him.

"There she is," a man who was riding a narrow-headed white horse said. Les knew he was Jay Creswell, a bum from Tombstone, the typical specimen of a VO hand. A cowboy would never call this bunch cowboys. They were gunsels, the kind of green hands who wished they could be a cowboys, called themselves cowboys, but would never be cowboys if they worked cattle and horses a hundred years. All a gunsel candidate needed in order to qualify for the crew of the VO was to be a loudmouth and a back-shooter.

"Where?" asked another hand, and Les was surprised to see Snider had returned to the VO. The Cowdens had put Snider in the breeze twice, the second time after he stabbed Ben in the back. Snider had promised everybody that he was ashamed of himself and would leave the country and start a new life. Well, he was back and would be fair game for Les. Les was glad to see him back. He liked to be able to count his enemies.

"She's standing there in the front yard with all the pretty Cowdens." Creswell said.

Packrat Packer moved his horse up beside Creswell. "Which ones would you call the ugly ones, the sonsabitching brothers?" He was riding a big, heavy, brand new, mail-order saddle. He wore a pistol in a holster on his left hip, another pistol stuck in the front of his belt, and a round brown hat tied on the back of his head with a Yaqui string. His boots were new and so were his spurs. His mustache was of the size and fur of a packrat and hung down both sides of his jaw bone. It was so thick with blond, scraggly hair that it covered his mouth like a brush thicket and muffled his speech. His adolescent head was so small, Les could squash it in one hand. This was the enemy.

"You fellers get down and come in for a drink and dinner while you're waiting," Les said. "If one of the ugly sons of bitches you're asking about gives you a fright, just call me or one of my brothers, and we'll take you by your little hand and comfort you."

"Naw, we'll just sit our horses and wait," Snider said. He acted as though he did not know Les.

Les was unarmed and had positioned himself so the VO would have to strain to turn and see him. One by one they turned their horses to face him. The Indian came in sight by another tree on the hill behind them.

The twins walked Doris and Royal to the barn and helped Les hitch their buggy and team. Not one of the VO offered to get off his horse and help, but when Les drove the team out into the yard Snider dismounted, handed his saddle horse to Packrat, climbed into the buggy, and took the lines. Snider was good at being polite to ladies. He had once paid polite court to Maudy Jane Pendleton when he camped with her brother near La Noria, Maudy's home.

Doris kissed Les a wet one on the cheek before she boarded the buggy with Royal and drove away. People did not have to do much to make Doris start doing them favors.

Les stood in the barnyard and watched until the VO was out of sight. The Apache was still at the base of the tree on the side of the hill. Les said to him in Spanish, "Come down and have a plate of my brother's wedding dinner."

The Apache was young and wore the red headband of an army scout, a trooper's blue cap, and *teguas*, the Apache mocasins with the sharp, curved toe and hard, thick, rawhide sole. He untracked slowly, languidly, and picked up a rifle and a reata, a rawhide rope, from behind the tree. He walked unself-consciously down the hill, stopped a few paces away from Les, and leaned on the rifle.

"Who are you?" Les asked.

"*Hijo de* Jose, son of Jose Santa Cruz," the Indian growled the words deep in his throat as a gentle rebuke that Les had not recognized him. Then he said the name given him by the whites, "Patch."

Jose Santa Cruz, his father, had been a warrior foe of A.B.'s when A.B. ran a freight line between Tucson and Tubac. Patch served as a scout for the soldiers at Camp Huachuca from time to time. Les knew he was part Yaqui. His mother's father, Casimiro, was full-blooded Yaqui and an old friend of the Cowdens.

"And your father, old Jose?"

"Killed last summer."

"Nooo, how?"

"In the ambush of the Yawner at Los Bultos in Sonora."

"Are you sure? I was there and did not see him."

"That's what they told me."

"Where have you been, friend?"

"Huachuca."

"Have you been serving the army as a *batidor,* a scout?"

Patch nodded.

"Ahhh, you've grown into the size and hair of a man. You were small when I last saw you. I didn't know you. Come and eat."

Les was only twenty. Patch was probably sixteen or seventeen. Les had been looking over his shoulders for enemies since he entered his teens. Patch had been a warrior since he was thirteen.

Patch would not untrack. "I heard El Jinete, the Horseman, and the little *partera,* midwife, were getting married."

"An hour ago. How do you know Maudy?"

"She helped the people as a nurse and midwife when she lived at Canela."

"She'll want to see you."

Patch stood fast. Apaches were not invited into homes. The Cowdens might ask him in, but the other whites would not like it. "Where's the Horseman?"

"You want me to bring him?"

"'*Saaabe.* I don't know." The man would not budge.

"I'll go get him."

Patch looked exceptionally strong. He was of average height, leggy, broad-shouldered, and handsome. He knew he was handsome and showed it in the way he moved, like a stud horse. He was modest enough not to preen, pose, or strut, to speak loudly or stare, but he kept himself clean and well-groomed.

The only sign of the pride in his appearance, the only plumage he flaunted, was his hair. The straight black mane hung below his shoulders and had been washed and combed to a sheen. His face was unlined, his eye clear, and Les was sure he was a better traveler, hunter, and fighter afoot than most men would be horseback.

Les knew he was poor, with few possessions and no tribal status. He did not know of any other family Patch might claim except the Apache and the Yaqui, but like a lot of other native southern Arizonans and Sonorans, his eyes were green.

Ben came through the barn carrying a big slice of wedding cake and a glass of whiskey. He handed them to Les and shook hands with Patch.

"I saw you, Jose *Hijo*, Jose Junior," Ben said. "Welcome."

Patch gave Ben the reata. Ben held it up and admired it because he knew Patch would not have given it to him if he was not proud of it. He passed the length of it through his hands and measured it in *brasadas*, a brasada being the length of a man's extended arms. *"Siete y pico,"* he said. "That's seven brasadas and a little bit more. It must be made from one hide."

Patch nodded.

The tail of the reata showed that it was braided in eight strands, but it was no bigger around than a pencil. The rawhide was soft and pliant as buckskin, though it was probably made of bull hide, and it had been carefully and evenly tallowed with kidney fat.

"It's never caught anything, has it, Jose?"

Patch shook his head.

"Did you make it?"

Patch nodded, picked up the tail and examined it critically, searched along its length, and showed Ben one spot in the braid where a strand was slightly narrower than the others.

Ben picked up the even coils and shook the reata in front of his face. "This is the finest reata I have ever seen in my life."

Les knew he was not lying. The lariat was more a work of art than a tool.

"This one will never be broken, because I will keep it to adorn the wall when I build my new house," Ben said.

Patch had never looked at Ben. He looked away in a new direction and sighed.

Ben, Les, and Patch squatted against the barn, ate wedding cake with their knives, and shared the whiskey. Ben was especially grateful to Casimiro, Patch's grandfather, for the help Casimiro had given him when he fled through the Rincon Mountains recently with the Live Stock Association's constables chasing him.

"What news of Casimiro, your *abuelito?*" Ben asked.

"I helped him harvest his *verano* of vegetables, melons, corn, and chile and bundled his *tasol*, his cornstalk fodder. Now he is hunting." Patch smiled. "He is much at peace."

"The ground on his mountain yielded well?"

"Very well."

"And Casi, his little granddaughter who lives with him? Is she your sister?"

22

"My sister. She is well." Patch sobered, as though having a small, healthy sister was a serious matter.

"She likes to live with her grandfather."

"She has to."

"Why?"

"Chato would steal her." Patch laughed softly, but the statement was not meant to be funny. He laughed at the queerness of Chato.

"Chato is related to you, is he not, Jose?"

"Uncle."

"I thought he was killed with the Yawner at Los Bultos."

Patch was serious. "He was not at Los Bultos with the Yawner, but he is with him now."

"Then the Yawner is still alive?"

"Si." Patch said this softly with an intake of breath through his teeth.

"We thought so."

"Yes."

"How did he escape?"

"He left himself for dead on the killing ground, then was able to walk away when you, Horseman, saw he was alive and turned away from him."

"He said that? You've seen him?"

"It's what he says to the people when he tells what happened."

"He said I let him get away? We were many scouts and soldiers. Les was there, too."

"He says that you and your brothers were the only ones who could have overtaken him and surprised him the way you did. He says you saw he was alive after the battle and turned away so he could escape. He sent you a present."

From inside his shirt, Patch brought out a skinning knife in a beaded buckskin sheath. The sheath was lined inside by thick, hard, raw bull hide. The buckskin cover was adorned with delicate fringe and tiny tin bells. The crude figure of a horseman was fashioned in red beads along the cover. Ben drew the knife. The four-inch blade was old and well balanced against a heavy elkhorn handle.

"This is the finest knife and sheath I have ever seen," Ben said.

Patch said, "Only . . . El Bostezador wants a dime for it."

Ben stood up, dug in his pocket and came out with a dime. "Will you look at that? My pocket is empty now. I only had one dime." He turned the pocket inside out to prove it, then gave the dime to Patch. Patch put it away without looking at it.

Ben took the whiskey glass from Les and passed it to Patch. Patch sipped, then sighed, and his eyes showed he felt better as he handed the glass to Les.

"Still, the old Yawner is too long in the *colmillo*, the fang, not to take care when he gives his enemy a knife, is he not?" Ben pointed to the tiny bells on the sheath and laughed. "He added the bells in case I tried to sneak up on him."

Patch nodded once.

"If you see the Yawner and Chato, tell them I am married now and through with war. I want to raise children and good horses and watch my cattle fatten."

"I will tell Yawner, but Chato is the enemy of all men, even the Yawner."

Les said, "Then he is like Duncan Vincent."

Patch looked Les in the eye and looked away. "El Alacrán. The Scorpion," he said, and almost smiled.

Les laughed. "Is that what you call the *jefe,* chief, of the San Rafael ranch, Jose?"

"The Apache calls him that."

"That's saying something. The Apache does not like the scorpion, does he? He squashes them."

"The Apache pulls off his stinger first. That way he kills him twice. Chato will always be an enemy of people, even when the wars are finished and the warriors have bought each other's knives, until someone kills him twice."

Les wanted to remind his brother of his big worry. "See, Ben? You can't make peace with Vincent. The poison is in him and his stinger will always itch to sting."

"Scorpions are many on the Santa Cruz," Ben said. "I can't kill them all."

"You'll kill them when they sting you, won't you?"

"Yes, brother, but I'm through killing people."

"Vincent won't stop stinging until he's dead, brother. Especially when he finds out you won't swat him to protect yourself."

Ben lifted the reata and examined the *honda* on the end, then hefted the loop to see the spring in the rawhide. "This thing is alive."

Les could see Ben was not going to let anyone bring him back to the war. He had not argued, confided, commiserated, or listened to anyone but Maudy since Margarita Elias was killed.

Maudy came through the barn to get Ben and shake hands with Patch. She knew Patch better than the Cowdens did. As they shook hands, Patch soberly looked away so she would know he was not predatory toward her. Maudy had changed out of her wedding dress, because she and Ben were leaving soon for the train in Patagonia. She told Ben it was almost time to go, then extended her hand to Patch again. Patch reached inside his vest, brought out a pair of beaded buckskin gauntlets, and gave them to her.

She put them on and they fit perfectly. "A gift for me? Who made them? You, Patch?"

Patch nodded.

"How did you know the size of my hands?"

"All the people on the Santa Cruz know your hands."

"No one ever gave me so fine a gift."

Ben and Maudy went back to the house and Les stayed to finish the whiskey with Patch. When it was gone, Patch went up and sat by the *bellota* again. Les and Mark caught their father's team of blacks and hitched them to a surrey for Ben and Maudy's ride to the train. The Cowden sisters helped bring the luggage and they boarded to join the bride and groom for the ride to Patagonia. Mark drove the team and started away with a fifteen-man escort of mounted wedding guests. Patch followed the cavalcade on a powerful bay horse.

Les watched the surrey until it was out of sight. Willy Porter, his oldest Porter cousin, walked up beside him, leading his saddle horse. "I got busy hitching and saddling other peoples' horses and everybody left before I could saddle one for myself," Les said. "If you want to catch them, you better hurry, Willy."

Willy was tall and rawboned and as towheaded as his Cowden cousins were dark-haired. All the Porters were capable cowmen and handy carpenters and knew how to build and work all kinds of machinery, but Willy was the handiest of them all. The Porter–Cowden clan bragged that Willy could build a china closet with a stone ax if he wanted to. He said, "I have to get home, Emily and Willy Fly are alone."

Les was surprised. Willy's wife was pregnant. He would never leave her and their three-year-old boy alone at the ranch on purpose. "My lord, Willy. How did that happen? Why didn't you bring them to the wedding?"

"I didn't come for the wedding myself. Emily didn't want to come because she's getting too big. I've taken the job riding shotgun on the Tombstone stage, so I hired that Snider and his wife to stay with Emily when I'm gone. I finished my run in Nogales last night and just rode over here on my way home to congratulate Ben and Maudy."

"Snider was here a while ago."

"I know. I met the son of a bitch driving his boss's wife up the road. You know what? He didn't even wave when he went by. I was so surprised to see him, I didn't say anything, but you can bet I'll drop a load on him when I see him again."

"Is there anything I can do? Do you want me to ride home with you?"

"No, but I better get going."

"Well, stop a minute and have a drink and dinner. It'll at least make you stronger for the ride."

"No. After I saw Snider, I didn't even want to stop here."

"You ought to eat."

"No, I couldn't eat a damned thing, but I'll take a drink along if you have a fat one handy."

Les took Willy's *amphorita,* a long, slim, pint bottle he carried in a

morral that hung from his saddlehorn, and filled it from the jug in
A.B.'s office. Then he handed him a drink in a tin cup. "Here, cousin,
el estribo, a drink for the stirrup."

Willy's eyes and thoughts were already a long way down the road
toward home. Les did not think he even tasted the whiskey. Willy
handed him the empty cup, mounted, and headed out without looking
back.

Les went back to the house to make sure the fiesta continued. He
decided he'd better get with it and have his own dinner, drinks, and
dancing. Maybe that Lorrie only needed to be charged and caped
around the floor a dozen times in order to find peace with the Cowdens
once and for all.

About ten o'clock, just before he got too drunk to remember anything,
Les remembered the dynamite. He faded away from the party and went
to his father's office. He sat down in the dark, leaned his chair against
the wall, and fell asleep.

He was awakened by the squeak of the barn's front door and the
scuff of boots approaching the office. His feet and the front legs of the
chair were off the floor. The sleep had numbed his legs and stiffened
him. He let the chair down off the wall. He sure felt dumb. Only a
drunk would have come here unarmed and alone to wait in the dark for
his enemies. Now the drink had worn off enough to show him how
muddled his thinking had been. If the visitors were Stiles and Teddy
Briggs and they struck a match when they came in, and they had their
pistols in their hands, they would probably shoot him.

The door to the office opened, the young men whispered, then one
came inside and one stopped at the door. The edge of the door opened
to within a foot of Les's face. One of the men went past him so closely
that he felt the wind of him on his hands, but he was not discovered.
Thanks to Joe Coyle's attention to its maintainence, the door swung
easily on oiled hinges. He took the edge in his hand.

The office was so dark Les could not tell who was standing at the
door, but he was reasonably sure only two men had come back to spark
the dynamite. The mariachis at the party began singing *"Cuatro Vidas."*
"If I had four lives, I would give four lives for theee . . ."

One man scuffed on his hands and knees underneath the desk. Les
heard him slide a searching hand on the floor and drag the heavy
whiskey jug out of the corner. "What the hell? It's not here." The man
under the desk was Stiles.

"Nooo, don't kid me, it's gotta be." The one at the door was Teddy
Briggs.

"No, by damn, it ain't here."

"Then they found it."

"Well, the goddammed alcoholic sonsabitches. All that whiskey up at the house and they had to come down here and drink some of this, too. How else could they have found our powder?" He slid both hands all over the floor under the desk to make sure. "No, it ain't here, and that's all they are to it."

Les realized if he let Stiles stand up, he might miss his chance to put knots on his head. He could barely see the dark shape of him straighten, come around, and sit on the desk. He heard him uncork the bottle and slosh the whiskey as he took a drink. "My, that man keeps good whiskey," Stiles said. "Want a snort?"

"No. Let's get going. They found the powder. Maybe they're watching the office."

"Naw, the drunken bastards're all drunk by now. I ain't giving up yet. I'm gonna look for that powder. It's a cinch they didn't take it to the house. Sure you don't want a drink?"

"We better go."

Les decided it was time to move when he heard the whiskey slosh in the jug as Stiles lifted it to drink again. He bashed the heavy oaken door into Teddy Briggs's face with all his weight and the driving force of his legs. In another stride he fell upon Stiles. He could not see Stiles but he struck ahead with the palms of his hands at a spot where he guessed the man's face would be and struck the bottom of the jug full force. A loud, wet, popping sound announced that the forefinger Stiles had hooked inside the jug handle snapped. Immediately thereafter one tone that was almost a whistle sounded in the jug as Stiles blew into it when Les rammed it into his front teeth. Les grabbed Stiles by the shoulders so he would not miss him in the dark and butted him three times between the eyes. Stiles wilted and Les disarmed him.

Les hurried back to the doorway. Briggs had been standing inside the door, but the door was so heavy and struck him with such force that it had slammed shut. Les opened it and kicked ahead in the dark until he discovered Briggs crawling on his hands and knees in half a swoon. Les disarmed him, dragged him inside the office, and lit the lamp.

Stiles was moaning and writhing weakly on the floor with his hands over his mouth. Les tied the hands of both men behind their backs. He found the jug lying on its side behind the desk. It was not broken and still held half its whiskey. He poured himself a drink in a tin cup, took a swallow, and waited for his enemies to revive.

When they could fully understand him, he picked them up and sat them in chairs side by side. Stiles kept spitting blood and fragments of teeth on the floor.

Les said, "You should have all the junk cleared out of your mouth by now, Billy, so just quit spitting on my papa's floor."

Stiles was too concerned with his condition to pay attention to Les. He spat another glob of blood on the floor. Les walked over and stomped down hard on his toe.

2 7

"Ohhh, you son of a bitch," groaned Stiles.

Les stomped on his other foot and Stiles looked him in the eye and yelled angrily, "You dirty son of a bitch." So Les stomped on the first foot again. "Ohhh," Stiles said again.

"Let him alone, Cowden," Teddy Briggs said.

"I will, now that I've finally got his attention," Les said.

"Anybody can act tough with a feller when he's got him tied up."

"You think I like this, Teddy? You're wrong. I don't like to tie people up and stomp their toes. I wish to hell you hadn't decided to blow up our barn, but here you are. What did you think I would do if I caught you, kiss you?"

"What are you going to do?"

"I don't know. What would you do to a pair of gunsels who tried to blow up your brother's wedding party?"

"I don't know and I won't ever know. You and your brothers killed two of my brothers before they were ever able to marry."

"The Apaches killed your brothers and you know it, so don't try to tell me something we both know is a lie."

"You sonofabitchin' bully," Stiles murmured.

"Billy, if you call me a son of a bitch again, I just don't know how I'm going to stand it. I thought I killed you at the Nogales cowpens and felt awful about it. Please don't make me have to kill you again. This time I guarantee it'll stick and you'll sure as hell end up in hell."

"Yum bedda dit."

"What? Better not try to talk with your mouth full."

Stiles enunciated. "You better do it. Kill me now, because if you don't, I'm gonna come back and get you."

"No, I won't kill you now. If I was going to do that, I wouldn't have tied you up. Get up. I'm sending you home COD."

Les walked his enemies outside and caught and saddled their horses. He left the horses tied to the corral and helped them mount. He tied their ankles to their stirrups. He took his quirt off the wall, looped it on his wrist, and led the horses out to the road.

"What're you gonna do now, Cowden?" Teddy Briggs said.

"I told you, I'm shipping you home COD."

"Well, goddam it, you're going to untie us, aren't you? We can't ride without holding our reins."

"You better be able to, or you'll soon be in the dirt, that's all I've got to say."

Les tied their reins to the saddlehorns, left enough slack in them so the horses could have their heads, then turned them both loose. The horses' ears turned back to their riders for a signal of what to do.

"Wait a minute," Teddy said. "Turn us over to A.B. He's the law and it's against the law to do what we did. Tying us on these horses is murder."

28

"Hell, don't tell him to do that," Stiles said. "That would surely be worse, if that old man found out we planted dynamite in his barn."

Les said, "All I'll do for you is hope your horses take you home safe."

"Hell, these horses'll go all the way back to the VO," Teddy said. "That's over twenty miles in the dark. We don't want them to do that. Do something else to us."

"I'll give you some advice. Whatever you do, don't fall off. Stay alert, so you can stay in the dead middle of those horses. If you fall off, or your saddle slips and you get dragged, they'll scatter pieces of you from here to the VO."

"You're giving us a death sentence, tying our hands and feet like this," Stiles said. "If we do get there in one piece, it'll be hours and hours from now."

"No, it won't." Les screamed like a banshee and quirted both horses across the hips. They sprang ahead like racehorses, shied away from the dark hill, veered toward Harshaw, sold out up the road, and ran quickly out of sight around the first bend. Les listened to the hoofbeats rattle on the hard road, the shouts echo in the canyon until they were gone.

Four

THE APACHES Chato, Arco, and Fausto coursed like wolves along a rimrock of Huachuca Canyon toward Manila Peak. They did not have a purpose, except to scare up prey. They hiked swiftly, for they were often in full view of the lookout at Camp Huachuca. From time to time they glanced over their shoulders at the soldiers' camp, not because they feared pursuit, but because it was their habit to keep their enemies in sight. Even if the soldiers saw them, they could not catch them. The Apaches had gone afoot farther across the steep, rocky ground of the Huachuca Mountains in half a day than a troop of cavalry could hope to cover in a whole day.

They climbed steadily toward the peak, sweating pleasurably at midday, through black and white oak forest spotted with snow, into pine forest where the snow was deeper. Chato was in the lead. He stopped on the brink of a cliff on the southwest side of the peak and pointed down at a flock of ducks. They flew by high above the valley below, but lower in altitude than the Apaches. The men looked down on their backs. The ducks flapped on against a wind current around the peak, keeping a safe height above the valley, unaware of the three predators above them. The Apaches watched them with quiet, speculative excitement. This privileged sight of the dutiful, soldierly fliers was the sort of prize they sought when they coursed. The Apaches knew places where the ducks would alight. They were fun to snare and good to eat broiled on oak coals. This year they carried a good load of grease on their backs.

The Apaches were surrounded by moisture. Clouds hung on the shoulders of the mountains. An intermittent drizzle of rain kept the ground spongy, but did not wet the men. They wore mostly buckskin that did not absorb their sweat or ventilate the heat they generated in the climb. They would take whatever prey they scared up that day, and cotton raiment would be much appreciated if they could find it.

They sniffed the air for game that might start up ahead of them and try to get away. Their coursing was as much play for them as it was a necessity; the hunt was as much fun as the capture and dispatch of prey. The Apaches were playful when they coursed and would playfully kill anything they caught.

They did not stop on Manila, because the clouds closed around them and masked the Babocomari Valley below. They went down off the peak and took a trail along a high ridge where they could see the ranches of El Relave, Cocono, Babocomari, and Canela.

When they got down off the mountain, Chato hurried into the willow thickets and cottonwood forest of Cocono Creek. He followed the creek to a spot where an ancient Spaniard had fashioned a *tauna*, a round stone trough in which a millstone had been rolled by mules and oxen to crush ore. Fausto and Arco moistened *pinole*, a mixture of cornmeal and *panocha*, brown sugar, with water in the palms of their hands and licked it up. Chato mixed his in a *cuchara*, a large spoon fashioned from the shell of a cow's horn.

He licked up the *pinole*, rinsed the *cuchara* in the stream, and searched up the side of the mountain until he found a spot against the *peña*, the bedrock, that he knew held placer gold. He filled a bandana with fine dirt that he scooped and brushed out of cracks, corners, and wells in the bedrock and went back to the *tauna*. He uncovered a stone bowl he kept hidden there. He put his dirt into the bowl, covered it with water and carefully rocked the bowl to wash away the dirt and keep the metal.

When all the dirt was gone and the residue in the bottom of the bowl was so clean that the water remained clear, Fausto and Arco moved closer to see if Chato would uncover gold.

"Black sand. That's all you have this time," Fausto said. He was only about sixteen, but in his entire life he had not accumulated an ounce of baby fat or gentleness. Fierceness fueled his body and dictated his actions.

"Only black sand?" Arco said. Arco, the bowman, was a tall, leggy young man about eighteen, the eldest son of Jose Santa Cruz. He was the best archer of the Yawner's warriors. His bow was taller than he. When people first saw him coming they thought he carried a bundle of lances. The arrows he launched with that bow were small lances. The Yawner's warriors laughingly called Arco's great, implacable arrows "the Death" and enjoyed watching him send them into flight.

"Only black sand after all that washing," Fausto said.

Chato grinned and washed the black sand out of the bowl into the *cuchara*. He was twice the age of his companions. To them he was twice the age a man ought to be, a grandfather, probably. He was not a grandfather, though, because he had sired no sons. He was too mean to have sons. No woman would sleep with him, none wait on him. He was fit company only when he went out to scare up prey, and then only if he did not take a position behind a man. A man could not turn his back on Chato. He considered all men and beasts his prey and could not be trusted, but these two young men enjoyed coursing with him. His cunning and imagination made him a good maestro.

Now he plastered the black sand down against the bowl of the *cuchara* with his thumb and dripped water on the upper edge of it. Fine, flat, yellow kernels of gold, all smaller than half a grain of wheat showed themselves in a bright arc.

"There they are, the *oritos*, little golds," Arco said.

Quickly, by squeezing small amounts of water out of the palm of his hand, he washed the black sand off the gold and laid it bare. The gold was not enough even to make a button. Chato held it under the noses of his companions and looked away while they examined it. Then he opened a pouch that hung around his neck and put it away.

Chato had not said a word since before sunup. He rose and led his companions upstream. The leaves of the creek forest had fallen and the trees did not hide the men as well as they did in the summer, but the rain helped conceal them.

El Relave ranch was on the west bank of the creek. The barn and corrals were near the creek below the house. The people drew their water from a well between the house and the barn. Smoke rose from the chimney on the house. Three horses languished in a corral under a *ramada* against the barn. Winter weather was always the best time to catch the Americans' horses inside the corral. They were hard to catch by Apaches out in the pasture, especially when Apaches wore buckskin. The smell of the wild Apache was foreign, strange, and intimidating to Americans and to their horses, for good reason. Apaches would eat them.

The dog began to bark as Chato knew he would. He barked every time Chato stopped to spy on the ranch. He was such a regular barker that the people did not pay attention to him. His tone was the same for coyotes and javalinas as it was for Apaches. He even barked the same for crows who flew by playing.

31

In a little while the dog came down to the edge of the stream. He was not a brave dog, only dutiful. He kept himself away from the brush so that if he scared anything into the open, or anything happened to him, it would be seen from the house. He probably thought the people would come down and save him if they saw him in danger. He was a smart dog. Chato would not order Arco to pin him to the ground with an arrow as long as his dying could be seen from the house.

The Apaches were careful not to look at the dog. Looking at him would make his barking more frantic. He would feel safer if he was not looked at. They might as well throw a rock at him as look at him. After a while, when he did not get a reaction from the Apaches, the dog did as Chato knew he would do: he strutted over to the corral, shielded himself from view of the house, and squirted on a post. Chato nodded at the bowman.

Arco had already fitted an arrow in his bow. He sat, took hold of the arrow and bowstring with both hands, stretched the bow with his feet, and clucked to the dog. The dog whirled to face him and struck a belligerent pose. The flint tip of the arrow pierced his throat, hurtled him backward off his feet, and pinned him to the fence post.

Chato's skin fit over his face so tightly his mouth did not have lips. He showed his teeth in a sort of grimace for his own humor as he thought, Apaches would eat their dogs, too.

The Apaches were on the downwind side of the horses, but the wind died and the horses smelled them. They threw up their heads, wheeled, glared at the Apaches, and snorted to relieve themselves of the scent, but they could not be seen from the house.

The house was in a clearing and would be difficult to reach unseen. Chato did not intend to be seen before he went inside. He was content to wait until the man came out in the late afternoon to milk the cow and feed the chickens and horses. He did not mind if no one showed until then. He wanted to know who was in the house before he decided to make his move to take what he wanted from the ranch.

This was not the first time Chato had been here. He knew the American the Apache called Huesos, Bones, lived here. He was a fierce man, unafraid of the Apache. He remained unintimidated after his every encounter with the Apache. He had been with Horseman and his brothers in the fight when the ranchers and soldiers tried to trap the Yawner against the Huachucas at Los Metates. Huesos rode good horses, was a good hand afoot or horseback, and would not be easy to overcome. If he was there, Chato would like to kill him with Arco's big death from the thicket. He was too vigilant to be easily killed any other way, even when he sat down under the flank of his milk cow, or made noise at his chores. Chato would rather wait for Huesos to just turn his back on Arco's thicket. That way would be sure.

Chato signed for Fausto to circle to a spot behind the house. The front of the house, the east side, faced the Apaches. The back faced the prevailing wind. The Apaches could see a girl stirring laundry in big kettles under a shelter beside the house. The kettles were set on a fire and she stirred the clothes with a club that had been scalded and bleached many times over. Chato wondered how mean the girl could be with that club. She was not too smart, washing clothes on a day when the sun could not dry them from behind rain clouds. The firelight glowed on the girl's face in the half-light of the stormy day. She was a strong Mexican. Her sleeves were rolled up for handling the wash. Chato liked the glow of the firelight on her skin. The sight of the fires under the laundry kettles made him feel contented and at ease.

Another man, husband of the Mexican, lived at El Relave with Huesos and his wife and boy. Chato hoped Huesos was away with the stage and the other man was inside. The other man was not formidable. He was not handy, strong, or vigilant. He liked to stay in the house, but when he came out he always came heavily armed with pistols and a rifle or shotgun. If he came out to milk the cow and feed the horses, Chato would take him by the hair of the head and sever his spine at the base of the skull as quickly as a fox killed a chicken, with one bite of his incisor and one jerk of his hand.

After two hours of watching the house, Chato asked himself, "Can it be they have no man with them?" He sent Arco around to ask Fausto if he had seen a man.

Emily Porter entertained her troubles. Her feet were swollen, a sign to her that she would probably have another boy. Frank Wong, the grocer in Harshaw, said swollen feet was a sign that a woman carried a boy. Emily's feet had swollen when she carried Willy Fly. Also, today was her third day of being angry at Bob Snider. Teresa, Snider's wife, said that he just could not stand to be idle any longer, so he had gone to the VO to see if he could have his old job back. That was fine. More power to him. That was three days ago. When was he coming back?

Emily said out loud, "The only way we could be worse off would be if Snider had taken the ax. Then Teresa couldn't have chopped our wood." She laughed when she realized she was talking to herself. Snider could have saved himself the pain of being idle by splitting up the firewood. He stayed in the house when Willy Porter was away. He had promised to spend a day on the woodpile ever since he and Teresa came to stay at El Relave. Now the women would have to cut the firewood. Emily pictured herself swinging the ax over her big, pregnant belly and swollen feet and laughed again. Well, Teresa didn't seem to mind doing it. She heard a footfall and held her smile to welcome Teresa.

The shock of seeing the Apache come through her door wrenched a quick scream from her. Chato took hold of her hair, yanked her face into his, ground his teeth like a javalina, chewed her face, swallowed her screams, and drove his knife into the back of her neck. He dropped her to the floor and began to strip her. He heard a sniffle and looked up. Willy Fly was standing in the doorway to the next room. Chato took the child by the heels and bashed his head back and forth against the doorjam.

Arco glided through the front door, used his body to cushion the child's head, and wrenched him away from Chato. Chato turned away from Arco's glaring eyes to finish stripping the woman. He straightened in surprise and pointed at her. "Look." The fetus inside her, near the end of its term, had discovered the trouble it was in and was leaping, kicking, and squirming against the wall of her abdomen. "An American thunders there." Chato laughed. He stooped, raised his knife overhead and brought it down in a swift arc the way he would disembowel a deer. The tip of the blade laid open the wall of the abdomen, broke open the placenta without touching the fetus, and gave light to Willy and Emily Porter's child. Chato rolled the woman with his toe and the child tumbled out on the floor. Arco saw that Chato had already killed the other child, so he dropped him beside the woman and went outside.

Fausto ran down the Mexican girl and stripped her. He carried her clothes and prodded her back to the house with the stirring club. The girl was in a turmoil of fear, anxiety, and shame, but Fausto could have been prodding a calf back to her pen for all he cared about the way she felt. He poked her with the stick only to keep her moving. He was more concerned about watching the horizon for intervention and keeping her on a straight line to the house than he was for her turmoil. He entertained no proprietary notions about her either. He had stripped her only to assert his domination as quickly as possible. Now that she was sufficiently cowed and helpless, he brought her back as a prize for whatever she might be worth.

Chato appeared at the door with blood on his nose, his cheeks, his chin, and wiped the blade of his knife on the edge of the door. The girl balked. Without looking at her, Fausto whacked her across the buttocks with the stirring club. He knew how to make any animal jump ahead when she tried to balk. The girl scrambled toward the wash shed. Fausto headed her off in two steps and whacked her on the side of the head to right her course.

Chato's hands were bloody to the wrists. He went around behind the girl, held the blade of his knife so only the tip of it protruded from between his fingers and jabbed it into the cheek of her butt, caught her by the hair when she jumped, and shoved her toward the barn. Arco and Fausto ransacked the house and carried armloads of clothing and other boodle to the barn.

Chato stood over the girl while she milked the Porter's cow into a gallon coffee can. When the can was half full, he took it and handed her another so she could keep milking while he drank milk. When the second can was half full, he took it from the girl and led her into the saddle house by the hair. He took two reatas off the wall and draped the coils around her neck. He piled other tools and saddle blankets into her arms. He found a long machete, tested the sharpness of the edge with his thumb, rapped it against a post, listened to the ring in the blade, and liked it.

Arco cut his arrow out of the dog, saw the tip was intact, and washed it clean in the horse trough. He turned to help Fausto catch the horses. The smell and sight of the Apaches made the horses afraid for their lives. Fausto and Arco walked them down. They kept walking to the horses' heads when they turned away until they surrendered to be bridled. When the horses finally stopped, they planted themselves and trembled in their tracks until the men goaded and slapped them to the barn to be saddled. By the time the Apaches mounted, the horses were bathed in sweat.

Chato braided the girl's thick hair into one long plait and looped the end on his wrist. He sat her in the saddle in front of him. The Apaches rode back to the Spaniard's *tauna*, dismounted, tied the girl to a tree, and went back to the ranch. They would not try to escape with stolen horses with hours of daylight remaining. They returned to the ranch on a different trail so they could watch it for pursuit.

They reached the house with two hours of daylight remaining and spread out in the brush on the stream, saw that Huesos and the *flojo*, the lazy American, had not returned. They lay down to wait until Huesos or the *flojo* came home and discovered the bodies. That scene was always worth hiding and waiting for.

Willy Porter almost killed his horse getting home. He never slept on his shift with the stage, but he usually stopped for one night in the hotel in Harshaw before he headed home. Those nights were usually short, but they were restful. By the time he reached his ranch, he had not slept for forty-eight hours, his eyes were red, his vision blurred, he was soaked to the skin, and every bone ached. When no one came out to greet him, not even his dog, he began to pray that the women had taken the horses and buckboard and gone to stay with neighbors.

His throat tightened so painfully with worry that he could not swallow. He was so afraid for his family that he was not afraid for himself. The ranch was too quiet. Not even a bird sounded from the house, barn, or corrals. He rode around to the front and saw the smear of blood on the wide open door. His horse was too tired and wobbly to even realize he was home. Willy ran through the door, and found the mutilated bodies of his wife and son.

He sat on the floor by his family for a while, then realized he needed to move them while he could see. He did not want to risk lighting a lamp. He laid the bodies on his and Emily's bed and covered them with a blanket. He went to the door and looked at the mountains he had loved all his life, the same mountains that hid and sheltered the murderers of his family.

He went to the barn and took his horse inside to unsaddle him. He fed him grain and rubbed his back and kept watch for murderers. He was not afraid. He wished they would come back and show their faces. His only hope to find them was to find Teresa alive. He hoped she had been taken captive. Apache captives were not tortured and abused forever. They had not killed her on the spot, so she had a chance to live her life.

He found Apache *tegua* tracks and Teresa's barefoot tracks in the mud of the corral, saw where an Apache lifted her onto a horse. He saw the Apaches had lined out on his horses for the mountains. Then he found his dead dog staring starkly with his tongue hanging out, the terror and anger at his killing still in his eyes.

He knew the Apache trick of riding away after stealing horses, leaving the horses, and doubling back to ambush the pursuit. He stayed inside the corral for cover against arrows. He did not follow the tracks.

If the Apaches killed him and took his last horse, they would have a better chance of keeping Teresa, the horses, and their loot. They would insure themselves against pursuit. The rain would wash out their tracks and cover their escape.

Willy knew it would be hard for them to resist watching his homecoming. After all, this theater of their depredation was way out in their country, not his. This was their favorite form of entertainment, to torture and kill and watch all the painful effects of it.

He went back into the stall with his horse and closed the door behind him. He watched the creek forest through the cracks between the boards while his horse finished his grain. The murderers would not want to attack him without first trying to snipe him with a rifle or an arrow. They must be disappointed. He was not shaking his fist at the sky and screaming for revenge. He had not bawled and sobbed and torn his hair in anger and grief.

His craving for revenge would not go completely unsatisfied. He would deliver unto Snider his death because of this. Snider, that lazy, rotten deadbeat who had camped on Willy and his family for six weeks, was going to die before God could call him to his glory and Willy would make sure the whole territory knew what he had done to deserve it. After that he would try to find Teresa and the wolves who killed his family.

Willy saddled his horse, mounted in the stall, swung the gate open and spurred his horse outside. He was halfway between the barn and the house when he heard the close whistle of the arrow. He threw himself off his horse as the arrow pierced the stirrup leather where his thigh had been. His horse followed him and stumbled through the door of the house behind him, bumped him, and caused him to slip down on the bloody floor, then fell dead inside the door. The shaft of the arrow was three-quarters of an inch around and had pierced him through the heart. Willy regained his feet, looked down at a jumble of bloody innards he had been reluctant to examine before, and recognized the tiny body of his unborn son.

Chato was disappointed, but not surprised by Huesos's behavior. He had hoped for more diversion, a more emotional reaction from the man whose family he had mutilated. He stayed under cover and kept Arco and Fausto from attacking. He did not explain to them that there was no reason to risk killing Huesos. He had plenty to suffer about, now that he was trapped in the house with the corpses. He'd gone away from the corpses once to get help and sympathy before he buried them, only to be driven back inside with them. He would have to sleep with them tonight. He could not risk coming out.

At full dark Chato and his companions went back to the horses and the girl. He was tired. He was happy he had the girl to cushion his rocky bed.

Five

LES WAS COMING BACK TO LIFE and dreading it. He felt all right the moment before he became fully conscious, but he knew when he came wide awake he was going to be sick. He had been drinking, running, and playing continually for three days since the wedding. Besides being so sick in the head, he would want to die. His conscience would hurt with the kind of hangover the Mexicans called "La Cruda Moral" and his moral sense would bother him like a raw wound. He did not remember what he had done wrong, but he knew he'd done something so awful he dreaded remembering it.

He revived and the impact of withdrawal from the long debauch took him in such an awful grip that he moaned out loud. He reached down beside the bed, found his mescal bottle and opened one eye to see how much was left. Thank god, he had a few swallows left, enough to get him started, washed, dressed, and downstairs to the bar.

He took a swallow, collapsed in the bed, and waited for the spirit to seep down and soothe his sensibilities. Someday the use of this drastic remedy would have to stop, but not today, not before he washed away this hangover and was able to see, hear, smell, think, and talk clearly again and step out in a straight line.

"Well, good morning, Sunshine," someone said. The voice was familiar because Les had been listening to it for three days. Lorrie Briggs. He turned toward the other side of the bed and opened his other eye. He had not suspected there was another human being within a mile of him and here was Lorrie Briggs in bed with him, naked as the day she was born, and *that* was what had been causing pain to his moral sense.

Les's other eye popped open. "What are *you* doing here?"

"Don't you remember, Sunshine dear? We got married last night. Was it last night? Maybe it was night before last, or maybe *day* before last."

Les watched her stretch under the covers and relax comfortably, as though perfectly content to stay abed the rest of her life. His eyes widened with purpose and intent. "Don't say a thing to anybody and we'll get it straightened up." Top-heavy, he sat up on the edge of the bed to dress.

"What a wedding night we had," Lorrie said. "Didn't we have a fine time? Why leave now? The room's paid for and I'm sure we can stay another day if we want to."

Les groped for his bottle. He looked around and saw that he was in a room in the Palace Hotel. He took another look at the woman to make sure it was Lorrie, and killed the rest of the mescal. "You stay if you want to. Stay as long as you like. I think I have business to attend to."

"Now, isn't that just like a man? You practically kidnapped me to get me in bed and now that you've had all you want, you discover you have business somewhere else."

Les saw that she was mocking him. "All right, I get it. This is a joke, isn't it?"

"I'm grinning, Lessy, but it's sure no joke. We're really married and I have the paper to prove it."

"Listen, I know I'm numb when I'm drunk, but I'd never get so soused I wouldn't remember I married Lorrie Briggs."

Lorrie kept talking, but Les quit listening. He dressed, washed his face and hands, and put on his hat. He did not have his jacket and the place was drafty. He went down to warm himself at the fireplace in the hotel bar.

The bartender was in the stockroom. Les waited for him to come out and A.B. came in. A.B.'s cheeks were ruddy and his step was light. The three-piece woolen suit he wore fit him like a warm, crisp, clean, rough hide. Les remembered how warm his father's vest had been, so tight over his breast, when Les sat in his lap as a child. His father's suits were always freshly brushed and buffed and smelled of the rich cigars he smoked with a trace of his whiskey.

"Well, son, are you back with the living for a while?" A.B. said.

"Yes, Papa. I think my hand slipped a little and I spilt too much down me, but I'm back on my feet and I'll be all right in a little while."

"It looks like we're in for good weather. You and Mark promised Ben you'd move his camp and livestock to the Vaca ranch."

"I'll go home and see what Mark's doing."

"That might be a good idea."

The bartender came in and A.B. asked him to give his son a swallow of whiskey from his private stock. Les swallowed a double and father and son stood by a moment while it did its medicinal work, then they thanked the bartender and went out.

"Oh, there you are, Lessy," the voice sounded again. Lorrie was in the lobby. "You devil, you went in the bar where I couldn't follow. Good morning, Mr. Cowden . . . Papa."

A.B. did not approve of Lorrie Briggs, but he was a gentleman. He bowed to her, looked her in the eye, and wished her good morning. The word "Papa" rolled over his head like wind over a glacier.

Lorrie walked up to A.B., hugged him and kissed him on the cheek, then threw herself on Les, grappled him around the neck, and kissed him on the mouth. Les maneuvered into a position to see his father's reaction.

A.B. stared at him. "What have you done to make this young woman feel she can fondle me and call me 'Papa'?"

Lorrie came down off the front of Les with a smile for A.B. "Why, sir, I thought you would have been told by now. Lessy and I are married."

A.B.'s ruddy face did not change expression, but his eyes softened with hurt. After watching Lorrie kiss his son, there was no mistaking that they knew each other's bodies well enough to be married. Les's face might try to lie to him, but his body could not.

A.B. had never liked the girl, even when Ben wanted to court her. He and Viney had put the quietus to that. They did not approve of her stock. A.B. told Ben that she came from people who made bread in the morning before they washed their hands. Now Les had fallen for her and she already thought she could call him "Papa."

For Les, this was a disaster. Usually, when he did something he knew his parents would not like, he took himself a long way away from home to do it, most of the time even to another country that spoke another language. Now he knew if he told one lie, he was sunk.

"Is this true, son?" A.B. said.

"That's what Lorrie says, Papa. To tell you the awful truth, I don't know what we did. I don't remember."

"You Cowdens have never thought much of me, I know, but I'm not a liar." Lorrie might have been mocking Les and A.B. before this, but now she was serious.

"Why would you want to marry Les?" A.B. said. "The only feeling you've ever had for the Cowdens was hate."

"That doesn't have to change. You can call me Les's hateful wife now."

"Then one of those titles has to go, the wife title, or the hateful one, it seems to me."

"Papa, don't concern yourself with this," Les said. "We'll work it out. I'll stand by anything I've done, drunk or sober."

Lorrie backed up against Les and looked down her nose at A.B. "Yes, Papa. Don't worry about us. We're married and that's that."

A.B. looked way off toward the Patagonia mountains. "I won't concern myself about it at all, son, except don't take her home until your mother's been notified."

Down the street in Frank Wong's restaurant Paula Mary Cowden and Garbie Burr sat at a table talking Chinese with Frank's fiancée and waiting for Jimmy Coyle to finish his chores. Frank's intended was only twelve years old, younger even than Paula Mary. The girl's name was May. Garbie could talk Chinese and was teaching her English. Paula Mary listened and learned some Chinese. To Paula Mary's satisfaction, Garbie and May established that it would be be a few years before she and Frank were married.

Jimmy Coyle was mopping the floor when the VO hands, Snider, Jay Creswell, Packrat, Teddy Briggs, and Billy Stiles, came in. The young men had spent all night in a saloon and were acting rowdy. They were so loud that Paula Mary, Garbie, and May moved to a booth in a corner across the room and turned their backs to them. Paula Mary warned the other two girls to be quiet. She knew they would be in for a hoorawing if the VO heard them talking Chinese.

The VO sprawled out on chairs in the last unmopped section of the place. Jimmy kept his head down and bore down on them. He mopped the floor for Frank Wong every morning and was used to moving in on drunks. They seldom noticed him.

He straightened and looked the VO bunch over, to see if they were sober enough to pay attention if he asked them to move. He saw they were not, so he probed with the mop to open a space between Packrat and Teddy Briggs.

Packrat and Teddy were dickering over a set of silver conchas Teddy owned and Packrat wanted as an adornment for his spur leathers. Packrat always wanted something somebody else owned.

Teddy and Packrat sat on the same side of a table facing each other with their feet stretched out in front of them. Jimmy nudged the feet with the mop. Teddy and Packrat did not pick up their feet or move them out of the way, so he mopped and nudged their feet from time to time. He always did that and everybody usually moved their feet without seeming to be bothered.

Jimmy took his mop to the bucket and sloshed it and rinsed it, squeezed some water out of it, but left it good and sloppy. Then he went back and plopped the mop down next to the feet. The mop was a lot wetter than he thought and splattered dirty water on Packrat and Teddy. Teddy had spent so much time down in his father's mine wearing brogans that he was overly proud of his shiny boots. Packrat's boots were brand new and the first pair he had acquired in his whole life. He was in absolute love with those boots and the new spurs he'd fitted to their heels. He became antagonistic toward Jimmy at once.

"Just what in the hell do you think you're doing with the mop, kid?" Teddy Briggs demanded.

"I'm trying to mop the floor." Jimmy straightened and looked Teddy in the eye.

"Here, let me see." Teddy extended his hand for the mop. Jimmy, thinking Teddy meant to mop the space around himself, gave him the handle.

"Come here," Teddy said. "Come over here, closer."

Jimmy took a step closer to him and Teddy cracked him solidly on top the head with the handle. Jimmy fell back stunned, his face contorted in angry pain.

Packrat was pleasantly surprised at Teddy's action. The older VO hands roared with laughter at the expression on Jimmy Coyle's face and the style Teddy had shown in causing it.

Teddy turned and showed his companions a straight face. "Damned little wart smudged the new boots my daddy gave me." He slapped the handle down on the floor, turned toward his laughing companions again, and grinned, proud of himself.

Paula Mary had been watching Jimmy, hoping he would not have trouble. She could have predicted that Teddy Briggs would try to bully him. She also knew Jimmy would not let himself be bullied.

Jimmy recovered quickly, picked up the mop, swung it with all his might, and slapped the wet end against the back of Teddy Briggs's head. Teddy's hat flew off and Snider snagged it in midair. Teddy's forehead hit the edge of the table and he fell off his chair in a faint.

Jimmy backed away and swung the mop to his shoulder again. Packrat rocked his chair back on two legs and threw his hands up to protect his face from the spray of dirty water. "Whoa, you little son of a bitch. Pull up!"

Jimmy smacked Packrat full in the face with the mop and spilled him over backwards out of his chair. Packrat sputtered with mop water pouring out of his mustache. He stood up and looked for his hat, found it, and examined the dirty splotches on it.

The older VO hands sat in line with their backs to the wall, laughing.

Jimmy moved in to swing the mop at them, but Frank Wong came up and grabbed his arms from behind. Packrat wore skin tight, leather gloves and he stepped up and slapped Jimmy on both sides of the face. Packrat was not big, but he was a foot taller than Jimmy. This made Frank Wong angry and he was bigger than Packrat. He charged Packrat with the mop.

Packrat did not expect that. Frank Wong was usually humble and subservient with his customers, no matter how rowdy they became. Now he choked up on the mop handle and poked it at Packrat's belly. Packrat retreated.

Snider stepped between them. "Whoa, whoa, whoa. Who do you think you are, chink? You don't do that to a white man. Not when I'm around."

Frank Wong spoke little English. He was not able to speak English at all when he was angry. He began shouting Chinese at Snider, pointing to the door and menacing him with the mop. Snider was a head taller and fifty pounds heavier than Frank Wong. He struck Frank on the side of the head with his pistol, split his ear and knocked him down by the door. When Frank tried to rise, Snider kicked him down.

Paula Mary screeched, "Bob Snider, you leave Frank alone," and ran into Snider's leg.

"Get out of the way, you little snort." Snider hit Frank with the pistol again. Frank rolled over on his back, his head bloody. "Yellow little leper," Snider said.

"Snider, you darned bully," Paula Mary cried. "Wait until my brother Ben finds out."

"You going to wire him way out in Long Beach? Bring him back from his honeymoon?"

"I've got two more brothers and a lot of big cousins."

"Fine, go get 'em."

Jimmy, Paula Mary, and Garbie helped Frank to his feet and sat him in a booth. Billy Stiles went to the kitchen for beer for the VO.

Paula Mary and Jimmy went out and found Les in Uncle Vince Farley's saloon. Les turned grouchy when Jimmy led him out to the street and he saw his little sister. "Paula Mary, what are you doing, calling people out of bars?"

"I can't help it, that bunch from the VO is up there bullying Frank Wong and somebody has to stop them."

"Well, why do I have to be the one to do it?"

"All right, then. If you won't help us, I'll try to find Papa."

"I'll go, but you just do not have any idea how much I don't want to."

On their way up the street Paula Mary and Jimmy told Les the names of the men in the VO bunch. "Also present was your new brother-in-law, Teddy Briggs. He's my relation now too, isn't he?" Paula Mary said. "Is he supposed to be a Cowden, or am I supposed to be a Briggs?"

Les sighed. "Paula Mary, *why* do you have to act so smart?"

"I know you and Lorrie Briggs got married."

"Who told you that?"

"Huh, it's all over town. Is it true or not?"

"It might be."

Les left Paula Mary and Jimmy outside and went in the restaurant. Frank Wong was on the floor and Garbie was standing between him and Snider. The rest of the VO were drinking beer and watching.

"Les, this man beat up Frank," Garbie said. "He needs to be arrested."

"Haw!" shouted the VO, laughing.

"Who's going to arrest us," Snider said. "We're the county constables."

"We'll get Undersheriff Cowden, then," Garbie said.

"Aw, I don't think we need him, do we, Snider?" Les said.

"You might."

"No, I don't need the help of the sheriff to handle cowards."

"Are you calling me a coward?"

"Yes. What do you want to do about it, stick me in the back with your pocket knife like you did my brother?"

"I've apologized to everyone in the country about that. I'm sorry about it. What more can I say?"

"You're being sorry is not enough for me. Now that you're back, I have to at least break your nose. My brother Ben almost died of that wound."

"I'm no match for you, Les. What do you want me to say? I won't fight you."

"What are you doing here? Why aren't you protecting Willy's family at El Relave like you hired out to do? Wasn't he depending on you to stay there?"

"Some men just can't spend all their days with women. Sooner or later a man has to go out and look for work. That's what I did."

"Yeah, it looks like it. You better hope nothing happens to your wife and Willy's family while you're over here at your new job beating up our town Chinaman."

"You don't know what happened. The chink took a club to a white man. I couldn't stand by and allow that."

"Everybody knows how big, brave, and loyal a citizen you are, Snider. The VO must be glad to have you back. I'm sure glad you're back. I was afraid you'd learned your lesson and left the country before I could break your bones for knifing my brother."

"I don't want any trouble with you, Les. I only went back to the VO because I needed work."

"Yeah, it's easy for a gunsel like you to get work at the VO. Easy to gang up with the VO and stab a man in the back with your pocket knife. Easy to bully a person like Frank Wong. It's also easy to say you don't want trouble with me, but you've got it anyway, Snider."

"Listen, Les, why don't I just take my friends and get on out of here? This argument is out of hand and I'm probably to blame. What can I do to make it right with you?"

"What do these men owe you, Frank?" Les asked.

Frank shook his head, nothing.

"You don't owe Frank anything, but you'll have to get out of town to suit me."

"Thank you, Les. I appreciate it, believe me."

"Don't thank me. I'm still going to break your nose, if there's anything left after Willy Porter finishes with you. If I was you, I'd get back to El Relave as quick as I could and make up with Willy Porter. You're going to be in awful trouble if he has to look you up."

The VO slowly stood up and started filing out. Teddy Briggs was the last in line. He turned and grinned at Les with a big lump shining in the middle of his forehead. "Take good care of little Lorrie," he said. Then he drew his forefinger along his throat from ear to ear, and went out.

Les helped Frank into his quarters and turned him over to his old parents and his fiancée and then took Paula Mary, Garbie, and Jimmy back to the hotel. A.B., Lorrie Briggs, and her father and mother were seated in the lobby.

When she saw Les, Lorrie kept her seat and her mouth shut in a good imitation of a lady. Les took a deep breath and walked to Mr. and Mrs. Briggs and shook their hands. "Is there anything I can do for you?" he said to Indiana Briggs, Lorrie's father.

"Yes, you can be a husband to the vixen, that's what you can do," Indiana said. "If you keep her two years, I'll buy you the best ranch in Arizona. I want to tell you, though, I don't think there's a chance in the world you'll even live that long if you stay with her."

Six

"WE CAN'T UNDERSTAND how anyone, especially a Cowden, would want to marry our daughter," Indiana Briggs said to A. B. Cowden. The Briggses, A.B., and Les Cowden were seated in council in the lobby of the Palace Hotel. "The only answer must be that Les was either forced into it, or didn't know what he was doing."

"Huh! Lorrie's too good for any Cowden, I'll tell you that," said Hattie Briggs, Lorrie's mother.

44

In the two-hour council between the heads of the two families, Les was surprised to learn that Indiana Briggs was apparently a hardworking and successful farmer, rancher, and miner. The man grew the highest corn in the county, forged his own plows, raised fat cattle for beef, and trained his own work oxen. He also owned the Chalkeye mine, one of the richest silver and lead mines in the territory. Some people said the Chalkeye made more money in the gold it mined as a side product than most of the country's other full-scale silver mines made on silver. He owned a string of small farms along Sonoita Creek that yielded four hundred acres of chile, vegetables, corn, barley, alfalfa and barley hay, fruit, and irrigated pasture.

Indiana Briggs seemed to be trying to sell Lorrie to the Cowdens by revealing what her dowry would be, so they would keep her. He said he hired only one cowboy, one farmer, and one miner to help him and he and the two sons who remained at home did all the rest of the work. He admitted that he and Hattie had done well with the farms, ranch, mine, and livestock, but they certainly had not enjoyed the same success in raising their children. Four had left home wilder than outhouse mice. The two who remained were only dumb laborers. Indiana Briggs made it plain to A.B. that he would do anything to see his daughter accepted into the Cowden family. Wild and mean as she had turned out, the only other way for her to go was to the penitentiary.

To hear Hattie Briggs tell it, Lorrie's good looks and hardworking ways and her father's wealth made her the Duchess of Arizona. People often thought Hattie was Lorrie's older sister because she was almost as handsome and graceful as her daughter. Her grace did not extend to her dealings with other people, though. Her voice was so strident that even her whisper put people in a bad mood.

"I thought we were always going to have trouble with the Cowdens," Indiana said. "I was sure our kids would keep fighting and butting heads until they were all dead. My lord, how could anyone have guessed that two of them would come together long enough and fit together well enough to marry?"

Les wondered how this seemingly hardworking and successful man managed to raise hoodlums like Hoozy, Whitey, and Teddy Briggs. Those three acted as though they had no father, no mother, and had never been to school.

The Briggses had raised their children in Indiana. Les knew that Hoozy and Whitey never thought of anything but mischief from the time they arrived in southern Arizona until the Apaches lanced them both to death a short time later. Lorrie and Teddy were exactly the same kind as their deceased brothers, smart, mean, vicious, poisonous, and proud of it.

Lorrie's two remaining brothers were still prowling down in the Chalkeye mine. Les figured he and Lorrie would not stay together more than fifteen more minutes that day, so sooner or later he would probably have the fists, boots, knives, and pistols of the Chalkeye miners to face. He figured Hattie Briggs was the fountain of all the meanness in her sons and daughters. She did not show one expression of good nature in the two hours she sat with the Cowdens, so the Chalkeye miners would undoubtedly be as mean as all the rest.

"It's beyond me how Lorrie could have been so stupid as to marry a drunken Cowden," Hattie said. "If I'd caught this one so drunk he didn't know what he was doing like she did, you can bet your diddly dot I wouldn't have done any petting on him. When I got through with him, he wouldn't have been able to marry anyone. The only woman who'd have wanted him anymore would have been his mama."

"Aw, you're just saying that, Hattie dear," Indiana said. "You wouldn't harm a flea."

"Well, if I'd had him at my mercy the way Lorrie did, you can bet he'd be walking spraddle-legged and suffering from a lot more than a hangover headache this morning."

"That does not bode well for future nights they might spend together." A.B. laughed. Les looked away from everybody and smiled.

"What reason did you have for marrying our daughter?" Hattie scolded. "Don't the Briggs and the Cowdens have enough trouble? You, Les Cowden, I'm talking to you."

"I'm the last one you ought to ask that. I didn't even know I'd done it until Lorrie told me I did."

"That's a big lie. Drunk or sober, a person needs a reason for marrying. If there ever were two people in the world who didn't have a reason, it's you two. Whose idea was it?"

Les just raised his hands, let them fall, and shook his head.

"We both got the idea at the same time," Lorrie said. "Don't you remember, Les?"

"No."

"He remembers, all right."

"It seems to me they ought to be sure they want to live together," A.B. said. "If they decide to go on, I'll help them. If they decide not to, they ought to put an end to it now. They certainly didn't like each other before they married and their wedding night doesn't seem to have improved their relations."

"Oh, they're not going to live together, but Lorrie is sure going to get everything that's due her as a wife," Hattie said. "That's an official proclamation from the mother. We know our rights."

"Now, Hattie, let's not threaten these people or invent grievances," Indiana said. "The kids were partying and maybe a little drunk, but they must have liked each other to do what they did. Let's go from there and not make up mean things to say."

"Yeah, I shouldn't be mean to this Cowden who killed my sons. I am sure he had a good reason for getting my daughter drunk and taking her to bed, the oldest reason of all for a man. Lust. Why wouldn't the murderer of our boys also come along and lust after our daughter? Well, the Cowden got what he wanted, as usual. Now it's time for Lorrie to get what she wants."

"I don't think there's a thing we can do about that," Indiana said. "Judge Dunn confirmed that he married them. They're old enough and have the certificate. It's up to them to decide whether to be nice to each other, or kill each other. You and I are out of it."

"All I have to say is, they can quit now or live together a hundred years, but Lorrie has the right to be paid off as a wife. She did all she needed to do to make it legal, so she better go home with us now before she gets murdered like her brothers."

Dick Martin came in the front door. Dick and Lorrie had been living in the same house since he was the Briggs brothers' partner and she was their housekeeper. Dick stayed after Hoozy and Whitey were killed. He stayed when Lorrie became Duncan Vincent's mistress. He welcomed her back and supported her when Doris Vincent found out about her and sent her packing. Lately he had announced to Les that he and Lorrie were to be married. He truly loved the black-hearted bitch.

Dick stopped in the center of the lobby and stared at Lorrie. She would not look at him. He said, "Well, Lorrie, I heard you and Les got married. I see Briggses and Cowdens sitting together, so I have to believe it, but I'd like you to tell me, for God's sake, why you did it."

Les had never seen Lorrie act humble before, but now she seemed to try to shrink down and disappear into her shoes. He knew Dick had been good to her when she was acting mean as a scorpion with her tail mashed to the ground. Dick knew how low she'd taken herself. He'd seen her gamble her body and reputation for money and prestige as Vincent's mistress. He'd seen her conspire with Vincent and Frank Marshall to murder Ben Cowden. He'd still wanted to marry her and Les believed Lorrie had promised him she'd do it.

"I . . ." Lorrie faltered, then cleared her throat so she could start again. "Me and Les are married, Dick. That's all there is to it."

"How did it happen? Why did you do it? You promised to marry me. Do you think he's better than me?"

"No one is better than you, Dick. I don't know why we did it. We went on a party the night of the wedding and we didn't stop until we got married."

Dick turned to Les. "Can you tell me why you did it? Do you Cowdens have to have everything? You've never even liked Lorrie."

"Dick, I'm the only one here who doesn't know what happened."

"I thought you were my friend. You knew Lorrie was going to marry me. Were you trying to get back at me because I worked for Duncan

Vincent? I thought you knew I was sorry for that. After all, his man shot me and left me for dead. I turned to your family after that. Now you've counted me dead just like all the other poor bastards you've killed in your war."

"It's not that, Dick. We were so drunk, we didn't know what we were doing."

"I don't believe that. I've seen you drink enough mescal to kill a tribe of Indians and not even yawn. Lorrie's too smart to drink because it makes her sick as a cat. You weren't too drunk to drag each other over to Judge Dunn and hold each other up while he married you."

"That's the first account of it I've heard from anybody but Lorrie."

"That's fine. You know what? I'm glad you ended up together. The tart dragged the drunkard she hated to the judge rather than marry me in a decent way. Neither one of you is worth the spit that holds you together."

Dick walked out. Les followed and stopped him on the veranda. He had never respected Dick much, but he did now. Sparse tears showed at the corners of Dick's eyes and he would not look at Les. He had been trying to be a friend to the Cowdens for a long time and part of the reason he joined Duncan Vincent when he did was because the Cowdens had not paid enough attention to him. Now Les wanted to be his friend and it was probably too late.

"I apologize for this, Dick."

"Les, I could have believed she would marry anyone else in the county, even a complete stranger, even maybe an Apache Indian, but not you. Sometimes I'd see the way you looked at each other and wonder if it was possible, but I was sure it could never happen. Even if I could have believed she'd marry you out of spite, or to get close enough to kill you, or to take something that belonged to you, I was sure you knew I wanted her and were too good a man to take her away from me."

Les could not answer because he was as surprised at what he'd done as everybody else.

"You've made me an enemy for life, Les. Don't count on me for anything."

"Am I going to have to fight you, too, Dick?"

"What do you care? I'm no match for you. You're a rich, strong, big, broad-shouldered Cowden. No, I won't fight you, but don't ever count on me for anything, not even a good morning." Dick Martin walked away.

Lorrie came and stood by Les and watched Dick disappear into a saloon. She said, "Well, that's that. I was worried he'd get nasty."

"Gosh, Lorrie, don't you have any feeling for the man at all? He's hurt worse than anyone I've ever seen."

"Sure, I do, but I'm can't worry about his troubles. I want to know what you plan to do about me."

"All of a sudden you need to know my plans? When did my plans become important to you?"

"After you and me got married."

"The only plans I have were made long before I woke up this morning. I have to go home and get my brother, load up, drive a bunch of horses to the Vaca ranch, and finish building corrals for Ben and Maudy."

"Oh no, you don't. You find something to do closer to home. You're married to me now."

"My home is where the work is. Later on, if we decide to stay together, I might take you to a ranch the Cowden Livestock Company sells us. For now, home will be in the adobe house at the Vaca ranch until Ben and Maudy come back from their honeymoon."

"Oh no. No ranch life for me. We're gonna live in my house here in Harshaw where you can come home to me every night and I can send you off regularly to work every morning."

"What will we do with Dick? He still lives in your house, doesn't he?"

"I'll take care of Dick. You just worry about taking care of me. You can start by moving your stuff up to my house."

"No. I'm loading up for the Vaca ranch. When I get back, if you want to live with me, we'll camp under the trees on the Temporal until I can build a house."

"Not me. You won't get me in a tent like an old squaw. Can you see me cooking beans and jerky over a fire? Your brain gone wet?"

"All right, we better go our separate ways while we still can without a lot of legal trouble. We're not even consummated."

Lorrie sang softly, "Oh yes we are."

"No, we're not. My brain might have been numb for Judge Dunn's ceremony, but I would not have slept through the fun part that made it legal."

"I agree. No man active as you could have slept through that. So, my friend, don't try to deny you had your fun. Get in harness, follow orders, and take up your duties as a husband."

"I'll tell you what. I'm going to my Uncle Vince's for a beer and bowl of *menudo*. I'll look you up later when you've had time to make a list of the orders you want to give me. I can't take orders when I'm hung over."

"I'll just go in the saloon with you, serve your *menudo* myself, and give you your orders while you fill your face."

"Oh no, you'd probably spit in it. Besides that, I won't allow any wife of mine to go in a saloon."

"You forget I work in that saloon. It occurs to me, we might not have any argument at all about where we're going to live. Much as you like

49

saloons, you now have an excuse to come and live in one. I'm sure your Uncle Vince would give you a job as a bartender. You can drink and fight to your heart's content from now on and get paid for it."

Indiana and Hattie Briggs came out to the veranda. Hattie said, "Why, imagine the gall of that Dick Martin. How could he think our Lorrie would marry him? He hasn't got a suit of clothes or a gunnysack to carry his overalls in or any prospects for the future at all."

Lorrie said, "Mama and Daddy, you can go home now. I have a good, safe place to sleep tonight, no matter what me and Les decide."

"You've made your decision, then?" Indiana asked.

"You bet she has," Les said.

"I'm staying right here in this hotel until I see how my daughter's treated," Hattie said.

"We're not staying" Indiana said. "We're going home. Come on." He took Hattie by the arm and walked her down the veranda stairs. When they landed on the street, Hattie jerked her arm away. "To *think* of the shabby way my beautiful daughter became a wife. And to make it worse, she had to marry a stinking, drunken Mexkin. It's more than any decent mother should have to bear."

"I don't think the Cowdens are Mexkins, Mama," Indiana said.

"Well, they talk it, act it, and look it, so you tell me what they are if they're not Mexkin."

Les was off to the saloon before Hattie got all of that out of her mouth.

Royal Vincent and the two cattlemen, John McClintock and Jack Akin, passed the Briggses on the street and walked up the stairs to the hotel veranda. They tipped their hats for Lorrie, went through the lobby and tipped their hats for A.B., then went upstairs to the VO offices on the second floor.

Vincent wore stylish, tailored clothes and shiny eastern boots. His one concession to frontier dress that day was the wide-brimmed, brown hat that he situated at a sharp angle over his brow. He hung his hat on the wall, gave cigars to his companions, and took a seat behind the desk. He kept his eyes lowered and took his time snipping off the end of his cigar and lighting it while the other men settled in their chairs.

"Have you heard?" Vincent narrowed his eyes against the thick smoke of his cigar. "Les Cowden married Lorrie Briggs on a drunk. Boy, wouldn't that be a pair to draw to in a fight? Now maybe the tart will get off my brother's back." He said this last to remind everyone that his brother Duncan Vincent knew the famous, beautiful Lorrie Briggs better than anyone present. Almost every man in southern Arizona lit up with pleasure at the mention of her name.

Akin and McClintock gave Royal blank looks. They were gentlemen.

They would not have made a comment even if Lorrie had been the Darling Clementine.

"Where's Duncan?" Jack Akin asked.

"He went back to New York at Christmastime to see the doctor."

"What's wrong, is he sick?"

"Oh no. Doris thought he needed a checkup."

"Is it his belly? He's always complaining about his belly. He been eating too much chile again? Is he worried about something?"

"It damned sure can't be the chile," McClintock said. "I eat barrels of it. I expect the Cowdens have given him ulcers or gas or something."

"They haven't done him any good, that's a cinch."

The cattlemen were in Harshaw hoping to be paid for several thousand steers Duncan Vincent had bought from them and shipped east before Christmas. Now they were finding out he had skipped without paying.

"How do you like those cigars, gentlemen?" Vincent said.

Akin and McClintock were not strangers to expensive cigars. They bought and sold tens of thousands of cattle the year around. They owned thousands of cattle on expensive pasture, in feed pens, and standing in the stockyards of California, Kansas City, and Chicago. They owned private railroad cars and spent more time traveling by rail between the far west and Chicago than they did in their own homes.

The Vincents represented a large eastern syndicate that was much wealthier than Akin and McClintock, but the Vincents were only employees of the syndicate. Akin and McClintock represented themselves in all aspects of their dealings. They did their own work and they gambled with their own assets. They spent a lot of time horseback, cutting and shipping cattle. California had been a state since 1850 and the two cattlemen kept their families on big ranches there. California was not having Indian trouble or range wars over public land. Royal Vincent's attempt to impress them with dollar cigars only showed them how much a gunsel he was. They did not need cigars, they needed Vincent to pay them for their steers.

"I hope you didn't invite us up here just to give us a cigar, Royal," Jack Akin said. "We want the checks for the steers we sold Duncan and we've come an awful long way to get them."

"Let me see what our secretary knows about it. I don't know how Duncan planned to pay you."

"He was supposed to have our money for us here today," Akin said.

"We didn't know he'd gone back east," McClintock said. "I guess we're lucky to find you here. We sure would have hated to waste the trip."

"Excuse me a minute." Vincent left the room and went down the hall to the secretary's office.

McClintock turned to Akin. "Jack, I think we stand about as much chance of being paid as the two whores who gave the soldiers credit until payday."

The cattlemen sat quietly and smoked their cigars for the rest of the time Vincent was out of the room. John McClintock was big as a grizzly and as voracious, but he was honest, openhanded, and often full of fun. When he traveled horseback, as he did that day, he wore the same canvas trousers, work shirt, big hat, and sheepskin jacket as an ordinary cowboy. He was able to give as good an account of himself defending his hide against Apaches in a remote canyon as he did in the drawing rooms of rich capitalists in Chicago.

Jack Akin was a slight, pale man. He seldom inquired about the health of a neighbor's family, but that neighbor knew he could expect a fair business deal from him.

When Vincent came back into the office, he said, "Well, I can't find any record of your checks. I'll get right on it and wire Duncan. Can you wait a few days until he answers? I imagine you're busy."

"Listen, I only came down here from Prescott, but that's still a week by stage," Akin said. "John came all the way from San Diego on the train. Duncan said he'd have our checks ready here today. He also promised to give us information about new public grazing land that's becoming available."

"Well, I'm sure sorry. He didn't tell me anything about your checks."

Akin said, "The secretary, what's his name, knew about our checks being due today. Can't you write them?"

"I'm afraid not, Jack. I'll have it straightened out in a day or two, though. I can tell you about the public land that's going to be available soon. Duncan needs your advice on that matter."

"Would that have anything to do with how quick we want you to pay us our money?"

"No, but it concerns a problem that plagues all the large land and cattle interests such as yours and ours."

"What's that?"

"It's these damned squatters like the Cowdens who forced this range war by hogging the public land. They're standing in the way of the progress that only businesses like yours and the VO's can bring to this country."

"You know I've been wondering why you call the Cowdens squatters and claim they stand in the way of progress." John McClintock said. "I sure never thought of them as squatters. Where did you get that?"

"Why, isn't that the best you can call them? They're only homesteaders. They use the public land around those homesteads as though it belonged exclusively to them. The only livestock they know is those scorpion-looking natives that are all horns and bones and tails that drag the ground."

McClintock became scornful. "What do you know about anything?

52

That family was named right when the top half of it was called cow. They're cowmen from the heels of their boots to their hatbands. The Porters, their forebears, have been here longer than anybody but the Apaches and the Mexicans. The only difference between them and us is, they've raised their families horseback and stood off Apaches and all kinds of desolation in order to keep the use of the public grass. We bought our way here. They came here when the country was still part of Mexico. They lost it in the Mexican war and then stayed and home-steaded it so they could get it back. I don't call that hogging the public land. I call it holding on until the goddamned death."

"That's not the opinion I expected from you, John. I hoped you would want to hear about the program Duncan and I have drawn up for the redistribution of public land. Your position in this matter should be the same as ours. Your help is required if we are all to continue to profit by the use of this land. The program is based on our mutual need for profit. With your help we can systematically and legally dismiss our competition while we make the country safe for settlement and new enterprise."

"Listen, we know what the VO's been trying to do. You want to fence the public land for yourself. You want to buy steers and run them on grass that people like the Cowdens need for their cows. You want more than your share of public grass and you'll fence your neighbors' cows off water to get it.

"I don't approve of the killing you've ordered, or the calumny you've spread about your neighbors, or the beatings your hoodlums gave A.B. and Ben Cowden so you could get them out of the way. I've lost horse races to the Cowdens and neighbored with them five years on the public land, and they're still my friends.

"In fact, they even helped your brother when he first came here. He could not have made it without them, yet he insisted on making ene-mies of them. Now you're trying to draw me and Jack into the damned war you've started with them. I don't appreciate that and it makes me feel that I've traveled seven hundred miles out here for nothing. I want to tell you, I don't like it when a man skips out on paying me what he owes and then tries to make me like it by inviting me into his war as though it would profit me."

McClintock stood up and put on his hat. He was so angry his hand shook. He missed the ashtray with his cigar, stubbed it out on the desk, and let it roll off to the floor.

Akin picked it up, dropped it in the ashtray, and followed him out.

Seven

AFTER THE CATTLEMEN left Vincent's office, Judge Richard M. Dunn went in with the five VO hands. Royal Vincent stood up and handed them constable's badges that the regulator rangers for the Pima Live Stock Association were empowered to wear. The young men took off their hats and stood up straight while Judge Dunn swore them in.

Royal moved out from behind the desk to shake hands and congratulate them. Judge Dunn helped himself to a handful of cigars from the box on the desk while he admonished them to just be sure they didn't do anything as constables that they would have been ashamed to do before they were given the badges.

Royal looked in the box to see if any cigars were left, picked it up so the Judge could not take any more, handed one to each of the constables, then put the box away in the desk. He unlocked a cabinet in the corner of the room and brought out a bottle of brandy and a half-dozen shot glasses and poured shots for the judge and each of the men. He then brought out a crystal snifter and poured a dram for himself.

"Well now, here's to the brave new crop of lawmen for lawless Pima County," Royal said, raising his glass.

The VO hands crowded to the desk and picked up their shots. Judge Dunn swallowed his drink and headed for the door, then paused before he went out. "Now that you're sworn lawmen and before you get to feeling too juicy, do some detective work and find out what happened to the six men who wore those badges before you."

"Where do we start, Judge?" Packrat said. "Give us a clue."

"Just ask your boss there," the judge said, and went out.

Royal refilled the empty shot glasses.

"What did happen to the men who wore these badges?" Packrat asked.

Stiles, Snider, and Teddy Briggs smirked and turned away.

Royal said, "They moved on to another line of work. It's time I told you what your duties as constables will be."

"Hey, I want to know what the judge meant," Creswell said. "What happened to those other rangers?"

"They're all dead, shot in the back," Snider said.

"By the Cowdens?"

"That's right. So now you've solved your first case. Shut up and let Mr. Royal give us our orders for the next one."

"I thought you knew the Live Stock Association and the VO were at war against the Cowdens and others of that faction," Royal said.

"I knew we were joining a war, but I didn't know other constables had been killed," Creswell said. "Who were they?"

"Greenhorn Texans who didn't know how to handle themselves," Snider said.

"How many were killed?" Packrat had turned pale.

"Five."

"I thought the judge said there were six. What happened to the other one?"

"What happened to the other one, Snider?" Royal said.

"He turned yellow and joined the Cowdens," Snider said. "He's that Joe Coyle who's flunkying around their barn with his kid."

"Any more questions?" Royal asked.

Creswell shook his head.

"I'm glad this meeting started out with that little bit of history to enlighten the new recruits," Royal said. "Thank you, Snider. You all might as well know, we're in a fight to the death against Cowdens, Apaches, miners, Mexican bandits, and cow thieves. If we are to bring progress to this frontier we need to fight for more grass and water. We've been losing the war. All the hopes of the VO are now in you native-born rangers. Your ability to regulate the policies of the Live Stock Association will determine the future of the VO."

"What does a regulator or ranger do?" Packrat asked.

"I'm sure your companions Stiles and Snider have told you something about it or you wouldn't be here. You've been sworn in as peace officers to uphold the law against cattle thieves. The squatters make their living branding mavericks. They carry running irons and steal cattle. Your main job is to stop that.

"The VO is only trying to fence and control the public grass that it's been allotted. The amount of public land we have the right to use is based on the amount of private land we own adjacent to the public land. Mavericklers like the Cowdens are trespassing on public land that only the VO has a right to use. You have been commissioned to keep the squatters off the VO's public land.

"You are authorized, even encouraged, to kill in self-defense. Don't fool yourself. Those badges make you targets for the Cowdens. They will kill you if you don't shoot first. They are dangerous. They've managed to eliminate our ranger force time and again by splitting it apart, killing some, and scaring the rest away."

"What makes you think we can do a better job than the Texans?" Creswell asked.

"The best asset you have is the same as the Cowdens' best weapon. You're native born. You know the country; you're young and reckless, and good horsemen. Three of you know the Cowdens well and have survived several fights with them. The other two come to the unit well-recommended. You are all fluent in Spanish and can get along as well in Sonora as Arizona. Those badges give you an automatic appointment to the ranks of Kosterlinsky's Rural Police called La Cordada."

"Whoa!" Creswell said. "Don't just go on and on with that crap. I'm from Holbrook, can't talk a lick of Mexican, and as far as being young and reckless, huh, I'm a devout coward when I'm being shot at."

"That's news to me. You were recommended for this job by Marshal Owens because of the work you did against rustlers in northern Arizona."

"Yeah, I know that, but it wasn't because I do things in a young and reckless manner. I work as an old coward and stay alive. If you think me or the Packrat are going to dash out and swashbuckle the Cowdens into their graves, you're crazy. So don't start out by lying to me and telling me what I can do and what my style is."

Royal smiled. "I stand very much corrected, Mr. . . . er . . . Creswell. I take it you still want the job?"

"Want the job? Hell no, what man in his right mind would want the job? I'm taking it though, because it's what I do best and nobody else in the territory likes me enough to give me a job."

"Well, *finally* we got that settled. Have I offended anyone else? If not, I'll give you your orders." Royal looked into the faces of his rangers.

"The first thing you have to do is discourage the Cowdens from taking possession of the Vaca ranch. The deeded land on that ranch borders the VO on the north and is only about twenty miles from our headquarters. By buying that ranch, Ben Cowden thinks he can help himself to all the mavericks in the country, turn his damned old cows out to graze the whole San Rafael Valley, and make a general nuisance of himself. I'm sure he thinks my brother Duncan is whipped and that's why he's gone in there and bought that ranch."

"Isn't he whipped?" Snider asked. "It seems to me, if Mr. Vincent had any brains at all, he would have known he was whipped after the Cowdens cooled all his mercenaries and sent him home from La Acequia."

"I admit Duncan was discouraged after that, but he isn't whipped. One little victory will bring him back, one like the crippling of a Cowden, the acquisition of the water rights to another mine or two, the packing up and shipping out of another squatter or two, the sudden mysterious death by long-range rifle of a Cowden, or one of their cousins."

Billy Stiles said. "That's right. You want to beat the Cowdens? Catch them afoot, then shoot them. Shoot those good horses out from under them first. Nobody'll ever be able to outrun them, or have the range they do, as long as they're mounted the way they are. In order to make targets of them that we can hit, we have to put them afoot.

"Right now might be a good time to take the offensive. Ben is off on his honeymoon and Lorrie Briggs has got Les all screwed up and confused. He's no good without Ben, but now that he's hung up in Lorrie's sheets, we can forget about him. If we can do something to make A.B. go crazy, the whole outfit'll go to hell. I think somebody ought to shoot Mark."

"You think they'll fall apart if you kill Mark, Billy?" Royal asked.

"Don't get the idea I'm the one to do it, because I ain't," Stiles said. "I just think that would be the best way to start winning this fight. The way to do that is just lay for him and potshot him from a long way off like you would a deer, then whoever does it should get the hell out of the country. But I ain't going to be the one to do it."

"Why not?"

"I'm too softhearted. I'm a terrible deer hunter. I've only been the Cowdens' enemy because I was paid to be. They've always given me a fair break and they've even been friendly. I think all the enmity has been on my side. I think they'd just as soon be friends. I couldn't potshot anybody like that."

"Well, who wants to do it?"

"By god, I'll do it," Teddy Briggs said.

"You want to shoot your brother-in-law?"

"You're damned right. Don't think I haven't thought of it. I've just been waiting until somebody offered to pay me to do it."

"Well, you're being paid your constable's and VO wages now, so you can have at 'er."

"Those wages ain't enough."

"What is enough?"

"Just give me five hundred bucks and my pick of two horses from the Cowden remuda after they fall," Teddy said.

"Done," Royal said. "You're not such a bad fellow. I thought you would try to hold me up."

"Listen to the rest of the deal. I want to be left alone to do it. I want to come and go as I please."

"That's fine. How soon can you do it?"

"Real soon."

"Why don't you shoot Les while you're at it?"

Teddy laughed. "Why Les?"

"It seems to me Les is tougher than Mark any day."

"Hell no, Les ain't tough anymore. Before the month is out Lorrie'll have him so tame he'll have to sack up his ass to keep from dragging out his tracks. He won't be any good to himself, his family, or even a wood hauler. Lorrie's going to turn Les Cowden into an orphan. We ain't never going to have to worry about Les Cowden again. Believe me, I'm Lorrie Briggs's brother."

After the rangers went out, two middle-aged men came through the door from an adjoining room.

"Did you listen?" Royal asked.

The men nodded.

"What do you think?"

"They're awful green," the tallest, a man named Randolph, said.

"That's probably the biggest bunch of wastrels in Arizona territory," the other man, Von, said. "They might be good cannon fodder, but I'm not even sure of that."

"Yes, and you know why the VO will be happy to draft their checks every month? Because they'll pester the Cowdens. That's all I need from them. It certainly doesn't matter if they get hurt, or the Cowdens run them off. There's plenty more like them in Arizona. Right now there's an overabundance of gunsels trying to learn how to be bad in Arizona."

Lorrie looked out the window of her house and tried to decide what to do with herself. If she was to make a stand, she would have to go to work in the saloon that afternoon as usual. The job was still hers and she did not think she ought to quit and depend on the support of Les Cowden.

Dick Martin's clothes and all the rest of his outfit were still in the house. Sooner or later he would probably come to get them and want to put on another sad show. For the next show he would probably be full of beer.

Yes, she guessed the thing to do was get ready for work. Once she found herself in the swing of it again, she would probably get along as though she had never thought to make a change, or spend her days another way.

She was very much surprised to see the Cowdens's bay team swing a spring wagon into her yard with Viney Cowden driving. All the Cowden girls were with her. Lorrie was so surprised to see them, she couldn't get away from the window before they saw her. They got down off the wagon and headed for the house. Lorrie was damned sure not afraid of them, so she opened the door.

Viney said, "Hello, Lorrie," and led her daughters into the house. Lorrie paused and looked outside to see if any more were coming. She closed the door and Viney took her by the shoulders and hugged her. Then Eileen, Betty, and Paula Mary each came up, looked her in the eye, and hugged her.

"Are you packed, yet, Lorrie?" Viney said. "We know Les won't be any help, so we've come to help you pack and take you home."

Lorrie may have been wild, vindictive, and mean when she wanted to be and was capable of cheating anyone else in the world, but she never lied to herself. She had always wished she could belong to a family like the Cowdens and have a decent life. That was one reason she stood Les Cowden up on his hind legs and married him. She had other reasons for marrying him that were as much fun, but being able to go live with the Cowden women was the best.

"Mrs. Cowden, what makes you think I want to go home with you?" Lorrie said. She wanted to be wooed a little. After all, everybody knew she was rotten. Why disappoint them?

"You're a Cowden now and we hope you'll come home with us."

"Aren't you even a little bit disappointed in the person Les chose for a wife?"

"Lordy, young woman, I've never been able to imagine what kind of girl Les would bring home. I've only worried that no one would have him. Now I don't have to imagine who his wife will be. You're the girl and thank the Lord you're sound and probably in your right mind. If you'll have Les and his family, we'll have you."

"I don't know. We didn't do right by marrying the way we did and Les wants out."

"Les doesn't know what he wants. Do you want out of the marriage?"

"If he does."

"Was it your idea to get married?"

"We got the idea at the same time."

"Then, little lady, if you want to try and make a marriage with my son, we're here to take you home. Want to give it a try? Me and my girls promise you, you'll never be lonesome in our house. We're on your side. Any time you decide you don't want to stay, we'll pack you up and bring you back."

"If you put it that way, I guess I can try."

The Cowden ladies helped Lorrie pack, loaded her in the spring wagon, drove back to town, and stopped in front of the saloon. Viney enlisted a boy off the street and sent him in for Les.

"My gosh," Les said, when he emerged and saw his womenfolk.

"We've got your wife," Eileen called. "I wouldn't stay in there too long if I were you."

"You better find a way to beat us home, Tomcat," Viney said, and she drove away.

"Let's go, brother."

Les turned and Mark was standing at his elbow. "What?"

"I've got Papa's buggy with orders to load you any way I can and take you home," Mark said.

"What about my horse?"

"What horse?"

"The horse I rode to town the other night."

"Papa sent him home with Jimmy Coyle days ago."

"What if I'd needed to run home in a hurry?"

"I don't know what you would have done, but you were unfit to ride."

"I can ride anytime, drunk or sober."

"Let's go, then."

"I'm not ready to go home."

"All right, I'll wait."

"Then come in and have a drink."

"Nope. I don't want a drink. You drink and I'll wait."

Les looked at his brother's stubborn face. "Hell, it won't be any fun if I know you're out here waiting."

"That'll be tough, won't it?"

"Aw hell, let's go home then."

El Durazno was altogether a new place for Les that first evening he found himself home with a wife. Viney and the girls made a fiesta of Lorrie's joining the family and gave Les to know he would have to go if he did not make her welcome.

Les guessed he should have tried to be more polite when he woke up in the hotel and found himself married. He might have tried to be a gentleman, but at the time he had been sure she would make some smart remark about it.

Now he could not keep from looking at her and she looked back when no one else was watching. This time his damned running and playing had not ended with only a hangover and a little guilt for being a cut-up and a brawler. This time he'd made a partnership with another person, and of all things, a wife, and of all people, Lorrie Briggs the enemy.

Lorrie did not seem like the enemy when she looked at him now. She looked prettier than anyone he'd ever known and the disdainful look was gone out of her eye. He even felt protective of her. From the standpoint of the tough Lorrie Briggs, she was not in a good situation. She was in a place where she was not supposed to have a friend in the world.

As far as Les knew, Dick Martin was the only friend Lorrie ever had. She was in the habit of flaunting her looks, giving men the lure, and then sinking the hook, not to reel them in, but to play them on the line until they went to pieces trying to get away. If they spurned her, she shot them.

That night before supper everybody was served a cup of brandy that the family made from the peaches of El Durazno. A.B. stood at the supper table, raised his glass to Lorrie, and said, "It seems that alcohol might have caused Les and Lorrie's adventure to start off bad, so to help right their course let's toast them with the tamest peach brandy in Arizona. I propose that we back Lorrie and Les with all our hearts, that they love one another as Viney and I do, and I hope that Lorrie learns to love us."

Just then a rig passed on the road. The family looked out and saw Lorrie's parents headed home. A.B. quickly ordered Mark to run and see if he could stop them and, if he could not, to saddle a horse, overtake them, and bring them back.

Lorrie only glanced once at her departing kin, then at Les, then away. "Don't bother going after them," she said. "They won't come back."

"I invited them to stop on their way home, but that was before I knew Lorrie would be here," A.B. said. "I should have insisted that they stop for supper. We should have let them know that we brought Lorrie home with us, Viney."

Viney only looked at him.

Lorrie said, "They knew I was here."

"How could they, Lorrie?" Paula Mary said.

"Your mother and I saw them watching us from the hotel veranda when we stopped in front of the saloon to get Les."

The Cowdens said no more about it. Their way was to leave another's personal business alone, even if she was another Cowden.

Eight

PATCH THE APACHE was on his way horseback to El Durazno from the army camp at Huachuca. Low clouds covered the top halves of the Huachuca Mountains on the south, the Whetstones on the north and the Canelo Hills that lay dead ahead as he rode west. A steady, cold drizzle of rain soaked the country. He followed an old wagon route to Santa Cruz, for he was in a hurry. He was not much concerned about cover or concealment, for he had just visited the Yawner. He wore the black blouse and red headband of the army scout, so he did not think he needed to hide his movements from the Apaches or the U. S. Army.

He rode into a willow thicket to cross Slaughterhouse Wash and his horse Colorado's ears perked up at something moving upstream. Patch stopped in the thicket and waited. The short, low murmur of a man's voice made him duck his head over Colorado's neck to hide. He dismounted and made Colorado lie down, as the horse was trained to do.

Colorado stretched out flat on his side and lay as motionless as a dead horse. Patch lay beside him with an arm over his neck. He watched Colorado and listened for the travelers. Another twitch of the horse's ears located them again and then Patch plainly heard them moving closer.

Colorado barely moved one ear once more at a sound Patch could not hear, then he lay still, barely breathing. Patch grinned at his horse. Colorado loved to act dead. Patch had not taught him to hold his breath, only that it was his duty to lie still when ordered to do so. The horse had been in some bad fights in his short life and seemed to appreciate being able to lie low and still instead of taking flight. He liked to run, though, and he was fast. Patch felt no great need to hide himself and his horse. Soldierlike, he did it for fun, and for drill.

He could only see one clearing across the wash where the travelers might show themselves, so he listened and admired the acting of his horse. Colorado's eye was half-open and glazed as a dead horse's. Patch moved closer against him, hugged his neck and watched for the travelers. The horse even seemed to be turning cold.

The first person who came in sight was Patch's brother Arco, and his heart sank. He had been informed by the Yawner that same day that Arco had been running with Chato, Patch's enemy. Chato meant "pug nose." The man was also called "bloody nose" for his habit of biting the faces of the people he killed and snorting his nose in their blood. Patch saw that Arco's buckskins were smeared with new blood.

The next man who came along was Fausto, cousin of Arco and Patch. Fausto carried a bundle of clothing on his back. The thighs of his buckskin trousers were smeared with blood. Behind him came Chato, riding a horse and leading another horse. The Mexican girl Teresa who lived with Huesos's family at El Relave was on the horse Chato was leading.

Arco was so wildly vigilant as he hunted the brush on all sides that Patch felt lucky he had not been discovered. Arco looked jaded as a deer that had been run for days by the Tarahumara.

To make a game of the hunt, the Tarahumara Indians enjoyed chasing deer and running them down on foot. Patch had seen deer that were being chased by the Tarahumara stumble into an Apache camp for sanctuary. After a deer found that he could not find safety through ordinary flight, he became so frantic to get away from the invincible Tarahumara that he sought any haven. He was never touched and hardly even saw the Tarahumara until exhaustion made him quit and the man caught up and cut his throat.

By the evidence he saw, Patch knew Chato had raided El Relave. He knew the girl and recognized the horses. His brother's expression was the same as a deer's who was about to be run down as prey, as though his flight was being channeled by pursuit. A girl, horses, and booty had been taken, and someone would inevitably come after them. Of the three Apaches, Arco was the one who would fear the consequences of a raid the most, and that was probably the reason Chato put him up front.

Fausto did not fear anything, not a fight, or the flight after a raid. He only strode quickly along and sweated under his load without letting it bother him. Except for being brave, he was another Chato.

Chato was the most vicious Apache. His main vice was killing. He took care to exercise his viciousness completely, so that he might savor it and make it last. The more defenseless his victim, the better. He never attacked an enemy face to face or man to man. He would only thrust his lance at a victim if he could draw first blood from the rear or surprise him from a blind side.

Patch knew Teresa, for he often stopped at El Relave to visit Huesos, but he did not know her well. He never stopped at a ranch where a woman lived unless the man was there. He seldom entered a ranch house. The inside of a house seemed to be a place where he would surely find his doom.

Patch waited until the Apaches were out of gunshot range before he made Colorado stand up. He mounted and backtracked them. If Arco and Fausto had been alone he would have stopped them and talked, but he did not want them to even see him when they traveled with Chato. Anyone with Chato did as Chato ordered. Chato would have entertained himself by tormenting Patch and making Arco and Fausto help him.

Patch found where Chato had stopped on Manila Peak, slaughtered a horse, and eaten the *menudos,* the heart, liver, and kidneys. Patch had seen the rest of the meat drying in sheets on the horses Chato and Teresa were riding.

The smell of blood was fresh on the place and Colorado did not like it. "There, see, Colorado? Always run away from Apaches when you see them." Patch laughed. Colorado's ears showed that he was sufficiently astounded by the things Apaches did to horses.

Chato was headed north toward the Whetstone Mountains. Full of meat as he was, he would probably not go much farther than the Whetstones until he was through feasting on the fresh meat he carried. Patch hoped he did not go to the Rincons. Patch's grandfather Casimiro and his little sister Casi were camped there, the next range north of the Whetstones. Chato's mouth would water if he knew Casi was with the old Yaqui.

Patch hoped Chato would be so full of meat and so comfortable with Teresa to use as a pillow, that he would stay in the Whetstones a while. Patch needed to find out what had happened to Huesos's family. He had seen both Snider and Huesos at the wedding of the Horseman, so he knew the women had been left alone at El Relave.

He found the spot where Chato rested at the *tauna* on Cocono Creek and dismounted to see what he could see. Because of the rain, he almost missed the spot Chato had brushed clean on the bedrock above the *tauna.* He only found it by accident when he squatted to rest beside it and saw the small bundle of willow twigs Chato had used to brush placer out the cracks in the rock. He knew Chato was fascinated by gold. Chato's blood was cold and he placed great value on cold things. He would rather see a little girl cold and dead than warm and

63

alive. He wanted gold. He knew how to spend it, too, but he seldom spent any.

Patch backtracked Chato to El Relave. Huesos's milk cow was grazing on the creek. She bawled and her eyes bulged with blame for her misery when she saw him, for she had not been milked and her udder was full to bursting. Her milk squirted when she bawled and kept streaming out when she walked. He drove her through open gates to the milk pen and shut her in. A horse nickered to Colorado and Patch saw he was not one of Huesos's horses. He wore the grandfather Porter's brand.

Patch saw Huesos's tracks in the corral. He unsaddled Colorado, put him in a dry stall and gave him grass-hay and grain. He found a bucket, milked the cow, and carried the milk to the house.

He saw blood smeared on the door and began to whistle softly to send out a mild alert for anyone who might be inside. For slipping up on this house, an Indian could lose his life before he even spilled a drop of milk out of the bucket. He saw more of Huesos's fresh tracks in the mud. The deep silence of the house made Patch stop whistling.

He went in and put the milk on the kitchen table, saw that blood had been spilled on the floor and someone had tried to wipe it clean. He wanted out of there and began to move stealthily. If Huesos was near, Patch was in danger, even though they had always been friends.

The bodies of Emily and Willy Fly were on the bed in the next room covered by a blanket. Patch heard someone digging and he looked out the bedroom window. He saw Huesos swing a pick into the ground on a hill behind the house. Patch went back to the barn and was careful to keep Huesos located by the sound of the digging until Colorado finished his hay. He saddled and rode back to the river, using the barn and corrals to hide him from Huesos. He would have liked to help dig the grave, but he knew the last thing Huesos wanted to see was an Apache.

The Cowden family rose in pitch dark rainy weather at 3:00 A.M. to help Les and Mark start for the Vaca ranch. The brothers went down to the barn to grain the horses and lay out the gear they would pack. Joe and Jimmy Coyle were there to help. When they were done, they all went to the house and Viney and the girls served a breakfast of beefsteak, eggs, potatoes, hotcakes, and wild honey.

Paula Mary went out to the Arizona room and brought in a blue enamel bowl of fresh milk. A thick layer of yellow cream had crusted on top. Les broke through the rich crust with a big spoon and scooped out a great dollop for his coffee, then more for his pancakes. The layer of cream was more than an inch thick and the family spooned it out until all the heavy, lumpy part of it was on their hotcakes or in their coffee. Viney stirred the finer cream to mix it down into the rest of the milk, poured the milk into quart jars, and put them away in a cupboard in the screened Arizona room.

Les had not been resting well. He and Lorrie may have enjoyed a wild spree in the hotel, but none was being enjoyed at El Durazno. The Cowdens did not worry about bunking the newlyweds together. Privacy was at a minimum because the house was only equipped with three large bedrooms. A.B. and Viney shared one, another was used by the girls, and the other by the boys. With Garbie and Lorrie, five young persons were using the girls' bedroom and sharing two big beds.

The boys' room was the logical place for Les and Lorrie, now that Ben was married and gone. Mark offered to give up his bed and sleep on a cot in some other part of the house, or in the barn with the Coyles, but Les and Lorrie would not have it. Now that they had sobered up from their spree, they were too shy to share a room surrounded by so many Cowdens. They preferred to be modest, single persons who were content to steal looks at each other from time to time.

At mealtimes, Les kept his eyes on his plate when Lorrie came around. He felt the whole family wanted to catch him making eyes at her. He was relieved that she took hold of the work with his sisters in the morning. He would have been embarrassed if she turned out to be sullen or windy or sat on her butt to be waited on by his mother and sisters.

Lorrie had been making points with Les from the first moment she came to live with the family. She had only visited with the Cowdens once before when Ben took her to a family dinner in Harshaw. That time she'd been snooty as hell, sat and looked down her nose at everybody while they waited on her, and never offered to help prepare the meal or clean up afterwards. That was the worst way any ablebodied girl could behave when she was invited to a frontier home. If she could not at least offer to make a hand when others were working at making a nice dinner, she wasn't worth killing.

Les and Mark, A.B., Joe and Jimmy were in the middle of breakfast and the women were through serving when Paula Mary sat down beside Les. Les knew she'd been laying for him and would not be able to go on living unless she could pounce on him and victimize him. He winked at her to encourage her to get it over with.

Paula Mary put on her innocent tot's face and said, "Leslie, when are you and Lorrie going to set up your own housekeeping?"

"What's the matter, little sister, you want us to leave?"

"Gosh, no."

"Then why do you ask? Don't you like your own sleeping arrangement?"

"I like it fine. Me and my sisters are used to sleeping together. Garbie and Lorrie seem to get along all right in the other bed, but isn't the husband supposed to take his wife to his own house or something when they get married?"

"Sooner or later, I guess."

Everybody else kept so still, not even the floors creaked, not even a hot coal rolled over in the stove.

Straight-faced, Paula Mary said, "Then you're not afraid Lorrie'll shoot you in the toe the first time she gets mad like she did Ben?"

Eileen laughed. "Don't worry, Leslie. We've been kidding Lorrie that you deserved to be shot by an angry female a long time ago, so she must be just the right girl for you."

"And why is that, Paula Mary?" Les said.

"Why?" Paula Mary said. "She proved she can't be messed with. You mess with her, you get the boolet."

"Paula Mary, what did I do to deserve a hoorawing by you this morning?"

A.B.'s eyes were cold as the blue ice on a high, deep, shady canyon lake in winter as he turned to his smallest daughter. Paula Mary opened her mouth to begin a smart retort, was bitten by the frost in her father's look, closed her mouth, and swallowed. Lorrie laughed and turned her back to the table. She was still smiling when she took the coffee pot off the stove and poured Les's cup full.

"What were you about to say, Paula Mary?" asked Viney.

"Nothing, Mama," Paula Mary murmured.

"Good. Maybe you could get the dishwater ready."

Paula Mary nodded seriously, stood up, and picked up Les's full coffee cup. "I guess that's a good idea," she said in a low voice, and the whole family laughed.

Surprised in the act of reaching for his coffee and finding his cup gone, Les said, "Paula Mary . . ."

"Oh, excuse me." She turned back and took the saucer, too.

Feeling that he had come away from another Paula Mary ambush nearly unscathed, Les left the table almost happy. He was ready to hit for the *tules* and get back to work away from women. He went to the corral and caught a horse called Snake from Ben's mount.

He would not ordinarily touch an animal from another man's mount, but that morning he was not thinking. He saw Snake standing in a pen by himself and remembered that Ben had put him there because the horse needed work. The horse was naturally snaky, mean, and untrustworthy. The only way to get along with him was to work hell out of him. Ben had caught him up because he'd pulled too many tricks. He had vowed to ride him every day for a while, then quit riding to prepare for his wedding. The horse still needed work and Les was in the mood to mash something that needed mashing.

The brothers intended to camp at the Vaca for a while, so they were taking plenty of horseflesh and provisions. They were also taking ten head of big bulls and oxen to sell for meat to the soldiers at Huachuca. Mark intended to work five colts during the trip. He packed his and Les's beds on two colts, their provisions and camp gear on two more, and saddled a colt to ride. Les was taking two extra cow horses.

When Les and Mark were ready to go, Joe and Jimmy saddled horses to help them start the livestock down the road. A.B. blocked the road with his horse and buggy to keep the remuda and cattle from turning toward Harshaw. Les and Mark positioned their horses outside the corral so they could point the stock down the road when Joe and Jimmy drove them out.

The cattle and horses felt good and started running when they splashed through the creek. Les was on the hill in front of them and he turned them down the road. The hill was steep, so it helped turn the cattle. Mark was in the creek below the cattle inside the turn. Joe and Jimmy came on behind the cattle.

Les spurred Snake across the steep slope of the hill intending to get out ahead of the stock and ride point until they settled down. The livestock felt good in the light rain and bucked and kicked and clattered on the road. Snake looked for an opportunity to unload Les while he could still smell his full bin of hay in the corral. He humped across the hill while Les tried to hurry him to get ahead of the cattle. When Les turned him downhill toward the road, Snake bogged his head and pitched off the hill in wild, headlong, writhing jumps.

The entire brood of Cowden women were out in the front yard to watch the cowboys start for the Vaca. A.B. drove along in his buggy behind the cattle with Joe and Jimmy. Les was given a second to realize he looked awfully good making a bronc ride on Snake down the hill. The horse could not swap ends with him while his momentum carried him downhill. Les knew he would have hell when the horse hit the road though. The road was like a wall in front of him and Snake was falling toward it without looking where he was going. Les would never be able to pick his head up and stop him before he hit the road. Snake's ass was going to do a houlihan when he butted his head against that hard road. "Oh me," Les murmured, and he looked across the creek into Lorrie Briggs Cowden's eyes.

The main traffic on that road was made up of ore wagons drawn by eighteen- and twenty-mule teams to and from the railroad in Patagonia. Ore wagon roads were the hardest, most abrasive surfaces in the world. Snake's head bored into the barpit beside the road as Les expected, Les heard sharp twin cracks as both Snake's cannon bones snapped and the horse cartwheeled and skidded on his back across the road.

Les spilled on his face across the rocky surface ahead of the horse. The cattle, cow horses, and packhorses were close upon him. The only way for them to go was over the top of Les and Snake. They balked, skidded, lifted their tails, snorted, squirted manure, scared themselves, and stampeded over the top of Les and Snake and ran on. Mark was so intent on getting ahead of the livestock that he did not even look back to see if Les survived. Jimmy at least gave Les a worried look before he ran on to help Mark.

A.B. dismounted from the buggy and peeled Les off the roadway. Les hurried to see how badly Snake was injured. The poor horse tried to get his feet on the ground ahead of him to rise, but his forelegs were broken. Before Les even wiped the mud and blood out of his eyes, he unbridled Snake, drew his pistol, and shot him.

Les leaned against the hill, found his handkerchief, and began cleaning the mud out of his eyes. A.B. pushed Les's hat back and spit on his own handkerchief to help him. Les wiped on one eye and A.B. wiped the other. A.B. noticed he was helped by abundant tears. He stepped back and saw his son was weeping.

"Well, son, that was quite a *catatumba* you took."

"I know, Papa. I couldn't pull him up. What am I going to tell Ben?"

"Did he ask you to ride his horse?"

"No, but the horse needed work. How's my brother going to take what I did to him?"

"Come on, son. Help Joe drag Snake off the road."

Joe had gone back for a team of workhorses and a doubletree to drag Snake away. Les undid his cinches and Joe hitched the horses to Snake and dragged him off the saddle. Les loaded his saddle, bridle, and blankets in the buggy and looked down the road for the cattle. They were clear out of sight.

Then Les, A.B., and Joe heard a shot. Les thought everything that could go wrong that day had already gone wrong, but two more gunshots sounded and were interspersed with the faint, high-pitched yelling of Jimmy Coyle. Joe swung aboard his saddle horse and spurred him down the road at a run. A.B. jumped on the buggy and whipped the team after him. Les boarded on the run and jerked his rifle out of its boot on his saddle.

The rain quickened to a downpour as A.B. warmed the hindquarters of his team with a buggy whip. Around the first bend the team almost collided with Mark's horse Colonel on a riderless runaway toward home. Mark's saddlehorn had been shattered and it wobbled on a last shred of leather. Les was suddenly so worried for Mark that it made him sick. The horse must have landed hard on his back to shatter the horn like that. As the buggy careened across the creek, Les saw that the tracks of the livestock left the road and followed the creek. A.B. stayed on the road and climbed the next hill. Les saw the cattle running a half mile further down the canyon. The packhorses were a hundred yards behind the cattle, but Les's saddle horses were long gone.

Shots sounded in the canyon below the buggy and one of A.B.'s bay team fell dead in the harness. A.B. picked up his rifle to fight back. In a hail of rifle fire, Les hugged his father against his chest and jumped to the ground for cover.

The rain increased as Les and A.B. fired into a rampart of boulders on the brow of a cliff across the canyon. Three men left that cover and ran over the top of the hill. Les threw off his slicker and ran down into the canyon, calling for Mark. Joe Coyle answered him.

Mark was sitting on a rock, holding his bleeding arm. Jimmy Coyle's Texas pony lay dead and Jimmy was sitting by his head, his own forehead streaming blood. Joe put a clean handkerchief on Mark's forearm as a compress and tied it on with his bandana. Mark's blood splattered on the rock with the rain. The storm darkened.

A.B. came to help Mark, so Les mounted Joe's horse and rode after the bushwhackers. He climbed a slick, wet slope through a stand of white oak and found the spot where four horses had been held. The ambush had evidently been laid in the rampart of boulders before Mark and Jimmy ran down the canyon to hold the livestock. The brass casings for two .30-30's and a Sharps .4570 littered the ground behind the cover of the rampart.

Joe Coyle's buckskin horse seemed tired, so Les dismounted to rest him while he read the bushwhackers' tracks. He turned to remount and saw blood streaming from the horse's nose. He stepped back, mortified that he had been riding a wounded horse. The buckskin groaned, swayed, fell over on his side, stiffened, and died.

"Aw hell," Les said, and he sat on the wet ground. After a while he took Joe's saddle, bridle, and blankets off the horse and carried them down the canyon's steep side.

The first ball fired at Mark had shattered his saddlehorn, broken his arm, unhorsed him, and sent Colonel home. A well-aimed ball killed Jimmy's little Texas brown and when he fell he banged Jimmy's head against the ground. Joe caught up during a lull and left his horse standing ground-hitched in the open while he sought cover. Joe had not realized that the buckskin was hit. The whole Cowden outfit had been put on the ground afoot. The cattle, packhorses, and cow horses were gone, and the killers were probably headed for someplace warm and dry for a drink and a meal.

Les sat down on a rock and used the rain on his face to clean out his eyes once and for all. "How did anyone know to lay an ambush here by the road?" he said. "Did we tell anyone we were going to the Vaca today?"

A.B. shook his head. "Who did you tell outside the family, son?"

Les's head ached. He said, "The Lord only knows."

Nine

A.B. TIED THE BUGGY'S TONGUE to the harness of the surviving horse, a gelding named Barney, so he could haul his crew home. The Cowdens and Coyles headed home in silence, except for Jimmy Coyle's sniffles. Les felt beaten. If A.B. or Mark had been killed, he might as well have slashed his wrists for all the good he would be in continuing the fight against the VO.

Les did not doubt that the ambushers were VO. Their tracks showed that they had waited by the road in the rain, followed Mark down the canyon where they tried to kill him, then ran away in the direction of Harshaw. The VO was ahead in the score by the count of three dead horses. The Cowdens were lucky to come away without losing any people. Les's carelessness in spurring Snake and jumping him out when he knew he might buck was the batterass blunder that had allowed the ambush to succeed. He decided he'd better give up trying to be a showoff bronc rider until the war was over.

Les felt as ordinary and helpless as everybody else in the world, because he had practically helped the bushwhackers put his family afoot. Now he realized how much the Cowdens needed their horses. Les's top horse, Sorrel Top, had been shot out from under him and killed early in the war. Les wondered if the VO had decided to eliminate the Cowdens' best weapon by shooting their big horses. They could hardly miss. Even a poor shot could hit a horse.

The Cowdens would never have thought of shooting a man's horse. The Cowden women were not being respected in this war, and back-shooting by the VO was common, but Les would never have expected them to start killing horses. Both sides needed horses. The VO certainly held the same esteem for their saddle horses as the Cowdens. Well, that barrier was down and the VO horses would be Les's next target.

"Papa, the VO did this to us. They saw that they put us afoot, so they probably won't go far," Les said. "In this weather I bet they headed straight for Harshaw and the saloon."

"I'm going after them as soon as I leave Mark and Jimmy with your mother," A.B. said.

"I want to be deputized, Papa."

"You're deputized."

Just before A.B. rounded the last bend by the ranch, Barney nickered. Les thought he was only anxious to get home, but then he almost collided with Viney's doctor's buggy on the turn. Viney had hitched the one-horse buggy in a hurry and she'd been whipping up, so her horse was taking long breaths and was hard to stop. Viney, Paula Mary, and Lorrie were crowded together on the narrow seat. A.B. and Viney hauled back on the lines to keep from tangling the horses.

"My God, one round of that .4570 would get both our wives," A.B. said. "Then what would we do?"

"Mr. Cowden, we heard guns," Viney said. "Lorrie and I decided to arm the other girls at home and see what we could do to help you."

"The boys are hurt. We'd better wait to talk about it when we get home." A.B. backed Barney to a wide spot in the road so Viney could go by and turn around. Nobody said another word all the way home.

Les wondered at the Cowdens' change of fortune. They were getting more vulnerable by the minute. Now the VO had them bunched like a herd of goats. Every Cowden wife, father, ablebodied man, and even the smallest child could have been killed in the past hour by two volleys of rifle fire.

After recouping at the ranch, Joe and Les saddled horses and headed back to locate the livestock. They met the horses coming home, drove them in and corraled them. The cattle could be gathered another day.

Back at the barn, Les hitched a team of sorrel geldings for A.B.'s ride to town. Paula Mary came to the barn just as Les was about to mount his saddle horse and head for Harshaw alone.

"Mama wants you up at the house, brother," Paula Mary said.

"Tell Mama I went to town."

Paula Mary stamped her foot. "Mama told me to tell you to do right for a change and come to the house."

Les took his foot out of the stirrup, put his horse in a stall, and he and Joe followed Paula Mary to the house. He went to his room, sat on the bed, and took a drink of mescal. His sister Betty came in without knocking and caught him putting the jug back under the bed. She was carrying an enamel basin full of warm water, a bar of lye soap, and a bundle of clean rags. She did not admonish him about the jug. Les figured that was because she did not want to talk. She had not said ten words to him since Frank Marshall, the VO thug, tried to rape her two months ago.

Betty sat down on the edge of the bed and looked at his eyes, then lathered one of the rags in the warm water. "Lie down," she said. "Right there on the edge of the bed." Les was surprised Betty was finding time to attend him. She loved Mark a lot more. Les wished she had stayed with Mark instead of surprising him with his snoot in the jug. She sat lightly beside him and cleaned the mud and blood off his face with the strong soap, then washed the embedded dirt out of the palms of his hands. Les liked to have his sisters by him. "Ow," he said.

Betty went out with the basin and bloody rags and came back with clean water, and a clean shirt that she laid on the bed. She rinsed all the soap off him and when she was done, pressed one warm, clean hand on his cheek. "You and your damned mescal," she said, and went out.

The kitchen always served as the Cowden operating room. Viney and Eileen had already washed, set, and splinted Mark's forearm. He looked pale and sick as Garbie wrapped the splint in a clean cloth. A.B. set a hot toddy of his good whiskey and sugared lime water in front of him.

Jimmy's head was doctored and bandaged. His eyes were red and teary. Grief for his little horse brought a sniffle out of him from time to time, but he made no complaint.

"I've been telling Joe and Jimmy we're grateful for their help," A.B. said. "I want you, Les, to bring in the remuda and have Joe and Jimmy pick mounts to replace the good horses they lost today. Those horses brought them here from Texas."

"They can have any horse we've got," Les said.

"You don't have to do that," Joe said. "Nobody told us we had to ride our own horses. You gave us Cowden horses to use."

"Well, we want you to have horses you can call your own," A.B. said. "That's the way you came to us and it's only right. You asked not to be included in our war. The least we can do is replace your losses. I also want to apologize to you."

"For what, sir?"

"For involving you in our war with the VO."

"Listen, you're not to blame for what they did. Me and Jimmy were fired on. We got in the war when I fired back."

"Well, I'm sorry you've been drawn into it."

"I was a fool to think we could stay neutral. The VO is my enemy now. I'm giving Jimmy a pistol to carry so he can defend himself."

Jimmy got up from the table and went out to the back porch. Paula Mary followed him.

"That certainly is a brokenhearted boy," A.B. said.

"Jimmy and Little Brown grew up together," Joe said.

Les had always admired Jimmy's Steeldust pony, a brown gelding who got his size from his berber mother and his muscle and short-distance speed from his Steeldust sire. The boy would be a long time taking another horse into his heart.

A.B. and Les rode to Harshaw in search of the four bushwhackers. They trotted up the length of saloon row. No horses were tied in the street in the rain or in the alley behind the saloons. The Cowdens stabled their horses in a barn behind the hotel and walked a block to the town livery.

The livery was run by Eddie Newton, called Eddie the Newt, a sneaky, wormy little blacksmith whose two-faced ways had made him an enemy of the Cowdens. Mark especially disliked him, not only because he had taken sides with the VO, but because he liked to buzz like a fly around Garbie Burr when she was at work waiting table.

Les and A.B. could hear Newton hammering at the forge, so without saying anything to each other they walked up to the blind side of the barn and split before Newton could see them. A.B. went around to the back to talk to Newton, and Les went in the front.

Les waited until he heard A.B.'s deep voice murmur at the forge, then searched down the line of stalls. Steam rising above two stalls led him to two sweat-soaked VO horses. He knew there had been three bushwhackers and one who held their horses, but seeing only two hot horses did not dissuade him from believing they belonged to the culprits. It only told him two of them had gone elsewhere to hide. He walked quietly toward the forge.

"Then you say no one's come in with their horses during the past few hours, Eddie?" A.B. said.

Newton was standing on Les's side of the forge, with his back to him. "Nossir, I just told you, nobody. You expecting somebody special?" Eddie the Newt prided himself on his large forearms. He always kept his sleeves rolled up to the elbows and he never wore a jacket, winter or summer. He was a strong, sooty-armed, dirty-handed little man who looked like a toad.

"I'm searching for three cowards who came to town about three hours ago."

"What cowards would that be? I expect you're not asking about some other Cowdens."

"Cowards who bushwhacked my sons and killed three of our horses a few hours ago."

"They did? Well, nobody's brought any horses in here since last night."

"Then why is steam rising off those horses back there in the stalls."

"Oh, that? Those things happen sometimes with horses. Maybe you could tell me why."

"It happens, young man, when warm horses are brought inside shelter on a cold day."

"Awww, yeah? Well, those came in yesterday."

"Eddie, do you want to be my enemy?"

"Me? Who'd be dumb enough to want that?"

"If you insist on lying, I'll fall on you like a tree. I hate a liar."

The man knew better than anyone that he was a liar and he respected the consequences of becoming A. B. Cowden's enemy. A.B. could be dealt with as long as he did not become angry and cease to act the gentleman. Eddie the Newt realized he had been a fool to give him cause to become impatient.

Newton murmured, "Well, I don't know how to take being called a liar by you . . . er . . . Mr. Cowden."

"You don't?"

"Nossir."

"You say, 'Undersheriff Cowden, I apologize for being a liar, and yes, two saddle horses were brought in and stabled in my barn a while ago.' "

"Yessir, I guess they were."

"What?"

"Yessir, Undersheriff Cowden, I apologize for being a liar. Two horses were brought in a while ago."

"Whose horses?"

Newton made a show of looking in a tablet for the names. "A man named Creswell and one named Packer."

"Did they speak to you?"

"Nossir. I don't know them very well."

"Only well enough to lie to me as a favor to them?"

"Uh, well, I . . ."

Les stepped up behind Newton and tapped him on the shoulder. Newton jumped and flinched away before he even recognized Les. "Don't hit me, Les. I was only trying to stay out of your war."

Les was not angry. "Well, you're not out of it. We knew we couldn't trust you, but we've been trying to leave you alone. Now you lie for the VO and still want to be neutral. That's insulting, Eddie."

Eddie was practically sure Les would not hurt him because he was talking instead of hitting, so he regained his composure. "Oh hey, I don't want to insult anybody. I'm in business."

"Come on, Les. Let's go, son," A.B. said.

"What is your business?" Les said.

"Can't you see? I'm this town's blacksmith."

"Damned near every man in this town is a smith. You're a liar and a two-faced little toad and that's what your business is."

Newton backed up and shut up.

"Where are the saddles for those VO horses?"

Newton pointed to the saddles on racks nearby. The saddle blankets were laid on top and Les turned them over. "Hell, they're still wet. Now take your sharpest knife and cut their offside latigos in two."

Newton quickly did as he was told.

"Now get your horseshoe nippers and cut the curb chains off the bridles."

Newton did that too.

"Now, you won't tell them I made you do that, will you?"

"Nossir. I'm in business. I won't tell nobody nothin'."

"Fine, so I'm going to tear your head off the next time I see you unless you've at least been given a black eye by the VO."

"Wait a minute. I don't want trouble with the VO, either."

"Eddie, you seem to be happy to go through life as a liar, so from now on we'll count on you to be a liar. Either lie to these cowards so they won't be able to trust you enough to leave their horses and saddles with you anymore, or disappear from the Santa Cruz. Because if this doesn't turn out to suit me, I'll hurt you."

A.B. and Les entered Vince Farley's saloon through the back room and separated again. Les stopped behind a curtain that separated the back room from the back of the bar. A.B. went into the saloon where the customers milled.

Creswell and Packrat were standing at the bar. Les saw the brims of their hats go up and their eyes narrow when they discovered A.B. They might be gunsels who didn't know how to keep from making targets of themselves and didn't know how to hide their tracks when they were out in the country, but they damned sure could handle themselves in town in the saloons. They would have held all the advantage over A.B. at that moment if Les had not taken up a bushwhacker's position behind the curtain.

Les drew his pistol and sighted at Creswell, because he was the man nearest A.B. If they wanted bushwhacking, dammit, he'd give them bushwhacking.

Creswell and Packrat lowered their eyes and hatbrims to their drinks. Les kept his pistol aimed at Creswell's left cheekbone. He knew his ball would strike a fraction high and to the right at that range and he wanted to put it between the son of a bitch's eyes.

As A.B. walked up to Creswell, Les realized he did not want to shoot a man from behind an old bar curtain. Ben would have known a better, more honorable way to get even for the bushwhacking. He would never have considered skulking behind a dirty bar curtain. The quality of Les's actions always seemed to deteriorate when Ben was not there to give him backbone.

When A.B. was close enough for Creswell to poke him in the belly with a pistol and shoot him, Creswell drew the weapon. Les was forced to squeeze his trigger. His ball struck Creswell's nose and Creswell's bullet drilled the floor between A.B.'s feet. Creswell dropped his pistol and took his face in both hands. A.B. drew his pistol and clubbed Creswell on the top of his hat, rendering him oblivious to the pain in his nose. Packrat thought A.B. was going shoot him and dropped for cover into the gutter at the base of the bar where everybody spat.

"The son of a bitch wanted to shoot my papa," Les yelled as he ran into the saloon. Still, he was ashamed he'd potshotted the man and hoped he had not disfigured him.

Packrat put up his hands to protect his face. "Don't kill me, Les," he said. A.B. saw the miserable look on Les's face and said, "No, son, everything's under control."

Les rolled Creswell over with the toe of his boot. Sure enough, a large chunk of the man's nose was gone.

"Tell the truth, Packrat," Les said. "Which one of you shot my brother a while ago?"

"It wasn't me."

"Would you remember if I did a military drill with the heel of my boots on your head? You were there, weren't you?"

"Yes."

"Which rifle did you shoot, the .30-30, or the .4570?"

"I didn't shoot anybody. I held the horses."

"Then you aren't to blame for anything your partners did to us down in Harshaw Canyon a while ago?"

"I didn't do any shooting."

"Where are your partners who did?"

Packrat sat up and Les could see his fear go away. Gunsels were so dumb.

"Well now, don't expect me to rat on my friends, Les."

"Les!" A.B. said, alarmed.

Les brought his boot down on Packrat's ear, then punted him in the face, then stomped him on the other ear. He lifted the boy's face with the toe of his boot. "That would be the last thing I'd ask you to do, Packrat," he said. "I only want to know where they are."

"At the Chinaman's."

"Thanks. Next time you hold their horses, you're gonna lose your nose too. Listen to me." Les prodded Packrat until he looked him in the eye. "Next time your ratty friends kill anything, I'm gonna take off your nose. Now, are you going to let your partner bleed to death and choke on his blood, or are you going to help him?"

"I can't help him. He's on his own."

"No, he isn't. Roll him over so he won't choke. Hold something on his nose to stop the bleeding."

"I'm hurting too much myself to help anybody."

"Well, then I guess I'll kick your nose off, too, Packrat."

"Les, don't hurt him anymore," A.B. said. "Help me take the two of them to jail. Les!"

Les headed for the front door. Miners, cowboys, and townsmen gave way for him. "Son!" A.B. ordered, but Les walked out into the cool night rain.

A man rode out of the darkness toward him. Les recognized his cousin Willy Porter. Willy would not have been that far away from El Relave at night alone unless something had happened to his family. Les let him ride by without speaking to him. He was riding a big dun horse that his grandfather owned. The horse was tired and the look on Willy's face showed that his heart was sick and his hope gone. Les watched him dismount in front of Uncle Vince's saloon and go in. A.B. would probably keep him there.

Les walked up the street and cleansed his thinking with fresh air. He would not be any good to his family if he did not learn to control his rage. The dim light inside Frank Wong's gave him hope that nobody was there.

He went around the back and found two VO horses tied to a tree. The rain increased, poured off his hatbrim, and chilled his shoulders through his jumper. He went back to look in the street for enemies, then entered Wong's through the front door. Snider and Stiles were sitting at a table in a corner with their backs to the wall. Les took off his wet jumper as he walked toward them.

Snider saw that Les was not coming at him to say hello. Stiles was as quick to realize his danger. The men skidded their chairs apart and Les hurled his jumper into Snider's face. Stiles reached for his pistol but stopped when Les pointed a finger at him.

Les pounded on the jumper with his big fists as Snider snatched to get it off his face. Les owned big hands and he knew how to hurt people with them, but his right shoulder was stiff and ineffective. He had injured it when Snake spilled him on the road. He beat on Snider through the jumper as best he could, but he did not seem to be able to hurt him. He uncovered Snider's face to see if he could strike it in the eyes and on the end of the nose and cause pain.

"That's enough, Les," Stiles said.

Les straightened. Stiles pointed his pistol at Les. "Come at me like that and I'll kill you, Les."

Les did not see the two big men that came through the door of Frank Wong's private quarters until they were about to hit him. He had time only to hide his jaw under his bad shoulder.

They knocked him down and danced on his head with hobnailed miner's boots. When he tried to stand, they whipped him with pistols. He knew he would have to regain his feet or die. The boots muddied and bloodied his head all over again. One stomped him in the kidney and, when he arched his back against the pain, the other sank the toe of his boot into his solar plexis and paralyzed him. The pain was so bad he almost fainted, but the miners did not pause. They stomped him until he did faint.

A blast of shot from Willy Porter's shotgun splintered a beam above the miners' heads and stopped them. Snider crowded into the corner next to Stiles. Willy backed the miners into the same corner while he wet a bandana with water from a pitcher on a table and bathed Les's face.

"Boy, am I glad to see you, Willy," Snider said. "I was afraid these men were going to kill Cowden there."

"Oh, you were, you dirty son of a bitch?" Willy said.

Les moaned, revived, rolled over on his back, and went away again for a while.

Willy pointed the shotgun at Snider. "Now, Snider, get away from those other fellers so I can kill you."

"Kill me where I stand, if you have to," Snider said. "But I want to know why."

"You yellow bastard, you left your own wife and my wife and son for the Apaches to butcher."

"My wife? Oh, my God. Teresa?"

Willy pointed the gun at Snider's sternum.

Les stirred and sat up. "Kill him, Willy."

"I'm sorry," Snider said. "Are they all right?"

Willy sighed. "You rotten bastard, didn't I just tell you? They've been butchered. You promised to stay home. My wife and babies have been murdered."

"Oh no," Snider said miserably.

Willy started to cry. The shotgun wavered.

"But I didn't leave them alone, Willy" Snider said, weeping.

"What do you mean?" Les said.

"Our friend Patch the Apache said he would stay and help them until you came home."

Ten

THE *CANTON DAWN,* a clipper out of San Diego, lay off the desert coast of Puerto Libertad, Sonora, in a night rain. Captain Wilhelm Clayton looked up into the ship's dark, naked rigging as the deck rolled in a thirty-knot wind.

Captain Clayton was a yankee from Gloucester and his ship was one of the last of its kind, a 185-foot ship-rigged China clipper. The ship was forty years old and Captain Clayton had been its skipper for thirty-eight years. To make room for its fragile and valuable opium and human cargo, the *Canton Dawn* was undermanned with a crew of only eighteen.

Colonel Gabriel Kosterlinsky of the Sonoran Rural Police and Indiana Briggs of Patagonia, Arizona, were on board to receive and pay for the ship's cargo. The cargo was to be off-loaded to a small fleet of *canoas,* wooden dugouts, that lay alongside the clipper in the storm. Each dugout was manned by two oarsmen and an armed guard from La Cordada, Kosterlinsky's elite Rural Police.

Sailors formed a chain on deck and began handing bricks of packaged opium down a ladder. "Wait just a minute," Briggs said as the first package was handed over the side. "I want to examine and tally the bricks before they go in the boats."

"Then I suggest you stand by the crew at work," Captain Clayton said.

"But you should stand there with me and the bricks should be weighed."

"The weight is stamped on each package and affixed with the seal of Whitelaw and George of Great Britain and Hong Kong, the suppliers from whom I received the cargo. You shall receive the cargo with the Whitelaw stamp and guarantee just as I did. The ship's clerk is standing there by the off-loading crew. Take your count with him."

Briggs groped down a slippery ladder off the bridge and stood by while a stream of five-kilo bricks of raw opium gum were counted off the ship. Kosterlinsky was impressed by the discipline and spareness of effort of the crew. Captain Clayton was a tall, weathered man with a closely trimmed white beard and no mustache. Kosterlinsky could not keep his eyes off him. Even though every roll of the ship made the Mexican skitter to keep his balance, the captain only swayed like the masts on his ship. He never looked away from his ship, cargo, and crew. In the few instances that he turned toward Kosterlinsky, he either looked past him to keep track of the work being done, through him as though he was a window to the shore, or over his head at masts and rigging.

Kosterlinsky was not backward. His curiosity had caused him to brave death to come aboard this ship. He had not been intimidated by his fear of the thrashing sea, the tossing of the ladder upon which he was forced to climb aboard the pitching deck, or by this cold monument of a man. After all, he was one of the businessmen who paid for the voyages of the *Canton Dawn.*

"Captain Clayton, have you ever heard of a *chubasco?"* Kosterlinsky said.

The captain lifted a megaphone to his mouth and shouted, "You, Perkins, stand fast there. Stay at the head of that ladder lest your shipmate lose his hold. Be alive and let us finally be rid of this confounded cargo."

"Captain . . . ?"

The captain turned to Kosterlinsky angrily.

"Do you know what a *chubasco* is?"

The captain turned back to watch his crew.

Kosterlinsky waited for an answer. He only wanted to have a conversation with the man.

"It's a storm peculiar to this sea," the captain finally said.

Kosterlinsky decided the captain was pleased to ignore him, so he subsided. When the packages had been off-loaded to the *canoas,* the captain drew a slate out of a slot on the bridge and chalked figures on it. He then turned to Kosterlinsky. "I assume you allude to the chuback, the sudden storm that occurs in gulf waters such as these. Yes, it's a small cyclone that has been known to hit ships in these waters."

"Do you know they are dangerous?"

"A chuback might cause damage if it hits a ship. As far as I know, it does not often do so. From what I have been told, a chuback can pass a ship within a quarter mile and not harm it."

"No, senor, I don't know what kind of storm you're talking about, but a *chubasco* is not that tame a monster. It overtakes a ship suddenly and covers a large area with violent winds that vary extremely in velocity and direction. *Chubascos* have been known to tear ships apart."

Clayton turned away and said, "Colonel, tell your oarsmen to return from shore quickly. I want you and the remainder of the cargo off the ship in case the storm does become more severe."

Kosterlinsky conveyed the order to the guards on the boats. He did not inform the yankee captain that Mexicans did not do anything quickly, especially when threatened by a *chubasco*. Mexicans were more likely to wait until the sun came out again to complete jobs such as these.

When the dugouts were bobbing toward the shore the captain ordered Kosterlinsky and Briggs to join him in his cabin. Inside, he remained standing by the door and offered no hospitality. The place was furnished only with the captain's chair, desk, and bed.

"I have been directed by Whitelaw and George to collect $27,000 from you at this time," the captain said.

"It was my understanding that the price was $25,000," Briggs said. "The same as last time."

"In gold, sir. Pay now."

"No, sir, not until I see the remainder of the cargo. I don't like to wait until it is being handed over the side to examine it. I also want you to explain why the price has been raised by $2,000."

"Two of the younger, smaller packages died during the last voyage and you did not pay for them. This time, Whitelaw and George sent two small males and an older couple as servants to the females and they all made the voyage in good health. They have instructed me to charge you for the servants."

"I was not prepared to pay an additional $2,000 for little boy chinks and a pair of old ones, only to pay $4,000 for the opium and $1,000 a head for every live, healthy young singsong."

"You will pay the cost or forfeit your deposit."

"That's piracy. I have to require that they all be in good enough health to withstand the journey across the desert. I won't pay for sick ones."

"The contract stipulates only that I deliver live packages. They are all breathing, so pay."

"First, I want to see the chinks. *Then* I'll pay."

Captain Clayton bellowed for his first mate, who came on the double and brushed his brow in a heavy, offhanded salute.

"Take these . . . er . . . Mexican gentlemen to the hold for an inspection of the cargo," the captain ordered.

Kosterlinsky was amused. He wondered how Briggs liked being called a Mexican. Briggs hated Mexicans. To a yankee slaver and dope smuggler who spent his life at sea and never stepped ashore unless it was in a town of seafarers, everybody in that part of the world must be either a Mexican or an Indian. Captain Clayton could show real ignorance after all.

The hold where the Chinese were housed was small. The smuggler's clipper sacrificed cargo space for a sharp bow, trim lines, and speed. The place was lighted by one lantern. A cluster of spent candles flickered at a place where a religious shrine had been erected. The shrine had been removed and the candles were burning out. Kosterlinsky expected to be laid low by the stench of bodies after the one hundred-day voyage, but he only smelled incense.

The first mate spoke to the people in soft, pidgin Chinese and they came forward carrying their bundles of personal belongings. They seemed spry enough. This cargo had the faces of children and was dressed in dark tunics and pants and black peacoats.

Briggs stepped forward and made a show of counting heads. "One's missing," he said.

The first mate went to a bundle of bedding in a corner where the old couple stood and uncovered another child lying on her side. He spoke softly to the couple and they lifted the child to a sitting position against the bulkhead. The bearded old man explained something to the mate.

"What's the matter with that one?" Briggs said.

"The old one says it's weak, but will regain its strength if they can find the medicinal herbs they need ashore."

"I guess I'm expected to pay for the sick one, too," Briggs said. "And I suppose it's a singsong."

"It's a female. The old one tells me you should not worry, he and the boys will carry it."

"Carry it, hell! Where they're going, nobody gets carried. If the chink can't walk, the chink gets deep-sixed."

"What's this 'deep-six'?" Kosterlinsky asked.

"The package goes over the side."

Kosterlinsky was still puzzled.

"Over the side. Sent to the bottom of the sea," Briggs said.

"You mean, the child would be thrown away like trash?" Kosterlinsky was amazed.

Briggs ignored him and pulled one of the children away from the others by the arm, unbuttoned and removed the peacoat, unbuttoned the tunic and exposed the undergarments. "Well, dammit is it male or female?"

"It's a male," the first mate said.

"Get their clothes off so I can see their limbs and parts. Dammit, I'm going to see what I'm buying."

Kosterlinsky looked into the boy's face. "Anybody can see this is a boy." He stepped over to another. "This one's a girl . . . and this one . . . here's another." He moved among the children until he had looked into all their faces. "All the rest are girls. You've got fifteen girls standing, one sitting against the wall, and two boys. No need for them to strip. What's the matter with you, Briggs?"

"Nothing's the matter. Nothing at all. I'm glad you're an expert on bull and heifer chinks. You can be the one to explain your examination to Duncan Vincent if the tally doesn't come out right."

"The tally's right."

Captain Clayton came down into the hold and stepped away from the ladder. He stepped fastidiously, as though unused to the footing in the hold. "You gentlemen satisfy yourselves about the cargo now and get ready to leave the ship."

"I don't want to pay for the sick one," Briggs grumbled. "Do I have to take it?"

"You don't have to take the package, but you have to pay for it, or refuse the entire shipment and forfeit your $10,000 deposit."

"What if we leave the child here?" Kosterlinsky said.

"All damaged or refused cargo goes over the side," the first mate said.

"I won't take any sick packages ashore," Briggs said. "I don't want to be responsible for causing an epidemic."

The captain turned to the first mate. "The man has seen it. Deep-six the one and take the rest of the cargo topside. I want it all off the ship the minute those dugouts bump the side." He turned and went back up the ladder. A moment later his voice boomed again and two sailors shinnied down the ladder and picked up the sick child.

"Wait a minute," Kosterlinsky said. One sailor went up the ladder with a hand around both the child's ankles and the other lifted from the bottom. The child's black eyes locked on Kosterlinsky's until she disappeared through the hatch. Kosterlinsky stared at the clean bare heels of the second seaman as they clambered quickly through the hatch and disappeared.

He hurried up the ladder, ran to the side of the ship, and looked down into the blackness of the sea. The captain stood by as the seamen lifted the child to drop her over the side.

"Wait!" Kosterlinsky shouted. The captain growled a command to stay his crewmen and they rested the girl on top the gunwale. She did not make one move to save herself. She might as well already be dead. "How can I stop this?"

"Why would you want to stop the disposal of waste from my ship, Colonel?" the captain said.

"My God, man. The child is still alive. It's murder."

"The package is not a child as you know one, but a sick heathen that is contaminating my ship."

"I'll pay you to spare her. Tell me how I can stop you from doing this."

"You cannot. Rules are rules." The captain turned to his crewmen. "Carry on," he ordered.

With a quick, effortless motion, the seamen flipped the child off the rail and away from the side of the ship. She spiraled lazily, hit the water head down and was sucked into the roiling sea.

The captain turned and bellowed angrily into Kosterlinsky's face. "Now, send your partner to my cabin with that money while you off-load the remainder of your cargo. *Move* before I deep-six the lot of you."

The first mate herded the Chinese on deck. Their bundles were lowered over the side in a net while the people climbed down a ladder that swung and jerked in the gale. Kosterlinsky stood at the gunwale and guided their hands when they first took hold of the ladder and felt them tremble and their feet skitter with fear as they groped their way off the ship. The boats rode the crests of the swells and banged against the side of the ship. Kosterlinsky was afraid the people would be crushed against the ship or lost in the blackness between the ship and the boats. He shouted threats at the oarsmen and guards and promised them death against the wall of a firing squad if they did not take all the people safely into the boats.

After he and Briggs climbed into the boats themselves and saw the risks that had been taken by the children and the old people, Kosterlinsky was sure that someone must have been lost or crippled in the dark. When they landed and counted heads and found that all the people were on shore and sound of limb, he shouted his gratitude to the oarsmen and guards. Then he ordered everyone to board the three covered wagons that would take them to the border.

He stopped at the door of a fisherman's shack and shouted for the Campana brothers. The Campanas were excellent scouts, knew the country and the Apaches, and were responsible for guiding the party safely to Tucson.

A *cachimba*, a lamp made of a small can with a wick sticking out of a hole in the lid and fueled by fish oil, burned on the fisherman's table. When the Campana brothers stood in front of Kosterlinsky, he said, "Tell me again your route, your rest stops, and the time you will need to take these children to Tucson."

Antonio Campana, the eldest, said, "The same as always, my Colonel."

"All right, tell me. How, as always?"

"Tonight we go to rest at Trincheras. From there ten short night journeys by wagon to Manzanita Canyon on the border. We leave the wagons there and travel by mule two nights afoot over the *laja*, the flat rock trail in the creek beds, through Manzanita, Penasco, and Calabasas canyons to the *via*, the railroad, where we will put them on the freight car."

"You don't only put them on the freight car. You board with them and ride the car to Tucson. My guards will be there to take the mules to their garrison in Santa Cruz after you leave Calabasas."

"Yes, my Colonel."

"You know the man Chee Lee, who will take charge of the people in Tucson. Wait on the train until you see him. Then come back to Santa Cruz and report to me."

"Yes, my Colonel."

"Your wagons are well provisioned?"

"Yes, my Colonel, just as you ordered it."

"Good. I want these people to *gain* weight on this journey. Woe to you if they arrive in Tucson malnourished."

"Nooo, my Colonel."

"No, I'm sure you are incapable of cheating on the purchase of provision for Chinamen."

"Nooo, my Colonel, I would feel it if you thought we could cheat."

"You are suitable for the job as scouts and guides. I have every confidence that you will deliver the people in good condition in a minimum of time."

"Thank you, my Colonel."

"But take your time. Are you sure this is the best route? What danger of attack by Apaches?"

"I don't think there is any danger, my Colonel. I think the renegades moved south to the Sierra for the winter."

"Let us hope to God they did."

"Yes, my Colonel."

"Sargeant Roblez is waiting for you with his squad at the wagons. Be gone."

Ben and Maudy stayed for their honeymoon at the Hotel Camarillo in Long Beach. When he was not looking at Maudy, Ben liked to look at the ocean. The sight of all that great mass of water was balm to the spirit of a man from Arizona who had been plagued by drought most of his life.

Ben and Maudy managed to keep to themselves for the first ten days, even though Maudy's Pendleton relatives tried to draw them into California society. Ben and Maudy resisted by not answering any messages or collecting calling cards that were left for them at the desk of the hotel.

The relatives became so persistent that the honeymooners were forced to hide when they saw them coming. Ben found himself more on the alert than he would have expected to be that far from home. "Apaches!" he would say when he saw a relative coursing the beach looking for them or coming through the front door of the hotel. Once, they lay still on their bed for a quarter of an hour while Richard Eliot, one of Maudy's cousins knocked persistently on the door. They knew that he knew they were in the room, because they had been having a happy conversation when he first spoke their names from the hallway, but they shut up and did not answer. They did not care if he knew they did not want to see him. When Eliot finally got tired and went away, they laughed and forgot about him.

Maudy's mother, Mrs. Pendleton, lived in Long Beach and after ten days they relented and went to see her, only because it was their duty. Early the previous summer Mrs. Pendleton had taken her youngest child and left Arizona to get away from the lawlessness and Apaches. She left Maudy behind as though she was only a piece of furniture that she would not need in California. Now she had decided to invite every available Pendleton and Cowden relative to a family reunion in honor of the newlyweds. Ben and Maudy consented to it, but would have been happier to be done with it.

On the first day of the reunion, relatives arrived at the Hotel Camarillo from as far away as the Russian River and San Francisco, the Napa Valley and San Diego. A reception was held in the hotel where Mrs. Pendleton and her brother introduced Ben and Maudy to all the relatives. Mrs. Pendleton came to the affair dressed in satin and pearls and a fancy tiara as though she was the great dame of Long Beach. She made Ben and Maudy line up beside her on a platform while the relatives passed a foot below them and had to look up to them to shake hands.

No Cowdens showed up. Ben was not surprised at that, since Mrs. Pendleton was the one who had sent out the wires of invitation and she had never been high on the Cowdens or the Porters. The only Cowdens in California were a brother and a married sister of A.B.'s. The brother was a cattleman on the Nevada border between Sacramento and Carson City and the sister was married to his neighbor. They were frontiersmen and had more important work to do than intrude on their nephew's honeymoon in Long Beach.

The Pendletons and Eliots were townsmen, merchants, and professionals. Ben and Maudy had nothing in common with them, except that most of them were Ben and Maudy's age.

Ben did not like any of them. The only one he had known before this trip was Richard Eliot. Richard had visited the Pendletons in Pima County once, "looking for business opportunities." After one week he fled, never to be heard from again.

By the time Ben spent two hours visiting and drinking with Maudy's male relatives he knew not one of them had ever heard a shot fired in anger or been confronted with any kind of danger to his life. He would have been happy for them, but not one seemed to have done anything of note, right or wrong, except make sure he was not available to be of service to anyone else.

Ben would have bet a new hat that not one of them had ever felt a passion for anything, because they seemed to be the kind of people who felt having a passion was unnecessary and should be avoided at all costs. Not one would even admit to ever being drunk.

Ben did not blame them for being townsmen, or being lucky their lives allowed them to keep a level head at all times. He did not dislike them because of their good fortune, or the tameness of their lives. He disliked the disdain on their faces when they addressed him, as though they wished they could say, "How can anyone who lives the way you are purported to live *enjoy* life so much."

The phonies did not like him because he was what they would have been if they had not chosen to be phony. They had not liked the sacrifices it would take to become real, so they had become phonies. He disliked them because they showed the bad manners and poor judgement to disapprove of him before they even knew him, when he was perfectly ready to accept them as friends the way they were. He liked to have friends. He had some real friends back where he came from.

Ben did not think a person had to be a drunk to be a good person. Everybody knew alcohol was poison. Being hypocritical about drink was bad. Maudy's relatives seemed disdainful because Ben enjoyed his drinks wholeheartedly. They seemed to want Ben to believe they could drink whiskey and wine without getting any of its poison in their stainless carcasses.

Maudy did not drink because she knew it was not good for a body. She disapproved of swallowing any kind of spirits, but did not mind too much if Ben did. The relatives separated Ben from Maudy and engaged him in a lot of drink and talk while they held their drinks in gloved hands, did very little drinking, and a whole lot of watching, listening, and speculating. It did not take Ben very long to realize that Maudy's relatives were inordinately intolerant of him.

Right or wrong, when Ben Cowden was given a party and alcohol was served, he drank with both hands. Drinking was fun for him. He never drank for business, social, or sinful reasons. He drank for fun and sometimes for medicine. Very few men in his experience used alcohol any other way, so it was new for him to run into a group of

California salamanders with drinks in their hands, but intolerant looks in their eyes for the way he drank. Nevertheless, he tried to be friendly, even though that sentiment was kept off balance by their constant, persistent questioning about matters that he considered to be only his own personal and private business.

Looking for an escape, he spied a band of mariachis walking through the lobby. He trotted out, brought them back, and lined them up beside the table where Maudy was sitting with the girl cousins. When the Mexicans formed around their table, some of the girls looked at each other with expressions of disgust, but they did not say anything. Ben was sure he was about to remedy any prejudice they might have against Mexican music and asked the musicians to play '*Sonora Querida*,' one of his and Maudy's favorites.

"Maybe the girls would like to hear something else," Maudy said. She must have known they would not like it and wanted to save that song for a time when she and Ben could be alone again.

"Play '*Raincho Grandy*,'" the most talkative and self-assured of the girl cousins said. She was the one who had been telling Maudy about all the fashion, culture, and cuisine that Maudy would be exposed to when she made Ben take her for a visit to San Francisco.

"No '*Raincho Grandy*' at any party of mine, by god," Ben said and turned to the musicians. "Please play 'Lovely Sonora.'" Then he stood back to watch the change that was bound to come over the cousins when they heard the beautiful song of the ranchers of his country.

Their faces changed all right, to lifeless masks. It was as though a veil of dead tissue enveloped Maudy's relatives' faces. They seemed to decay before his eyes, and he realized that must be more their normal state than the phony facades they had showed before the music started. The song was so beautiful and they were so dead to it that Ben yelled, "*Yiii, haiii, haiii,*" with all his heart and sent a shudder through them that might have been their first, or last, sure sign of life.

Later, when everyone was seated for dinner, Maudy's relatives began another critical examination of him. He had moved the mariachis away from the table so the diners could talk, but he and Maudy could still hear the music. He gave all his attention to Maudy, hoping to hold off the questioning. Waiters poured champagne and he could smell the roast beef, potatoes, and gravy that were on their way to their table. With all he had to enjoy, Ben felt it would take a lot of salamandering to ruin the rest of the party for him. But he had never known salamanders such as these.

"Ben fought in the battle of Apache Pass, he says," Mrs. Pendleton said. "We all read about it soon after I returned to California this summer. That must have been quite an experience, to be completely fooled and defeated by a horde of savages."

The woman acted as though Apaches were as foreign to her as dirt, even though she'd been closer to Apaches in battle than Ben had ever been. She'd fled Arizona vowing never to return after Apaches came so close to her in a raid on her home that she shot at one, missed, and killed her own child.

Ben and his brothers, uncles, cousins, and even his grandfather had tried to help the U. S. Army in the battle of Los Metates and he and his brothers had been in the battle of Los Bultos, both during the summer of 1885. He had never been in the battle of Apache Pass. He did not want to make his mother-in-law out a liar, so he did not say anything.

"The battle of Apache Pass? Was he in that one? Wasn't that when Cochise whipped the hell out of the U. S. Army? Did he survive that one?" A male cousin said.

"He says he did."

"Any white man who survived that battle is quite remarkable, since none are supposed to have survived."

"Los Metates, Mother," Maudy said. "Not Apache Pass. Ben and most of the men in his family were in the battle of Los Metates last summer. That battle was fought near our place at La Noria."

"Oh, your father was in that one, too, then," Mrs. Pendleton said.

"No, Mother. Father was not there. Ben and his family were."

"Oh, is that right, Cowden?" Richard Eliot said. "I thought you were a rancher. I didn't know you were a soldier."

"I'm a cattleman," Ben said.

"Oh yes, that's right. You say you're a cattleman. Is that different from being a rancher? How do you raise cattle if you don't have a ranch?"

"We have ranches, but there are all kinds of ranchers: hog ranchers, sheep ranchers, and even goat ranchers. A cattleman is a cattle rancher."

"You say you have ranches. How many? How many cattle do you have?"

"Oh, that's not important."

"Not important? How big are these ranches?"

"Big enough to make a living when it rains, too small when it doesn't."

"I was out there. I know how much landscape your ranches cover. There's hundreds of acres of land, but it's so desolate only the lizards and cactus can survive. The cattle even look like lizards."

Maudy's cousins remained silent and straight-faced as they stared at Ben and waited for him to answer.

"If you've been there and seen for yourself, why ask me all these questions?"

"Pardon me, but your new relations are interested in you and anxious to know all they can about you. Tell us, doesn't ranching in that desolate land keep you busy? You must have a veritable mountain of work to do. How can you be a rancher if you have to fight so-called battles against so-called savage Apaches?"

"We have plenty of work to do; we like it and try not to let anybody keep us from it."

"Yet you say you were in the battle of Los Metates? We read about that battle. How could you have soldiered in a battle that took place so many miles away from your ranch? Have you invented a way to fly? It seems to me you'd have to be three men to have done everything you say you did."

"The U. S. Army wired us requesting our help with men and horses and we dropped our personal business and joined the army for a while."

"Did you get right down where you could smell the fire and blood?" This came from another cousin who was sitting close to Ben. Ben saw the man's wife prod him with her foot and give him a look to shut him up. Ben was embarrassed enough to be grateful to her.

"We got as close as anybody, except the Mexicans. The Apaches overran the Mexicans and killed a squad of their cavalry." Ben decided that was the last honest answer he would give the sonsabitches. He'd had enough. Anybody fool enough to ask these questions in Pima County would have found himself in a fight long before this.

"Well, so we find you're a rancher . . . no, a cattleman, pardon me . . . and a soldier," Eliot said. "What else? Oh yes. Didn't you tell someone you'd also been a highwayman, a rustler, a gunfighter, and along with all that, quite a ladies man?"

Ben looked at the man a long moment before he answered. "I would not have said that, because I don't insult myself. I don't think anyone said that, because where I come from you could lose your life for it. Maudy, my mother, and sisters are the only ladies whose man I am."

"No one calls you a rustler, gunfighter, and holdup man without losing his life? Do you know a man from your town of Harshaw named Royal Vincent? He spent a lot of time here last summer and fall and told us a lot of stories about you. The last I heard he was still alive."

Ben was struck dumb.

"Please don't take me wrong, he didn't say anything real bad about you. He only implied that most of the tales we'd heard about you were mostly windys you spread about yourself."

"Don't believe that," Maudy said. "Royal Vincent is Ben's second-worst enemy in the world. If you've heard that Ben is a rustler, it's a lie spread by enemies like him."

"How does a good man make enemies?"

Ben was about to answer, "By mashing snoopy smart alecs," but at that moment Maudy's Uncle Fred stood up, raised his wine glass, and tapped a spoon against a water glass. "A toast," he announced. "To Mr. and Mrs. Ben Cowden."

Maudy did not have champagne and Ben did not drink with the sonsabitches. Hypocritically they all smiled at Ben and Maudy and drank to them. Ben did not drink again until the meal came.

He would have liked a real drink for a bracer when everybody rose from the table after the dinner and the headwaiter handed him the check. Maudy acted as though she did not notice it and he would not have given her relatives the pleasure of thinking it bothered him to pay for the music, dinner, and drinks at his own party. He never looked at their faces again. He paid with *alazanas*, the sorrel gold coin of Porfirio Diaz, gave a generous tip, and the honeymoon was over. He had only enough cash left in his money belt to settle the hotel bill. He and Maudy were going home, and it was about time.

Eleven

AS HE AWAKENED, Les thought, I think this all happened before. He did not know where he was, did not care, and was not grateful to be coming back to life. He lay on his back and when he opened his eyes his sight was funneled as though he was looking out from inside a cave. The sides of the cave were the swollen flesh around his eyes. He tried to touch his brow, but found he could not raise his arm. When he touched his face with the other hand, it was tight and numb with swelling and stuck out away from his head. His ear was swollen and sore again. He thought, I have not helped my cauliflower ear get well.

He turned his head at the creak of a chair and saw Willy Porter sitting by the side of the bed with his hat on. "Well, at least I know I ain't dead," Les said. "'Cause you ain't no angel. Where am I?"

"In the hotel."

"How come my folks didn't take me home?"

"Doc Tucker wanted to see if your skull was broke before he'd let them."

"Ain't it?"

"Naw. The Doc said your skull's your soundest bone. Every ounce of your meat is pounded black and blue, but you ain't broke."

"What's wrong with my arm?"

"Your shoulder was dislocated. Doc popped it back in while you were out and couldn't feel him do it."

"I think it's broken."

"Naw, Doc said your bones're hard as bedrock. He was scared the thugs had put both your eyes out and kicked your ears off, but after he sewed up your head he said all you needed to do was stay out of trouble a while and you'd heal right up."

"How'd I get here? I wasn't clear out when you came in Wong's and stopped the fight."

"What fight? There sure wasn't any fight. Those fellers just kicked the hell out of you. Doc came to Wong's and gave you laudanum and you went off to dreamland while we were walking you to the hotel."

"Who were those burly bastards that put the boots to me?"

"Those two, cousin, were Indiana Briggs's oldest sons. Those are his good, hardworking sons."

"Lordy, I forgot he still had those two. Hell, they're my *brothers-in-law*."

"That they are."

"Lordy Lord, they didn't show me an ounce of pity. How did you get to know them?"

"Indiana introduced them to me once when he took me up to the Chalkeye to sell me some scrap iron. I've been up there several times since and I sold them some bulls. They're the ones who do all the work on his mines and farms. They're nice fellers."

"I wondered who that was could be so damned mean to my head."

"They haven't been here very long. They only came to Arizona after Hoozy and Whitey were killed. I guess they blame you and Ben for those deaths the same as the rest of their family does."

"Aw, how long are we going to be accused of that same old stuff? Lorrie still accuses me of that, even though we're supposed to be married. Where's . . . my folks?"

"Betty and Eileen have been taking turns sitting with you. They asked me to spell them while they went off to do something more important."

Les thought, well, that ought to show how married I am. Old Lorrie's got other things to do. Not that I'd want her to see me with my head all swoll up. This looks like the room she and I slept in. She didn't mind being with me then, but she was busy getting her legal clinch on me that time.

Les knew he had been beaten to within an inch of his life. His resolve was weak and he felt like bawling.

Then somebody—he thought it was one of his sisters—came in the room with the clink of dishes and a starchy rustle of skirts. Bones's expression became respectful and decent and he stood up, patted Les on the hip, told him he would be back after a while, and went out.

"I've got a pot of coffee over here on the table," his sister said. "Can you roll over on your back? Want me to help you?" Les could not tell which sister was talking to him. He hoped he didn't have brain damage. His sisters' voices were a lot alike, but he could usually tell them apart.

This one was probably Eileen. She was taller than Betty and Paula

Mary and sure of her strength. She took hold of him and rolled him over. "Ow," Les said.

Lorrie Cowden's eyes smiled down at him. She was trying to keep from grinning. He knew how sweet her mouth tasted. "Big baby," she said.

"I thought you had something else to do."

"I did. Betty and Eileen took over for me so I could go home and sleep. I slept from seven yesterday evening until five this morning without waking up."

"How long was I out?"

"Three nights and two days, but you weren't out all the time. You've got an awful concussion. Don't you remember talking to me?"

"When were you here?"

"I was here the first two days and nights. Don't you remember? I deserve a gold star and you don't even remember."

"Aw, I remember. I just wanted to see if you did."

"I don't see how you could remember a thing. You did a lot of crazy talking."

"Yeah, what did I say?"

"Never mind. I brought coffee, so scoot up as far as you can and I'll help you drink it. You want coffee, don't you?"

Lorrie gave him her hand and helped him sit up. He held on to the hand loosely so she could take it back if she wanted to. She stopped as though she could not move away until he let go her hand, as though she had no other purpose except to stand there and give him her hand to hold. He tightened his hold and she sat down on the edge of the bed. She sat so that her hand did not move, so he would not have trouble holding it. She put sugar and cream in his coffee the way he liked it, stirred it, and carried it to his breast with one hand while she let him hold the other. Les was not holding it tightly, either. She could take it away any time she wanted to. He did not see any meanness or connivance in her eyes. They only seemed full of caring and good humor.

Willy Porter met A. B. Cowden on the hotel veranda and they had coffee while Willy reported what he had found at El Relave.

"You never go in the dining room in the morning for your coffee like you used to, Uncle Ahira," Willy said. "Your coffee time in the dining room used to be like a town meeting, the way people came in to see you every morning. What happened?"

"Bones, the war between us and the VO happened. I can't sit in there and draw a crowd because some crazy thug of Vincent's might try to get me and shoot everybody else. I'd rather sit out here with my back to a wall where I can see everybody coming. People don't like to sit outside very long in the winter, so I don't draw a crowd anymore."

"I didn't know your feud with Vincent had gone that far, Uncle Ahira."

"You and the rest of the Porters have been too busy with your own affairs. You mind your own business and that's good. The damned war is complicated enough without the Porters getting into it."

"Well, I didn't know it had become a war."

"It has. It's the VO, the Live Stock Association and most of the Pima County government against the Cowdens, Farleys, Eliases, and all the other Sonorans who neighbor the VO. That should include the Porters."

"As undersheriff aren't you part of the Pima County government, Uncle Ahira?"

"I am. The county government has tried to get me out, but the folks here in Harshaw have been able to keep me in the job."

"Well, I've been so busy I haven't known much about the trouble. We're . . . we *were* pretty isolated out at El Relave . . ." Willy fell silent a moment. "Too isolated, I guess. I knew you were in some kind of feud with the VO, but I didn't hear much about it until I took the job as messenger for the stage . . ." He fell silent again. Then, in an absent minded way, he said, "Is there anything I can do to help you, Uncle Ahira?"

"No, you just take care of yourself. This trouble with the VO can be handled a lot better if everybody allows the law to take charge when people do wrong. Now that Ben's off on a vacation and the other two are laid up for a while, maybe I'll be able to find the ones responsible for your tragedy without a big fuss being made."

"You won't have to bother about that, Uncle Ahira. I know who butchered my family."

"You do?"

"Patch the Apache did it."

"How do you know that, Bones?"

"Patch told Snider he would stay at El Relave when Snider went off to look for work. Patch is responsible for the murder of my family."

"I can't believe Patch would do a thing like that. He's from good people. Me and my sons have always liked him."

"So have I. That's how he was able to do what he did."

"I'll tell you, I'd trust Patch a whole lot more than I'd trust Snider. Snider's a sneak. When you give a sneak a break, he'll always make you sorry. I caught him in the act of burning my barn and felt sorry for him and let him go. If he'd had an ounce of decency, he'd have left the country and never come back like he promised. When I saw he'd come back to the VO, I knew it wasn't because he wanted to be a peacemaker."

"You think Snider lied to me about Patch?"

"I'd believe that before I'd believe Patch killed your family. Didn't you know Patch showed up at Ben's wedding?"

"No. I was there and I didn't see him."

"He followed Ben and Maudy to Patagonia when they left for the train."

"I didn't know that. I guess I just didn't see him."

"Patch would have to be an eagle to kill people at El Relave and be at El Durazno at practically the same time."

"Then it's just Snider's word against Patch's."

"That's about it. It's easy to accuse an Apache, especially if Apaches probably really did the killing."

"No doubt about it. My dog was killed by an arrow and the killers left *tegua* tracks in my yard and corrals. Apaches did it."

"The question is, was Patch in on it? If he wasn't, he might know who was."

"That's a question only one person can answer without leaving any doubt."

"Teresa can, if she's alive."

"That's right. I guess it's up to me to find her. Now that I'm thinking more clearly, I'm sure it's what I have to do."

"Snider doesn't seem to care what happened to her."

"Speak of the devil."

Snider and Royal Vincent came up the hotel's steep front steps and stopped in front of Willy.

"Bones, I've been doing a lot of thinking and I want you to know I only trusted that Indian because you told me I could," Snider announced. "I'm really sorry, but I wasn't the only one fooled. He fooled you, too, so I'm not to blame for losing our women."

Willy stared at Snider and did not say a word or change expression. Snider backed toward the front door of the hotel. "I just wanted you to know what I think. I've been taking a lot of criticism and dirty looks from people over this."

Royal addressed A.B. "What are you planning to do about retrieving Teresa Snider from the Yawner?"

"I'm not going to lead an army of men after the Yawner, if that's what you mean."

"What are you going to do?"

"I telegraphed reports of the affair to the Army at Fort Lowell and Camp Huachuca, also to General Bustamante of the Mexican Army at Hermosillo and Kosterlinsky's Rural Police at Santa Cruz."

"Is that all you intend to do, send wires?"

"It's not all I'll do, but it's all the explanation I'll give to the likes of you."

"Listen, Cowden, our feud has to wait until these butchers are caught and hanged."

"That sounds good."

"Tell me what you plan to do."

"No."

"Then I'll have to take the initiative. I've sent a wire to Sheriff Perkins in Tucson and he's dispatching me fifty rangers. With those men, the VO hands, and other good men who want to join, I'll form a fighting force that will wipe out the Yawner once and for all."

"Dream on, Prince Royal."

"Is that all you have to say to me? As undersheriff, I'd think you'd want to take a hand in helping me organize the cadre."

"You are a dreamer, aren't you? You haven't got any more chance of catching the Yawner with your bunch of worthless constables than I have of reaching New York in backward strides."

"I'll quote you on that when I've finally succeeded in ridding our land of that butcher and make my report."

"I hope you live to make a report."

"How about you, Porter? You ought to come along with us. After all, it was your family that was murdered."

"I don't need a jackass like you to tell me who was murdered or what I ought to do about it," Willy said. "I'd go with you if I thought you were worth a damn. Who would you get to scout for that horde of stumbling gunsels you call the Pima County Live Stock Association Rangers?"

"I'd like you to be our scout."

"I wouldn't know who would be more dangerous to me, the Apaches ahead of me, or the shiftless bastards behind me. The rain wiped out the killers' tracks before I ever left home. Are you so much a gunsel that you haven't even noticed how much it's rained since my family was killed? Do you think I'm dumb enough to get out ahead of a gang of ignorant, trigger-happy gooberlips like you and Snider and have all your guns pointing at my back?"

A.B. saw Snider's face turn pale and sick as he looked at something across the Harshaw pond. He lowered his hatbrim to hide his face and inched backward toward the lobby. A.B. looked across the pond and saw the Indian in a black blouse and red headband standing under a tree by the schoolhouse. Patch.

Snider was almost out of sight inside the lobby. A.B. did not have to be told why the sight of Patch made Snider ill. He breathed a sigh of relief that Patch and Bones would be reconciled because Patch had come to town to see to it.

"We don't need tracks to follow," Royal Vincent said. "All we need to do is run down the Yawner and his band and wipe them out. You can't tell me those Apache scouts at Camp Huachuca don't know where to find him."

"And you think you know how to get them to help you," A.B. said.

"Hell yes, I do. Money. That's why they joined the Army in the first place, for money. If they'll sell themselves to the Army for a black blouse and a red headband and three squares a day, they'll join me when I show them some real coin."

Just then Doris Vincent came out of the hotel, smiling and wiggling from stem to stern with cheerfulness. She greeted A.B. fondly and rubbed him on the shoulder, introduced herself to Willy, then took Royal into the hotel.

Willy said, "Uncle Hirey, I think I'll stay with you until Les and Mark get well. You can use a hand, can't you?"

"Yes, we can. That's good, Bones."

"Now I'm positive Snider is as much to blame for killing my family as he would have been if he'd locked them in a room full of rattlesnakes. I know it and he knows it. All I have to do is find Patch to prove it."

"Well, you don't even have to leave town. Patch is right over there in the schoolyard."

A.B. pointed across the pond, but Patch was gone.

Doris hustled her brother-in-law up the stairs toward his office. "Honestly, Royal, you ought to try not to publish your ignorance. You and Snider were talking so loud, everybody could hear you in the restaurant and I'm sure also up the street at the post office as well as clear on down inside the saloons." She knocked on Les's door, left Royal standing in the hall, and went in.

Lorrie was sitting in a chair beside the bed. Les looked like a purple ogre. Doris had never seen any of the VO look this ruined after a fight with the Cowdens. The Cowdens seemed to be having so much hell she did not know how much longer they could keep up the fight. "Well, Leslie," she said. "You don't look so bad. People said you were at death's door."

"I'm only a little sore and mad," Les said.

Doris stood at the side of the bed and smiled and patted Lorrie instead of speaking to her. She hugged Les and kissed him on the mouth, then straightened with both hands lightly on his chest, patted him, fluffed his pillow, and looked into his eyes to make sure he appreciated her. Lorrie read both their looks and did not like it.

Doris retired to the foot of the bed. "Is there anything I can do for you two? I heard you married. Congratulations."

"I was about to leave so Les could get some rest," Lorrie said.

"I'm sure he can rest better with you here to look after him, Lorrie. I'm the one who's in the way."

"You're not in the way, Doris," Les said.

"Well, I don't want to be another nuisance to you like all the other Vincents. I just came in to see what I could do for you."

"He's doing fine," Lorrie said. "He's got a big family of women to look after him."

"Well, I'll be gone. Get well quick. 'Bye."

Lorrie glided out of her chair and followed Doris to the door, shut it behind her, and locked it. When she turned to Les, she was so mad her mouth was a straight, bloodless slash across her face. When she spoke, her voice was a growl. "How come that woman thinks she can come in here and ignore me, kiss you on the mouth, pat your butt, and fluff your pillow? When did she learn to do that, anyway?"

"She never did that before, as far as I can remember." Les laughed.

"Oh yeah. It seems to me you have an awful short memory when it comes to the things you've done with women. How many thousands more women think they can come in here and give you soulful looks in front of me? What am I, the ten-damned-thousandth in the line?"

Les could not answer that, so he laughed.

"You think I'm funny, do you? Laugh at this, then." She drenched his head with a whole pitcher of water. She was not satisfied with the effect, so she brought the bottom of the pitcher down on his head. The heavy crock pitcher remained intact, so she chunked it away and dashed it into a thousand pieces. She stalked to the door, grappled with the lock and wrenched it open, stepped out, paused to gather strength, and slammed the door so hard the building shook.

Les was so angry he got out of bed, dressed, and dragged himself downstairs to the bar. The bump Lorrie had put on his head began to seep a little blood, but he wiped it off and nobody even looked his way. The bartender served him as though not surprised that he looked like he'd been run over by a train.

He thought, why would I think anyone who knows me would be surprised to see me like this? Everybody knows how drunk I get, so this bartender that I've known all my drinking life probably only figures I got drunk again and fell down in front of a team of horses, or got run over by a bull, or clobbered by a madwoman. He doesn't even say hello, because there's no telling how mean and wild I acted the last time he served me. I ought to quit drinking, but dammit, not today.

Lorrie's anger lasted until she walked out on the veranda where A.B. was sitting. He said, "Well, howdy, pretty daughter. How's your world today?"

Lorrie sat down on the veranda and took a deep breath. "Not too darned good, but I'll make it."

"Are you doing what you like to do?"

"I just did something I sure wanted to do."

"What was that? You didn't shoot Les's toe off, did you?"

Lorrie laughed. "No, but I tried to knock his head off."

Willy Porter rode by and tipped his hat for A.B. and Lorrie, then hit a trot for El Durazno. He wanted to give his horse a good feed of grain and a brushing.

El Durazno was only three miles from Harshaw. Halfway, Patch the Apache stepped out into the road ahead of Willy and leaned on his rifle. Willy stopped and sat his horse. "I've been looking for you, Patch," he said in Spanish.

"I am carrying a message for the Horseman," Patch said.

"Did Snider leave you to look after Teresa and my family?"

"No, he left them alone to be taken by Chato."

"How do you know Chato took them?"

"I saw him in Slaughterhouse Wash with Teresita and your horses."

"What else did you see?"

"That he killed Emily and Willy Fly."

"When did you see that?"

"I milked your cow and when I carried the milk to the house, I saw them on the bed. You were on the hill digging."

"You were the one who left the milk on the table?"

"Yes."

"Why didn't you tell me you were there?"

"You wanted to kill someone, maybe an Indian."

"Not you."

"I did not need to find out who you wanted to kill."

"Will you come back to town with me and tell the Horseman's father?"

"Yes."

"Let's go and get this settled."

Snider had followed Willy out of town. He dismounted with his rifle when he heard Willy stop to talk to someone by the road. He climbed a hill above the road, crawled forward into oak brush and looked down and saw Willy and Patch together. He had never killed anyone, but he needed to decide quickly which one to kill first.

Willy Porter smiled at Patch and Snider decided he'd better kill him first. Patch must have satisfied Willy that Snider had lied about Patch being to blame for the deaths of Willy's family. Willy was mounted and would light out for town in a hurry if he was not hit first.

Snider took a deep breath, held a bead between Willy's shoulder blades, and squeezed. All Willy's limbs went rigid when the bullet struck him and the horse sprang forward. Paralyzed, Willy's body stayed on the horse a few jumps, then toppled onto the road like a plank.

Patch poured three accurate shots into the oak brush so fast Snider had to stick his nose in the dirt to keep from being hit. Then Snider scrambled backwards into a cover of boulders quick as a centipede, ran and mounted his horse, and hit for Harshaw.

Patch was afoot and Willy's horse had run off. Patch would not have followed the assassin anyway. He figured the assassin was Snider. All he needed to do to confirm it was to find his tracks. He knew Snider's track. He always made it a point to know the tracks of friends and enemies. He had never liked Snider at all.

Patch heard a wagon coming up the canyon. He put Willy's hat under his head for a pillow. He was already dead and stiff as a lodgepole. Patch left the road before the people in the wagon could see him and gained the same cover the assassin had used. The boot track in the boulders was Snider's all right.

Twelve

LES STOOD UP STRAIGHT at the end the bar and decided to do some serious thinking. Getting his ass kicked would make any man quicken his thinking. Les's ass had been pink and virgin, as far as an ass-kicking was concerned. He'd never been whipped in a fight before the Briggs brothers jumped him. So maybe he ought to start using his head for something more than a corral gate.

He decided his best course was to get out of town until he healed up. He did not have any good reason for being in that bar either. People could look at him and tell he'd had the worst of it in a fight. He did not want that to encourage more enemies to try him. If he wanted to face the truth, he did not feel like fighting, could not put up a fight even if he wanted to. He was not armed and did not have enough strength in his right arm to scratch his nose, let alone draw a pistol. He was drinking left-handed and his ribs on that side were so sore he almost had to bow to his glass to get a swallow.

After three drinks he felt better. One more and he might feel loose enough to climb the stairs back to the room, get his pistol and jacket, and go home.

Then the two large Briggs brothers walked in. Les heard their heavy, hobnailed boots coming when they were still out in the lobby. He recognized them the minute they straightened up after they came through the door. They were half-a-head taller than the door frame. Les did not know how he recognized them, but he was sure they were Lorrie's brothers. Their imprint on his brain must have been tattooed indelibly by the hobnails.

Now he looked at them to see what their faces were like. They were blond-headed and clean-cut and wore the open expressions of good-natured working men. They were better looking than Hoozy, Whitey, and Teddy. They smiled while their eyes became accustomed to the dark room. They walked past Les and took stools halfway down the bar.

One of the Briggses straightened and saw Les's face in the mirror behind the bar. He leaned toward his brother and told him about Les. The brother turned slowly to look at Les, turned back to his brother, said something in a low voice, and they both laughed.

Les took stock of himself and found he was short of everything he needed if he was to live another hour. Both sides of his ribs were kicked in, his vision was impaired, his legs and arms barely functioning. His mouth was so sore, his lips so mashed, he could not even engage the Briggses in a cuss fight. He could not for the life of him even make a resolution to fight. He bent over for another swallow of his drink. He knew the wise course was to avoid another ass-kicking, but he just could not bring himself to take the first step toward the door. He wanted one more drink. His resolve to fight might be crippled, but his stubbornness to have that drink was not.

He was about to order the other drink when the bartender brought him one and inclined his head toward the Briggses. "Those big fellers said for me to give their brother-in-law a drink."

Les let it sit. Now he wouldn't be able to have another unless he accepted this one. Wormy Hoozy and Weasly Whitey Briggs had suddenly resurrected inside the carcasses of two giants. Les had hoped Lorrie would be the only Briggs who would ever bother him again. She was more than a sufficient bother for any man. Now these two monsters wanted him to refuse the drink so they could stomp him again, or he would have to *pelar,* peel away and run like a coward.

"I'm not going to drink this, bartender, so get it out of my sight," Les said. Now, why did I say that?, he thought. Worse than that, he started dragging his sore carcass toward the Briggses. He thought, what the hell, might as well take my lumps, so I can have my other drink and go home.

The Briggses did not let on they knew he was coming until he stood behind them with one Briggs on his right and one on his left.

"What made you think I'd drink with you?" Les said. "Did you think I'd ever forget the ass-kicking you gave me?"

The Briggses leaned with their forearms on the bar and both hands on their drinks. One Briggs grinned and stared straight ahead into the mirror. The other turned his head, grinned at Les over his shoulder, and said, "It looks like we did a good job on you, all right. We thought you deserved a drink for getting well so quick."

"I think I'll just buy you a drink for stopping when you did," Les said.

"Well now, that's decent. We'll take it. It ain't often somebody shows us gratitude after we almost stomped him to death."

"It's not gratitude. I figure you might need a drink to help you get your breath back. You must have been awful tired and wore out to stop dancing on me, puny as you are. Now, if it had been me, I never would have stopped. You'd either be a jelly, or I'd still be stomping you."

"We didn't get tired of stomping you and you didn't get tired of the stomping. What's it gonna take to make you tired?"

"A week of stomping on your two heads."

"When would you like to start? I think you ought to know, we never fight one against one. We even team up when we beat our wives."

The bartender brought the drink Les had ordered for the Briggses and the one the Briggses bought for him. The Briggs who had been watching Les in the mirror handed him his drink. "Here, if we can accept your drink, you can accept ours."

Les looked at it. Refusing a drink was something he did not truly want to do. "Well, all right, but this one makes us even in the drink department, so let's not have any more."

The Briggses stood up straight and faced Les and drank down their drinks. "I'm Elkhart, called Elk," the one on Les's left said. "I'm Wabash, called Wash," the Briggs on the right said. Their hands were big as scoop shovels, their shoulders wide and heavy as oxen yoke. Elk was taller and wirier than Wash.

"You Cowdens and us Briggses might become friends, if you ever get over having to murder or marry us," Elk said.

"We haven't murdered any of you. Apaches did that. As for marrying your sister, well, it hasn't been established that I married her. I think she married me."

"Now, strange as it might sound, we believe you," Wash said. "We know our sister real well, and we don't object to her marrying you. If there ever were two people who deserved each other, you two are it. We've been saying we really piled injury on top of insult when we put the boots to you the other night. We're kinda sorry we did that. The insult that was already on your head was our sister."

"You apologize for doing it?"

"I guess maybe we do. We thought you were Ben. We figured Lorrie was bound to already have Les Cowden plumb whipped worthless and kept at home. Then, when we found out we'd kicked the hell out of Les, we were not surprised that he gave us no fight at all. How long you been married to our sister? You're weaker'n a lepe calf."

"Weak as a lepe, am I?"

The Briggses looked him up and down and grinned. Les knew his mouth was about to overload his black-and-blue butt.

"Look at you," Wash said. "I know what you're thinking. You still think you're tough. Aren't you tired of being stomped? Look there in the mirror at your sore old head and ask yourself, 'Do I want the Briggses to go back to work on me and make me look worse?' If the answer is yes, remember that both of us will be doing the job, not just one. That's a double Briggs stomping you'll get again."

"I know what you mean," Les said. "I believe I'll wait a while, maybe until I catch you apart. I would like a fair chance to see how you handle yourselves with your fists man-to-man."

"We'll be looking forward to it, brother. We're perfectly willing to let you go back to our sister until you feel ready. We wish all our enemies would have to live with her. Believe me, she can take the fight out of gangs of mean fellers like you."

Lorrie came to the swinging doors and looked over the top, saw Les with her brothers, and came through in a hurry. "What, have you taken up drinking with the very riffraff that almost crippled you for life? Have you lost your mind, Les Cowden?"

"No, Lorrie, I was about to see if they would break their rule and fight me man-to-man."

The Briggs brothers turned their backs to Lorrie, leaned on the bar, and stared into their drinks. Lorrie started shoving Les toward the door and poking him in his sore ribs and back. He knew she probably thought he was reluctant to leave because he wanted to fight, but he was too crippled to move fast enough to stay out of her reach. She inflicted so much pain on him that he was forced to sit down in the lobby.

"Look at you," Lorrie said. "What made you think you could fight those two big brutes?"

"I didn't really want to fight anybody."

"Then what were you doing with them?"

"I was hoping a miracle would happen and I'd just disappear from there and then reappear home in bed, or something like that."

"So, what do you have to say to me?"

"Thank you. You're the miracle I was hoping for. You saved my hump."

"All right, then, let's get you back to bed."

"I'm ready. I just need you to go up and get my pistol and jacket and we'll go home."

"Oh, no. You're coming up with me."

"Well, Lorrie, to tell you the truth I don't think I can climb those stairs up and down and then get home. I might make it if I don't have to climb the stairs."

"You don't have to climb back down the stairs, just up the stairs. We're staying here in our own room together while we have an excuse to do it. Now come on, I'll help you. You can make it to our second honeymoon bed, can't you?"

"Well, since you put it that way, yes, I can."

The walk to bed was painfully slow, but Les did not stop to rest, catch his breath, or wipe his brow. Lorrie helped him undress, sponged him off with warm water and soap, rubbed him with mescal, petted him a little, blew out the light, laughed, and piled in bed on top of him.

Eileen, Paula Mary, and Joe and Jimmy Coyle had set out with the spring wagon and team for Harshaw to bring Les home. Jimmy and Paula Mary stood up in the back. Joe drove the team at such a brisk trot that the spring wagon skimmed the hard road.

Joe's passengers were having fun. He had just tightened every bolt and board and oiled every joint, hinge, and spring of the wagon and made it tight as a new cabinet. The earth swelled in the evening cold and brought up the fragrance of cottonwood, willow, arrow weed, oak trees, and brush, and the mulch of the summer's crop of high, old grass.

The wagon was hitched to Barney, the horse that had survived the VO ambush down Harshaw Canyon, and a new horse called Pete Reynolds. Pete Reynolds, the man, had come along one day with his bay hitched to a buggy and the horse matched Barney so perfectly that A.B. bought him. Pete Reynolds had been such a gentleman when they made the trade that A.B. named the horse after him. This was the new horse's first day working with Barney and he had fallen in step with his new partner and worked with the same ease and grace since they wheeled about and made their first turn.

The road to Harshaw had one U-curve against a hill and around a bend of Harshaw Creek. The family always liked whoever was driving to take the slope of that turn as fast as he could. Joe tapped the team into a measured lope. The horses' heads bobbed together in a cadence that was almost slow, but the spring wagon seemed to glide and lower a wing to swoop around the turn without a sound or a creak in its joints and wheels. That brought shouts and giggles out of Paula Mary and laughing from Eileen and Jimmy.

Joe's eyes watered against the cold wind as he concentrated on holding the wagon along the edge of the road above the creek. He was lucky the road rose steeply as he left the turn. The grade slowed the horses in time for Joe to stop them before they ran over a person lying face up in the middle of the road.

The horses shied at the form as Joe drove around it. He looked down as he drove by and was almost sure the man was dead. He stopped the team, handed the lines to Eileen, and went back to examine the body.

"My gosh, that man's sure a sound sleeper," Paula Mary said.

Joe knelt between the body and the wagon to hide the man's dead face from Jimmy and Paula Mary, felt for a pulse, and found none. The staring eyes told him the man was dead, but he was still warm. Then he saw blood had seeped into the ground underneath the body.

"Who is it, Joe?" Eileen asked. Barney and Pete Reynolds kept looking back over their shoulders at the form and were becoming hard to handle. They knew the thing in the road had caught the death and they did not like to stand so close to it without being able to watch it and see what it might do. They were light-mouthed and ordinarily easy to handle, but Eileen was getting scared and could not help pulling too hard on them. When she took too tight a hold on them they almost came over backward, but if she gave them slack they threatened to bolt and run away.

"That's Willy Porter," Paula Mary said. "Why doesn't he get up from there? Is he drunk?"

Eileen spoke up in a carefully controlled, even tone, "I don't know what's going on back there, but, Joe, you better come and take these lines, because this team is about to leave the world."

Jimmy jumped down off the wagon to see what he could do and that startled the horses, so they decided to leave the place once and for all. Eileen held them and they backed too quickly against the wagon, then lunged ahead again.

Paula Mary was about to jump off the wagon when it lurched ahead and threw her off the back. She landed on a rock, sprained her ankle, and squalled like the owls had snatched her. The horses stood up and pawed at the sky. Eileen gave them slack to keep them from coming over backwards and they hit the ground running. She turned them into the hill to keep them from getting away. They sprang over a bank and up a forty-five-degree grade. The wagon came to a stop when the front wheels struck the bank. The horses were jerked short and teetered on their hind legs over Eileen's head. They came down in a tangle of harness, scrambled for footing over a pile of boulders, and lunged up hill again. Before they reared again, Joe reached their heads and held them.

Joe led the team down off the hill and untangled the harness and traces. He climbed up beside Eileen and drove the horses up the road to air them out. He turned them around, brought them back and stopped a safe distance away, so they could have a clear look at the man in the road. Jimmy stopped rubbing Paula Mary's ankle, took hold of the horses, and stood at their heads.

Joe loaded Willy Porter in the back of the wagon, then loaded Paula Mary right in beside him, turned the wagon around, and headed for Harshaw.

Jimmy was holding Paula Mary's shoe. He started rubbing her ankle again and she sniffled.

Eileen turned to look at her. "What's the matter, Paula Mary?"

"I hurt my ankle."

"What in the world's the matter with Bones? Is the poor man drunk?"

Paula Mary looked up at her sister and said angrily, "Can't you see he's dead? He's got blood all over him."

Les awakened and listened to a commotion gather momentum in the town. First, a downstairs door slammed and the wooden hotel reverberated and trembled like a drum. Feet walked in and out, then trotted in and out, then another door slammed and voices began sounding, then someone shouted down the street. He wanted a drink, but he did not want to wake Lorrie. Her head was bowed on his shoulder and her little breaths puffed against his chest in slumber.

Somebody tramped by Les's door and pounded on Royal's door to wake him up. A while later a quiet step stopped outside and knocked on Les's door and Jimmy spoke softly.

"Yes, Jimmy?"

"Can you come downstairs?"

"What happened?"

"Your pappy would like you to come down."

Lorrie stirred and Les detached himself. Lorrie moved over an inch and went on sleeping. Les dressed in the dark with a sense of doom. He did not light the lamp because he was afraid a light would make him a target. He was halfway down the stairs to the lobby before he realized how sore he was. Doctor Tucker was administering to Paula Mary. He had pulled off her stocking and bared her foot. Her ankle was red and swollen. A.B. told Les that Willy Porter had been shot in the back and murdered.

The lobby filled with people. Snider staggered drunk out of the saloon with the Briggs brothers. Royal Vincent and Billy Stiles came down the stairs and joined a knot of people listening to Joe Coyle tell how he found Willy in the road shot in the back.

Another dense knot of men carried a burden through the front door and laid it on the desk. Les saw it was Willy and went over to look at his face. He looked like a child who had been playing hard at kick-the-can after supper and had been made to go to bed before he wanted to stop playing. When they were growing up, Les had seen him lie down in bed still excited from the game and knock off to sleep before he even finished breathing his last sigh of the day. His eyes looked like they had just lost their focus in that instant before they closed in sleep. Les had known Willy all his life.

With Judge Dunn standing nearby, Les emptied Willy's pockets of a watch, a few coins and a stock knife. He took off Willy's pistol belt. Les knew the coins might be all of Willy's money that anybody would ever find. He did not use banks. If he had any other money, it was buried or hidden somewhere. Somebody in the family should go out and stay at El Relave to keep scavengers from looting the house and barn.

"Where's his horse?" Les asked. "He was riding a dun of his grandfather's."

"I don't think anybody's seen his horse," Dick Martin said softly. Les knew Dick was sad about Willy. He might be angry at Les, but he was softhearted and he'd played plenty of kick-the-can with Les and Bones when they were small.

Snider shouldered his way through the crowd around the body and said to Les, "Have you found out who murdered the man?"

Les stared at Snider. "Somebody like you who couldn't face him, shot him in the back."

"Well then, I know who it was. That gut-eater Patch did it."

"Patch, the scout?" Judge Dunn asked. "What makes you think Patch did it?"

"Porter left Patch in charge of his ranch when he went off on the stage and Porter's family was murdered and my wife taken by Patch's damned relatives. He knew he had to potshot Porter or Porter would have come after him sooner or later to even the score. The Indian killed him. I saw him down in the schoolyard this very morning. I'm sure he did it."

"Well, that cinches it," Royal announced. "I'm asking all you men to volunteer for a posse. My rangers will arrive in full strength tomorrow."

A.B. came up and spoke to Snider. "You saw Patch this morning?"

"I sure did," Snider said.

"Why didn't you say something about it? You knew Willy wanted to talk to him."

"Something took my mind off it and I forgot to tell him."

"I see." A.B. stared at Snider speculatively. Snider's squirm was almost imperceptible. He inched backward. "But you're absolutely sure he did it?"

"Yes," Snider said. He saw that A.B. knew he was the murderer.

"Who will volunteer?" Royal shouted. "Who's joining my posse?"

A.B. moved Les away from the crowd. "How do you feel, son?"

"Just a little sore, Papa."

"What do you think we ought to do with Willy?"

"I think he'd want to be buried with Emily and Willy Fly at El Relave."

"Then I'll send Mark to tell Uncle Billy and Aunt Mary that he's been killed and to bring the folks to meet us and bury him at El Relave. Willy'll be all right for several days in this weather."

"Sure he will."

"You'll have to start making a hand a little too soon. Can you do it?"

"I don't feel much pain anymore, Papa."

Thirteen

NONE OF THE TOWNSMEN who came to gawk at Willy Porter's carcass volunteered to join Royal Vincent's posse. When Royal's appeal for volunteers was ignored, he turned away and went into the telegraph office off the lobby to see if his wire to Tucson had been answered and his fifty rangers were on the way.

Jim Porter, Viney's brother, was the telegraph operator and he was busy receiving another message. Royal waited by the door and heard A.B. tell Les that he would send Mark to Porter Canyon to notify the family of the murder. Jim Porter copied the incoming message and went out to deliver it. Royal went behind the desk and looked through a stack of messages for his answer from Tucson. He read a message from Ben Cowden that notified A.B. he would arrive in Patagonia the next evening. Coincidentally, the message Royal expected was there notifying him that his fifty constables would arrive on the same train as Ben.

Royal took Snider, Billy Stiles, and Teddy up to his office. The sound of so many feet passing by in the hall and bunching in the office next door awakened Lorrie. She lay next to the wall and did not move. She could hear all the talk in Royal's office.

"Teddy, I want you to get on your horse and follow old man Cowden wherever he goes," Royal said. "I heard him say he was sending Mark to Porter Canyon. That's your chance to shoot Mark."

"No use getting in a hurry," Teddy said. "Mark won't leave the ranch tonight."

"I want you to stay close to the Cowdens so Mark won't get away."

"Yeah, and where am I going to sleep if he doesn't head out tonight? What do you expect me to do, sit on a rock and watch the house while the Cowdens sleep?"

"That's right. That's what I want you to do."

"I thought you said I could be my own boss on this."

"You can kill him any way you want, but I want you on his trail tonight."

Teddy stood up and angrily scraped his chair out of the way. "Hell, it's just a waste of time. I don't even have a blanket with me."

"Then you better get one quick. Nobody said the Cowdens would keep their hours to suit you."

"All right, but it's stupid for me to go out and sit in the cold all night."

"That's what makes assassins so mean, I guess."

Teddy tramped out of the office, slammed the door, tramped down the hall and down the stairs. The office remained quiet until the sound of him was gone.

"Say, Royal, aren't we going to celebrate?" Snider said. "Give us a brandy."

"Celebrate what?"

"Somebody killed a squatter, didn't they?"

"Who killed the squatter, Snider?" Billy Stiles asked.

"Not me."

"He was shot in the back, wasn't he?"

"Yeah, he was."

"You did it, didn't you?"

"Hell no. I never shot anybody in my life."

"You've knifed one or two, though, haven't you?"

"Well, one. I cut Ben Cowden, but that was kind of an accident."

"In the back, too. You have to get awful close to a man to do that, so how was it an accident?"

"Well, it wasn't altogether an accident. We were in a fracas and I just kind of lashed out to keep him away from me."

"Yeah, you just kind of got scared and threw out your hand and happened to be holding a knife and it cut him in the back."

"That's about it. Everything happened so fast, Ben got cut."

"After such a close quarter fight with Ben, it must have been easy to shoot Bones in the back from behind a bush."

"What the hell are you saying?"

"If you would stab Ben Cowden in the back, you would damned sure shoot Bones Porter in the back. Wasn't Bones mad at you for leaving his family alone at the ranch? You were scared to death that sooner or later he was gonna getcha, weren't you?"

"We settled that. I left Patch, the Apache, at the ranch."

"Listen, Snider, we're your partners. We knew when you followed Bones out of town this afternoon, and we saw you sneak back with your face all yellow."

Snider's face began to turn yellow again.

"It doesn't make any difference who killed Porter, or how he was killed," Royal said. "He was just another Cowden as far as I'm concerned, one we won't have to fight."

Stiles was angry. "That kind of thinking is the reason we're losing this fight. Decent people don't shoot other decent people in the back. You said you hired me as a ranger because I'm a native of this country. Well, listen to me, then. Every newspaper has come out against the VO in this war. They call Duncan Vincent 'Would-Be King Vincent.' Believe me, nobody's going to join your posse. The VO is just, dammit, unpopular as hell.

"It was my idea to go out and bushwhack the Cowden horses the other day, because I don't mind being suspected of being a horse-killer. I won't get hung for that. Bushwhacking Bones Porter is something else. You think people don't know one of us did that? What's worse, the Porters will join the Cowdens in the war now. When they hear about the killings at El Relave, they're going to take a long look at Snider and do more than just give him a contemptible name. They won't only come after Snider, either. What they do to him they'll want to do to the rest of us."

"You want out of this, Billy? Take a walk," Royal said.

"No, I have my own account to settle with the Cowdens and I wouldn't stand a Chinaman's chance alone. I'm just trying to show you that we can't take on every decent person in the territory. Face it, everybody likes the Cowdens and nobody likes us."

"They will someday, when they see what Duncan is trying to do."

"Hooray."

"Believe me, I understand your point. That's why I'm making such a fuss about going after the Yawner. We can keep people from bothering about our war with the Cowdens by getting them riled up against the Apaches again. If we keep talking that up and then go out and get the old Yawner without any help from the Cowdens, we'll build up a lot of credit for ourselves."

"Well, I hope so," Billy Stiles said. "I just wish we knew what we were doing."

"I know what I'm doing," Royal said.

"No, the Cowdens do, and they do their best work when they're mad. They were happy when Ben got married, but now we've made them mad again."

"So who's left to be mad at anybody?" Snider said. "Ben's off in Honeymoon Land. Les's carcass has been mashed to the bone and the leavings are in Lorrie Briggs's hands. Mark's arm is broke. I don't know how many of their horses we killed. Hell, we ain't doing so bad. Who cares if we're unpopular? We've split 'em up good."

Von and Randolph knocked and came in with a nattily dressed Chinese. Royal sent his rangers out to prepare for their campaign against the Yawner. He waited until they were gone before he spoke to his visitor. "What have you got for me, Lee?"

Lee was a pale, thin, delicate man with a high forehead and a feathery mustache that was hard to see. He smiled. "Girls," he said.

"Here in Harshaw? Now?"

"Not yet, on the way."

"What are you doing here? I thought you were supposed to wire me when they arrived."

"I must have more money."

"I don't owe you any money, do I?"

"I did not say you owe it. Only that I must have it."

"What is this? My brother already paid you an outrageous amount for this shipment. When are we going to see the results?"

"Soon."

"I've paid you all you have coming."

"This small sum I ask for is to stop a certain authority from suspecting that you are a smuggler and a slaver."

"What? Do I hear right? You think you can blackmail me? Bribing officials is your department, not ours."

"I am only here to receive $1,600 for protecting you from the authorities, nothing more."

"Why, you damned chink, I'll have you tied to a tree, skinned alive, and whipped to death."

"No, no, no. That is the kind of action my organization employs, not yours."

"I guess you think I'm afraid of your tong, or whatever you call that bunch of chink hoodlums you run with."

"I am not here to intimidate you. We have provided a lucrative business for you that we will continue to protect. My organization's pipeline for the products your organization brings into the country provides you with a good market and protection from discovery. We want you to make a profit, but you must be ready to give us money when we ask for it. We don't need you unless you can supply money."

"Oh, is that right? And how would you move little girls and loaded pack mules through the Mexican and American authorities, Mexican bandits, and Apaches? By sampan and rickshaw?"

"We would find a way, but we won't need to if you keep your word and continue to supply us with the money we want, including, at times, small unforeseen amounts, like the $1,600 I want now."

"We paid you all the money our agreement provided for and more. What you're demanding now is blackmail and I won't pay it. Extortion is another word for it."

"I agree. I rejoice that you understand."

"Mr. Lee, I think you'd better leave."

"I understand your anger. I don't understand why you would sacrifice your good name and go to jail over so small a sum as $1,600. I'll go up the street to Mr. Wong's. You can send the cash by messenger."

"Get out, you blackmailer."

Lee rose and went out without a rustle.

Vincent turned to Von and Randolph.

"What are you going to do?" Randolph asked. "The man can damned sure get what he wants."

"You're my partners. What do you think I ought to do? I'll tell you, I think I'll do what any self-respecting partner would do, get you to shoot his ass full of bullets and drop it down a mine shaft."

"You want to start a war with the tong now?"

"So what? What's so tough about the tong?"

"Listen, we know Chee Lee's tong. It's plenty tough, plenty mean, and never, never plays fair."

"It occurs to me your knowledge and advice on chink hoodlums and their business ventures brought me the tong."

"Yes, we did, and we've made a lot of money on the venture. Now, my advice to you is, pay Lee like a gentleman, don't fret and don't rant, and you'll make a lot of money. Threaten the man, hurt him, fail to pay, and you'll find yourself in a war that will make your fight with the Cowdens seem like a game of singing tops."

"Maybe we should get out of the chink traffic."

"You want out?" Von joined in. "I'll take it all myself."

"You want to pay blackmail?"

"Sure. $1,600 in blackmail is a lot better than being exposed as a slaver and dope smuggler. Me and Randolph have made $75,000 since we started. Why would I want to give it up?"

"I hate to pay graft, bribes, and blackmail. It's against my nature."

"Oh yes, Senator Vincent, I realize how much your nature as a fine, upstanding, sterling member of the community must be offended by Mr. Chee Lee's demands, but look at it the way you should. The business is lucrative as hell and the personal and legal risk is small. The danger of losing the perishable merchandise is large, but the merchandise wants to make it to America as badly as we want it to. The livestock willingly risks its own life so that someday it can become American and that shows up in an extra measure of profit for us."

"It doesn't seem right to look at these people as livestock."

"Ah, that sounds like our Senator Vincent, all right. Listen, hasn't your brother been trying to make a name for himself as the pioneer who brought the first Hereford cattle into this country?"

"Yes, of course. That's been one of our most prideful projects."

"How much money has it made him?"

"Not much, yet. If we ever get these squatters out of the way, it'll be the best business in the west."

"I've made $75,000 on about a hundred Chinese and you've made more than that. The Chinese wanted to come here. We haven't whipped them or chained them and the traffic flows smoother all the time. Chee Lee's tong provides the old country stock, then protects and markets it for us in this country. The stock lives happily ever after. Tell me that's not better than trailing a bunch of old, pink-eyed bulls into the country and fighting over their grass. Tell me which stock yields the most profit over the cost per pound gain. You want out? I'll buy you out."

"I can't believe you're willing to pay the chink $1600 just because he demanded it out of the clear blue sky like that."

"Yes, I'll pay it. Besides that, I'll treat him like a friend."

"Well, I guess I'll stay in, but you two'll have to be the ones who deal with the tong. You're right. I guess this is not the time to stand on principle. We do little enough for the money we make."

"That's a good way to look at it."

Lorrie loved her listening place on the other side of the wall. She wriggled happily under the blankets, kicked with pleasure, rubbed cozily against the sheets. The blinds and curtains were closed on the windows of her room and she felt as alone and unseen as a ghost. She could have laughed out loud with the glee she felt, but she did not want to be discovered. She loved the fun of lying quiet, safe, and comfortable while she listened to Royal Vincent's awful scheming.

A new crowd of feet stopped out in the hall. Lorrie thought her door was locked, but to her surprise it opened and the feet tramped into her room. She was not surprised that Les would bring a gang of cowboys or relatives into her room. He was not used to privacy and did not consider that anyone else might want it. She turned to smile at him. Instead, she smiled at Dick Martin, Creswell, and Packrat.

The men just stood and gawked at her.

She said, "What in the world are you doing in here, Dick Martin?"

"Oh, hi . . . er . . . Lorrie. We're looking for the VO office."

"Are you new around here? Does this look like it?"

"I'm awful sorry, Lorrie. This is awful. You see, uh, Sheriff Cowden just released these VO men from jail and I brought them up here to get the money for their fine from the secretary. I guess I opened the wrong door."

"What do I care? Do you think I want you to stand over my bed while you explain why you're so damned dumb?"

"Well, no, Lorrie, I . . ."

"I advise you to get out of here before my husband catches you by my bed. If he doesn't shoot you, I'll have to, or he might believe I invited you in."

The three men only stood and gawked. Lorrie was only dressed in her nightgown, but she had to risk giving them more to look at. She reached for her purse and set it on her lap. She cocked a derringer pistol as she drew it out of the purse. The three pairs of eyes switched from her pretty breasts to the weapon. She let fly at their eyes.

Even though she was a notoriously bad shot, everybody in the county knew Lorrie enjoyed any occasion of firing her pistol and always shot to kill. All of a sudden, Martin, Creswell, and Packrat realized their carcasses had lost all their value. Martin and Creswell whirled and launched their worthless selves at the open door, knocked Packrat down, and trampled the length of him. Packrat's face took splinters off the floor as it skidded toward the door, but that did not deter his effort to escape. He looked back once to see if more bullets were coming and scurried after his partners like a cockroach.

112

The sight of the absolute panic she had caused made Lorrie laugh so hard she could barely move to shut the door. Then she sat down and let the pistol dangle on her finger while she brought her mirth under control and listened to the VO tell about its latest encounter with a Cowden.

"I didn't know they were right next door, for hell's sake," Royal said gruffly. "She was in bed, you say? Where's the bed? Against which wall?"

"I don't think she heard anything." Dick Martin said. "I think she was asleep when we went in."

"Shhhhhshut up!"

After that no one spoke in a normal tone again and Lorrie could not understand them. Then Les came in and said, "Who did that shooting up here?"

Lorrie held her finger to her lips so he would speak quietly.

"What's the matter? How come your door wasn't locked?"

Lorrie made frantic signs for him to be quiet and he subsided. She quickly dressed and packed their valise and took him down to the lobby.

Next door, Creswell said, "Did the Cowdens go downstairs? Damn, that's a pretty woman."

"Pretty?" Royal said. "I wonder how much she heard."

"Like I said, I think she was asleep," Dick Martin said.

"That's right, you were her work ox for a while, weren't you, Martin? I guess you ought to know what she looks like when she's been asleep."

"I do."

"You know, my brother had her. Ben Cowden probably had her. You had her. I could have had her, too. She'd have done anything for me if I'd wanted to have her when Duncan kicked her out. I should have kept her in the family. I wouldn't have to worry about what she was doing behind my back now. I sure didn't know she was right next door."

"I don't think you have to worry about Lorrie."

"She's a Cowden, isn't she? I'll tell you one thing. She'd better not be spying on me. She can fall in the war the same as any of them."

"Over my dead body, she'll fall, Vincent."

"Oh, ho, ho. Listen to our cavalier defend the maiden's honor."

"Shut up, Vincent," Dick Martin said.

"Martin, you're wasting your breath. She's not in the next room listening anymore. I distinctly heard her leave with Cowden. I hope you don't think your defending her will make her shine up to you again. You were never more than just another one of her foolish oxen."

As A.B. drove his buggy away from the hotel, Lorrie kept looking back. She sat with A.B. in front so Les could have the back seat to himself. Les wondered what she was watching, but was too sore to look. Outside Harshaw, he finally followed her look and saw Teddy coming along behind them with his rifle over the saddlehorn.

Lorrie did not say anything about her brother, but when he left the road and disappeared, she seemed relieved. Les watched her after they got home and after a while she went out and walked quickly to the barn. He told himself he was too sore to follow. He did not want to move, but she never went to the barn, had no business there. He figured if she wanted to meet her brother, it was none of his business. Teddy was the only one in her family she seemed to like.

Lorrie walked up Harshaw Creek for a half mile as fast as she could go, then crossed the road and climbed through the oak brush and trees to a ridge that ran parallel to the creek. She was no tracker, but the horse tracks she saw on the ridge looked fresh. She followed them until she saw the horse tied to a tree above the Cowden house. Teddy was huddled in a blanket down in a pile of rocks watching the house.

Lorrie walked up behind him and stopped. He sat with his knees under his chin and did not move. He'd leaned his Sharps .4570 against a rock beside him. Lorrie sat down behind him to wait until he discovered her. His face was turned toward the house. He always seemed like a young bobcat to Lorrie, short-coupled, short-nosed, square-jawed, tufts of wild hair over his ears, always a watchful look, and bobtailed. He'd been born bobtailed, which meant to Lorrie that he'd been born to fight and never have anything to lose.

Lorrie said in an even voice, "Teddy, what do you think you're doing?"

Teddy yelped and went three feet in the air. The rifle clattered down a small cliff out of reach. He did not even think about pulling his pistol. When he recognized his sister, he put both hands on his chest and allowed himself to breath. Lorrie laughed until her sides ached. Finally, Teddy smiled and climbed down after his rifle.

"A fine assassin you make," Lorrie said.

"Well, who in the heck would believe somebody'd come up behind him like that?"

"I would think you should expect it. If you want to make a business of killing people, you ought to know they're gonna want to stop you."

"Not them Cowdens. They're so crippled Ma could finish 'em with her broom."

"You underestimate the Cowdens, little brother."

"Naw, I don't. We've about got 'em whipped."

"Well, I'm a Cowden who's not whipped, so you better go back to town and practice before you try to shoot us all."

"Aw, I wasn't going to shoot anybody."

"Yes, you were. You've turned into a bushwacker like the rest of the VO."

"No, I haven't. I was just watching the place."

"Yes, you have. You helped them shoot our horses the other day, too, didn't you?"

"No, I didn't. Your horses? Why you taking their side? What's in it for you? Nothing."

"I'll tell you something. Either walk down there and call Mark outside and shoot him face to face, or get your butt back to your bushwhacking, back-shooting, horse-killing ranger friends. Rangers! You're a helluva ranger."

"I ain't leaving just because you tell me to."

"Oh, you're not? You want to make me mad?"

"I don't care if you get mad. You can't whip me anymore, so I'm warning you, sister, if you come at me with your fists like you used to, I'll knock your block off."

"I might not be able to whip you, but I can sure give it a try."

"Try away, lady." Teddy stuck out his chest and strutted toward Lorrie. She swung a haymaker at his head and he caught her wrist and twisted until she went down on her knees. "Nyaaa, nyaaa, nyaaa," he said, and wagged his tongue in her face.

Les's fist connected with the side of his head. Teddy fell like a bull axed in a slaughterhouse. He went down so hard and so suddenly that he jerked Lorrie down on her back. Les helped her up and looked down at Teddy, concerned that he might have killed him in front of his sister. Teddy's eyes were open and glazed and his limbs began to jerk. Lorrie walked around Les and looked down at Teddy. "Well, he's a goner," she said.

Les knelt by the boy and rubbed his wrists and hands.

"He's a goner," Lorrie said again.

"He'll be all right in a minute," Les said. Then Teddy breathed a great sigh and relaxed.

"You think so?"

"Yeah, see?"

Teddy raised a hand to his eyes. Les helped him get on his horse, headed him toward town, and whacked the horse on the rump. The horse trotted all the way down off the hill to the road before Teddy revived enough to gather his reins.

As Lorrie helped him off the hill, Les said, "What did you think you would accomplish by coming up here, Lorrie?"

"What would you have done if you'd caught my brother laying an ambush for your family?"

"I would probably have snuffed his lights."

"I know you would. You already snuffed two of my brothers. Teddy's the only one I ever liked."

Les looked in her face. She was working hard helping him off the hill and the climbing had made her sweat. Her hair was wet at the temples and her upper lip was beaded with sweat. She met his gaze and he shook his head in disbelief and wonder. "You still believe we killed your brothers, don't you?"

"Well, I didn't want Teddy to shoot Mark," she said. "I love Mark. If anybody from the Briggs family shoots any Cowdens it's gonna be me."

"Why did he want to shoot Mark instead of me?"

"He was waiting for Mark to head out to the Porters, I think."

"We did Teddy a favor, then. He would have frozen his butt off waiting for Mark to ride out. Joe Coyle left for Porter Canyon hours ago."

Fourteen

BEN WENT TO THE TRAIN DEPOT to confirm his and Maudy's reservations for the trip home. The ticket agent told him he was sorry, but he had no record of their reservations.

"Our compartment was reserved when we bought our round-trip tickets in Patagonia before the New Year," Ben said.

"I have no record of it."

"When's the next train to Arizona? Reserve us a compartment on that one."

"The next train does not have compartments on it."

"Well, reserve us a compartment on the next train that has one."

"I'll see what I can do."

"When will you be able to confirm our tickets?"

"Try me in two days."

Ben thought, in two days I won't need a reservation, because I will have gone plumb nuts.

He walked out to the platform by the tracks, sat down, and packed his pipe. A black man was tidying the platform. He was not working hard, because the space was already spotless. Every brass knob and plate was polished to a gleam. Every iron pole, seat brace, luggage-cart wheel, and even the man's dust pan was painted shiny black. Every wooden door, seat, cart bed, and even the man's broom handle was painted shiny green.

The man roved about with his broom and a long-handled dust pan, flicking up specks of debris that Ben could not even see. A stubby pipe smoked and made juicy sounds in the center of his mouth. He roved back and forth across the shiny floor toward Ben. When he was close, Ben smiled and said, "Hello, Joe."

"Hi, Joe," the black man rumbled. His head was slightly bowed, the lower lids of his eyes drooped and caught the smoke of the pipe. The whites of his eyes were smoky. Ben smelled the pipe ten feet away.

"I know you," Ben said.

"I think I know you, too, young man."

"I'll tell you where I saw you last. You were with a troop of the Tenth Cavalry under Lieutenant Hughes. You fought against the Yawner last summer at Los Metates, didn't you?" Ben was one hundred percent sure he was right, but the man kept his old soldier's poker face. Ben said, "You were Lieutenant Hughes's sergeant. I was in that battle with my grandfather, William Porter, and a bunch of cowmen. I went up to translate for Lieutenant Hughes when he tried to pursue the Yawner through the Mexican Army. Don't you remember me?"

"Yessir, you're the outlaw Ben Cowden." His eye brightened with good humor, but he did not smile.

Ben laughed softly and lit his pipe. "What are you doing here, Sergeant?"

"Retired last fall. Working for the railroad now."

"Were you with the Tenth at Los Molinos too? We flashed you some heliograph messages. Me and my brothers scouted against the Yawner when you drove him to us at Los Bultos. Who was your Lieutenant?"

"Bode."

"That's right. Lieutenant Carl Bode."

"I knew it was you when you and your lady stepped off the train a week or so ago."

"I'm trying to get home. I've had my full quota of California. How do you like California, Sergeant?"

"Good. I had a full twenty-year ration of the desert."

"I miss Arizona. I got down homesick the minute I turned away from my first look at the ocean."

"Arizona's too hot and thirsty. I stayed hot and thirsty all the time when I joined the horse soldiers on the Great Plains, then in Texas against the Comanches, through the fight against Victorio in New Mexico, and all the time in and out of Sonora and Chihuahua. . . . Too much heat and thirst."

"Anyway, it's good to see a friend. I was beginning to think I wouldn't find a white man in the whole state of California."

"I'm black as any man can be, but I know what you mean."

"Huh! You're more like me than anybody I've seen out here, including my own relations."

"Do you Cowdens still raise good horses?"

"You bet. Do you still ride?"

"I have an old horse to take care of and he takes care of me in that department."

"I could see an old cavalryman getting tired of the sun and dust of the desert, but he'd never get far away from his horse."

The sergeant smiled. "That's right."

"Now I'm worse homesick. I want to get home. Don't know why I ever came out here."

"Those were some horses you Cowdens and Porters rode at Los Metates. Your horses compared to ours the way that private car yonder compares to a cattle car."

A private railroad car was parked on a siding nearby. No name of any company was printed on it, but it was freshly painted and polished. A large MC monogram was painted in fancy scroll on the side and the rear grate that protected the platform was decorated with a Diamond MC. Lace curtains adorned the windows. The brass adornments on the rear safety grate and the lamps over the boarding steps were freshly polished.

"Who does it belong to?"

"It used to belong to Colonel Francis Cavanaugh, but he died last Christmas."

"My, isn't that a handsome thing? Is it nice inside?"

"It is, sir."

"It probably doesn't even squeak. Wouldn't it be nice to ride home to Arizona in that thing?"

"Mr. Cowden, would you like to see the inside?"

"I sure would."

"I'm the one keeps it tidy, so I have the key."

The sergeant told Ben his name was Lawrence Broussard. He'd been born in Louisiana, joined the Army when he was sixteen, and spent twenty years in the cavalry.

The car was a palace inside with cut glass window dressing and chandeliers, polished hardwood floor, bar, and sideboards. The room was fitted for extreme comfort with stuffed chairs, Persian carpets, a four poster double bed, and a shiny, hardwood, privy cabinet. A closet was packed with linen embroidered with the initials MC. A complete seventy-six-piece set of china and a newly polished silver set were decorated with the same monogram.

"Didn't you say the man's name was Francis Cavanaugh? What's the MC for?"

"For the colonel's wife, Mary Cavanaugh."

Outside, Ben asked the sergeant if the lady used the car.

"She comes down to see that I keep it tidy, but hasn't used it since the colonel died."

"Does she come regularly?"

"Oh, yes. She walks down here with her dogs every Wednesday."

"That's tomorrow. What time, Sargeant?"

"Ten in the morning."

"Do you think she'd sell it?"

"I don't know, sir."

118

"Would you mind if I bought it and took it back to Arizona?"

"I couldn't think of a better man to ride it than a man like you who rides good horses."

"I'll be here tomorrow morning at ten."

Ben met with Mrs. Cavanaugh and bought the car lock, stock, and barrel for $8,000 as a wedding present for Maudy. He paid with a bank draft on a deposit of golden *alazanas* that he'd taken from Duncan Vincent. He could not help but gloat at that. After all, his papa never said gloating was a sin. Duncan Vincent would never have been able to spend that gold in better style and the good Lord surely meant for Maudy to have a railroad car. The MC on the car, linen, and silver stood for Maudy Cowden now.

On the day Ben arranged for the car to be hooked to a train bound for Benson, Arizona, he hired Sargeant Broussard to help Maudy stock it with food, drink, and fresh water and to show her where to stow their clothing and luggage. After he paid the freight, Ben found them at work in the car.

Maudy went to the bar and dropped two drams of brandy into the toney, new snifters and handed them to the sergeant and Ben. "Ben, I think you should say something sensible to make this extravagance right," she said. "Then you and Sergeant Broussard should drink a toast."

Ben stood up and raised his glass to the sergeant. "To our good luck in running into a comrade who looked out for us."

The sergeant said, "To good people who deserve good luck."

They drank and Maudy took their glasses to wash and put away. Ben reached for his wallet. The sergeant anticipated him and stayed his hand.

"I want to pay you now, Sergeant," Ben said. "Our train leaves tonight."

"No, you can't pay me."

"Sergeant Broussard is going home with us," Maudy said.

"That's a good idea," Ben said. "He can make this trip to show us how to keep the thing fed and watered."

"No, Ben." Maudy's smile had an uncertain edge on it. "I hired the sergeant to come help us on the Vaca."

Ben did not bat an eye. "That's a better idea," he said. That was a first class extravagance Ben had not expected, but he could see it as a gift from Maudy. A soldier horseman like the sergeant was exactly the kind of help he needed on the Vaca ranch. His brothers were needed at El Durazno until they married and moved to their own ranches.

"How do you think you'll like working cattle, Sergeant?"

"I helped with cattle on the farm where I was raised before the War of Northern Aggression."

"Good. You know a thing or two about a cow. We'll be friends from now on, so we won't have to call each other 'sir.' What do you want to be called?"

"Sergeant, sir."

"I thought you had your fill of the desert."

"I have, but I'd rather work out in the open again than police a train depot. Anyway, I was always in some kind of a fight when I was a buffalo soldier. That's why I was always so hot and thirsty. I figure helping you move a few old cows around will be something I'll like. I won't have to shoot them and they won't have to shoot me."

"Oh, if you throw in with us, you still might get hot and thirsty from time to time."

"Oh, well, I can go to the shade, get a drink, and cool off, can't I?"

"If that's all you need, we've got plenty of shade and water. What about your family? Do you want to bring anyone?"

"I have no family, sir."

"Not even in Louisiana?"

"We were slaves in Louisiana. My relations were bought or bred and then sold. None that were sold were ever bought back."

Sergeant served Ben and Maudy supper on the car that night as it rolled back toward Arizona and established a routine he would follow whenever they used the car. In the car, he was the mess sergeant and did the cooking, bussing, washing, cleaning, and tidying. When Maudy was in the car, she was on vacation. Sergeant slept and ate with the porters on the train and Maudy and Ben enjoyed complete privacy except for the time each day when he came in to clean and cook, and joke with them.

That first night, rolling toward Arizona in Maudy's car, was the most comfortable and restful of Ben's life. After that night he never again minded going on long trips, as long as he could go in Maudy's car.

In Benson, their car was shuttled to Chamiso siding and another car was hooked to Maudy's car. While they waited to be switched to the New Mexico and Arizona line to Patagonia, a crowd of young men stepped off the other car. Prominently on each of their chests was displayed the shield of the Pima County Live Stock Association constable. Ben recognized several of the youngsters who had filibustered in Mexico at La Acequia with Duncan Vincent before Christmas. These were the gunsels Ben and his brothers and Don Juan Pedro Elias had turned back with their tails between their legs. These were the little, no-good, Tucson transients who had been given badges so they could come after the Cowdens in the name of law and order.

Now it was plain they had not learned their lesson. They strutted and grinned, laughed and slapped their legs at each others' jokes, and smoked. Every one of them had his skinny fingers wrapped around a cigarette. Now they could all afford smokes. The Live Stock Association gave them a wage and the VO would give them a bonus for joining this posse.

"What are those kids doing way out here?" Maudy asked.

"They're Vincent's regulator rangers headed for Patagonia again," Ben said.

"What for?"

"The Lord only knows. Les and Mark probably stirred up Royal Vincent and he needs to try to regulate the Cowdens' lives again."

"What does he need those wormy kids for, I wonder?"

"I don't know, but I'm not a bit sorry to see them. They're helpless. Royal will never be able to sneak up on us if he rides at the head of that bunch. I can't understand why the VO keeps calling them up. We've put 'em in the breeze so much, I'd think the VO would learn to leave them in the Tucson alleys and saloons where they found them."

The regulators were called back aboard and the two cars were switched to the New Mexico and Arizona line. The day was sunny and crisp. Maudy raised all the blinds and opened the curtains. Ben asked Sergeant to ride with them so they could talk about the country he had ridden with the Tenth Cavalry.

The train rumbled down beside the San Pedro River and Ben watched for and pointed out the spot where he and Les had crossed the tracks a few days before Christmas. They had ridden from El Durazno to Benson to meet Mark and then on to the Dragoons to take their sisters Eileen and Paula Mary back from the Bonner family. He felt a glow of pleasure now when he saw the very trail he had ridden tiredly with Les, because this time when he crossed the junction of the trail and the tracks, he was headed home in great comfort.

The train went on through other places where Ben had cowboyed and Sergeant had soldiered. The train's right of way was through as good a summer grassland for cattle as laid outdoors anywhere in the world: south beside the San Pedro River between the Whetstone Mountains and the Dragoons to the Boquillas ranch, west along the Babocomari River to Camp Huachuca.

This was the first time Sergeant had been back in the country since he was separated from the service. A corporal met the train at Camp Huachuca. Three private soldiers stepped off and fell instantly into the corporal's sphere of authority. Sergeant knew the corporal and stepped off to say hello and shake his hand. The corporal kept a serious eye on his charges and was too prepared to administer discipline to even give Sergeant a hello smile. The train moved and Sergeant returned to the car. The corporal marched the new men down a street between long rows of white tents into the U. S. Army.

The train passed through Uncle Billy Porter's Babocomari ranch to Sonoita, then south again down Sonoita Creek between the Santa Rita Mountains and the Canelo Hills to Patagonia. The dry grass was high and thick and most of the cattle Ben saw along the way were full, lying down, and chewing their cuds. The waters of the San Pedro, Babocomari, and Sonoita were running slow and heavy and looked hard and jewellike. Ben knew how that winter water tasted when a man, being careful to keep from wetting his clothes, lay on his belly beside it and drank, felt its hard weight on his tongue and then its lump of coldness drill his brisket down inside his heavy garments.

The train arrived in Patagonia an hour after dark. Eileen, Paula Mary, Betty, Mark, and another, heavy-faced man were sitting in A.B.'s landau coach with the top down. Ben wondered how they figured to carry everybody home. The landau would seat eight with the driver, but that would leave no room for luggage. Then he saw Barney tied nearby, harnessed to a shay. He wondered who the heavy-faced man in the landau was. He did not look unfamiliar and he was wearing Les's hat. Was that Les?

"Maudy, is that Les sitting up there beside Mark in the landau?" Ben asked.

Maudy looked at the man a moment. "My Lord, what happened to his face?"

The Cowdens in the landau tried to find Ben and Maudy among the regulator rangers as they stepped off the train. VO cowboys sat their horses by the platform holding saddle horses for the rangers. The rangers carried their saddles off the train and took charge of the horses. Everyone of them cast admiring looks at the Cowden girls and a coyote's over-the-shoulder look at Mark and Les, but the Cowdens ignored them.

The Cowdens finally recognized Ben and Maudy unloading their baggage with Sergeant by Maudy's car. Mark wheeled the landau around and pulled up beside the luggage. The VO rode away and the Cowdens were finally able to smile and be happy.

Sergeant was introduced and, while the luggage was loaded, Ben took Les by the arm and moved him aside. "Let Mark and Sergeant load the stuff, brother," he said. "You're barely able to move. What happened?"

"It'd take all night to tell you and you wouldn't like it all at once. I'll tell you little by little as time goes by."

"What did that to your face?"

"The Briggs brothers that work the Chalkeye mine. I didn't know they were within a hundred of miles of me when they walked up and knocked me down and put the boots to me."

"That does sound like a long story. Let's go home."

"Let me just put a period on it before we go."

"I'm still in a good mood, so you better not."

"A lot has been happening between us and the Briggses."

"Dear Lord, I can imagine."

"It all started at the wedding party."

"Don't tell me Lorrie threw one of her fits and tried to shoot somebody again."

"No, she didn't do that."

"Did she try to poison anybody? She didn't spit in the ice cream, did she? I knew she'd stayed at the party to pull something when I saw Dick Martin leave without her."

"You saw that she stayed at the party when Dick left?"

"Damned right I did. I *always* keep an eye on Lorrie Briggs when she's that close."

Ben could see that Les was going to tell him all the bad news. He dreaded finding out how much his brother had fouled up. He said, "Well, brother, what did she do, set you up so her brothers could stomp you?"

"No, but you're gonna think what she did was a whole lot worse."

"What did she do this time?"

"She caused me to get married."

"To who, for god's sake?"

"To her."

Ben felt his face darken, but he only showed his wrath by turning away. Ben had always hated Les's tendency to commit damned foolishness. He knew what had happened. Les got drunk. Les got wild. Les got down in the slop like a pig, then got married to the sorriest piece of trash in Arizona territory. Now Les wanted his big brother's blessing so everything would end up just right.

Ben helped Maudy into the shay and absentmindedly climbed in and took the lines. Les untied Barney for him, then hugged Maudy and gave her a kiss. "Lorrie's getting along good with the whole family, Ben. She's a changed girl. She's been good to all of us."

"OK, we'll see you at home. Follow us," Ben said.

He drove along without speaking for a while. Maudy hugged his arm and smiled at him. "Come on. It's all right."

"I might be able to live with it if I knew that all he'd fouled up while I was gone was his own life," Ben said. "What bothers me most is wondering what else he screwed up while he got down with Lorrie."

"Well, be kind to your brother. He worships you."

"I know it. That's just the trouble. I can't tell him anything because he acts like he's going to cry if I even look at him wrong. He acts like he's afraid of me or something."

"Darlin', everybody's felt that way around you since Margarita Elias was killed."

"You mean everybody but you."

"Me too, darlin'."

Fifteen

AT SUPPER Les thought Ben looked and acted more like an elder statesman than a brother. His hair was trimmed to a sculpture, his mustache gone. He was much paler and older-looking than he had been before he got married. He almost looked citified.

He might have been a visiting dignitary for all he seemed to enjoy his home. He was especially cool and formal to Les and he treated Lorrie as though he had only just met her, as though she was another daughter in a family he was visiting on business.

Maudy was full of happy stories about her relatives and enthusiastic about her mother's good health and involvement in the civic affairs of Long Beach. All Ben said about Maudy's mother was that she had complained a lot about the oily, greasy water in her well. A Mexican brought her a barrel of sea water and a barrel of sweet water every week because she could not drink her well water and it was not even good for washing clothes or mopping floors.

Les could see Ben did not think much of Maudy's relatives. He was already on the outs with Maudy's father. Will Pendleton blamed Ben Cowden for the war between the Cowdens and Will's neighbor Duncan Vincent. Will kept himself steadfastly neutral, even though Vincent had decimated two of his other neighbor families.

Les had been nervous about the meeting between Maudy and Lorrie. Les and Mark had turned their room over to Ben and Maudy, and Lorrie was changing the bedding when Maudy arrived at the house. After Maudy hugged Viney, she went to her room. Les followed her to make sure war did not break out. Lorrie was smoothing a bed with her back to the door and Maudy spoke to her. Lorrie turned slowly and gracefully, recognized Maudy, read her open, affectionate look, and embraced her happily. They did not pay a bit of attention to Les, so he left them alone.

After supper A.B. repaired to his office with his sons. The Coyles had laid a fire in a potbellied stove in the office and A.B. gave his sons cigars and whiskey. Ben kept himself apart from his brothers. He did not spill an ash of his cigar, or even seem to enjoy the glow of A.B.'s whiskey.

Ben listened quietly, expressionlessly to A.B. and Les tell everything that had happened since he left on his honeymoon: Snider's abandonment of the women at El Relave, his re-enlistment in the VO rangers, the murder of Willy Porter's family, the kidnapping of Teresa, and the back-shooting of Willy, and he did not show any of his usual passion or make a comment. The story of Les's stomping by Lorrie's brothers finally disturbed his calm.

"How could anybody get you down like that, brother? I can't believe you didn't put in a good lick or two."

Carelessly, without thinking, Les said, "I wasn't as fit as I should have been after old Snake fell on me."

All sound and movement went still. Ben's gaze turned much colder. "You rode Snake? What were you doing on Snake?"

"Well, we had to drive ten big steers to Camp Huachuca, so we thought we'd take your horses and provisions to the Vaca ranch at the same time."

"You wanted to drive cattle and horses to the Vaca? What happened to stop you? It's a wonder the VO or old Yawner didn't waylay you. You ought to know better than to make targets of yourselves like that."

Les was forced to tell him that they had been waylaid and bush-whacked and lost three horses.

Ben only shook his head, gave a wry grin and said, "Aren't you lucky? You could have lost your lives, too."

Les, relieved, said, "Yes, I guess we were lucky."

"And did they shoot Snake, too?"

Les knew he was in for it. The worst thing a man could do was ride somebody else's horse without permission. Worse than that was to hurt the horse. He'd done even worse than that, he'd hurt the horse so bad he had to shoot him.

"No."

"Well, I'm glad of that."

"He . . . uh . . . I . . . had to shoot him, though."

"You did? Why?"

"He . . . uh . . . broke both front legs. I . . . uh . . ."

Ben stood up. "Don't tell me any more. Just shut up. Excuse me, Papa. Maybe in the morning we can talk about moving me to the Vaca. I'm going to bed."

"We still have a lot to talk about," A.B. said. "You must have seen Royal Vincent's rangers in Patagonia. He's building trouble again."

"He can't cause me any trouble. I'm out of it. No more war for me. I've got nothing against anybody. I just want to take Maudy and Sergeant Broussard out to the Vaca and get some work done with our cattle."

The next morning, the three brothers loaded the packhorses again, tied them head to tail, mounted Maudy sidesaddle on her horse, Little Buck, tied the remuda head to tail, and lined out for the Vaca ranch. Les felt greatly relieved when the house was finally out of sight behind him. He had worried that he would never get away from all the different kinds of society that had shut him indoors since the wedding.

Ben put him out ahead to ride the ridges and scout for ambush. Mark stayed on the ridges behind the packtrain and remuda, watching their backtrail. Ben and Sergeant stayed on the wagon road with Ben leading the packhorses and Sergeant leading the remuda. They kept the horses at a trot whenever possible. Maudy came along behind with her quirt to keep the horses from lagging. Ben did not want to stop in Harshaw Canyon because it would make them better targets and keep them from reaching the Vaca before dark.

Les was happy to be doing right for a change. He regretted that Ben had turned cold toward the Cowden troubles, but he was bound to return to his forgiving, good-natured self after he had been out in the open a while. After he did some work outdoors, he would be able to face the trouble again and find a resolution for it.

The whole family was getting a new start with Ben's return. Ben was their leader and that was all there was to it. He seemed to be an altogether different man that day in his brand new work clothes. His work hat was even brand new. His neck was pale where his honeymoon haircut had bared new skin.

Viney always washed their new work clothes before they wore them so they would fit better. Les knew Ben would warm up as soon as he started to wear a little. That was why Les had not said a word in his own defense when Ben showed his extreme exasperation for the way he fouled up. The truth of it was, nothing had been lost by Les's incompetence, except a lot of Les's hide. Old Snake had been lost, but if he fell with Les he could have fallen with Ben and maybe Ben would not have been so lucky as to walk away from the pileup. It was a whole lot better that Snake had fallen with Les, because Les was used to pulling batter-asses and having wrecks. He always walked away from them more or less intact. Ben always got hurt when he had a wreck.

Les liked riding out away from everybody with the responsibility of reading the country. He was good at it. He could read the country ahead for cowards and cow feed with equal ease and enjoyment. The winter had been wet and almost balmy. No hard freeze had hampered the start of the coming season's cow feed. Thick clumps of last year's grass were greening up at the stem. The sky was so clear it hurt his eyes and the sun on the damp earth made the country smell good. He could smell everything. Even his hat smelled good. He could see a hundred miles almost any way he turned. Meadowlarks, redwing, or cardinals tuned up every minute.

Les was riding Codger, a stocky, smooth-muscled, bald-faced, brown gelding. He'd been trying to get Codger into a project of sustained hard work. Cranky Codger liked to exasperate men and other horses with malicious mischief. When he did not have hard work to do, he liked to paw holes in troughs and bite other horses. He liked to make runs on unsuspecting horses and rake his lower teeth down their backs. That always fixed a horse so he could not be ridden for a month or six weeks. Les hoped if he used Codger hard for a while, the horse would forget to do mischief.

Codger was a smooth traveling horse and the ground was spongy and damp from the rains, so he made little noise. The hills and ridges along the wagon track were steep, high, and brushy. Les kept off the skyline, watched all sides of the road, and crossed the road often so when Ben came along he could see his tracks.

Two hours before sundown, he sat Codger on the side of Saddle Mountain and waited for Ben to top out of a canyon onto the San Rafael Valley. From there on, the country was wide open all the way to the Vaca. He saw a horseman ride down the Mowry Mine road and stop and wait by the spot where Ben would top out. The rider was Patch the Apache.

Les reached Patch at the same time as Ben and the horses. Ben and Sergeant were able to stop and let the horses blow because the open San Rafael provided no cover for bushwhackers.

Mark was the only one who did not dismount. Ben no longer seemed cold. As Les suspected, the good old Arizona sun had perked up his blood. Les and Sergeant held the horses and Ben and Maudy hunkered down to talk to Patch and find out the truth about the tragedy of El Relave. After Patch enlightened them about that, he told Ben the Yawner wanted to see him.

"Why me?" Ben said. "I'm still his enemy, especially now that Chato butchered my cousins."

"He is tired and does not want to have to run and fight because of Chato."

"Every time he winters hard he wants to talk. Where is he? Why didn't he go to Mexico where he winters well?"

"He's on Pajarito Mountain. He was on Huachuca Mountain and ready to talk when Chato killed Huesos's family. He ran to Pajarito because he did not want to be accused of the raid."

"I gave up all wars. I am nothing but a cowman."

"The Yawner says he knows you will see that he is treated fairly."

"I'm not sure the soldiers won't hang him."

"He says, if the soldiers want to hang him, he will fight."

"I can only ask Lieutenant Buck what he wants to do."

"The Yawner wants to see you before you tell anyone he wants talk."

"Why?"

"He wants you to take his peace terms to the soldiers."

"What are the terms?"

"I don't know."

Maudy set up housekeeping at the Vaca that evening. The next morning, A.B., the Cowden women, and the Farleys came along with

Willy Porter's body. That afternoon all the Cowdens, Porters, and Farleys met at El Relave to bury Willy.

Chato and his companions walked into a camp at Cabeza de Vaca spring on the north slope of the Rincons. They found a fire going, a bean pot cooking, a can of freshly brewed coffee, broiled quail, a small stack of hot corn tortillas wrapped in a clean cotton cloth, and no people. Chato wrapped a quail in a tortilla and, while he ate it, found a gourd filled with mescal. Arco and Fausto left Teresa to shift for herself and began to eat.

This was Arco's grandfather Casimiro's camp. Arco's little seven-year-old sister, Casi, was Casimiro's only companion.

"Where are they?" Chato said.

Arco spooned beans onto a tortilla, folded the tortilla, and sat back on his haunches to eat it.

"Casimirooo," Chato called in a low voice. "Come out. Here we are with your grandson El Arco."

Casimiro, the old Yaqui who lived in that camp in peace, stepped out of the brush behind Chato. "I see him," he said.

Arco glanced at his grandfather and went on eating. Fausto left the fire.

"Where is the child?" Chato asked. "I want to see her." He watched for Arco's reaction. As a game, he had once stolen the child from her mother and sold her to a Mexican on the Mulatos River for a pouch of gold. He won the game when he killed the Mexican and took back the child. Casimiro then stole her from Chato and came here to hide.

Chato had never fathered a child. Casi was beautiful and possessed a poise that Chato respected. Everybody knew he coveted other peoples' children. He did terrible things to some of those he captured, but he seemed to want Casi more as an ornament or precious toy.

"I have mescal, frijoles, tortilla, and I have coffee," Casimiro said. "Drink and eat."

"How do you have coffee?"

"I trade squashes, *calabaza*, pumpkin, corn, *tesguino*, corn beer, and mescal for coffee and clothes with the Mexicans in Tucson."

"You will be rich if you do that."

"No, I don't need anything."

"Where's the *teguequita*, the little brown girl? I may want to take her away from you." He watched for apprehension in Arco's eye, but the boy showed none.

"She's not here. Fausto won't find her."

"You call her."

Teresa was trying to warm herself by the fire. Casimiro offered his hand to Arco. Arco looked up at his grandfather and took the hand loosely, looked at Chato, turned back to his food, and released the hand.

"Eat and go, Chato," Casimiro said. "I don't want you here." He found a bowl, rinsed it at the spring, measured beans and soup into it, found a tortilla, and gave the food to Teresa. He went to his *ramada*, brought out a blanket, unfolded it, and spread it over the girl's shoulders. "What do you need with my Casi?" he said. "Look at this child. She is too footsore to go another step. You want to do that to my Casi, too? Leave this girl and go."

Chato grimaced and cocked his head toward the brush where Fausto had disappeared. He looked at Arco and Arco left the camp. Chato sat on his haunches and bared his teeth to the fire.

Casimiro looked up and said, "No!" as Fausto and Arco coaxed Casi into the firelight. She was wrapped in a blanket.

Fausto said, "I would not have found her, but I stepped on her." He began to feed himself.

Casi sat as close to her grandfather as she could, poked her toes to the fire, wiggled them slightly as they warmed, and stared at Chato. Arco wrapped himself in his blanket and lay down to sleep with the soles of his bare feet to the fire. His feet were sore. The day had been so wet, his *teguas* got soggy and stretched and he had not been able to wear them.

Casimiro stood up and took his granddaughter by the hand. "Eat. Rest. Then leave," he said to Chato. He led Casi to their pallet under the *ramada* and lay down. After a while Fausto lay down with his feet to the fire.

An hour before dawn, long after he allowed the fire to die, Chato rose, picked up the rock upon which he had been sitting, and went and stood over the old Yaqui.

He raised the rock high and brought it down on Casimiro's skull. The rock rolled back toward his feet and made him skip away. A wire the Yaqui used to dry jerky under the *ramada* caught Chato's shirt at the neck. He fell into a fearful panic, then abruptly broke free. He panted as his fear subsided, then grimaced and picked up the sleeping child.

Fausto then bashed Arco's head with a rock.

Chato kicked Teresa awake, handed her the child, and quickly ransacked the camp for goods. Fausto led the horses in and Chato loaded Teresa and Casi on one, mounted the other, and rode up into a forest of ponderosa pine. An hour later, they let the horses blow on *El Puerto de Cabeza de Vaca*, Cowhead Pass, then headed back toward the Huachucas.

Casimiro followed until he saw them ride down the other side of the pass, then returned to his camp. Arco was gone. Casimiro wondered how Arco could have survived the crush of the rock. He went to his pallet and picked up his blankets. They were wet with the ruins of the pumpkin he had laid under the blankets instead of his head. Chato's gold pouch dangled from the wire that had snatched it off his neck in the dark.

He found Arco's track and followed it. Arco had staggered away aimlessly, leaving blood in his track. Casimiro found him standing on a slope in thick manzanita brush.

Casimiro walked up on the downhill side of him and touched his shoulder. Arco swung his arms around like the limbs of a tree, collapsed, and rolled down the hill. Casimiro dragged him to camp.

He applied *yerba del pasmo* from his medicine pouch, a healing herb that stopped the bleeding on Arco's head. He built up the fire and boiled water to make a tea of the *pasmo* to promote healing. He also prepared a large portion of *pinole* with a broth of venison jerky. He needed to feed his patient so he would get well. Arco needed all the food and medicine he could hold. Casimiro the Yaqui knew how to care for the sick and injured. Later he planned to give his grandson the tea of *oja de palvia*, the leaf of a gray weed that would calm his pain. Its effect was better when it was chewed fresh, but in the winter he had no fresh *palvia*.

Like most Yaquis, Casimiro was a devout Christian. He believed Chato had also inflicted an evil wound into Arco's soul. He prayed to the Blessed Mother for him. He bathed his head with cold water from the spring and prayed to Saint John the Baptist for his cure.

When Arco was resting, Casimiro thought about his Casi. He did not think Chato would abuse her. The demon admired the child. The demon still loved the purity of the child. He would not hurt her until the love turned to envy.

Sixteen

LORRIE WAS NOT with the folks when they arrived at the Vaca with Willy Porter's body. Betty said that Lorrie would rather meet the rest of the family when it came together for some other reason.

Les understood how she felt. He did not feel married yet, anyway. He could not picture himself going to the funeral with a wife at his side. Most of the family would think his bringing her home had been another batterass he'd pulled during a drunk. He was sure nobody in the family was ready to congratulate him and give Lorrie housekeeping presents.

The Cowdens and Farleys from Harshaw were the last to arrive at El

Relave. All the Porters who lived on the Santa Cruz River, fifty souls, were already there.

Every door and window in the house was wide open. The place had been swept and washed. Busy grown-ups and playing children hurried in and out. The Cowden women carried food into the house and pitched in with the preparation of the big meal the family would have before everybody went home.

A large fire had been built in the open between the barn and the house so people would have a place to stop and stay warm while they visited. Les carried four big Dutch ovens filled with raw biscuits to the fire and covered them with oak coals. The Cowden brothers often speculated on why the Porters had stayed out of the range war. Even though they often told the Cowdens they would always be ready to help when they were needed, they never came forward to fight. The Porters worked hard to keep their cattle business alive and there were a lot of Porters. They owned three times more cattle than the Cowdens and their range was that much larger. They were more than a dozen men and a dozen boys old enough to work horseback. The Porters did not use outside help. They could furnish the entire roundup crew when they gathered their own cattle. They were so independent, they seldom even offered to help their neighbors anymore.

The Cowdens were only three men, but even with the war their land and cattle holdings were growing fast. The Porters were no longer growing. They were becoming clannish, even to the exclusion of the Cowdens and Farleys. In another two generations, the Porters would not own enough land and cattle to keep all their progeny busy. Some of them would have to find new territory to run their cattle, or find new ways to make a living.

Someone had brought Willy's chairs to the fire for the women and all the men were standing. Everybody liked the fire. Women visited in twos and threes among themselves and seldom joined the conversations of the men. The men did not say anything they did not want the women to hear.

A few miners came to Willy's funeral, but they cheerfully built their own fire and stayed apart. No townsmen came because El Relave was too far for them to travel under the threat of Apaches and road agents.

Men came representing the Heredia, De La Ossa, Apodaca, Salazar, and Romero ranching families. Because they were neighbors and life-long friends, they stood at the fire as family. Those old Mexican families had taken more losses in blood and property in various wars than any of the Cowden–Porter clan. They had been in the country a hundred years longer than anyone except the Apaches. The Porters and Cowdens could not even have owned ground in which to bury their dead if not for them.

The miners and the men from the Mexican families did not bring their women and children to the burial because of the danger and difficulty of the trip. The Porters and Cowdens did not take their families when they attended burial services of their neighbors on distant outlying ranches, either.

Les was the last of the Cowdens to reach the fire. After he arranged the Dutch ovens in the coals, he shook every hand and stood beside his brothers.

Roy Porter said, "How could this happen? Bones didn't have an enemy in the world. Somebody must have mistaken him for somebody else. He wasn't robbed, was he?"

Les thought, that's just the damned way all the self-centered Porters think. He can't see that a Porter could have an enemy in the world. The Cowdens have been fighting his damned battles for him and he refuses to acknowledge it, even after a Porter gets bushwhacked.

"There's no doubt in my mind that Bones had an enemy," A.B. said. "The killer followed him out of town and shot him in the back."

"It's hard to understand why anybody would want to kill Bones."

"You ought to come up that road by our house more often, Roy. Stop and visit once in a while."

"Don't have time to go to town. How would that change anything?"

"You'd know what was going on. We're in a fight. The VO's trying to take over the country."

"The VO hasn't strung any wire around my country."

"Yes, they have. They fenced your cattle and ours off the American Boy range last summer."

"Well, I'd made up my mind to move those cattle away from there anyway, so it didn't bother me in the least."

"It didn't bother you because Ben let your cattle in to water when he found them dying of thirst."

"What has that to do with somebody bushwhacking my nephew? He didn't have any cattle on the American Boy. Nobody knows who shot him, do they?"

"Bob Snider did it. He was afraid Bones was coming after him for leaving Emily to the Apaches."

"I don't know anything about that."

"You've been ignoring the fight too long, Roy. All you Porters have."

Uncle Billy said, "I gave Snider a rifle and sold him a horse and saddle last summer so he could quit the VO and get a new start. How could he kill my son? Bones took him and Teresa into his home and treated them like family."

"For the same reason he was able to leave his wife unprotected and throw in with the VO again. He steps on people to make his life easy."

"I don't think that's evidence enough to get me in a range war with the VO," Roy Porter said.

"It's evidence enough for me to have a short talk with Mr. Snider," Uncle Billy said.

"Talking won't do any good," A.B. said. "I can't arrest him for leaving the women to the Apaches or for killing Bones, because the only witness was Patch the Apache. An Apache's testimony would never hold up in a Pima County court. You people have to weigh the evidence and do what's right, like we do."

"If you as undersheriff can't do anything by law, I don't want to do anything by lawlessness," Roy said.

The Porters and their neighbors defended their eyes from the smoke, warmed their hands over the fire, smoked their pipes, whittled sticks, and listened.

A.B. said, "My point is this: the VO has carried this war into our bedrooms and barns, against our men and women, children and grown-ups alike, and we've held them off. We'll keep holding them off, but we're getting tired. If we quit and give Duncan Vincent the range he wants, do you think he'll stop taking land? He has another brother and a bunch of lawyers lobbying in Washington with a claim that could make them owners of this whole country. In the meantime, while the government examines their claim, they're taking everything we don't nail down. You Porters are lucky my sons have been doing the nailing."

"Nevertheless, I don't want to do anything illegal," Roy Porter said. "It's against my nature to shoot a man who wears a badge."

"Well, it ain't against my nature," Uncle Billy said. "You can just count me in your war. That includes the sons I've got left and my livestock, weapons, and credit. Count on my women, too."

Les left the fire and walked up the hill to help finish digging the grave. Ben was the brother who liked to stand around and talk at these gatherings. Mark usually helped Viney. People never liked the way Les talked or helped women. They only liked him when he made a hand.

The only other graves on the hill belonged to Emily and Willy Fly. It sure hadn't taken Bones long to come here, build a house, build a family, lose it, and join it in death. There were plenty more Porters, but no more Bones.

When Les got down into the grave and began to dig, he felt he'd finally reached the bottom of the pit of his life, the place he had always tried to avoid. He dug so furiously that his uncles Jim and John Porter ordered him to quit. When he did not seem to hear them, Jim jumped into the grave and took the shovel away from him. Les picked up the pick, and Jim took that away from him. "That's deep enough, now," Jim said. "There's nothing left to do, Les. All we need to do is shape it a little."

Les crawled out and sat on a rock in the sun. He was on the Canelo Hills and could see across the San Rafael Valley. He could almost see the house on the Vaca ranch. He wanted to get away from all the society and back to work.

Digging in the bottom of the grave had hurt his heart. Poor old Bones and Emily and Willy Fly. Everybody called the little feller Willy Fly because he liked to run.

That's how they'd be remembered a hundred years from now, maybe, if there were any Porters and Cowdens left in the country who were proud of being Porters and Cowdens. Maybe they'd come here and say, "Look, here's where Willy Bones and Willy Fly and Emily the young wife and mother and her unborn baby are buried. They were all wiped out the same week. Imagine that."

He watched a cloud of dust a while and saw it was being made by a gang of riders.

"Well, here they come, Jimmy," John said to his brother. "I was hoping they wouldn't interrupt the funeral. We better tell Ben."

"Hell, you better tell Les first," Jim said.

"Tell me what?" Les said.

"That's Royal Vincent and his rangers with a warrant for you Cowden brothers."

"What for?"

"The murder of Jack Odoms."

"Aw, how can that be? How do you know?"

"Royal wired Judge Black in Tucson that he received the warrant papers in the mail yesterday from my office."

"Papa wasn't notified, was he?"

"He didn't get an official notice, but we told him the warrant had been issued several days ago."

"This is just fine," Les said. As he hurried down off the hill, he thought, thank our holy Lord, it's probably the spur we need. Ben'll have to wake up and get a'moving. Papa probably didn't tell us so Royal would surprise us and Ben would have to get high behind, or go to jail again. He swore he'd never go to jail again.

The Cowden brothers were ready to go in six minutes. A.B. stopped them, told them to wait, lined them up with Jim and John Porter, Roy and Uncle Billy Porter, and several more grown and able Porter men, and swore them in as deputy sheriffs of Pima County. He even had badges for them.

"Do you have the authority to do this?" Roy Porter asked.

"I have the authority when I see an emergency. A month ago, when Ben was on the run, I went to the governor in Prescott and laid out the VO's whole scheme. He told me I could use my own judgement in keeping the peace in my jurisdiction. The VO has a gang of constables? Well, from now on, we have sheriffs. We'll find out who is right in court after the shooting stops."

"Let's have the shooting now, Papa," Les said. "Let's face them down once and for all."

"No. It'll be better if you boys lead them away from here and make them chase you. We'll bury Bones and take our families home and settle with them on our own terms. You fellers just line out and keep them out of breath."

The Cowden brothers rode out of the yard and crossed Cocono Creek. As soon as they were out of sight of their relatives, they turned downstream and stopped in the concealment of a willow thicket. They wanted to stay and see what happened at the house.

Les hoped his brothers were ready to fight. Mark's arm was better, but still trying to heal in the splint. Les had no idea how Ben felt. The brothers were out ahead of their troubles on fast horses again, and that was a good start. They had to fight, whether they liked it or not.

Royal Vincent and his bunch rode into the yard at El Relave. A lanky, competent-looking, older man rode beside Royal on a good dun horse. The rest of the wormy little constables were as unformidable as usual. Even though they were fifty-strong, they might as well have been hiding in a corner, for all they would intimidate anyone that day.

Royal announced, "In case some of you don't know me, I am Senator Royal Vincent of the Pima County Live Stock Association rangers and I'm here to set you gents straight on a thing or two."

The Porters stared at him. Les was happy. Who could look at Royal's face and his George Armstrong Custer getup and still think the Cowdens were in the wrong? Royal was only what he appeared to be, an eccentric gentleman out for air.

The lanky man on the dun horse rode up and handed A.B. a sheaf of papers. "Undersheriff Cowden, my name is Ted Randolph. These documents identify me as a special agent for the United States Department of the Interior with the warrant and authority to take your three sons into custody. If you'll surrender them, we'll be on our way."

"My sons just left," A.B. said. "This family is here for a burial service, but you are welcome to get down off your horses and have something to eat. I am in authority here and I don't take orders from constables and agents hired by your association or honor your warrants, so if you don't want to eat, I'd appreciate it if you'd leave."

Randolph drew his pistol, pulled out a watch, and said, "We will give you one minute to deliver Ben, Les, and Mark Cowden to our custody."

The rangers bunched closer together as the Porters and Farleys spread out behind A.B. The women and children came out of the house to watch.

Les said, "The women might not know what to do if shooting starts, so they might get shot, but they will know what to do when they see our three horses running at them, they'll get out of the way."

Ben nodded, Mark nodded, and the brothers drew their pistols.

Ben said, "Who wants a quiet, decent life, anyway?"

Les said, "Shoot at their eyes and maybe you won't hit a relative."

Ben laughed. "Crease 'em. The poor little fellers have never done us any harm."

Mark was serious. "Yeah, crease 'em between the eyes."

"In a hurry now, brothers, so none of them will have a chance to stand still and take aim," Ben said.

With the sound of crashing brush to announce them, the brothers spurred their horses out of the thicket straight at the VO. Their horses made five jumps out in the open before the VO reacted.

Ben was riding Prim Pete, his top horse, a racehorse. Les and Mark's horses could run, but Prim had jumped out in front of them as though he was a running locomotive and they were flatcars that had come unhitched.

Randolph sighted down his arm at Ben and would certainly have killed him, but Uncle Billy Porter popped a cap on an old cavalry revolver that sounded like dynamite going off in a mine shaft and set the special agent's dun horse to bucking.

The VO had been keeping themselves in such a scared knot that when they tried to move they only ran together into a tighter one. The Cowden brothers rode horses that did not buck when explosions went off between their ears or in their faces. They aimed their pistols hat-high and rammed their horses into the VO. Two horses scattered away together from in front of Les when he fired into a man's face and Mark's horse knocked them both down. Another rider in front of Les turned loose all holds and tumbled over backwards off his horse as though shot. The VO horses piled and reared over the top of one another. Mark's horse, Colonel, glanced off the scramble of horses and vaulted over Codger's hips. Colonel's front feet passed so close to Les that he felt their wind on the back of his neck.

Ben made straight for Randolph. As the special agent fought to control his horse, he got his first look at Ben Cowden and Ben was coming to get him.

Royal's horse scattered some women and children and stampeded for the open country. Royal hollered, "Whoa, boy, whoa, boy, whoa, boy, whoa," reared back and pulled on his reins with all his might, while his horse got going so fast the wind flapped the brim of his hat into his eyes. When his horse was running faster than he could bear it, Royal hooked his spurs into the animal's flanks to hold on better and made him tuck his tail and buck. The women and children stood away from the melee and watched.

Les veered in behind Ben. Ben raised his pistol to shoot Randolph's hat off and the dun horse stumbled just as Ben fired. The bullet spewed dirt off the front of Bones's adobe house into a passel of Porter children.

Prim Pete flashed by Randolph and left for the races. Randolph straightened and aimed at Ben's back. Les rammed Codger's shoulder into the dun horse and brought his pistol down on Randolph's hat. Randolph and his horse went down in the meeting fire. As he left the fray, Les saw the cast-iron lid of a Dutch oven fly up like the wadding from a shotgun. Biscuits sprayed into the air out of the smoke and sparks of the fire, and Les saw that the biscuits were brown and done.

Seventeen

SNIDER WAS DRUNK. He had been hanging around town drinking since the day he murdered Willy Porter. His eyes were red, his hair in his eyes. He was dirty and talked all the time. When he was not talking, he whined, "Yow, yow, yow," to fill in the spaces, so there would be no silence to bother him.

Garbie Burr was about full of him. She had been waiting on him in the hotel dining room and at Wong's day and night since Willy's body was brought in. She worked separate shifts in the hotel and at Wong's: breakfast and supper at the hotel, noon and afternoons at Wong's. She did not like to have time on her hands. Except when she was with Mark Cowden, she was happiest working as a waitress.

Snider made Garbie wish she could have a week off. He had been closing her down every night at the hotel, showing up at the hotel the next morning when the dining room opened for breakfast, then following her to Wong's at noon. Now he and Garbie were alone at Wong's and he was yow-yowing and waving his pistol. He liked to have his pistol out when he drank beer at Wong's. He let it dangle on his finger and aimed it at Garbie when he wanted to stress a point. He liked to have it in the hand that carried his beer to his mouth. Sometimes he sighted it at Garbie with both hands like a rifle and said, "Pow! Pow! Pow!" pretending to shoot her dead.

He knew better than to draw his pistol in the hotel. No one would stand for that kind of behavior there. Dick Martin kept an eye on him when he was in the hotel and took him home when he got so drunk he was ready to collapse.

Snider did as he pleased in Frank Wong's, though. Wong's was a hangout for the VO and Frank ran a tab on their beer. Frank also kept a five-gallon jug of contraband mescal in the kitchen. The VO ran the tabs up high and seldom settled them completely.

Garbie knew the VO had something on Frank. She was sure he'd helped them smuggle Chinese into the country. Garbie knew many of the VO's comings and goings. They did business with that fancy, slithery Chee Lee, who came there and ordered Frank around, sometimes screamed at him and thumped him. Kosterlinsky and Indiana Briggs came to Wong's to do business with Chee Lee, too. Garbie had been telling A.B. everything she saw.

Teddy Briggs came in and sat down with Snider. This was the slowest time of the day and Garbie could have kissed Teddy for coming in. Snider pointed the pistol at Teddy and Teddy pushed it away. Garbie did not think it was cocked to shoot, but it was loaded and still plenty dangerous.

Another way Snider bothered Garbie was his whining about Teresa. Ohhh, poor Teresa. Pooor little old girl. She'd never had a chance. Do you know where I found Teresa? You'd be surprised. You really want to know? Well, I'm gonna tell you, anyway. I got her out of a. . . . She was working in a. . . . Selling herself day and night in a place in Juarez, Mexico. Did you know that? Sure she was, but I didn't hold it against her. Nossir . . . no ma'am. I brought her back to Arizona to start a new life. Did you know that's why I came back? Sure. I wanted her to have a chance to start a new life where nobody knew what she was."

Teddy asked for beer and Garbie went in the kitchen to get it. When she came back out, Snider was pointing his pistol at Teddy's face and going, "Pow! Pow! Pow." Teddy was so tired of trying to make him stop, he tried to ignore him. Snider cocked the pistol. The sound of it chilled Garbie's blood. When she set the beer down she was angry.

Teddy picked up his beer, walked away from the table and looked out the window at the street. Snider aimed the pistol at Teddy's back like a rifle with his trigger hand on the butt and his other hand under the barrel.

"Now, Snider, that's enough," Garbie said. "You'll hurt somebody. Didn't your mama ever tell you not to point a gun at people? We've had enough. Give it to me, you brat."

Snider waved the pistol recklessly so she could not grab it. Teddy moved to the other side of the room.

"Give it to me, you dunce," Garbie said.

"No, you're not my mama."

"Come on, quit playing with it. Give it to me."

Snider glared at Garbie and pointed the pistol dead center at her breast. "Get away, woman. Nobody gets my pistol. Not my mama, not you, not even my Teresa."

Garbie straightened. "You're a brave man to point that thing at a person who's trying to help you."

"You're damned right, I am. So just stay away from me."

"Yes, you're brave. If you're so brave, why don't you get on your horse and go find Teresa? She might be ready to come back to you now after a week with some bloody Apache."

"You watch what you say about my Teresa, you trollop, you."

"All right, brave man, start a fight with me, then."

"I will. I don't let anybody say anything about my Teresita."

"If I stop talking about her, will you give me the pistol?"

"No."

"Give it to me."

Garbie reached for the pistol, Snider waved it out of reach, then brought it back to bear on her chest.

Teddy turned and was suddenly afraid. "No!" he shouted. "For God's sake, Snider."

The pistol exploded with fire and smoke. Snider was holding it so loosely, the kick sprained his thumb and bucked out of his hand. The .45-caliber weapon exercised its killing power to perfection though. The bullet went through Garbie's heart.

"No!" shouted Teddy and ran to catch the girl.

Snider kicked his chair over, stumbled to his feet and bent over the table to look at Garbie. "Aw, she's all right. I was just playing."

"Goddam you, Snider. The girl only asked you to put your pistol away."

"Aw, she's all right."

"Yeah, you son of a bitch. Look at her."

Garbie died in agony.

Snider picked up his pistol and put it in its holster.

Teddy's knee was bent under the girl. He saw she was bleeding on him and let her down on the floor, took out his hankerchief, and wiped the blood off his trousers.

"What now? What are we gonna do now?" Snider said.

"What are *we* going to do? You son of a bitch, you're on your own," Teddy said.

"Now, you can stop calling me a son of a bitch, Teddy. I have a good mother and I don't let anybody call her a bitch."

"I doubt she has anything to do with you."

"What do you care anyway? You didn't shoot the trollop, I did. She was just another trollop friend of the Cowdens. I bet she carried everything she heard us say here right down the canyon to the undersheriff himself. I say good riddance."

"Oh, now you're saying you killed her because she was spying on the VO? You rat. You killed her for no reason at all. Don't try to say you did it for the great and glorious VO."

"Well, she was a trollop and a spy, so good riddance."

Teddy looked down at Garbie. "Poor darn pretty little girl. You son of a bitch, you make me sick."

"Now I told you not to say that to me. You don't want me to kill you, too, do you?"

Teddy drew his pistol and rammed it in Snider's face. "Yes, you son-of-a-bitch-in' bastard, that's what you are. You want me to do what I want to do?"

Snider pushed the muzzle aside. "You don't understand. That girl was not doing us any good here."

Teddy was so mad he was shaking. "You stay right here. I'm going to report this before I get in trouble. God, what's my sister going to say when she finds out I was here and didn't stop this?"

Teddy left by the street door. Snider went out the back and got on his horse. He was still drunk, but not so drunk he took to the main street. He rode down the alley behind the saloons. He was passing the last saloon in the line when he heard, "Fight! Fight at the chinaman's! There's been a shooting at the chinaman's!"

This was not the first time Snider had hidden from this town for shame. He'd snuck in here naked from El Durazno once when A.B. caught he and another VO cowboy about to set fire to his barn. A.B. took away their boots and burned their clothes and warned them to leave the country.

Maudy was at the Cowdens' at the time and Snider snuck back and got her to loan him an old woman's housecoat to wear into Harshaw. He'd courted Maudy before Ben Cowden noticed her and took her away from him. He'd been smitten with Maudy. She was good. After she threw him over for Ben, he'd felt dirty, felt he'd never have another chance to win a decent girl for a wife. Women were scarce as hell in that country and decent women could just hardly ever be found who would look at the likes of him. Lately, he'd been fixing it so the country was even a lot more short of good women by causing the loss of Emily Porter, Teresa, and now Garbie. He was quite a woman-killer. He only wanted to charm women, but instead brought them doom.

No use worrying about it. He couldn't bring them back. He'd just have to watch his own back for a while. If you killed a man, you could still count on a few friends who didn't mind. They might have even wanted to kill him, too. You killed a girl, and everybody, good people and bad people, turned away from you forever so you would never have another friend in the world.

Snider rode behind the hills and ridges along Harshaw Creek, past the brush and rocks that hid him when he killed Willy Porter, and came up behind the El Durazno orchard. Well, Lorrie Briggs was one woman who might talk to him, might even give him a drink of her father-in-law's whiskey.

Snider counted on the Coyles staying down at the barn, because Lorrie was alone in the house. That little Jimmy Coyle had been in the chinaman's sweeping and mopping earlier and he told Snider the

Cowdens were all gone to bury Willy and Lorrie was alone at the house.

Funny how things worked out. The only woman in the country for whom he was worthy was the only woman at the moment available for a visit. Maybe it was preordained that he go to Lorrie for solace. She was only a saloon girl, but she was bound to be unhappy living with the Cowdens. Snider smiled. Lorrie was ripe for a nice visit with one of her own kind, otherwise she would have gone off with the rest of them to bury Willy.

He stepped down off his horse, tied him, snuck through the back door of the Arizona room, and looked through an open window into the kitchen. Sorry as he was, he would not have walked into any house where he knew a decent woman might be found alone, but Lorrie was a different kind of woman. She was a mistress type woman, a real trollopy saloon girl. She'd flirted with Snider every time he went into Vince Farley's saloon and seemed to prefer his company to anyone else's.

Lorrie was sitting at the kitchen table with her back to him.

"Howdy, there," he said.

Lorrie turned to him with a smile that faded when she saw who he was.

"I didn't see anybody around, so I came right in. Sorry to bother you."

"What do you want, Snider?"

She was having a cup of coffee. "You know, I was just wondering if a man could get you to give him a cup of coffee."

"It's not far to town. There's coffee everywhere you go in town, but I can just bet it ain't coffee you need. You look like a drunk in need of a drink."

"Well now, bless you for an understanding girl, Lorrie."

"You don't need to think you'll find it here."

"No, coffee'll be just fine. I've made up my mind to sober up today."

"I haven't made up my mind to invite you in, though."

"Aw, Lorrie, you wouldn't deprive a man of the help he needs to reform, would you? I'm turning over a new leaf. I could have had a drink, but I decided to get out of town where I couldn't get one."

"You can sit down for one cup of coffee, then I want you to go away without being told."

"Oh, absolutely, Lorrie. I have to be on my way. I'm on a special errand for Royal Vincent."

"I bet that's really special."

"You know? It really is. Royal's been giving me a whole lot of special work to do lately. I get along with him a whole lot better than I do with ole Duncan. You and I both know how hard that ole Duncan is to get along with."

"What makes you think I know anything about Duncan Vincent?"

"Well, I really don't. I just thought you and ole Duncan were real close at one time."

Lorrie set a cup of coffee and a spoon on the table in front of Snider and pushed the sugar close to it. "Well, you're wrong."

"You're right, nobody can claim to be a friend of ole Duncan's. Royal's the one in charge now, anyway. Have you seen Royal lately? He sure thinks a lot of you, Lorrie. Just the other day he was raving about how pretty you are."

Lorrie sat down across the table from him. "Oh, yeah," she said. "I bet."

Snider told her how much she was missed at the saloon. She yawned. He told her Dick Martin was a devastated man for having lost her to Les Cowden. She picked soap out of a crack in the table. He told her he'd missed her more and more as each day went by, until it was downright painful to go into Vince Farley's saloon. The saloon's business had fallen off by half. The whole town was mourning her loss by marriage to Les Cowden. Lorrie yawned again and glanced at his coffee to see how close he was to being finished and gone.

Snider did some thinking while he kept his mouth going and finally decided to get to the heart of the matter. "How are you getting along with the Cowdens, Lorrie?"

Lorrie looked him straight in the eye. "How do you mean?"

"I mean, hating them as much as you do, I'd think you'd be unhappy living with them."

"Listen, Snider, my troubles or happiness are not any of your business. What made you think you could come here and pump me about how I feel?"

"Oh, excuse me. I didn't mean to pry."

"The hell you didn't. You'd never have come here unless you knew I was alone. You damned-well know what would happen to you if Les Cowden caught you sneaking around me when he was gone. If you don't know how unpopular you are with the Cowdens and Porters right now, you're stupider than I think you are."

"To tell the truth, I think I get along pretty well with the Cowdens and Porters."

"You're stupider than hell, then."

"What did I do to them? I see them from time to time and they speak to me."

"You know what you did. You signed the death warrants of those women when you went off and left them."

"I left a man with them, but I guess there's no need to try to explain that to you."

"No, I'm not interested."

Snider tasted his coffee as though it was most precious. "I'm interested in knowing how you get along with the Cowdens. You've lasted a lot longer with them than anybody thought you would."

"I get along real well. Why?"

"That's something, because I'm fresh in the market for a woman and I hoped you'd come and go to Tucson with me while I did my errand for Royal."

"I said you were stupid, not me. Stop being stupid, or you'll have to leave without finishing your coffee."

Both Lorrie's hands were on the table and she passed a fork back and forth between them.

Snider reached out and took hold of the fork. "Aw, come on, Lorrie. I know you're bored, otherwise you'd have gone off with the Cowdens to bury Willy."

Lorrie snatched the fork away from him and tried to spear his hand with it. He jerked the hand away before she could pin it to the table. The fork sprang out of her hand and clattered to the floor.

"Now, Lorrie, I don't mind you acting like a wildcat, so just do everything that comes natural." Snider walked around the table toward her. Lorrie got out of the chair. "That's what makes everybody think you'd be so fun."

Lorrie picked up a chunk of oak firewood that had been split off the trunk and threw it at Snider's head. It bounced off his shoulder and crashed into a cupboard.

Snider stopped, rubbed the shoulder and looked back at the cupboard. "Let's not mess up the house, Lorrie, just each other."

Lorrie moved toward the door and Snider cut her off. "Naw, let's just keep it inside. Let's not call outsiders."

"What the hell do you want, Snider?"

"I want a woman and you're the only one left in the world sorry enough for me."

"What for, to eat, to strangle, or what? What do you want me for?"

"I want you to be nice to me, Lorrie."

"Why didn't you say that instead of coming at me like a gorilla?"

"Aw well, that's just my way. I'm rough, but I'm gentle."

"Oh yeah? Come over here by the stove, then."

Snider grinned with disbelief. "Shouldn't we go somewhere more comfortable, Lorrie? How about your bedroom?"

"Too cold in there. Come over here by the stove."

"I don't trust you, damn it."

"Aw, don't be a chicken. You think I don't know how to satisfy a man's needs? I'm an expert. Come over here and I'll take care of you, but don't get any ideas that I'll ever do it again. I'm not going to fool with you very long, only long enough to satisfy your damned animal urges so I can get rid of you. You think I don't know what you want?"

"What do I want, Lorrie?"

143

"Come over here and I'll show you."

Snider could not help himself. He walked over to her. She took both his hands and pushed him gently against a counter. She embraced his waist, barely touching his front with hers. His eyelids drooped with pleasure. Lorrie reached up and pushed back his hat, caressed his ears. She picked his hat off his head, rubbed his scalp, then began to massage the back of his neck. He breathed heavily against her face, sighed deeply. She moved closer and put her head on his shoulder, her leg between his legs, caressed his ear.

With her right hand, Lorrie reached up beside a cupboard to a rack of knives and lifted out her favorite, a heavy cleaver. The blade was old and had been sharpened so many times that it curved like a headsman's ax.

She rubbed her leg between Snider's legs, carefully moved his hands off her hips and stepped in closer to him. He leaned back and braced himself with his hands on the counter. She tickled his ear between her thumb and forefinger. She raised the cleaver and brought it down hard to cut off all his fingers. When he squalled she raised the cleaver to bury it in his skull.

Snider went mad. The cleaver sliced all the way to the bone of his forearm as he fended it off. He hit Lorrie in the temple with his fist and knocked her down on her back, stood on her arm and kicked the cleaver away, then stomped on her face.

He looked down at Lorrie and began to weep. She was unconscious or dead. He had stomped her with all his might. She had cut off the three outside fingers of his right hand. He found a wet dishrag and wrapped it on his hand, wrapped a clean dishtowel around his forearm and tied it tight with his teeth.

He looked for his fingers, found them and put them in his shirt pocket. His anger overcame the sadness. He straddled Lorrie, sat on her and split open her blouse and underclothes. The sight of the pretty, bare breasts made him look for the cleaver.

He heard a shout from down at the barn. The screen door slammed and he staggered to his feet. He turned to the door and saw his blood spatter across the kitchen table. He searched for a better hold on his wound so he could stop the bleeding. He drew his pistol.

Teddy Briggs came in the door to the sight of the bloody kitchen and the half-naked woman on the floor. "Bob, you son of a bitch," he yelled. He recognized his sister and threw himself down on the floor beside her.

Snider ran outside to his horse. He mounted and rode into Harshaw Creek. "Lorrie?" someone called from the barn. "Are you all right, Lorrie?"

Snider rode on without looking back. He needed care. Maudy would help him. She was the only decent person left in the world. He would ride to the Vaca. She wouldn't know about Garbie and Lorrie. He'd tell Maudy he'd roped a big cow and lost his fingers in the dallies of his rope if she wanted to know.

Ben, Les, and Mark had just ridden up to the barn when they heard Teddy's shout in the house. Les rode through the barn and called up to the house for Lorrie. When she did not answer, he spurred his horse to the back door and hit the ground running. He almost knocked the door off its hinges when he banged through. The sight of Lorrie's body on the floor so startled him that he stumbled over Teddy's feet and fell on his face beside her.

Teddy turned his weeping face toward Les, but he just sat there, his hands idle while he bawled. Lorrie lay so still, her face was so smashed, anybody could see she was dead. Les tried to pull her dress together to cover her breasts. Her skin was still warm. He touched her graceful neck and a pulse beat jumped into the end of his finger. He carried her into a bedroom and laid her down. He ran back for a bucket of cold water and began cleaning her face. He said, "Oh God, Lorrie, please wake up and be all right."

Lorrie stirred, her eyes opened, she whimpered.

"Aw, baby," Les said.

Lorrie brushed at the cold cloth weakly. "Kaad breed . . ." she said.

"Aw, honey."

Lorrie pushed at his hand.

"Be still, honey, I'm wiping the blood off."

"Kaad breed, Les."

"What?"

"I'm drying to dell you to led . . . me . . . *breed.*"

"Oh, you can't *breathe?* I'm *sorry,* baby." He laughed softly, but Lorrie didn't.

Eighteen

MAUDY WAS NOT SURPRISED when Royal and his gang showed up at the Vaca ranch the evening after the burial. They had raced after Ben and his brothers at full tilt in the wrong direction when they left El Relave, and now must be coming back to see if they could find out which way they really went. They might find the hats and weapons they'd lost in their big hurry, but the Cowdens were long gone.

Maudy was sweeping the ground in front of her house when the VO appeared. She always kept a large expanse of ground swept bare, smooth, and clean around her house. That eliminated places for crawly things to hide. Sunshine on a bare yard discouraged animals and insects from venturing into her house. Her yard was so clean a person could run across it barefoot at night. After she had been at the Vaca a while, and all the bugs and snakes had found out they could not live there without being sunburnt or trampled, she would plant flower beds.

Royal and his rangers rode their horses across the swept ground to Maudy's front door. Maudy was not surprised they did not know any better than to trample a woman's yard, even though anyone could see it was neatly swept. She had neighbored with the VO ever since the Vincents came to the country and she knew how dumb they were. She smiled at them from a chair by her doorway. She planted the broom in front of her, held on to it with both hands, and did not fidget, fret, or budge.

The gang stayed on their horses as though in too big a hurry to get off for a drink of water. Not that Maudy would have offered them one. Royal wanted to know where the Cowden brothers had gone. Maudy naturally said she did not know.

Royal's horse would not stand still. He stamped and fretted and frothed at the bit. That helped Royal's pose. He was sure Maudy enjoyed the picture he made on a horse. Maudy only smiled at him so he would go on thinking it. He said he wanted her advice on how he could get in touch with the brothers in a peaceful way. Maudy said she didn't know how he'd ever be able to do that without a fight, no matter how peaceful he felt.

Royal said he reckoned the Cowdens would leave the country for a while, or at least that would be the smart thing to do. Maudy said, no, she believed they'd gone off to locate the Yawner. Royal asked where the Yawner was. Maudy told him she did not know, but Patch, the scout, had brought her husband a message from the old savage, and the brothers had gone off to find him. She did not think the brothers were running from the VO at all. The VO was plumb outdistanced again and the brothers were attending to more important business.

Royal said that was a lie. He knew the brothers were off down in Mexico hiding again. Maudy said she didn't lie, but if he thought the Cowden brothers worried about the Royal Vincent gunsels, all the rumors about him being on dope must be true.

Royal Vincent asked Maudy if she knew who he was and if she remembered him. She said she remembered him from the first time he had visited the San Rafael ranch a few years before. She remembered him without his chin whiskers and hair down to his shoulders. She said she liked the short cavalryman's cape he was wearing over his shoulders now. She wore a cape just like it sometimes when she went to town.

Royal tried to smile, then inquired about the health of her father and brothers. He said he sure liked her father and brothers. He was sure they must miss her cooking, since she had been the only woman left to care for them at their ranch at La Noria. Maudy said he did not need to bother himself about her father's care and feeding now, since he had never shown any concern for it before.

Royal then asked how long she intended to stay at the Vaca because it was on land that belonged to the VO. Maudy said the Vaca was Ben Cowden's own homestead, filed and proven long before the Vincents had ever even heard of the San Rafael Valley. Royal said he did not think so, he would have to check, but he was almost sure Maudy was trespassing.

Royal said his brother Duncan had always been able to get along with her father and brothers at La Noria, but now that she was a Cowden she was marked for trouble just like all the rest of them. Maudy said she reckoned she could handle any trouble a dude like Royal thought he could give her. He asked why she was being so cantankerous and calling him names. She was not acting like the Maudy he knew, the Maudy who had lived with her folks at La Noria in sight of the VO's big headquarters house, the Maudy who had always offered him coffee and biscuits. Wouldn't she offer him coffee and biscuits now, and be her old self? Maudy said she didn't have any coffee and biscuits made, but she had a mirror. He was welcome to come in and use her mirror, since that was what he seemed to need most in the world right then.

Royal said she talked real sassy for a woman alone in the middle of nowhere. He was not in the habit of molesting women, but he was not going to take sassy talk from a sorry Cowden, any kind of a Cowden, male or female. He thought maybe he would take Maudy into custody for being an accessory.

Royal ordered his gunsels to catch a team and hitch up the spring wagon so Maudy could load what she needed and come away. Maudy was under arrest.

Packrat hurried forward, eager to be the one who drove the wagon so he could sit close to Maudy. Maudy was still in her chair with the broom. As Packrat swung his leg off his horse to dismount, she jumped up, screeched like a banshee, and whacked Royal's horse on the nose with the broom.

That was the worse thing in the world Royal's horse thought could ever happen to a horse. He went absolutely loose in the bowels with fear and fell out from under Royal in his hurry to duck away from Maudy and leave her yard. His plan of escape did not include taking Royal with him, so he kicked high behind, came down on stiff front legs, and wiped the ground from side to side with his head and tail like a sidewinder. He loosened Royal's seat and began to hurry sideways.

Royal started losing his grip on the saddlehorn and swinging away from the horse. Then the horse stopped dead and stood him on his head in a pile of rocks that Maudy had stacked on the edge of the clearing.

With another screech and a clout of the broom on Packrat's horse's nose Maudy put the jumpy VO horses in the breeze again.

The entire cavalcade stampeded or bucked away from Maudy's yard with eyes starting, and hats, manes, and tails flying. Most of them ran across an open flat toward their home range on the VO. Six or seven riders left the yard running after their mounts afoot and hollering whoa. Two men who rode gentle horses gave chase after the riderless horses, but did more to run them off than turn them back.

Maudy had never been one to find great happiness at seeing people unhorsed as others did, but she was proud of the wreck she'd caused. When she heard Sergeant's deep laugh behind her, she started laughing too.

A troop of cavalry headed in to the Vaca from the direction of Camp Huachuca. When they were close, Sergeant recognized the guidon of the Fourth Cavalry, with Lieutenant Bill Buck and Sergeant Leroy Dodge in the lead. Lieutenant Buck stopped his troop on the edge of Maudy's yard and watched the scattering of the VO rangers in the flat. Royal Vincent had been able to hold on to his horse's reins, so he was still near the house. Ted Randolph had stayed in place with his horse under control.

Randolph showed Lieutenant Buck his written appointment as a special agent for the Department of the Interior and the warrant for the Cowden brothers.

Lieutenant Buck carefully inspected Randolph's commission and the warrant and handed them back without comment.

"So we expect your cooperation in the apprehension of these men, Lieutenant," Randolph said.

"I have a much more important mission at this time," Lieutenant Buck said. He dismounted and walked around Randolph's horse and saluted Maudy. "Mrs. Cowden, we're only here to welcome you as our neighbor and offer you our services."

Maudy smiled, shook his hand, and thanked him.

"I served with your husband and his brothers at Los Bultos last summer. He is one of the finest men I have ever known. I was pleased to make the recommendation for the government commendations Ben and his brothers received for their help in that battle."

"Thank you, I was at the ranch when the commendations were given to them."

"Now, what is this about your husband and his brothers being accused of outlawry?"

Randolph rode away toward the flat and waved and shouted orders to reorganize the rangers.

"I frankly don't know," Maudy said. "Royal Vincent seems to think he can arrest them for the murder of Jack Odoms. Odoms and his men murdered our neighbor Edmundo Romero last summer. Royal and fifty or sixty other people saw Odoms shoot and kill Margarita Elias, his own wife. Absolutely no one claims to know who killed Odoms. I don't see how that warrant for Ben and his brothers could be any good."

"Thank you, Mrs. Cowden." Lieutenant Buck turned to Royal. "Do you dispute what this lady says?"

"We have a legal warrant," Royal said. "Odoms's shooting of his wife was an accident. Will you help us apprehend these men or not?"

"When I rode in to this ranch I had the distinct feeling that these constable rangers of yours were causing a disturbance," Lieutenant Buck said. "Is that true, Mrs. Cowden?"

Maudy brightened. "Yes, some of them dismounted and turned their horses loose on our pasture without being asked, and others trampled our pasture under their horses' feet. They were all acting rowdy. I think they were trying to show off by doing acrobatics when they dismounted. I'd like to see them on their way before they do more damage, or hurt themselves."

"I guess you'd better be on your way, Mr. Vincent," Lieutenant Buck said. "You're finished here, are you not?"

"Then you won't honor this warrant, Lieutenant?"

"I do not have orders to pursue the Cowden brothers. Your warrant would have to be shown to my superiors."

"This lady says the Cowdens have gone to join the Yawner. Where is he?"

"I think he's in the Huachucas."

"Why aren't you going after him, if he's up there?"

"Mr. Vincent, if he's up there, he's already right where I want him. As long as he keeps still, I'll leave him alone. If I captured him, I'd have to feed, clothe, and shelter him. I don't have the manpower or the supplies for that."

"What are you doing out on patrol then?"

"Making sure the old savage hasn't moved."

"Well, we want him. Part of the mission of this patrol is to find and capture the Yawner and bring him to justice."

"Well, then I suggest you proceed on your mission." Lieutenant Buck pointed to Huachuca Peak. "My last report has it that the Yawner is up there."

"Thank you. If we bring him in, my report will detail your lack of cooperation, Lieutenant."

"Sir, I appreciate that."

Randolph had regrouped the rangers and their horses. Royal joined them in the flat and they rode away toward Huachuca Peak.

Sergeant Broussard shook hands with Lieutenant Buck and Sergeant Dodge and they watched the VO head for glory.

Sergeant Broussard said, "The old heathen can see all the way to this ranch. He can see them coming, count them, and assign individual targets to his bowmen."

"No he can't, Sergeant," Sergeant Dodge said. "Because he's not up there."

Ben and Mark found the weeping Teddy sitting in a puddle of blood on the kitchen floor and thought he was bleeding to death.

"Bob Snider did it. Look for Snider. He did it," he said. The brothers started to pick him up and carry him to a bed for care, found he was unscathed, set him down, and forgot about him. He sat at the kitchen table in ruins and could not stop bawling.

Lorrie revived. Les helped her undress and put on her nightgown. He made her get in bed under the covers, then piled extra blankets and quilts on her. He finished cleaning her face and stopped the bleeding. Snider's boot had bashed and cut her cheeks, brows, and lips, and broken her nose.

The brothers were cleaning up the house when Judge Dunn and Dick Martin rode in to see if A.B. had returned from El Relave. The Judge sat down in the kitchen and started a long-winded account of Frank Wong's discovery of Garbie Burr's bloody corpse.

Mark was struck dumb. He listened while Ben and Les asked questions. Then he walked to the barn, mounted his horse, and rode away toward town.

A.B., Viney, and the girls were home by dark. They did not even dismount from the landau when they heard about Garbie. They went into town to bring Mark and Garbie's body home. The girls laid it on the bed she had shared with Lorrie and bathed, combed, and dressed her.

Mark sat with his mother a while in the Arizona room and when he came out his sisters took turns embracing him. He said he'd found poor Frank Wong weeping by Garbie's body. The next morning the Cowdens buried Garbie in their family plot.

Patch had been left as a sentry on the road while the family buried Garbie. Les went up to relieve him. A fine drizzle was falling, but Les could see well. He found Patch sitting in the shelter of a boulder where he could watch long stretches of road. "Jose," he said in a low voice.

Patch raised his hand to quiet him. The rain increased and the sky darkened. Les stopped in his tracks and heard riders coming up the road. A crowd of bright yellow slickers came in sight. Patch jumped up and ran with Les down the hill into the barn to warn Ben and Mark. Their horses were already packed and saddled and feeding in their stalls. The brothers tightened cinches, picked up their rifles, mounted, and rode toward the orchard.

Les said, "Just a minute," and dismounted at the house. His brothers dismounted and followed him to the back door to kiss their mother and sisters and be given a sack of hot biscuits and bacon to pad their bellies while they rode.

Les knelt at Lorrie's bedside and hugged her against his damp Saltillo, kissed her, and told her to please take care of herself, heal fast, and not be sad. She nodded, looked away, and said, "Uh, huh," like a sad girl, but this time a girl with a family.

A few minutes later the brothers and Patch sat their horses down in the creek below the house and watched Duncan Vincent ride by in the lead of a band of horsemen.

When they were gone, Ben said, "Well, the old scorpion is back and he's got grown men to help him this time."

"Yes, he does," Les said. "They're riding good horses and sitting them well. Who do you think they are?"

"This time I recognized some homegrown Arizonans," Ben said.

Les expected Mark to say something, then thought, my Lord, how does my brother feel? He's lost the love of his life.

The brothers turned their horses and headed for the Pajaritos against the wind and rain.

Nineteen

ANTONIO CAMPANA stopped the Chinese people on the south side of Manzanita Mountain at dawn and walked up to the peak to look around. A breeze from the east promised more rain and carried the smell of wood smoke from the Pajaritos. He knew Apaches liked the Pajaritos in the summer, but he could not understand why they would be there in the winter. They liked to go a lot farther south in the winter. He was given to worry about Apaches and must now believe they were the ones with the fire on the Pajaritos. His route through Peñasco Canyon and then down the Peña Blanca trail skirted the Pajaritos and he would have to hide until dark before he could start.

The singsong girls did not travel well and the Campanas were overdue. They did not need to think Kosterlinsky or Vincent would come out to look for them, either. The singsong girls were not good riders of mules and did not know how to walk at all. Their bound feet were no good for walking.

The Campanas were long-legged Sonorans and good hikers. They were only a stroll from Calabasas where they wanted to put the girls on the train. Calabasas was only a half-day's walk for a normal female, but Antonio did not think he could get the girls to the train in less than an entire night now. He walked back down to the camp.

With their short legs and their tiny feet the *sonsonete* girls needed at least three little steps to his one. They could barely take themselves down to Manzanita Creek for a drink. They depended on the Campanas for everything. Every pair of eyes turned to Antonio the minute he reached camp. They watched him like little dogs. The *chinito* boys had filled the water gourds at the stream and the girls were drinking.

Antonio sat down with his brother, took a corn leaf from him, and cut it into a rectangle with his skinning knife. He took his brother's pouch of homegrown *macuzi* tobacco and rolled himself a *cigarro* in the leaf. He struck sparks with the top edge of his knife off a white rock into *hiesca,* oak punk, that he held in the palm of his hand, blew on it until he made a coal, and lit the *cigarro.*

"No fire today," he said. "No coffee. Apaches in the Pajaritos."

"I'm no good for fighting today," Ernesto Campana, the brother, said. "I don't think I like this business anymore."

Antonio grinned. "Not better than jail?"

"No."

"Not better than the mine?"

"Not better than the mine, either. I think I'll go prospecting with what I make on this trip, though."

"You mean, if you get home."

"Yes, if I get home. Where are the Apaches?"

"In the Pajaritos."

"Where in the Pajaritos?"

"This end."

"To finish me off."

"It'll be all right. We'll hide all day. I'll unsaddle the *bestias,* the beasts, and hide the saddles. I'll watch from the peak, you watch the trail from the other side of the creek."

"We haven't had Apaches before. What if they find us?"

"If Apaches find us, we let them have the *chinitas,* that's all."

"What about us?"

"I'll run. What about you?"

"Who knows?"

Antonio unsaddled the mules and hid the saddles under a thick stand of manzanita brush. He tied the mules head to tail, fed them corn in morrals, and hobbled them. They were so tired and hungry they put their heads down on the ground in the morrals and closed their eyes to eat. He cut a high stand of old summer grass out of a sheltered arroyo and carried many armloads to the mules.

152

The old couple and the three boys helped Ernesto hide the girls. The Campanas had dug gravelike nests for their human contraband on this spot long before the first trip was made and had improved them each time they stopped to bivouack with a new bunch. The nests were lined with dry grass and topped with lids of bamboo and rawhide and covered with grass and dirt.

The Campana brothers were experts at camouflage and the Chinese always stayed in their nests. Antonio did not think he could lie there like that all day, but he did not worry about the people. He could not explain to them what would happen if they did not stay in their holes, because he did not speak their language, but they always stayed down and rested quietly until they were unearthed.

The singsong girls were well-behaved. When they were ready to travel, the Campanas put them on their mules and they stayed on board until they were lifted off. They were fed cold tacos of meat and beans and they ate what they got and did not ask for more. They saw to their other personal needs on their own, were always ready to resume the march, and when it was time to rest they crawled into their holes without a whimper.

He only wished they could walk. He knew if he pointed to the trail and led the way, they would try, but it would be impossible for them to *caminac,* take to the road and make progress, if they ever had to use their feet.

Antonio's grandfather said God had not given the *sonsonetes* adequate feet, voices, bodies, or hands. They were dumb as lambs, but so far all of them on previous trips had stayed on their mules and made it to the train. Antonio imagined their little *nalga* butts were rubbed and galled the color of roses, but they never made a sound or even an expression of pain. They seemed so delicate, they might perish in the waft of a breeze. They were so small and quiet, no one but the Campanas even knew they moved on the face of the earth. Except for the Campanas, only God would notice if they perished. Even if the Apaches caught them, tortured them, and squashed them, who would ever know? They were so small, the Apaches could impale them all on one lance, salt them, and dry them to jerky with the sun of one day.

Antonio went to the peak again and was careful to stay off the skyline. He lay on his belly and watched the Pajaritos. He watched two hawks soar above Peñasco Canyon, but everything else remained still. At midafternoon, a wind blew in from the east and he watched a rain move toward him across the Santa Ritas. Two crows flapped out of the Pajaritos and tumbled and played on the wind ahead of the rain.

Antonio looked off across the country at the storm's thick black wall and knew the trail ahead would be rained on heavily until long after dark. He went down and uncovered his live packages, fed them again,

153

put them on their mules and headed for Calabasas. They were barely on their way when the rain caught and drenched them.

Later, in the final light of the day, Antonio looked back to make sure the mules were close together in the file, that all the saddles rode high over their withers, that all the packages had kept pace, and missed one. He counted heads and one was gone. He stopped the file and rode all the way back to Ernesto to make sure. He was short one mule and singsong girl. He did not remember the features of the girl, but he took stock of his mules and knew which one was missing.

He did not stop. He needed to cross a ridge out of Peñasco Canyon and find the trail that would lead him out of Peña Blanca Canyon before the light was gone. He felt a weight on his heart. A train of twenty-five mules was long. At a bend in the trail, covered by the storm, some *fiera,* haughty predator, had taken one, only one. Antonio could not stop for one and risk the rest. Everyone knew how perishable the packages were.

The Cowden brothers and Patch rode under the Red Mountain cliffs down Alum Gulch to Sonoita Creek. The dark night, rain and wooded trail along the creek covered them so only God knew where they were. The rain stopped for a while an hour before dawn and they made camp in a sheltered grove of cottonwood against Los Cuates Buttes. They grained their horses, folded themselves in their beds inside the tarps, and slept.

They were up and horseback again before dawn, crossed the railroad tracks at Calabasas, and rode up the canyon toward the Pajaritos. They were only just out of sight of the siding at Calabasas when they came face to face with Antonio Campana. They were amused at the serious expression on his face when they stopped and blocked his way. His expression as much as told them that he was in the lead of something he did not want anyone else to see.

"*Hola,* Campana, look at you, so far from home," Ben said. "We've been wondering how you were employed these days. I'm glad to see you took our advice and left the San Rafael."

Antonio did not want to talk, but he said, "You made it difficult for me there."

The brothers saw a mule's ears bob behind an outcropping of rock in the wash, then the mule and his small bundled and hooded rider came into view, then another rider just like her, then another, and another. The brothers moved their horses out of Campana's way so he could go on, but he did not move and the file stopped behind him.

"Imagine finding a crowd of people this size way out here," Ben said. "And look at them. They're from another world. Antonio, you're a surprising man."

"I don't want trouble."

"Well, we won't cause you trouble. We're glad you're doing well. I hope your employers appreciate you. Not everyone could do what you do."

Campana's mules untracked and went on. Not one child's downcast face showed suffering.

After they were gone, Mark said, "Singsong girls. Do you think Garbie was killed because of what she knew about this?"

"I wouldn't be a damned bit surprised," Les said.

"She told Papa about the smuggling at Ben's wedding," Mark said. "I wish we'd done something about it."

"I knew they were smuggling people across the border last fall," Ben said. "What could Papa do about it? When did we have time to mess with it?"

"I saw Papa and Mama laughing with her," Les said. "What did she say to them?"

"She quoted something in that singsong Chinese for Papa and then translated it."

"What did she say?"

"I guess she thought Papa better move to stop the smuggling, so she said the old Chinese saying was, 'When you wake up, *get* up. When you get up, *do* something.' "

The brothers and Patch backtracked the singsong girls up Calabasas Canyon. Patch took the lead when the canyon deepened at the base of the Pajaritos. Under Pajarito Peak he led them out of the canyon, along a gradual ridge, and into the Yawner's camp against a cliff.

The brothers and Patch caused no stir when they rode in. They did not look to the right nor to the left and no one in the camp looked directly at them.

The Yawner sat alone in front of a small fire with his back against the cliff. He looked past Patch at the brothers, examined each of their faces, and settled on Ben's. The brothers dismounted and the Yawner stepped forward and shook Ben's hand.

The Yawner and his band spoke Spanish, but no English. Ben sat near his side. Les and Mark sat across the fire from them. Patch moved away by himself and did not talk to his relations in the band. His role was such that he must show that he was loyal to the Cowdens' mission. That was a lesson in loyalty to Les.

This was the camp of the broncos. The Apaches called the white men Americans and Patch was Americanized. Patch was serving his country. When the Yawner's band was healthy, his band preyed on Americans and Mexicans alike. Sometimes they prospered, but not lately. Most of the band had been wiped out at Los Bultos.

Les was not comfortable sitting with his back to the camp, but he and Mark felt they should be courteous. Patch could face the camp but did not take advantage of his position by staring. Ben's attention was on the Yawner.

Les and Mark could not have taken a position from which they could oversee the camp, as though taking a license to stare. To the predator Apache, a stare was a threat. Even a glance could be taken as an insult.

The Yawner periodically made a sharp appraisal of the Cowden horses, but most of the time his eyes were vacant of human expression as the brothers knew it. The eyes were black and fathomless and did not show kindness.

The Yawner seemed to be a different person every time Les saw him. He was a stocky, heavy-shouldered man. From time to time, he rubbed the back of his shoulder against a rough surface of the cliff to please an itch. He sat cross-legged. His worn *teguas* were studded halfway the length of his shins with dime-sized, silver conchas. He wore several thin, worn silver bracelets on one wrist, nothing on the other. His mouth was so wide it split his face from ear to ear, like an old snake's. It did not look like a mouth that knew anything of supping, sipping, or kissing. It seemed to Les to be a mouth that stayed closed over the clenched jaws of the old savage so much that it might someday heal shut. The brothers had never felt any kindness for the savage. He had drunk more blood than any old wolf, so life was better for everyone when he kept his mouth shut.

Ben took the knife and sheath the Yawner had sent him, held it before him so the Yawner could see it, and told him he appreciated the gift. The Yawner only glanced at it when Ben put it back in his belt.

"Patch is a good man to bring me here so that I can thank you for the gift, Bostezador," Ben said. He called him Yawner, his Apache name, because he did not know him well enough to use his Christian name. He and the man only knew each other as foes.

"Good. You like it?"

"*Seguro que si,* be sure of it."

"Horseman, this was a hard trail for you to take only for that."

"I come only for that."

"Have you no messages from the American soldiers?"

"No. I have spoken to no one about you, except my father."

"Ah, the sheriff father who raises the horses of the horsemen. Is he well?"

"Yes."

"What message does he send me?"

"None."

"Is he not one of the chiefs who would like to see me hang?"

"My father would like to see you go back to San Carlos. Most Americans would rather see you dead."

"And you?"

"I'm my father's son. I thought you were dying the last time I saw you at Los Bultos. I did not want to see that."

"I know that. But I did not die at all."

"Nevertheless, I did not want to see you dead."

"That is why you did not finish me whan you saw me crawling under your horse. That is why you turned away when Ben Tom pointed his rifle at my eyes."

"Yes."

"How was it that you could let me live? Are you an authority?"

"No."

"I thought you were the leader of the soldiers who fooled me at Los Bultos."

"Me and my brothers tracked you and spied on you in your camp."

"You, Horseman, and your brothers, have prowled very close to me at times, as I have been close to you."

Ben smiled. "That's true. My small brother who sits here spied on your camp on Cerro Pelon one night last summer. He was so close, the smell of your meat made his mouth water."

"I know. We saw his tracks days later. He was close enough to step on us. I said, that's one of the horsemen, for he never dismounted." The Yawner showed a glimmer of teeth. "I thought it was you."

"No, it was our youngest brother over there."

"So now you come to my camp in the open light of day. What do you want?"

"Only to thank you for the present."

"Not as an authority to plead with me to give up my weapons and surrender my *gente*, my people?"

"No."

"Good, because I will not surrender."

Ben and the Yawner remained silent for a while. The women carried two small whitetail does into camp, laid them under a jack pine, and set to work skinning and quartering them on their hides. They ate slices of raw liver as they worked. The heads were taken aside by a woman and, with soft, deft, woman's blows with a hardwood club, she opened the skulls and scooped out the brains.

The women became aware that Les was watching them and began to entertain themselves with stolen glances at him. They were so deft with the knives, Les wondered how they would have entertained themselves with him if he had been brought in as a captive. Women and children captured by the Yawner sometimes survived. Men did not.

"Where did you go on the train?" the Yawner asked Ben.

"I took my woman to California."

"Your woman, the little healer."

"Yes."

"California. The country by the big sea."

"Yes."

"I would not go there unless to kill Mexicans." The teeth glimmered again.

"After I saw the ocean, I was ready to come home."

"We have the same home, you and I. You did not kill me at Los Bultos, so you must not want it all for yourself."

"No. Only to use for a while, I guess."

"You have not scarred it with wire, like the others."

"Not yet. It's for common use."

"Yes, for all the people."

Les knew the Yawner's acting tame was all a lie. He would not mind fighting to the death. He loved war more than peace because that was the Apache way. Ben had been summoned so he would go back and tell the soldiers how nice the Yawner had become. The Sonoita and Santa Cruz valleys had always been the Apaches' favorite "enchanted land." Why would the Yawner want to share it unless it was only to allow Americans to bring in goods and become his prey?

"I can stay here now, Horseman. I have many horses, many cattle. With all this rain, I am waiting for the *pastora,* the Indian wheat, to sprout on the desert by the sea, so I can fatten my livestock."

"Oh, the Seris want you there?"

"The Seris, the Yaquis, the Papagos, the Mexicans. What does it matter what they want?"

"The new feed must be sprouting at San Carlos by now, too."

"Maybe, but not like the *pastora.*"

"Why don't you go back to San Carlos now in peace?"

"I've been thinking about it. We miss our people there."

"If you took your people back to San Carlos you would have to stop fighting."

"We're not fighting. We want to visit our people for a while. The soldiers' horses are able to pursue us longer and come closer to us when the days are cold. Food is scarce. The cold subdues us and we have to stay by the fire."

"Why do you stay here? This is not good country in winter. You need a house here."

"Bah! A house, a tomb, what is the difference?"

"Why do you stay in these cold rocks?"

"I told you. We wait for the *pastora.* We will grind it and make meal. It makes light flour. Where it grows, our animals fatten in the open and we can see for leagues in every direction. Soon, we'll all be warm and fat." He showed a glimmer of amusement across the mouth, but not in the eyes.

A mule sounded off in its peculiar cross between a bray and a whinny that died in a strangled moan. Les looked down at his hands and wondered what had happened to the owner, who'd been forced to relinquish the animal.

"Santiago caught a *chinita* today," the Yawner said. "He took her with the mule. I want to trade her to you."

Ben laughed softly. "I don't want her." He looked toward his brothers. Les gazed expressionessly over Ben's head. Mark carved dried mud off his boots with his pocket knife. "Do you want a China girl, brothers?"

Les and Mark shook their heads slightly, uninterestedly.

The Yawner made a sign to someone and two women brought the girl and sat her down in front of him. She did not look up. Her back was to Les and Mark.

Les looked at the hand the girl used to hold herself away from the thorn tips of a clump of lechuguilla on the slope below her. The hand was tiny, shapely, smooth-skinned, and ivory-white. The veins were protected only by a transparent film of skin, the nails well cared for and shapely. It pulsed and trembled against the rocky ground.

Les thought, that's all right, girl. We can get you out of this. You don't know it, but you're lucky. The only people in the world who could help you got here in time. Les looked away from the hand so his concern would not show. He glanced at the Yawner and dreaded it, because the Yawner had been watching him. The Yawner was not the kind to miss a sign of human feeling that would help him make a trade.

"What will you give for her?" the Yawner asked Ben. "Some of your gold?"

Ben leaned forward and lifted the child's chin, looked into her face, sat back. "Who would want her? What good would she be?"

"She's very new. *Está nuevecita*, Horseman. Can't you see?"

"If she was any good she would not have been thrown away by her people. She is a long way from home and still only a child."

"What does it mean?"

"She comes from a people who don't want girls. They can't sell them and they can't give them away. They usually drown them when they are babies, or bash their heads against the rocks and throw them away."

"Why?"

"These kind of women are no good."

"What kind of man would do that to his child?"

"Men of an ancient race. You see how the Americans build and get rich? The Americans' buildings are caves compared to the buildings of the *chinos*. You and I are as *taquachics*, badgers digging in the dirt, compared to the *chinos*. Their wisdom has decided them that their women are no good. This China girl is nothing."

"Can't she work?"

"She can't do anything."

"She can't breed, either?"

"Ooo, they don't like to do that. Who would want them for that? Their *cria,* offspring, would weaken your stock. Look at the eyes. I doubt she can see across the canyon."

"Would you lie for her, Horseman?"

"She might be able to see across the canyon, but I am telling you the truth when I say she comes from a race that rubs out its females."

"How do they multiply, then? How is she here?"

"They must breed enough to raise the men they need, but they must not like to breed."

"Is this true?"

"Believe me, this one has been rejected by her people, or she would not be here."

"Take her with you when you go. Let her weaken the American stock."

"Shall we go now? What did you want me for?"

"I want to have my horses and cattle and live in peace as you do, Horseman. How am I to do that?"

"We can't live in peace without sacrifice. I don't know what sacrifices you would make."

"I would sacrifice all Americans." The glimmer showed again.

"There are too many, Bostezador."

"I want you to tell me how, then. The Americans have a place for me at San Carlos. They promised me I could have that place with my relatives. There no longer seems to be another way."

"As you say, San Carlos is your place."

"The reservation."

"Yes."

"I want to take my livestock, no matter whose brand is on it. I will not sacrifice my livestock. Will the Americans allow that?"

"I can't say. I am not in authority."

"Who can say?"

"Only the soldiers."

"Which soldiers? Bring me the Liebre, the Jackrabbit. I'll speak to him."

"Which one is he?" Ben turned to Patch.

"Lieutenant Buck," Patch said.

"Yes, that one, I think. Go right now," the Yawner said.

The brothers stood up to leave. Patch stood still.

The Yawner addressed Les. "Give me the *alazan,* the sorrel horse you're riding, for the *chinita.*"

"You like that horse, Jefe?" Les said. He took a last look at old Codger and cussed. If he only had been cold enough not to show he cared about that girl. Now he and Codger had fallen prey to the damned old savage. He knew he had no choice but to give up his horse, so he might as well not whine about it.

"I might not eat that one," the Yawner said.

"Take him as a gift."

"And the saddle, too?"

"You want the saddle?"

"No. I have a light soldier's saddle. Take the *chinita*, I won't take your *vaquera* saddle."

"I'll take her off your hands as a favor to you," Les said. "But I want the mule, so I won't have to walk."

The Yawner showed the glimmer once more and signed for the mule to be brought. "I will do anything to see one of the horsemen ride a mule," he said.

Les took the girl's hand and helped her to her feet. When the mule was brought, he saddled him, loaded her in the saddle and mounted behind her. Then he rode away with his brothers.

Twenty

MAUDY SANG and swept and danced with her broom. She had dyed new flour sacks bright red, yellow, and green and stretched them over her windows with tacks. The strong sunlight through these new window panes made her think of Japanese lanterns and summer dances, so she danced. She sang softly so as not to disturb the quiet of the day. The day was not so quiet. A cardinal had just called down by the corrals and Sergeant was chopping firewood at the woodpile.

He stopped chopping too soon. Maudy stopped dancing and listened. Sergeant spoke and was answered by another male voice. Maudy pulled back one of her window panes so she could see to the woodpile. She could not leave the windows tacked up on a warm day, anyway. With Chato sneaking up on women and cutting them open, she had to be able to see outside.

She saw a riderless horse standing at the woodpile and Sergeant was helping a man toward the bunkhouse by the corrals. She went to the door and called to stop him and ran to see what was the matter. She found poor Snider practically in a faint with a mutilated hand.

Maudy made Sergeant turn around and take Snider to the house. They undressed him and put him in her bed. She had to give an order for everything she wanted Sergeant to do, because he did not seem to want to help. She was surprised a soldier was so slow about helping a wounded man.

Exasperated, Maudy finally drew Sergeant outside. "Honestly, Sergeant, I shouldn't have to tell you what to do. I'm sure you've helped prepare a wounded man for treatment before."

"Yes ma'am, I have, but not a man like this one."

"Why don't you want to help this one?"

"I was taking him down to my bed first, then you said his name and I felt like putting him back on his horse."

"Why?"

"Isn't he the one that abandoned the ranch where Chato butchered Emily Porter and her child?"

"That's what they say, Sergeant, but he's been my friend for a long time and he's a friend of my brothers. I wouldn't judge him until I heard his side of the story."

"Yes, ma'am. Why does he have to take your bed? He would probably rest easier down in mine."

"Don't worry yourself about that, Sergeant. I'd rather have him up here handy to my stove, bandages, and medicines."

"Yes, ma'am."

Maudy washed Snider's hand, doused it with mescal, and brought him to life, then smeared it with carbolic salve. She did not have any trimming to do. The cleaver had amputated the fingers with surgical precision. She wrapped the stumps in clean bandages.

Snider wanted a drink of the mescal, so she gave him a thimbleful and refused him more until he began to whine. Then she handed him the whole bottle and turned her back on him. She picked up his clothing and examined it for stains and found the fingers in the shirt pocket. She gave a small shriek and handed the shirt to Sergeant. Sergeant dug a hole for the fingers out by the woodpile and buried them, then took Snider's horse to the corral, unsaddled him, and fed him grain.

When Sergeant was gone and Snider had taken a snort of mescal to warm his innards, he said, "I want to thank you for taking me in, Maudy. I'm always able to turn to you when I'm in trouble."

"Oh yeah, what makes you think that?" Maudy said.

"Well, it was you who helped me that time the old man Cowden stripped me and burned my clothes. You gave me that old lady's housecoat to wear and your horse to ride so I could get respectable again, remember?"

"I thought I was helping you get out of the country like you'd been ordered to do. I never dreamed you'd come back and cause so much trouble again."

"I'm in trouble, but I haven't caused any of it, Maudy. Listen, I won't stay long. Just let me get my strength back and I'll move on."

"Nobody's hurrying you."

"Thank you, Maudy."

"I'd do the same for a stray dog, Bob."

"OK. But you're just a good person, everybody knows that. And there

162

was a time when you were glad to see me coming. When I courted you. Remember? When you were up at Canelo with your mother and father and little sisters?"

"Boy, you've done a lot to change that. You became a horse thief and a back-stabber. You make a habit of breaking your word and that habit brought about the deaths of two very fine people and the kidnapping of your own wife."

Snider began to weep. Maudy was not a cold person and she could not stand to see anyone cry when he was hurt. She sat at the bedside and put her arm around Snider's shoulders. "Oh, I'm sorry, Bob," she said.

"My little wife is gone," Snider sobbed.

"Shhh, she'll be found."

"I miss her. You don't know how much I've blamed myself for leaving those poor ladies at the ranch, but I had to get out and find work. Nobody can go through life just sponging off other people."

"Shhh. You don't have to explain. Just rest now. Go to sleep. You can tell me about it when you wake up."

Maudy laid Snider's head on the pillow and covered his shoulders with the blankets and he seemed to sleep. She washed her hands, then set to work and cooked a pot of beans and a pot of stew, baked bread, and brewed a pot of coffee. She had brought a good supply of canned fruit and vegetables from El Durazno. She opened a jar of peaches, poured a cup of coffee for Sergeant, and went outside to look for him.

Sergeant was sitting quietly by the door. He asked how Snider was doing and she told him he was resting. Sergeant said he did not think Ben would approve of Snider being at the Vaca. Sergeant understood that Snider was a pariah. Maudy said she could see that Sergeant was worried about his responsibility for keeping her safe and she appreciated that. He said he had plenty to worry about with keeping watch over the good horses someone was bound to want to steal and a young woman who would be a temptation for other kinds of vicious thieves.

Maudy sat down on the bench beside him and said, "I can see this is not the kind of work you wanted when you retired from the army, Sergeant."

Sergeant sucked on his pipe and smiled. "Nooo. I told Ben all I wanted was never to be thirsty for water and to have a good, shady place to sit and bide the time."

"Well, you have those things. You're in the shade, anyway. Do you want a drink of water?"

"Nooo, I can satisfy my normal thirst any time I want to. I was talking about that terrible thirst for a cool drink a man gets five minutes after he goes into battle. That's the thirst I dread."

"Well, I've never known that kind of thirst, so I doubt you will again."

"I'm not too sure. I felt it coming on when that Mr. Vincent came by with his pack of recruits and I feel it now that this man has come to camp on you."

"Don't worry about him. He won't stay long after Ben comes back. Anyway, come in now and have your collation. I have fresh bread, canned peaches, and coffee all ready for you. You think that will taste good?"

"Yes, ma'am, I believe it will."

Snider had not budged. He was on his back and seemed to be sound asleep.

Sergeant knew a bad man from a good one and he knew to watch a bad one. He sat down and watched Snider while he ate the fresh bread and peaches with the coffee. After a while he said, "When did you say Ben and his brothers would be back, Miss Maudy?"

Snider stopped breathing.

"Soon, I think." Maudy's voice was sweet and expressed only innocence and trust. She was not suspicious of Snider.

Snider lay as still as a dead man.

"Maybe this afternoon or this evening," Maudy said.

Snider's eyes opened wide and stared at the ceiling.

"How did Mister Snider lose his fingers?" Sergeant asked.

"I haven't asked him yet."

"Where did it happen?"

"I didn't ask the poor man any questions at all."

"I imagine Ben will know all about it by now."

"I imagine so."

Snider rolled over, saw that Sergeant was watching him, closed his eyes, stretched, opened his eyes, acted disoriented, and looked for Maudy. "That bread smells good," he said.

Maudy smiled, happy that Snider had rested. She prepared him a bowl of stew, sliced him fresh bread, poured him a cup of coffee, and went outside while he dressed. She carried on a conversation with him from outside the door. He said he had been in a knock-down-drag-out fight with three Mexican miners in an alley in Harshaw and they had finally subdued him, held him down, and cut off his fingers. Maudy asked him what had brought him so far away from a doctor. Why had he not seen the doctor in Harshaw? He thought a minute before he lied this time. He had not anticipated the question. He sat down and took a bite of his stew.

"I just wanted to get away. They beat me pretty bad and I was not thinking too clear," Snider said. "All I could think of was to try and find you. You're better'n any doctor."

Maudy looked at him, sure that he was lying. He did not have a mark on him except the mutilated hand.

"Where did those Mexicans strike you, Bob?" Maudy asked.

He realized his face showed no sign of a fight, turned red, grasped the back of his neck. "They just kept hitting me on the back of the neck. That's a Mexican trick, you know."

"Why didn't they want to leave any marks on you, Bob?"

"I guess they didn't want me to be able to prove I'd been beaten if I told Sheriff Cowden. Those Mexicans are awful scared of Sheriff Cowden, you know."

"Why did they cut off your fingers, then? Didn't they think anyone would notice?"

Snider ducked his head. "I don't know why anyone would do that."

"How did you really lose your fingers, Bob?"

Snider looked up, embarrassed. He turned on Sergeant. "What are you staring at? Why do you keep staring at me?"

"I'm listening to your story, sir. No offense intended."

"Well, don't stare at me. I know I'm ugly and maimed. Don't keep reminding me of it. Don't you know anything about that?"

"About what, sir?"

"About people staring at you because of the way you look."

"Why would I mind if people looked at me, sir?"

"I'd think you'd be as self-conscious about your looks as I am. I'm maimed, but you're black. Don't people ever tell you they think you're a real ugly nigger?"

"Black people don't, and anyone who thinks that don't have to look."

"Well, don't stare at me. It bothers me."

Sergeant put down his spoon.

"You're kind of an uppity nigger, aren't you?" Snider said. He took the clean dish towel that Maudy had wrapped on the bread to keep it warm, wadded it up, held it in the palm of his wounded hand to absorb the seeping blood, and took another bite of stew.

"How is that, sir?"

"What, you think you can answer me back? You think you can argue with me? You sit there and stare at me and expect me to eat my meal with you and you want to start an argument with me, too?"

"No, sir, I sure don't want to start an argument."

Snider's eyes got wild. He stood up from the table and drew his pistol, but did not point it. "Don't *argue* with me."

"Oh no, sir, I never argue with a man with a gun." Sergeant stood up, but did not step back.

"Bob Snider, put that away," Maudy said. "I don't like people to draw their weapons in my house."

"This damned nigger's insulting me."

"I don't like that word. You better get on your horse and leave before you do something else I don't like. As it is, I don't think Ben's going to like it when he finds out I let you stop here."

"I'm going, but I'm taking your money."

"You figure on robbing me, Bob Snider?"

"Yes, I'm robbing you and your nigger man, too. Just get out your money." Snider cocked the pistol and waved it at Sergeant. "You, too. Empty your pockets on the table."

"Now, sir, please don't wave a cocked pistol in here like that," Sergeant said. "You don't want to hurt Miss Maudy. Come on down to my quarters and I'll give you all the money you need. I've got over a hundred dollars."

"No, Sergeant, you don't have to give him your money," Maudy said. "He's not going to rob anyone."

"The damned hell, I'm not," Snider said.

"What with?"

"What?"

"What you going to shoot us with if we don't give you our money?"

"Damn it, what . . ." Snider looked at the pistol.

"You going to shoot us without any cartridges?"

Sergeant raised a fist to hit Snider, intending to satisfy himself by landing one blow on his ear.

"You don't have to hit him, Sergeant," Maudy said. "He's leaving, aren't you, Bob?"

"What kind of a woman would unload a man's pistol while he slept?"

"The woman who nursed Ben Cowden back to life after you stabbed him in the back. He should have shot you then, instead of having pity on you and letting you go. Now you're back and expect all of us to tolerate you again. Get out of my house and off this ranch before I take a six-shooter to you."

Sergeant took the pistol out of Snider's hand and Snider did not resist. Sergeant and Maudy followed him down to the barn.

"I need a fresh horse. Can't I at least have a fresh horse?" Snider said.

"I think you better get on your own horse and be gone before I decide to have mercy on him and make you go afoot," Maudy said.

"Look at him, he's half-dead. We both need rest. Please let us rest. Look, I'll just lay down in the hay." Snider collapsed in the haystack.

Maudy snatched up a pitchfork and he jumped to his feet like a footracer.

"Here, sir, I better help you saddle your horse so you can get going before Miss Maudy lets all the juice out of you," Sergeant said.

Sergeant saddled the horse and Snider mounted. He said, "I'm not leaving here without my pistol and cartridges."

"Well, I'll not give them to you," Maudy said. "You'll have to find some other way to get along. Everybody in this country has bent over backwards to supply you with rifles, horses, clothes, saddles, bandages, and food. Instead of making a new start in life, you've betrayed us. Now you pay. Get on down the road."

"If you make me leave here without my pistol and cartridges, you're the same as a murderer."

"I'm treating you no worse than you did Emily Porter when you rode away and left her at El Relave. To do you justice, I'll treat you no better."

Snider wandered away, wavering toward El Relave. Maudy and Sergeant watched until he was out of sight.

Snider wandered for a while before he decided to go to El Relave. Nobody was there and nobody would look for him there. He'd fixed that, though not altogether on purpose. He had not wanted anything to happen to Emily, Willy Fly, and Teresa, but he'd just been too worthless to stay with them. He told Teresa he needed to find work. The truth was, he'd been going crazy with the solitude and the boredom and wanted to go to the saloon, hear some music, have a drink, make plans, and talk big with other men. He'd never been good at doing hard work on a ranch.

He rode up a trail that wound into the Canelo Hills and stopped in the pass to look back at the San Rafael Valley. Rain was sweeping over the Vaca ranchhouse. The sight of it coming to wet him down made him feel sorry for himself. He did not know why everything happened to him. His whole arm hurt as though a lion had taken it in his jaws and torn it off. He hoped all the food had not been taken away from El Relave and he could stay there for a while.

He would never be able to go back to a decent life, so he needed to figure out how to get some money and leave the country. It was going to be hard for him to hide, now that he was disfigured. He would go to Chihuahua where nobody would know what he'd done. People would put out a warrant for him in Sonora. Kosterlinsky's Rural Police would want him.

He had not been at El Relave since he left Emily and Teresa. The only thing new about the place were the new graves on the hill. He put his horse away in the barn and fed him hay. Everything else, even the corn in the bin down to the last kernel, was gone. The bucket was down in the well, so he hauled it up full and took a drink, then carried it to the house. The door was ajar. The relatives had not left a thing inside. He lay down on the floor in the empty house and closed his eyes in despair.

He slept. He awakened when the floor became uncomfortable and cold. Night had fallen and a strong wind buffeted the house with rain. He hated this place of desolation and solitude. He wanted company. He walked through the storm to the barn and lay down to sleep in the hay by his horse.

He awakened at dawn and turned toward his horse. Two Indians,

167

one young and one old, were sitting against the wall, facing him, an arm's length away. He sat up in terror.

"*Buenos dias,*" the old Indian said.

Snider's way to the door was blocked by the Indians.

"Calm yourself," the old Indian said in Spanish.

"What? What did you say?"

"*Calmate, calmate,*" the old Indian said calmly, and he motioned for Snider to settle down.

Snider saw that both Indians were eating jerky. The old Indian tore a strip off a large sheet of jerky by his side and handed it to the young Indian beside him. He did not take his eyes off Snider. The young Indian took the meat without looking at it. He did not look at anything.

The old Indian's hair was gray and he wore a hat of woven beargrass. He was very thin and dry. He picked up a cup made of half a gourd and poured dry *pinole* into it, unstoppered another gourd *bule* that he carried on a cord over his shoulder and poured water into the *pinole*. He stirred it into a paste and tried to hand it to the young Indian. The young Indian had not eaten the jerky, so the old one put it into his mouth for him. The young one started chewing it slowly and drawing it into his mouth.

The jerky and *pinole* had made Snider forget his terror.

The old Indian handed him the *pinole*. "Eat," he said and stood up. The young Indian stood up, too. The young one carried an immense quiver of arrows and a bow that was as tall as he. Both Indians carried large skinning knives. The old one had a horse pistol and a belt full of cartridges.

Snider took the *pinole*, about one mouthful, wiped it into his mouth with three swipes of his fingers, and threw the bowl away as though it was not worth keeping. The old Indian closed the *pinole* pouch and hung it around his neck beside another pouch.

Snider was hungry. He had only taken two mouthfuls of Maudy's stew before she ran him off. The thought of the stew made his mouth water. He stared at the sheet of jerky. The old Indian tore away a strip and handed it to him. Snider's saliva burst over it as he jammed it between his back teeth. He thought, I should have eaten that whole bowl of stew and brought all that bread of Maudy's with me. I should have killed her and the damned nigger before she had a chance to unload my pistol.

The old Indian led the young one over to the hay, took the quiver of arrows and the bow off his shoulders, and laid him down. He unwrapped a bandana from the young man's brow and inspected a poultice of green paste on a wound on his forehead. He took some leaves from a pouch that hung from his waist and put them in the young man's mouth. The young man closed his eyes.

Snider bridled and saddled his horse and went back to see if he might get a chance to steal the old Indian's food and pistol. Both Indians were asleep in the hay. Snider found an ax handle with which to bash their heads. He hefted it, and turned to hit the old Indian.

The old Indian was standing out of range. Snider made a lunge at him and the old Indian danced away and reached the door. Snider knew he would never be able to outrun the old devil, but he wanted the food and weapons. He gambled and used his head for once. He raised the ax handle over the young Indian's head.

The old Indian raised a hand and said, "No!"

Snider motioned for him to come to him and he took the pistol, cartridge belt, and jerky. He snatched both the pouches off the old man's neck. He swung the axhandle at the old man's head, but he dodged and got away. Snider laughed at him. The young Indian awakened and sat up. Snider grinned at the old Indian and clubbed the young one across the brow with the axhandle. He looked back and the old Indian was gone.

Snider picked up the gourd bowl, went out, and drew a bucket of water from the well and opened the heaviest *pinole* pouch. This time he was going to eat the whole sackful. He poured it out into the Indian's gourd cup. It looked different. There were some colored berries in it, too. Then he saw a diamond and the red berries were not berries, they were rubys. The other stones were blue, yellow, and green gems and the *pinole* was not *pinole* at all, it was placer gold.

Smiling, he very, very carefully, poured it all back into the pouch. He sat on the edge of the well, chewed on jerky, and felt prosperous for the first time in his life. He heard voices, and Royal Vincent rode into the yard. Snider looked around and saw his other VO comrades dismounting at the barn.

"Snider, where in the hell have you been?" Vincent said. "What are you doing out here all by yourself? Have you got anything to eat?"

Snider covered his wound. "I've been looking for you for days."

Somebody shouted that there was a dead Indian in the barn. Snider uncovered his hand. "I killed that Indian," he said. "He cut off my fingers."

Royal Vincent sat down on the edge of the well and drank water and chewed some of Snider's jerky while Snider told him a tale about how he had been jumped by two Indians. Snider had lost his fingers when one of the Indians tried to stab him and he was forced to grab the blade of the knife. He had chased that Indian into the barn and killed him.

Snider rode back to Harshaw with the VO and decided he would try to bluff his way back into respectability again as he had done before. He could always make a run for it to Chihuahua if it didn't work. After all, he was rich now.

Twenty-one

THE COWDEN LADIES went out into the front yard to holler and wave when they saw Les and his brothers on the road coming home. They laughed when they saw Les bringing up the rear on a mule. Les wished he could feel lighthearted. He had given the China girl the seat on his saddle and was riding behind her. His butt was sore from riding so far on the hair, gristle, and bone of a mule. He wished the trouble that caused him to have to do it was over.

He rode through the barn and straight up to the house and his sisters helped him put his cargo on the ground. The little girl was so wrapped and hidden in her clothes against the cold and travail that only a patch of her face could be seen.

The ladies took charge of her like a new doll and paid little attention to Les. Lorrie did not even come out. Les looked around for her and was about to turn away and take his mule to the barn, when he saw her face in a window. Her face was still very swollen. She smiled, though, and lifted her hand to wave. He hurried and unsaddled his mule and fed him, stopped to say hello to A.B. in his office, then hurried to the house to see Lorrie.

He was hugging Lorrie and trying to get her to give him a second kiss when Paula Mary and Betty came in. Paula Mary started laughing at him and even Betty smiled. Les asked what they imagined was so funny.

Paula Mary said, "You look like Mr. and Mrs. Paddy Ryan trying to kiss after they've been box-fighting each other."

Les and Lorrie were standing in front of a mirror with their arms around each other and they turned and looked at themselves. Both their eyes were black, the bridges of their boot-sculpted noses swollen flush with their foreheads. Les laughed, because he and Lorrie looked exactly alike.

Lorrie started crying and ran out of the room. Betty followed her. Paula Mary gave Les a dirty look and said, "Now what have you done?"

"Paula Mary, you did it again, didn't you?" Les said. He went out to find his wife, but she was not in sight. He looked outside and saw Betty disappearing into the orchard. Viney told him Lorrie had been going to the orchard when she wanted to be alone. Lorrie was used to privacy and the Cowdens did not provide enough of that for a newly married young woman. "But you know, son, it's not your family's responsibility to provide a private place for you and your bride," Viney said. "You will have to start building a place of your own pretty soon."

Les was not one to cross his mother in any way, so he did not try to remind her that he had been too busy to build a house.

"You know, son, you think too much is happening for you to think of making a home of your own. That might be true, but that's the reason people plan their homes years before they marry. You didn't plan anything and now, like it or not, excuses or not, your little bride is miserable."

Les thought, well, getting stomped in the face didn't help the poor thing, either. He went back to the barn to see why his brothers had not come to the house. He found them enjoying a drink of whiskey with A.B. in the office. He quickly looked away from their drinks so they would not see he wanted one. He knew A.B. and his brothers did not want to hurt his feelings, but they had seldom offered him a drink before he married Lorrie, so he sure did not want them to think they had to do it now.

Les drank three cups of water from an *olla* hanging by a window. A.B. gave him a cigar and he took a seat and lit it. He liked cigars. He didn't care if he did crave a drink, he didn't need the trouble it caused him. After a few puffs of the cigar, he would forget about it. He would take a drink when he could handle it better. After all he was twenty years old and ought to be able to handle his whiskey better than he'd been doing.

A new turn in the legal battle between Duncan Vincent and the U. S. government over Vincent's claims on the public land had brought Duncan home. He had lost the fight to own 200,000 acres of public land he had been trying to get. He had claimed the land was included in the San Rafael grant he bought from the Romeros in Santa Cruz, Sonora.

In truth, the Cowdens and Porters were more entitled to use the land than Vincent. Ben's Vaca homestead and Duke Porter's homestead were inside that land. Duncan Vincent was also found guilty of fencing the public land and the court ordered him to remove those barriers from the American Boy range immediately. In handing down his decision, Judge Bryan, associate justice of the Supreme Court, called the Vincent brothers "landgrabbers." Now the would-be kings were also being styled as land hogs, barn burners, and murderers by the *Harshaw Bullion, Arizona Star* and other territorial newspapers. Judge Bryan was an honest judge and had resisted all the pressures that were put on him by Vincent's lobbyists in Washington, D.C., the state capitol in Prescott, and in Pima County.

Another trouble that was being visited upon Duncan Vincent's head was the governor of Sonora's warrant for his arrest. Vincent was being blamed for murders his rangers had committed in Sonora and for leading them against Kosterlinsky's Rural Police at La Acequia. The governor called the La Acequia intrusion an invasion, a filibuster. The governor of Arizona had been asked to issue an order for Vincent's extradition to Sonora, but this request had been ignored because of Vincent's influence with politicians close to the governor.

Kosterlinsky was in Harshaw that day. Since everybody knew he could not serve his warrant on Vincent, A.B. figured he might be there to attend to his smuggling business with Vincent.

Lieutenant Buck's patrol was on its way to El Durazno with Maudy and Sergeant Broussard. A.B. had decided to bring the whole family under one roof. He expected the lieutenant and his troopers to arrive late that afternoon. Lieutenant Buck was bringing Maudy home as a favor, but the brothers were sure he would be glad to know they had arranged for him to talk to the Yawner.

A.B. warned his sons that Vincent had recruited seasoned fighters into his crew of cowboys at the ranch. The Cowdens could expect that Royal Vincent wanted to serve the warrant for Odoms's killing.

Les asked his father why he didn't arrest the Vincent brothers now that the VO had been found guilty of illegally fencing the public land. A.B. said that Vincent had only been ordered to take the fences down. He could not be arrested unless he failed to comply.

Paula Mary came to tell A.B. and the brothers that supper was ready and they all went up and washed on the back porch, then went in and put on clean shirts. The Chinese girl had been bathed and fed and put to bed in the girls' bedroom.

Les left the table early and went to the barn. He could be a wild, untiring man away from home. He could run and play, work and fight without ever drawing a long breath, but the minute he landed at home and ate supper, a great weariness came over him. He did not have time to wait and see what the sleeping arrangements would be now that Maudy was on the way. He climbed into the hay loft, collapsed, and was asleep before his carcass leveled itself in the hay.

He awakened late in the night, too late to go up and heat water for a bath, too sore to go right back to sleep. He would have liked to take a hot bath and soak out the soreness. He could hear Joe Coyle snoring. The lateness of the hour and the loss of the evening made him feel a sense of dread, because Maudy was not home yet and Lorrie was asleep. He regretted not having spoken to Lorrie after Paula Mary made her cry. His body ached, his heart ached, he needed rest because he might have to fight again at any time, and Maudy was not home.

The sound of horses on the road brought him to his feet. A cavalcade stopped in front of the barn and someone pounded on the double doors. Joe Coyle stopped snoring and opened the doors without even asking who was there. Les figured Joe must sure feel at peace, for he seemed not to care much about what might happen to him. If a Cowden snored and opened doors to anyone that came along, he would either be killed in his sleep or shot in his tracks.

Luckily for the Cowdens and Joe Coyle, the visitors were Lieutenant Buck, a platoon of cavalrymen, Maudy, and Sergeant Broussard. Les climbed down and gave the loft to the soldiers for a place to sleep. He walked Maudy to the house and was glad when he found Viney and Eileen awake. Maudy went straight to bed with Ben and Ben did not even have to get up. Now Les couldn't sleep in the loft or in a bed, so he unrolled his camp bed beside Mark in the front room and tried again.

He would have been able to sleep like a dead man if he did not have a wife. The thought of the one, solitary kiss that Lorrie had given him kept him awake. He thought he might even be able to sleep if he knew she would rather be with him than in a room with the warm, sweet-smelling covey of his sisters. The house was so dark he could barely see the outline of the girls' door. He lasted another quarter hour, then slipped out of his blankets, put on his trousers, and snuck into the girls' bedroom on his hands and knees.

He did not know where she was sleeping. He needed to sneak her out of there, if she would come. He should have known better than to go in there in the dark. He had never been in the girls' bedroom when they were all in there sleeping.

The Chinese girl had been put on a pallet with a down mattress and quilts and as he groped across the floor he grabbed her by the foot. He backed away from the small cry and the quiet stir he caused, remained still until everybody settled down, crept forward again, and saw stars from a blow on the end of his nose. The dealer of that blow must have been small, because it only made his eyes water. Before he could cry out and identify himself a dozen more blows were landed by much larger dealers and given with fists, or perhaps heavy bludgeons. Most of them only made lumps on him, but one landed viciously on his sore brow. He cussed, and another bashed him in the mouth. He was forced to cry out and run out the door before he was finally able to identify himself.

Betty lit a lamp and A.B., Mark, and Ben rallied to the room in a hurry. Viney and Maudy put on their wraps and went in, too. The family thought Les's trying to sneak in and kidnap his wife away from the Cowden tigresses was hilarious and Lorrie laughed as hard as everybody else.

Eileen took Les's hand and sat him down on the edge of the bed by Lorrie. She told him that as a reward for the extraordinary effort he'd made to be with his wife, he would be allowed to visit with her until everybody went back to bed.

Les smiled and took his ribbing, but he did not contribute a word and could not look at Lorrie. The only good that came out of the whole thing was the fun it gave everybody and the smile it gave Lorrie. He was not well enough disposed to public service to enjoy it much himself. When everybody subsided and he finally returned to his bedroll, he was so glad to find peace, he went right to sleep.

Les was the first one out in the morning. The soldiers were up with a cooking fire in the yard in front of the barn and he could smell their coffee. He walked out into the orchard to stretch his legs and found Patch and Casimiro sitting by a small fire. He returned to the house and brought back three cups and leftover coffee that he warmed on the Indians' fire.

Casimiro told Les about Chato's raid on his camp in the Rincons and Snider's killing of Arco and his rejoining the VO. He had tracked Chato all the way from the Rincons and suspected he was back in the Yawner's camp.

Patch wanted to go after Chato and had been waiting for the Cowdens to get up so he could make a *despedida*, a plea for his departure. He did not think the Cowdens needed him and he might have a chance to rescue his little sister, Casi.

Patch stood up to leave and shouldered Arco's giant bow and quiver. Les said that he had seen an arrow from a bow like that pass through Whitey Briggs's thigh and into his horse's heart and end both their lives. Patch said Arco was the only man in the country who had carried a bow that size. Les asked Patch if he would someday consent to tell Lorrie about Arco and the bow so he could prove to her once and for all that Whitey was not killed by the Cowdens. Patch agreed that she should be told the truth.

Les watched Patch and Casimiro hurry through the orchard at a pace they could keep for days, the Indians' peculiar, hipshot, almost lumbering gait. A man who did not know how smooth the gait was would think the Indians' steps were heavy on the ground, until he examined their tracks and saw that their feet scarcely brushed it.

Les watched them climb around the hill behind the house. As they reached a spot where the first sun of the day touched the hill, they saw something down at the barn that made them stop and turn back into the orchard. Les walked around the house to find out what they were looking at and saw Royal Vincent lead his VO rangers into the barnyard. The Campana brothers, Creswell, Packrat, and the Briggs brothers were in the bunch, but Les could not see Snider.

Les caught up to Patch and Casimiro and asked them to take horses from the corral so they could hurry and locate Chato and come back to the brothers. The Cowdens would go with Lieutenant Buck's patrol to the meeting with the Yawner. The Cowdens would meet with Patch and Casimiro at Thumb Butte before the patrol reached the Yawner's camp.

Les knew that Campana had told Vincent where the Yawner was

camped by now and Vincent would demand to accompany Lieutenant Buck's patrol. If Chato was with the Yawner, he had to be located before the great cavalcade appeared. He could not be captured and separated from Casi and Teresa unless he was taken by surprise. Patch agreed, and he and Casimiro went down to the corral to catch their horses.

Les carried the coffee pot back into the house. The ladies had risen and fixed themselves up and were cooking breakfast. A.B., Ben, and Mark brought Lieutenant Buck, Sergeant O'Kane, and Wash and Elk Briggs into the house, introduced them to the Cowden ladies and sat them down for breakfast.

Lieutenant Buck announced that Royal Vincent would suspend serving the warrant on the Cowden brothers if he and his men were allowed to accompany the patrol to the Yawner's camp. The Lieutenant agreed to allow the VO to go, only because he did not have the authority to stop them.

The Briggs brothers seemed to be in a good mood at first and began kidding their sister. The Cowden ladies warmed to them and told about the stunt Les had tried to pull the night before. The Briggses then became boisterous and said they didn't think Les should be blamed, because every miner, soldier, and cowboy who patronized Vince Farley's bar wanted to kidnap her.

Les did not like the implied insult to Lorrie or the way Sergeant O'Kane laughed and then stared at Lorrie's hips and breasts without raising his eyes to her face. Lieutenant Buck smiled into Lorrie's eyes so long it made her turn away. Les knew the soldiers frequented Uncle Vince's bar. His appetite turned into a pain in the pit of his stomach.

Viney said she was glad Lorrie's brothers finally came to see her and asked them why they hadn't brought Indiana and Hattie with them. The Briggses both smirked and Elk said they did not take their parents to ass-kickings. They had come to kick some goddammed Cowden ass because they heard Les was in the habit of beating their sister.

The room fell so silent that the ring of Joe Coyle's hammer on the anvil in the barn sounded clear as a church bell. The Briggses broke that silence by adding that they could see it was true that their sister had been beaten, so they would start kicking some goddammed Cowden ass as soon as breakfast was over. They made the statement in the same good-natured, easy manner they used when they kidded Lorrie. Then they began feeding themselves with both hands as though they ate breakfast with the Cowdens every morning.

Les held his tongue and ate some breakfast because he knew he needed to eat in order to be able to work and fight. He and his brothers would never have savaged the Briggses in front of their mother and Lorrie, even though the Briggses had practically asked to have it done on the spot and before another minute went by.

Nobody would get up from the table before A.B. either, so even though Les ate very little, he crossed his legs and asked for another cup of coffee. The Briggses finished eating, pushed their chairs back, lit their pipes, and were in no hurry to leave. They enjoyed the impression they made. They felt in control of the Cowdens. They mistook the Cowdens' good nature for fearfulness and foolishness.

Lorrie said to her brothers, "Now that you've had breakfast, do you want to hear my side of the story?"

Wash smiled through the smoke of his pipe. Elk pointed the stem of his pipe at Lorrie and said he did not give a particular god damn about hearing her story.

Mark had been sitting next to Wash, but now the Briggses had moved their chairs behind him. He was not finished with his breakfast, but his face darkened and he put down his fork and pushed his chair back against the wall.

Les envied Mark because he never turned pale when he was angry. All Les's blood left him for dead and retired to the pit of his stomach.

Before Lorrie could tell her brothers who had stomped her face, A.B. said, "Nor does the girl need to explain anything to anybody. Mr. Briggs, that was the third time you blasphemed at my table. You're welcome here, but I don't allow anyone to blaspheme or use bad words when my ladies are present."

"Well, I wasn't talking to your ladies," Elk said. "I was talking to my sister the barfly."

"Lorrie is a Cowden now, but even if she wasn't, I would require that you treat her with respect."

"Listen, old feller, I can see your women want people to think they're respectable and think they can make a respectable woman out of our sister, but that don't wash with us. We know our sister wouldn't be here if you were respectable. Hell, what kind of a man marries a barfly? All I see in this room are murderers, stage robbers, and cow-thieves. Hell, everybody knows Lorrie's new Cowden sisters stabbed Frank Marshall forty times with a pitchfork, then shot him full of buckshot. Now, we're sorry, but where we come from that just ain't respectable."

"You're wrong. I shot the coward," A.B. said. "And you just said another bad word at our table."

"So what, are you some kind of an old lady that can't stand to hear where you're going? Hell, didn't you know? You and our Lorrie're all bound for hell."

"That's it. That's all," Ben said. "Stand out of those chairs and head for the door."

The Briggses grinned, knocked the ashes out of their pipes in Viney's plates, shoved their hats back, and stood up. Les hurried out the door ahead of them so they would not get away. Elk hurried up close behind him.

Les was in the habit of leaving his spurs on his boots all the time. He usually took his boots off when he went in the house, because Viney did not like anyone to scuff her furniture with their spurs. He did not like to strap on his spurs when he went outside and have to unstrap them and take them off when he went back in the house. Every once in a while he snuck into the house with his spurs on and he had done it the night before.

Wash Briggs stepped on one of Les's spurs and nailed his foot to the ground. When Les stumbled, he released it and shoved him down on his face. Like soldiers in a drill, the Briggs brothers marched the length of him. Ben and Sergeant O'Kane pushed them off before they could do a countermarch over the top of him again.

"I don't care what you do away from this house, but I'll shoot the first Briggs who draws a gun or throws a punch in front of my wife and girls," A.B. said. "Take yourselves behind the barn for that business."

Sergeant O'Kane was a big, strong man the same size as the Briggses. He took them by the upper arms and started them toward the barn. "To the barn we go," he said.

The Briggses had stomped Les's sore shoulder again, so he could not lift it. He must have carried it badly for a moment, because Mark bravely stepped up and told him he would fight for him that day. Mark could not punch hard enough to kill a fly, was not vicious enough even to kill a fly unless he was angry. He was angry enough to be able to kill a fly that morning, but not a good enough fighter to whip even anyone as big as his little sister Paula Mary unless he used a pistol or a rifle. Les thanked him and told him he and Ben could watch his back so he would only have to worry about one Briggs at a time. He did not like sonsabitches walking on him single file.

Lieutenant Buck went back to his unit and informed the soldiers and VO rangers that an ass-kicking between the Briggses and the Cowdens was about to take place. The gang of soldiers and gunsels followed him to the south side, the sunny side, of the barn.

As much as the Cowden brothers fought, their mother had never seen them in a battle and never asked them anything about their fights. She did not think they liked to fight and she did not like them to fight.

Because of his mother, Les took off his clean shirt. He thought, by god, this time at least I'll save my shirt. He was being given more time to prepare for this fistfight than ever before.

He turned to hand his shirt, hat, and pistol belt over the top of the fence to Mark and caught sight of Snider. The north side of the corral was the barn's south wall. Snider came out of the barn and leaned against the wall to warm himself in the sun while he watched the fight.

Elk grinned for a bunch of shouting VO rangers as he took off his coat, hat, and gunbelt. Wash held his brother's things and stood against the wall by Snider. A.B. and Ben came out of the barn and stood on the other side of the door from Wash. Elk reached inside his coat pocket and took out a heavy pair of miner's gloves and slipped them on.

Elk and Les headed toward each other, but Sergeant O'Kane stepped between them and announced that he and his soldiers wanted a fair fight. There would be no stomping, kicking, gouging, hitting a man when he was down, or ganging up two on one. Soldiers of the United States could not be witnesses to an unfair fight and would not allow one. Then Sergeant O'Kane got out of the way.

Les Cowden had never lost an evenly matched fight and he was a fast learner. His last fair fight had been a kicking, gouging, stomping, toe-to-toe fistfight with Captain Jack Odoms. Odoms was an older and wiser fighter than Les. Les had not won or lost the fight, but he was the one who walked away from it, and he learned a lot about fighting a taller man that day. He learned how a man who knew the range of his punches could have an advantage over an opponent who did not.

Les walked up to the towering, grinning Elk Briggs and, as soon as he was in range, jabbed him in his grinners. Elk would have been able to keep him away if he had known his range, because his arms were a foot longer than Les's. Les was cool enough to step inside the danger zone and jab him again. He hit Elk so hard that time that Elk's mouth bled. Elk swung at him with bent arms and fanned the air a yard short. Les could not throw a straight punch with his right shoulder, so he walked in again and slammed Elk with a straight left, then shoveled a right uppercut into Elk's solar plexis that dropped him on his face as though he'd been shot in the spine.

Sergeant O'Kane shouted, "No boots, Cowden," and checked Les from stomping the gray matter out of Elk's head. Les stood over him so he could start punching the moment Elk's knees came off the ground, but the man did not get up. He rolled over on his back and closed his eyes.

"You killed him," Wash shouted. "You killed my brother." He looked crazy. Ben started toward him.

Les was out of his head with anger. "Get the son of a bitch on his feet," he said. "I'm not through with him." He stepped up and spurred Elk hard in the ribs.

"No boots, now, Cowden," Sergeant O'Kane shouted.

Les grabbed Elk by the hair and dragged him toward the horse trough. Wash threw down everything of Elk's except his pistol. As the hat and coat and pistol belt settled toward the ground, the pistol slid out in his hand. He cocked it waist high and pointed it at Les.

Ben pounded his pistol down on Wash's hat so hard he brought dust out of his boots. The bullet missed Les and Wash sat down hard between his heels, asleep with his eyes open.

Les tried to drown Elk in the horse trough, but he couldn't worry him enough to make him stand. Finally he realized the man's breath had not returned from the punch he'd taken in his middle. He let him lay down. Without looking at Snider, he headed that way.

Snider was wary enough, but he did not have a place to go to get away, unless he turned and ran toward the soldiers sitting on the corral fence. Cowdens blocked every other way out. As Les walked toward him, he watched Les's face for a clue as to what he intended to do. He took one uncertain step toward the soldiers and Les headed him off, then he took another toward the door and Ben headed him off.

Snider realized Les was indeed coming for him. He raised his hand in front of his face to show Les he had been maimed, but that was a mistake. Les grabbed the hand and squeezed it, then stuck a hook in his ear. Snider wailed as though Les was killing him and tried to throw himself on the ground. Les was not killing him, though. He gripped his hand tighter and did not let him go down. He began to drum his head against the barn with punches to the middle of his nose. He played staccato with his head against the barn until he was unconscious and then let him down to the ground.

Elk was on his feet bathing his face in the trough. Les fell on him, but only stunned him. He whirled to face Les with his hands down to show he was through fighting. Les stepped in close and began winging hooks into his head. He was six inches shorter than Elk. Elk's big target of a head towered above him and Les kept it up there. The effect of his blows on the head was almost as bad as it would have been if Les had been carrying hay hooks. He butchered Elk Briggs's head and kept flaying it, carving it, and fileting it until Elk passed out, folded in the middle, and sat down in the trough with his head against the fence. Les submerged the head with blows and was waiting for it to resurface when Ben and Sergeant O'Kane dragged him off.

Twenty-two

LES WAS NOT TIRED of thumping on his enemies. As soon as Ben and Sergeant O'Kane turned him loose, he looked for Snider again, but Royal had removed him from the battleground. A.B. wanted to arrest Snider for the murder of Garbie Burr and the assault on Lorrie, but Vincent maintained that Snider was as immune from arrest as the Cowdens. Lieutenant Buck backed Royal on that. No complaint had been signed against Snider. Royal maintained that Garbie's death had been an accident and Snider struck Lorrie in self defense. A full-fledged murder warrant had been issued for the Cowdens.

The brothers saddled their horses, packed another horse with their beds and provisions, and went to the house to say good-bye to their mother, wives, and sisters. Les could not find Lorrie and he did not want to ask anyone where she was. His mother and sisters coolly gave him their cheeks to kiss. He was about to head back to the barn when Betty pointed toward the orchard with her chin and told him Lorrie was out there. He found her sitting on a big, smooth rock that all the Cowdens used from time to time when they were sad or glad.

Les sat on the ground beside her. She turned away from him and said, "Well, did you kill any more of my brothers?"

Les laughed quietly. "Not hardly."

"You got even, though, I suppose?"

"I'm good until the next time they try to stomp me or shoot me, I guess."

"Well, that's something."

Mark called for Les. The patrol was mounted and ready to leave.

"Can we talk a minute?" Les said.

"What do you want to talk about?"

"Anything you do."

"What could that be?"

"I don't know. What do women like to talk about? Having homes, dishes, and things . . . babies . . . or something like that?"

Lorrie turned to him. "You beat up my brother and try to drown him in the horse trough one minute and then ask me if I want to talk about a home and babies in the next? What kind of nut are you?"

"You saw the fight? Where were you?"

"What fight? It looked like murder to me. Me and your sisters got up on the hill in time to see you knock my brother into the horse trough. You hit him from behind and never gave him a chance to fight back. Your sisters were as appalled as I was."

"Lorrie, you missed the whole thing. It was a fair fight. You only saw how it ended."

Lorrie shook her head. "You're a goddammed crazy man. How can you talk to anybody about babies?"

Les stood up and said lamely, "I didn't start it. You were there in the kitchen when your brothers started the fight."

"That part of it was just talk. That didn't compare with what you did to my brother. I didn't know anyone could do that to another person."

"My lord, Lorrie, don't act so innocent. Look what you and Snider did to each other. You were in a war, weren't you? Well, so was I."

Mark called again and Les said, "I have to go."

"Maybe that's what's bothering me," Lorrie said.

"What *is* bothering you, dammit?"

"What bothers me is the way we both act in a fight."

"Hell almighty, how's a person supposed to act in a fight?"

"I don't fight fair and you don't, either."

Mark called and sounded desperate. Les said, "Well, all I've got to say is, this is one hell of a courtship we're having here," and he left her.

Les's feelings were hurt, so he went back to the kitchen. His sisters did not turn to look at him. He stopped inside the the door and announced that it was not his fault that he was in trouble with the women in his family. It was too bad they had decided to sneak around and watch the fight, but they hadn't seen what they thought they saw. Before they made him out to be a madman they should talk to A.B. He saw the fight from start to finish. He guessed the only way he could get Lorrie and his sisters to care about him again was to let the Briggs brothers stomp him again. His sisters must prefer having to pick him up and patch him up and giving him soup to sip after a fight.

By the time Les made it to the barn and mounted his horse, everybody was gone. When he caught up to the cavalcade, his brothers were in the lead with Lieutenant Buck. The road between Les and his brothers was crammed with horsemen, so he had to be content to stay in the rear.

He liked being behind the VO where he could look them over. He would not have liked them giving the back of his neck hateful stares. The Briggses were not in the cavalcade, but Snider was. Les figured Royal would have to be as careful of Snider's welfare as his guardian angel. He would be a fool to let him be arrested and questioned. Of all the VO constables, Snider and Stiles knew the most about the Vincents' wrongdoing. Those two and Campana knew enough about them to put them in jail. Snider better watch himself. Les might not be the only one who wanted to see him dead.

Creswell was up in the lead of the VO. Les was glad to be behind him, too. Creswell could not be too happy with Les for shooting off the end of his nose. The bandage for his nose covered most of his face and was held in place by a gauze wrap around his head.

Lieutenant Buck stopped the column and Ben waved Les forward. To a man the VO riders turned to look at Les and not one moved his horse aside to make room so he could keep his horse on the road on his way to the front. Les was riding a horse he called Goose, a tall, big-footed horse with great balance.

The cavalcade was under a bluff. The hill was steep, rocky, and brushy on the downhill side of the road. Les put Goose off the road on the uphill side and rode above the heads of the VO so Goose could kick rocks on them. The rangers shouted their indignity at Les for being so discourteous while they scattered out of the way of the rocks.

The soldiers ahead of the VO moved aside so Les could come back to the road. The VO and the army had been at odds since the VO's arrival. The army considered the VO to be a threat to the success of the mission. Lieutenant Buck's troopers had soldiered with the Cowdens against the Yawner at Los Metates and Los Bultos and had rooted for Les in the fight.

The patrol was being guided by the Apache scouts Ben Tom and Lacy Greer, so the Cowdens left the column and hurried ahead. They followed the Sonoita Creek trail and reached Thumb Butte three hours before sundown.

Patch and Casimiro were resting by a fire and the brothers made coffee. The Indians had cleaned and widened a spring so the brothers could water their horses. They had made a careful reconnaisance of the Yawner's camp and found Casi and Teresa. Teresa was working with the women, Casi with the children. Teresa was not being mistreated because Fausto stayed close to her.

The brothers and Patch rode straight to the Yawner's camp. Casimiro circled stealthily to watch the camp without being seen. The brothers hoped to distract Chato when they went in to talk to the Yawner so Casimiro could take the child.

One of the Yawner's warriors led the brothers to an open flat on the northeast side of Pajarito Peak. The Yawner, Chato, and a warrior Les's age named Alfonso were waiting for them by a fire. Women and children held the band's livestock nearby. Les could not tell the women from the girls, but one of them caught his attention because she was limping, and he thought he recognized Teresa. She had covered a lot of country in a hurry in the past week or two and she was bound to be footsore and tired.

Casimiro would not be able to spirit Casi off the edge of the band because all the women and children were together on the open flat. Les counted fourteen warriors standing on the perimeter of the flat. The furthest was only fifty yards away. Only a few were armed with pistols or rifles, the rest with bows and full quivers of arrows.

The Yawner's savage old face was set like granite. He greeted the brothers, but did not ask them to dismount. He did not waste time letting them know that he was dissatisfied. He said, "We are warriors, Horseman. I agreed to speak to the Jackrabbit because he is a soldier and understands the load I carry in my heart. I did not expect you to bring the town dogs."

"The ones you correctly call the town dogs are mostly harmless and are here because of politics, Yawner," Ben said. "If they cause trouble, my brothers and the Jackrabbit and his soldiers will take your side against them."

"What is this 'politics'? I don't know what this is."

"Do you have a wife?"

"Yes."

"Does she have an old bothersome mother?"

"Yes."

182

"Does that old lady have an old sister who pesters her to bother you?"

The Yawner showed the glimmer of teeth. "Yes."

"The bother the *viejas* cause you is called politics. Have the old sister and mother-in-law seemed like enemies who think they have the right to govern you because they are connected to your family through your wife?"

"Yes."

"That's politics. All men who try to do good, honest work are bothered by it. The politicians attach themselves to us like ticks on our backs so they can be sure they get a share in everything we do. If we prosper, they fatten on our life's blood. If we fail, they jump off and grope around blindly until they can find another back to bite."

The Yawner asked the brothers and Patch to dismount. Patch squatted on his heels and held the horses.

Alfonso walked around the fire to shake hands with the brothers, then went over to shake hands with Patch. He and Patch did not smile at each other. He returned to his place by the fire to stare fiercely at the brothers.

Patch positioned himself slightly to Chato's rear, but Chato did not allow that for long. Without rising off his heels, he pivoted so he could watch Patch and the Cowdens equally well. He listened to Ben and the Yawner with an old coyote's expression on his face.

As crafty, greedy, and mean as he was, Chato was too unsophisticated to hide his crafty, mean, greedy thoughts. They showed on his face as plainly as his nose. Nobody, not even the devil, could tell what the Yawner was thinking unless he wanted them to. He still had not shown friendliness. The glimmer of a smile that he sometimes showed was never reflected in his eyes.

The Yawner told Ben that anyone could see his band was not strong. His experience with townsmen made him suspect that this day might not end well. He knew to expect respectful treatment from the Horsemen and the soldiers, but he did not believe the townsmen came to honor him. They probably wanted at least to bark and nip at his heels and force the lieutenant to hang him.

Ben spent the next hour placating the Yawner. He said that he and his brothers were there to defend the Apache from scorn, mockery, and treachery. He and his brothers would see that the Yawner did not have to deal with the townsmen. The townsmen were as much the enemies of the Horsemen as they were of the Apache. Their presence was only political and would not affect the disposition of the agreement reached by the Yawner and the United States Army.

Lieutenant Buck showed proper courtesy when he arrived at the flat. The bugler played ruffles and flourishes in honor of the Yawner and Lieutenant Buck was escorted forward by only an honor guard. The

Yawner asked him to dismount and his guard wheeled about and loped back to the main body. Lieutenant Buck gave the Yawner, Alfonso, and Chato tobacco. They immediately rolled it in cornleaf and began to smoke.

In Spanish, with Lacey Greer as Apache interpreter, Lieutenant Buck asked the Yawner if he or any of his band needed medical treatment or food. The Yawner told Lieutenant Buck that his band was small, hungry, defenseless, but not sick.

He said that, after most of his warriors had been massacred at Los Bultos by combined Mexican and American forces led by the Horseman and his brothers, he had lain wounded in the brush and watched Lieutenant Buck's soldiers bury the Apache dead. After the buffalo soldiers had come up from Los Molinos in the valley of Altar and joined the white soldiers, the Yawner and Chato had been forced to slip past the light of their camp fires one night in order to make their escape.

The Yawner's wounds forced him to travel a route that provided water. The only trail with enough water to accommodate him was the one back to the Santa Ritas. He and Chato had found Alfonso and these few men, women, and children when they reached those mountains.

Lieutenant Buck said that the Yawner and Chato might be tried for murders that had been committed on Apache raids during the past year. He asked the Yawner if he was in possession of the woman, Teresa, who had been taken captive by Chato at El Relave.

The Yawner told him that he would never surrender. He might make the decision to return to San Carlos if Lieutenant Buck promised that no harm would come to him or anyone else in his band. No one should be tried for fighting or taking prisoners in a war. Every warrior must be shown respect. The Yawner had fled San Carlos before because he had not been shown respect there. Respect must be shown him if he was to return. He did not consider being tried and hanged for fighting a war to be signs of respect. The band must also be allowed to keep all its livestock as it did when he had consented to return to San Carlos before.

Lieutenant Buck said he was not the final authority on the matter. His superiors would have to make the decisions on whether or not to grant the Yawner's terms. Now, would the Yawner accompany him to the railhead in Calabasas tomorrow? Lieutenant Buck wanted to load the band on the train and take it to Fort Lowell in Tucson.

The Yawner looked to Ben Cowden, as though he expected Ben to answer the question. Ben told Lieutenant Buck that the Yawner expected to be escorted to Huachuca. He wanted to travel overland and take his livestock.

Lieutenant Buck agreed to escort the band to Patagonia where the livestock could be loaded on a train for Camp Huachuca. Would the Yawner agree to travel by rail from Patagonia to Camp Huachuca if his livestock was carried on the same train?

The Yawner said he wanted the lieutenant to promise that upon his return to San Carlos, his people would be allowed the freedom of making *tesguino,* homemade corn beer, with no restrictions, no restraints, and no arguments. Were the Apaches considered to be such children that they be denied the right to make the beer they had enjoyed for generations? A fight over the white man's disrespect for the Apache and his right to make and drink *tesguino* had been the cause of his breaking away from the reservation the previous May.

Lieutenant Buck said he did not have the authority to make that promise, but he would recommend that the Apache be allowed to make *tesguino.* He asked the Yawner if he could be ready to be escorted to Patagonia early the next day and the Yawner went on to other conditions he would require, other needs he wanted satisfied.

Thus the discussion of terms went on and on Apache style until sunset. The foes tried each others' patience, for this was the last defense the old Yawner would make. If he was to surrender his freedom and keep his honor, he wanted to win peace and contentment. Les was almost sure the Yawner and Alfonso had decided to return to the reservation, but Chato's face showed plainly that he would not abide by any agreement they made. He could no more be expected to abide by a rational agreement between the Yawner and Lieutenant Buck than an old coon could be caught out of a tree, turned loose in a house, and expected not to make a mess.

The talk between Lieutenant Buck and the Yawner dragged on too long to suit Royal Vincent and he brought his men forward to make sure everyone knew he should be included in the contention. That brought Sergeant O'Kane forward to detain him. Royal began to argue in a loud voice and O'Kane was joined by two other noncommissioned officers. Royal motioned the VO forward until his rangers stood their horses ten yards from the Yawner's fire.

Royal saw that the Yawner's band was small and undermanned and shouted in English, "What in the hell is all the talk about? Let's take 'em down to Calabasas, lock 'em on the train, and be done with them. Me and my men have waited long enough. We're not camping here tonight with these savages at our throats."

The VO rangers were not content to sit their horses in a column behind their leader. They spread out in a half circle beside him to look at the Yawner. This move disturbed the Apache livestock and it began to drift toward a wash behind the Yawner with the women and children running to contain it.

Snider crowded Lieutenant Buck with his horse and said, "Mister, my wife is over there with that bunch of savages and I want her brought to me, *now.*" He was so excited his horse danced in place and made the three Apaches stand up and move out of the way. The Cowden brothers aligned themselves beside Alfonso and the Yawner with their backs to a boulder.

Snider's horse whirled away from the Indians. Chato lazily stooped and picked up a rock. Snider turned in the saddle, pointed at Chato, and shouted, "You sonofabitch, Chato. Babykiller!" He pulled his pistol and reined his horse around so he could fire at Chato. Chato bounced the rock off Snider's temple and Snider's bullet struck something way off target and whined away into a canyon. Snider slumped over his horse's shoulder. Chato screamed, grabbed him by the hair, snatched him off his horse, and before his legs cleared the saddle plunged his knife into his throat.

The Yawner and Alfonso stayed against the wall and did not raise their hands. Royal fired at Chato from his dancing horse and missed. The VO horses panicked and rangers fired in every direction. The Cowden brothers fired under the VO horses and over their heads to further their panic. Someone raised up behind the Yawner and the Cowdens and fired a volley that emptied three VO saddles.

Chato fell on his knees beside Snider, pulled back his head, chewed and ground his teeth like a javelina, and stuck his blade into the man's throat again. He twisted the blade and searched with it to find the artery, then pulled it out ahead of a fountain of blood. Then he jerked a leather pouch off Snider's neck and ran away.

Lieutenant Buck ran into the melee and shouted and waved his arms to stop the firing. The column of troopers split the VO in two and subdued the rangers with rifle butts and fists.

Les looked around and the Yawner and Alfonso were gone. He saw the women and children go over the ridge into Calabasas Canyon behind the troopers and the VO. Royal Vincent's horse ran away with him toward home.

The brothers mounted their horses and Les and Patch ran to find Teresa. They topped the Calabasas Canyon ridge in time to see the women and children fleeing down the hill.

Patch turned away from the women and ran along the ridge as though he knew what he was doing, so Les followed him. Patch began to pour the coal to Colorado and Les marveled at the horse's speed and endurance. He knew Colorado had not been given rest for a week. He was so thin his hip bones stuck out and a man could almost see through the hide of his flanks, yet he did not slacken.

Les stuck Goose on Colorado's tail and gave him his head. Goose followed the other horse as any rope horse should and gave Les freedom to look around. Patch was watching the ground for tracks and watching the terrain for footing. Les watched for the quarry.

They hit a wide trail that led straight south and struck the fresh, running tracks of two horses. Now Les and Patch could both give their horses their heads and watch for Fausto and Teresa.

Les knew the country. The trail was on a high, rocky ridge that rose steadily from white oak and *bellota* country into piñon, cedar, and jack pine. Les and Patch reached the side of the last peak in the Pajarito chain, looked down on lesser, rockier peaks, and could see a long way into Mexico. Good trails from Pesqueira Creek and Potrero and Walker canyons converged on this trail, and this became the only one to Mexico. Pedregoso Mountain across the line in Sonora was dead ahead. The tracks of Fausto's horses were so fresh, Les could almost smell the frogs of the hooves, could almost see the mud settle inside the broken ground.

Fausto would know he was being pursued and lay an ambush. Les and Patch were foolhardy to chase him with so much abandon. All he had to do was stop, take dead aim, and shoot them off their horses. Les only hoped they could sight him before he realized they were close.

Colorado shuddered, stumbled, and ran on as Les saw the smoke of a shot belch out of brush by the trail ahead. Les stuck Goose off the downhill side of the trail and out of sight of the shooter. Another shot sounded. Les dismounted with his rifle, climbed up to the trail and fired into the brush. Colorado was still running up the trail. Suddenly, he stumbled again and began to weave. He fell and Patch rolled out in front of him, regained his feet, and ran over the hill out of sight.

Les jumped up and ran up the trail after Patch. Colorado lay on his side, but he raised his head when Les ran by. Les topped the hill and saw Patch kneel on a slab of flat rock, string the big bow, and fit one of the arrows in it. He sat on the rock with both feet on the bow, drew the string with both arms, then relaxed.

Fausto was not in sight. Les heard rocks rattle in the canyon below. Fausto appeared horseback at the bottom leading the horse Teresa was riding. He started climbing the trail on the other side of the canyon. He must have thought he had stopped his pursuers, because his pace was almost leisurely as he allowed his horses to pick their own way in the climb.

As Fausto traversed the hill, he made the best target for Les's rifle. Teresa was below Fausto and away from the line of fire.

"Wait, Patch," Les said. He sat on the rock next to him, braced his rifle between his legs, and fired a round that stunned Fausto's horse to his knees. The animal recovered and Fausto tried to make him continue, so Les hit him with another round. The horse lunged under the impact, then reared over backward and tumbled down the hill on top of Fausto. Teresa's horse braced himself against the pull of the lead rope and jerked it free of Fausto's grip. Fausto's horse landed in a narrow, rocky wash on top of him.

Fausto lay still as Les slid down the hill toward him. Teresa dismounted and looked down at Fausto. He lay on his side with a leg under his horse. She picked up a rock as big as Les's hat, raised it overhead, yelled, *"¡Hijo de tu chingada madre!* Son of your fornicated mother!"* and smashed it down on Fausto's head. Her young voice was so pure and musical that it made Les smile. She looked around for another boulder suitable for smashing Fausto's head.

The wounded horse saw Les coming and used his last strength to stand. Fausto's foot was caught in the stirrup and when the horse stood up he rolled Fausto on his back. The Apache-made willow stirrup had been crushed in the fall and Fausto's foot was trapped inside. The horse was too near death to run and drag him. He stood on braced legs and trembled as his life waned. Les caught his bridle rein and freed Fausto's foot and let it drop. He led the horse away and shot him in the cavalryman's spot on his forehead, the place where two lines a soldier would have chalked between his ears and his eyes would have crossed. The horse dropped dead at Les's feet.

Les heard the sound of feathered hardwood and flint on the wind. One of Patch's big arrows buried itself in the middle of Fausto's chest and he screamed and came back to life to die. He had been playing dead, even after Teresa's rock nearly split his skull. The big shaft through his sternum was final. He flopped and arched his back and the tip came out of the ground under his back. He flopped again and gulped for air like a fish on a spear. He stared at Patch, but could not move as Patch picked up one of his hands and cut off the fingers.

Teresa hissed, *"¡Si, si, si!"* as Patch systematically mutilated Fausto so his body would not serve him in the next life. While Fausto squirmed and screamed, Patch bent over him and carefully, painstakingly began butchering him.

Les tried to help Teresa back on her horse, but she balked and sat on the ground to watch Patch finish Fausto.

Les mounted her horse and rode back up the hill to look for Goose. Goose had just made the decision to trail his reins and head for home. Les caught him and loosened the cinches of both horses, sat down, and waited. When Patch and Teresa caught up, Les tried to talk to her, but all she could do was cry and cuss.

Patch took his saddle off Colorado and put it on Teresa's horse. He knelt and cut a lock from Colorado's mane.

He and Teresa rode her horse double and Les led the way back to the flat. They met Ben and Mark coming up the trail tracking them.

Ben told Les that four warriors had been hiding and holding horses close by the Yawner during the talk. When the shooting started, Alfonso and the Yawner simply mounted and rode away. Ben and Mark tried to follow them, but pulled up when they were fired on. The Yawner had slipped away to his old haunts and would probably never talk to the Cowdens or any other white man again. Chato, Casimiro, and Casi had disappeared.

At the flat, half the VO constables were afoot and the other half had run off trying to catch loose horses. The brothers looked down into Snider's face and were not sorry he was dead. The soldiers had rounded up the Apache women and children. The brothers found their pack-horse dragging his lead rope and grazing toward home, left Patch to help Lieutenant Buck, and headed home with Teresa.

Twenty-three

DUNCAN VINCENT'S new constables made an armed camp of Harshaw. The forty men were tough, hardened, mature, neat in appearance, and in evidence everywhere except the saloons. Their leader, Ted Randolph, had ordered them to walk the town in pairs like policemen on a beat, so everyone could see them.

A.B. sat at his place on the hotel veranda during the morning as some of these new, more respectable constables trooped in for coffee in the dining room. They kept to themselves and barely spoke to anyone. A.B. guessed they were probably experienced former lawmen or veterans of security agencies such as the Pinkertons. They probably believed they were on a crusade to bring law and order to Harshaw and the rest of southern Arizona.

By weight of numbers and appearance, these men took over the town for the VO without a word or deed. A.B. was almost amused, because they would still have to go through him to make an arrest or use the jail.

Evidently Duncan Vincent had told these strangers that A.B. Cowden did not count at all. They ignored him, even though he wore the badge of undersheriff and they were junior officials who were technically and legally under his authority. Each man glanced at him out of the corner of his eye for a first look in the morning, but none greeted him. A.B. thought it was a shame they were on the wrong side, because they looked tough and well-principled. He could tell by the way they carried themselves and their weapons that they had good sense and were probably good marksmen. He had gone to Eddie Newton's barn to look at their horses and they were well-mounted. No doubt about it, they made a formidable impression on everybody in the town.

It remained to be seen how far they would go to win the war for Duncan Vincent. A.B. believed they intended to keep a grip on the town, but he would not worry about it until both of the Vincent brothers, Von and Randolph, and all their rangers were in town at the same time.

He tried to locate Von and Randolph as soon as he could every morning. He believed Von had gone with Royal to the Pajaritos, but he was not sure. He was not always able to keep accurate track of those two agents. They had been in Harshaw several days before they let people know they were special agents for the U. S. Department of the Interior. That was not great news to A.B. He had dispatched the Department of Interior's last special agent to other jurisdictions with a fatal load of double-aught buckshot.

The Harshaw people had been giving him questioning looks. Finally, Edna Farley, Viney's sister and the wife of Vince Farley, walked up to him on the veranda and asked what he was going to do about all the cold-looking constables who were crowding the streets. There were even more constables in Harshaw than there were evil thoughts. They were wearing such righteous looks that Edna had begun to examine her conscience to see if she had done anything wrong to offend some god she did not know. A.B. laughed, Edna laughed, and Edna went on down the street with her little daughter Myrtle, Paula Mary's best friend.

A.B. watched them. Every time Edna walked by a VO she swished her skirts and swung her purse on its string to make sure she was given enough room to pass. She would then make some remark to Myrtle and they would both laugh. That made other folks smile and soon the constables were looking around self-consciously to see who the people were laughing at.

At midmorning Antonio Campana and Royal Vincent showed up at the hotel. A.B. was surprised to see them alone and without the rest of Royal's rangers. He had not noticed when the VO returned to town. They must have snuck in the back way. Usually the rangers ran up the main street in a bunch, made a big show, and went straight in the saloons without even attending their horses.

Campana showed that he had spent a few ordinary days on the trail, but Royal was in a state of desolation. His hat had lost its crease, his splendid jacket its buttons, his cheek was smeared with blood from a nosebleed, his holster was empty, and he was walking spraddle-legged as though his trousers chafed tender surfaces. He climbed the veranda stairs by pulling himself up the bannister, barely glanced at A.B., and went up to his office.

A.B. had been waiting for Campana to come to town, because he intended to arrest him for his part in the smuggling of the Chinese children, and for conspiracy in the murder of Garbie Burr. A.B.'s sons had told him about meeting Campana and a packtrain of Chinese children on the trail, had even brought one of the children home, so A.B. wanted Senor Campana to tell him who his bosses were. A.B.

hoped the Lord would give him the singular honor of taking the Vincents to jail for trafficking, buying, and selling children and ordering Garbie's murder.

Any time was right for arresting Antonio Campana, but A.B. wanted to wait until the Vincents came out to make their usual show of arrogance. Showing arrogance was about the only offensive tactic they were able to exercise, so they did it whenever they could.

A.B. knew the Vincents had conspired with Campana many times to break the law. Anybody who hired Antonio Campana could tell by his looks that he owned a talent for conspiracy. Campana greatly respected and feared the Cowdens and he would blab his gizzards out when A.B. ordered him to talk about his association with the VO. If he did not want to answer A.B.'s questions, he could answer to Les. A.B. did not mind using his son's hard fists to make Campana tell his story. The Cowden brothers had warned Campana that they would kill him if he did not quit the VO, yet he kept right on helping them. He would not want to become the prisoner of A. B. Cowden. He could not expect the Cowdens to be tolerant forever.

Three of Royal's scattered cadre of rangers came straggling into town. They tied their tired horses in the street and went into a saloon. Two of them had lost their hats, a sure sign they had been running from something scary and not looking back. Their horses were sunken-flanked and hollow-eyed and the sweat had run through their long winter hair and dried to salt many times.

Duncan Vincent came out on the veranda with Campana, Ted Randolph, and Billy Stiles. Stiles remarked on the tired VO horses in front of the saloon. Duncan immediately dispatched him to the saloon to fire the men. He then caught sight of A. B. Cowden and was so surprised and offended by the sight of his enemy that he turned pale around the nose, threw back his head, and nodded a curt hello.

Randolph offered his hand to A.B. "How are ya, Cowden?"

A.B.'s attention locked on Campana. He stepped around Randolph and said, "Antonio Campana, I arrest you on suspicion of murder, conspiracy, and the unlawful transportation of aliens."

Campana's instinct was to jump and run, but he was too tired. A.B. grabbed him by the back of the neck, shoved his face into the wall, took his pistol and knife, and turned him around.

In Spanish, A.B. quietly ordered Campana to raise his hands above his head and walk ahead of him to his buggy behind the hotel. Campana assured him that he would not cause trouble. He was not a fighter.

A.B. turned toward Duncan and Randolph and drew his pistol, a beautiful, ivory handled Colt .45 with an eight-inch barrel. "If you think you can impede this arrest, do it now before my back is turned. Act now while I'm facing you. No? Then back up."

191

Duncan and Randolph dragged their feet back into the hotel. Two of the new constables started out through the same door, saw Campana with his hands up, stopped in the doorway, and stared at A.B.'s big pistol. "You hired trash back up with your boss," A.B. said, and waved them inside with his pistol.

A.B. chained Campana in the back seat of his buggy and headed for the new jail in Patagonia. That jail was manned by a jailer and a guard and equipped with an office. The one-room Harshaw jail would have been a dangerous place to keep Campana. A.B. might not even have been able to keep him alive in there.

On his way to Patagonia, A.B. met Joe Coyle driving Viney, Eileen, Maudy, and the Chinese girl to town. He stopped and told them that Harshaw was not the best place for a Cowden at that moment. They told him they only intended to visit Frank Wong so he would talk to the girl for them. Viney and the girls did not even know her name. Frank Wong's was the main hangout for the VO and not the best place for his family to visit, but A.B. did not try to stop Viney from going. Harshaw was Viney Cowden's town. If the VO threatened her, A.B. was confident the people of Harshaw would run them clear out of the county.

When Viney came to town, everybody perked up. The sight of the smiling Cowden women arriving in town at a brisk pace behind the big gray horses Smoke and Blue made the townspeople feel good. The Cowdens always dressed up when they went to town and seemed to feel a special joy when they arrived.

Frank Wong came out to help them off the landau. Joe stayed in the rig to hold the team. Inside, Frank's mother served them tea, while a dapper Chinese man introduced himself as Chee Lee and volunteered to translate for them. The girl was from a coastal region of China and spoke the same language as he and the Wongs.

She told the Cowden ladies to call her May Lou. Everybody laughed when she said the Cowdens fed her too much. Her body had been very sore from sleeping on the deck of the ship, from hiding in rocky holes, and riding bony mules. Now she had recovered from her trip and wanted to know when she would begin work as a prostitute.

Viney said, "Not in this century, at least," and the girls laughed. Viney told May Lou that she could stay on with the Cowdens and help milk cows, feed chickens, wash dishes, make bread, and help with other chores if she wanted to. Mr. Lee told them the girl did not know a thing about any of that kind of work. She barely knew how to feed and take care of herself. Viney said to tell her she was in America and if she stayed with the Cowdens she could learn how to work.

The child was beautiful, with coal black hair and eyes, full lips, and a small, aquiline nose. She told the Cowdens that she was grateful to them, but she thought she would like to visit with the Wongs for a few days. Mr. Lee's voice turned sugary when he translated this. Viney decided that would not be a good idea and hustled the girl out of the restaurant to the landau. The girl showed a good sense of self-preservation when she climbed back on the carriage without hesitating. Mr. Lee followed her and gave her a possessive boost into the carriage, then took off his hat for Viney and pledged his undying allegiance as a translator, friend, and supplier of spices from the east.

Viney asked Joe to drive down by the hotel so they could do some quick shopping. Royal and Duncan Vincent, Billy Stiles, and Ted Randolph were sitting on the hotel veranda.

Joe stayed in the landau and ignored the VO on the veranda. After a while, Billy Stiles and Randolph came down the stairs. Joe did not know either of them, but they came up to him and introduced themselves and shook his hand.

Joe was wary and they began to lean on him with quiet familiarity and cordiality, as if they owned him or soon would. Stiles told him they wanted to get to know him in a hurry before they might have to say good-bye forever. Randolph inquired about his health. Joe did not inquire about theirs. Thus the line was drawn between them and war declared. On the surface, Stiles and Randolph made it clear to him that he was in an unhealthy position and he made it clear that he would remain loyal to the Cowdens. Joe tried to figure out their other reasons for engaging him. They had come down for some other reason than to intimidate him.

He noticed that all the rangers on the street were watching the landau. Stiles and Randolph shut off the conversation with Joe when the ladies returned with Edna and Myrtle. They tipped their hats and only stepped back far enough to give the ladies room to board and it became clear to Joe they had acquired a proprietary interest in the Cowden ladies.

When Joe started the team, Viney asked him to turn around in a wide spot in front of the hotel and take Edna and Myrtle back to their house in the upper end of Harshaw Canyon. He swung the team wide to the edge of the pond, then across the street. In front of the hotel, Stiles and Randolph rode up on their horses, grabbed the check reins on the team and stopped the landau.

The landau was directly below the staircase to the hotel and Vincent and his retinue stared down at Viney. Joe Coyle knew it would be foolish to draw his pistol. That would only make the Cowden ladies the backstop in a firing range. He relaxed and sat quietly to see what would happen.

Viney said, "Duncan, tell your trash to let go my horses and move out of the way."

"Trash? The trash is in the carriage, Missus," Duncan said. "Maudy Pendleton, what are you doing down there with that pack of crones?"

"It's Mrs. Cowden. Cowden's my name," Maudy said.

"I can't understand how a girl as good as you could marry into a bunch like that."

Maudy smiled at him sweetly, took off her glove, and twiddled her ring finger at him.

"I guess you're wondering why my brother, Constable Vincent, ordered your carriage stopped, Missus."

Viney stared straight ahead.

"He has decided to arrest you women for being accessories to robbery, murder, cattle theft, trespass on the public land . . . I can't remember all the specifics of the warrant. You and your daughters, it seems, will have to be taken into custody. Your participation in these crimes has been all too evident. You're a threat to the public good. Don't blame me for this. Your menfolk made it clear at the outset of our differences that we could expect as much trouble from you as from them. Now Constable Vincent deems it necessary to remove you as obstacles to the peace of the community."

"How do you propose to do this, kill us?" Eileen shouted. "That's what you'll have to do to stop us from fighting you."

"Oh, no. I don't think Constable Vincent will have to take so drastic a measure. He'll keep you in our town jail until your brothers give themselves up."

"Why are we being treated so well? You killed the Romeros, the Johnsons, Margarita Elias, and the Lord only knows who else."

"Woman, I'm no killer. You can be sure I'll be a gentleman in this. Your new sister-in-law Maudy Jane knows I can be a gentleman when I am privileged to deal with nice people."

"What makes you think I'll say you're a gentleman?" Maudy said. "You're so common not even a lizard can deal with you."

Vincent nodded and Stiles and Randolph led Viney's team up the street toward the jail. A few more of Royal's VO constables had straggled in from the Pajaritos and gone into the bars. Townspeople heard the exchange between Vincent and the Cowdens and word of the arrest passed up the street. People shouted encouragement to the ladies and townsmen formed an escort to walk beside the landau as it rolled up the street.

Packrat Packer stumbled out of a bar ahead of Viney's carriage. He had suffered a terrible thirst after his flight out of the Pajaritos and had taken on a dangerous load of beer and whiskey in a short time. When he heard something about the Cowden women going to jail, he felt a great victory had been won for his side. He staggered out to the boardwalk as the Cowden carriage drove by. He gazed blearily into the faces of the beautiful and remote Cowden women who never, never noticed him. He charged into the street, waved his arms like a wild man, shouted, "Yippee!" and threw his hat under the noses of Blue and Smoke.

Blue and Smoke were not in the best of moods. They were used to stepping out ahead of their carriage. The two rangers had been jerking on their heads and snubbing them so they could not see where they were going. The rangers' horses stepped on their feet, bit them, and threatened to kick them. Smoke and Blue wanted to be turned loose.

The hat sailing underneath them was all the excuse they needed to go berserk. They reared up and whipped their heads from side to side to free themselves. Blue came down straddling the hips of ranger Stiles' horse, clubbed Stiles off his horse with his head, then tromped him and drew the wheels of the carriage over the top of him.

Smoke struck Randolph a glancing blow on the head with a front foot, freed himself, and sprang away with Blue. Randolph recovered and spurred his mount to catch up. The team outran him. As the carriage passed Randolph, Joe stood up and knocked him off his horse with the butt of his buggy whip.

Joe circled the pond and pulled up to leave town at a respectable pace. A cheer went up from the townspeople. The Cowdens laughed all the way home.

Duncan Vincent tried so hard to keep himself under control that his face pinched all the blood and most of the color out of itself. Some pockets of blood were not able to flee quickly enough and they made streaks of color between the trembling muscles. Royal Vincent looked like a man who had been whipped with a snake. Major Ted Randolph picked himself off the Harshaw street and barked orders to all the rangers within earshot to catch his horse and meet him in front of the hotel in five minutes.

Royal Vincent asked him what he intended to do with the rangers.

"I'm going to seize that witches' coven," Randolph said.

"Me and my men have been through hell," Royal complained. "We're not in any condition to saddle horses and chase after a bunch of women. We need rest and medical care."

"Don't trouble yourself. Rest assured, I'll handle it."

"Well, if you're sure you can handle it without me."

"Rest assured, I say."

Randolph chose Stiles and six of Duncan's new rangers and waited until four hours after dark to ride to El Durazno. He did not have to tell these rangers to keep quiet. They knew what to do. He rode up to the Cowdens' barn in the light of the moon. The rangers could hear Joe Coyle snoring. Randolph drew his pistol and pounded on the door with the butt, then he and Stiles dismounted and stood by the door.

Joe came quickly to the door without lighting a lamp.

"You sleep awful sound out here, don't you, Joe?" Randolph said. "Aren't you afraid somebody'll sneak up on you?"

Joe grinned. "I like it out here. Anyway, who could be worse than you?"

"How do you like this?" Randolph said, and he stunned Joe between the eyes with the barrel of his pistol, then shot him in the knee. Joe groaned and fell forward on his face. Randolph took aim and shot him through the back of the other knee.

The rangers surrounded the house and slammed in through every door. The Cowden women were sitting in the kitchen wrapped in their bathrobes.

"Well, well, after all that big show on the street, we expected more resistence, Missus," Randolph said to Viney.

"You should thank me for that, mister. My daughters wanted to shoot you, but I wouldn't let them," Viney said. "You would have hurt them and my husband and sons would have been forced to kill you."

"Who fired those shots in the barn?" Eileen asked.

"You'll come with us now, all of you. You're under arrest," Randolph said.

The rangers herded the Cowden women to the barn, and into the office. Joe Coyle was not there. The rangers harnessed the blue horses to the landau, loaded the women, and barely missed running over Joe in the yard in front of the barn.

Eileen screamed Joe's name and tried to jump out of the landau, but a ranger riding beside the carriage slapped her back to her seat. Joe never moved.

Randolph intended to lock the Cowden women in the jail, but Doris Vincent was waiting for them and made him unload them at the hotel. As Doris escorted them through the lobby, Elk and Wash Briggs took charge of Lorrie. The ladies had not uttered a whimper or a complaint since Eileen shouted Joe's name when she saw him on the ground in front of the barn. Doris escorted them to the hotel's best suite of rooms. In the hallway upstairs, she told Royal Vincent that she would be the Cowden ladies' guard.

Lorrie asked her brothers what they wanted with her.

"We don't know what to do with you, never have, but it's high time you got away from the Cowdens, that's for sure," Wash said. "They're finished. They're all going to jail."

"And you find that you have discovered great concern in your hearts for me?"

"No, we just thought you might want to get away from those Cowdens," Elk said. "Pardon us if we were wrong."

"You're always wrong when you try to do my thinking for me, but I'm glad you kept me from being locked up. I have something to do."

"You better come home with us before the Vincents decide to arrest you, too."

The lobby, bar, and dining room were full of townsmen and VO rangers. Lorrie saw the one man in the whole town who could help her and started toward him.

"Where do you think you're going?" Wash said.

"I told you, I have something to do."

"Naw, you just stay here with us."

"Yes, you stay with us, now." Elk blocked her way to the dining room.

"That's right, stand in my way so I can kick you in the privates in front of all your big, manly VO partners," Lorrie said.

The giant Briggs brothers looked around to see if anyone had heard Lorrie. She slipped by them and went into the dining room and asked Doctor Tucker if he would please go back to El Durazno with her to see what he could do for Joe Coyle. The doctor did not question her. He picked up his medicine bag and followed her to the street to look for the landau.

Packrat was standing at the bottom of the veranda stairs and, when Lorrie did not see the landau, she asked him where it was. He looked up and down the street instead of answering her, then acted as though he did not like her enough to give her an answer. "I don't know, why ask me?"

Lorrie slammed the heels of both her hands into his chest. "You worthless dolt, you have eyes, don't you?" She kept slamming him and backing him up. "For once in your life, be of some use."

"Eddie the Newt took it."

Lorrie made sure Doctor Tucker kept up and hurried to Eddie Newton's stable. His lamps were lit and he was about to unharness Smoke and Blue. He looked up and saw Lorrie coming toward him and prepared a smirk for her. She grabbed a long-handled shovel that was leaning against a wall and swung it over her shoulder and the smirk died.

Lorrie stopped one shovel handle length away from Eddie the Newt, ready to level him with the shovel. "Now, Eddie," she said. "You lead that team out into the yard and hold it while Doctor and I get on the carriage, or I'm going to dig a grave in your head with your shovel. I won't hit you with the flat end and bounce it off your skull. I'll hit you with the sharp edge and cut it in half like a watermelon."

Eddie led the team out into the yard and held it while Lorrie and Doctor Tucker climbed on. Lorrie picked up the lines and handed them to the doctor. "I think you better drive, Doctor," she said. "We have to hurry and I've never driven a team in my life."

They met Jimmy Coyle running toward town. He and Sergeant had hidden when they heard the shots that felled Joe. Betty had shoved

Paula Mary under their bed when she heard the shooting at the barn. Both children had helped Sergeant tie tourniquets on Joe's legs and carry him to bed.

Twenty-four

THE COWDEN BROTHERS and Teresa were lined out for home at a comfortable pace when Sergeant O'Kane hailed them from behind and told them Lieutenant Buck wanted them to stop and talk. Les longed to keep going and so did his horse. The brothers wanted to get home.

Teresa did not say much, but when anything was asked of her she nodded quickly and looked down the trail toward El Paso. She knew her way home and was eager to go. She was not in bad condition, either. She wore clean buckskins and the Apaches had made new *teguas* for her sore feet.

Lieutenant Buck rode up to the Cowdens and dismounted. The brothers were not impatient, but they sat their horses so they would not lose time getting on and off again. It was time to go. Night had fallen, but the moon had risen big and fat in a clear sky and the way home was plain to see.

Les lit his pipe to save his patience. Lieutenant Buck said he would not return to Camp Huachuca without the Yawner. He would make camp, pursue the Yawner the next day, and try to talk him into surrendering.

"Forget it," Les said. "You broke faith with him when you allowed the VO to come to the talk. The next time you see him, be ready to fight. That's the only way you'll bring him in."

"He doesn't believe my unit was to blame for this fiasco, does he?" Lieutenant Buck said.

"Why not?" Ben said. "You are to blame and so are we. We should never have allowed the VO to come along. Hell, you must want them to mess you up again. Half of them are still with you."

"I have to bring him in, or shoot him. Those are my orders. I'd like you to find him so we can talk again."

"You don't need us for that. He'll want his folks back and come after you."

"That's what I've been thinking. I sure wish you'd take Patch and try to intercede for me. I don't want a fight and I don't think he does."

The brothers looked at each other. They wanted to go home, but they had given their word they would help the Yawner. "All right. If you'll take charge of Teresa, we'll get on his tracks for you," Ben said.

"Good."

"Aw, hell," Les said.

The brothers dismounted and made camp under some ash trees by Calabasas Creek. Teresa stayed on her horse a long time. Mark coaxed her down and she began to weep. He walked her to a tree and made her comfortable. She cried while the brothers made camp.

Les went up to the soldiers' camp to find bedding for Teresa. The soldiers had made a pile of the gear left behind by the VO. Teddy Briggs was holding a cup of coffee in one hand and sorting through the gear with the other. When he saw Les coming, he turned his back and walked away to a fire in a separate camp the VO had made in a grove of oak trees.

Les found one blanket, but that was not enough for a bed. A soldier told him the VO had taken all the extra blankets. Les walked over, found the pile, and chose four blankets. He laid them neatly one upon the other, folded them in half, and picked them up.

"Hey, fellow, where do you think you're taking our blankets?" one of the constables demanded.

"See that grove of ash trees down in the canyon?" Les asked. "I'm taking them down there for a bed for your partner's wife, Teresa Snider."

"The hell you are." The constable walked toward him with the moonlight shining on his badge.

Les turned toward the man and stumbled. He looked down at somebody's boot at the end of somebody's leg. "Excuse me," he said, then realized he'd stumbled over a dead man. Four bodies were lying in a row covered with blankets.

"He ain't excusing anybody. He's dead." The cranky constable was Creswell.

"I need these blankets for Teresa Snider."

"Oh, you do? Well, you can't have 'em. These men need every one of 'em."

"Men? What men are you talking about? You call that bunch of running-off sons of bitches men?"

"Listen, Cowden, you can't come up here and loot our camp. I saw you and your brothers shoot at us when we tried to take that old Indian. I already reported you to the lieutenant and I'll be filing another report on you when I get back to Harshaw."

"Well, good for you. I'll be down by the creek if you need any help with it."

"Put those blankets back."

"Listen, Creswell, I've already argued with you more than I ever do with sons of bitches. I've only made an exception of you because it was me that shot off your nose and I don't need to hurt you again. I will appeal to your better nature. I don't want these blankets for myself, they're for your partner Snider's widow. She's been through hell and I don't want her to get cold tonight. Be nice, now, and don't give me any trouble."

"If that bitch needs a blanket, tell her to come up here and lay down with her husband's corpse. Why hasn't she even come up here and looked at his face?"

Les said quietly, "Have you ever thought what it would be like if somebody punched you on the end of your sore nose with all his might?"

Creswell scrambled backwards, tripped and almost fell. When he recovered, he was ten yards away and ready to keep going.

"Careful." Les headed for his camp with the blankets.

At camp, Mark carried a bowl of flour, a bucket of water, and a jar of bacon grease to Teresa and asked her if she would help with the supper and make tortillas. She took hold of the tools and soon patted out several *gordas*, thick Chihuahua-style tortillas. She found the right pan, raked coals out of the fire, browned them, and folded them inside a clean cotton dishcloth so they would stay hot. Mark cooked jerky gravy and eggs and made coffee. When he called Teresa and his brothers to supper, she smiled.

During supper the brothers and Patch quietly talked over the doings of the day. They looked to Teresa often to see if she wanted to say anything, so she would know they wanted her to join in, but they did not question her. They knew what she had endured, because they knew where she had been with Chato. Patch told about seeing her in Slaughterhouse Wash right after she was captured. She began to cry again softly, but she looked pretty, even happy. Les was almost sure she felt relief and happiness. That night her life had turned around.

The stocky special agent, Jonas Von, walked down from the soldiers' camp. He wore black clothes and a black hat that made him seem like a moving shadow in the night. He was a specter that swaggered with a seaman's roll down the hill to the Cowdens' firelight. He sat down near Teresa without being asked. Les figured he could stay a while, though he was on shaky ground with Les for butting in on Teresa's peace.

Les wondered where he had been when the VO started shooting and the Yawner ran away. He did not remember seeing him anywhere in the melee, and Les remembered almost everything that happened.

Von turned to Teresa and asked her if she could talk English.

Teresa shook her head slightly.

"What are your maiden and married names?" Von sported a little V of whiskers that clung to the center of his lower lip like a spider.

"Didn't you understand the girl?" Les said. "She shook her head no, she doesn't talk English."

Von did not look at Les. "Ask her if she was raped."

"We're going to bed now. She can tell her story to our papa when we get her home. If you want to find out what happened to her, you can get it from him."

"I'm the authority here. Just do as I tell you and ask her if she was raped and how many times and by who. Ask her also who killed the Porter woman."

Ben stood up behind Von and picked him up by the long hairs on the back of his neck. The hair pulling hurt so much the man was unable to move, like a cat caught by the nape of the neck. Ben was so angry he ground his teeth. "What is the matter with you dudes? Can't you understand Arizona English? Do you think we like to repeat ourselves?" He waved Von's head gently from side to side, squeezed the hair inside his fist so hard the man squawked, then pushed him away toward the soldiers' fire. Ben did not like to bully people. Relenting, he said, "Out here you can't come to a camp and start using the people and embarrassing them. This girl needs time to recover, not a grilling by some cold-hearted idiot."

"Listen to me, I'll send a squad of soldiers down here to get her and throw her in with the Apache women," Von said. "Let's see how you like that."

"She's not an Apache prisoner," Les said. "She's an American and our guest, so just get away from her."

"Your lack of cooperation is duly noted. You have no right to hinder my investigation. As an agent of the Department of the Interior, it's my job to interrogate this woman."

"Yeah, well, not now," Ben said.

Von turned and headed toward the soldiers' fire, a black shape that made Les want to look up at the stars to clean out his eyes.

When they were ready to go in the morning, the brothers gave Teresa into the care of Sergeant O'Kane and charged him with her protection. They asked Lieutenant Buck to put out scouts for his own defense, but to keep his route of march in Calabasas Canyon and to wait for the brothers at the railroad siding. The brothers would report to him that evening. They did not intend to follow the Yawner if he went to Mexico. They made Lieutenant Buck promise he would not use them to uncover the Yawner and then try to take him by force.

The brothers left their packhorse with the patrol and headed out on the Yawner's tracks. The Yawner must have prearranged a rallying point before the meeting, because the tracks of the whole bunch came together at a cottonwood grove in Pesqueira Canyon, a mile from the meeting place. Well-armed and with twenty mounted men who would want to retrieve their women and children, the Yawner was again a dangerous force.

Les was happy the old demon was able to rally so quickly. The VO might have massacred his band if he had not been ready to defend himself. The whole country wanted to see him vanquished, but the

Cowdens did not need the shame of leading him into a massacre. Les was glad the Yawner had not placed blind trust in the Cowdens' ability to bring honorable men to the meeting. He was too wary, wily, and cunning to trust anybody.

The Yawner knew the brothers laid down a volley of fire to protect him from the VO and the soldiers showed good discipline by not firing at the Apaches. Only the VO had gone to the meeting intending treachery, and that was plenty to send the Yawner back on the warpath. Les did not think he and his brothers had a chance in the world to catch up to him.

The brothers and Patch followed the Yawner's horse tracks south. The tracks led them in a straight line for a while and the brothers were almost sure they were long gone to Mexico, but then they abruptly turned east. The brothers loped down Pesqueira Canyon, parallel to Calabasas Canyon. The tracks were clear and deep in the sand. They entered a stream of water over a long apron of flat rock and landed in the sand again under an immense, white bluff that stretched between Pesqueira and Calabasas canyons. The two canyons converged under the bluff.

Patch stopped the brothers. All four men looked up at the bluff for Apaches. The day was almost gone. They woke up from their concentration on the tracks and realized they could be targets for ambush if the Yawner was on the bluff.

The tracks plainly continued down Pesqueira Creek, but not one of these four trackers would have raced on without suspecting the Yawner would like the bluff for a place to lay an ambush. From the bluff he would have a good field of fire in any direction and he had enough men to cover every field. He might not intend to retrieve his people back there, but he could start shaving and whittling on the patrol.

The brothers had stopped in a narrow place where the bluff rose straight overhead. They suspected the Yawner had used the flat rock upstream as a place to dismount and climb the rock to the bluffs. Apaches did not leave tracks to their place of ambush.

Just as the brothers decided to disperse to keep from being shot, someone shouted and fired gunshots in the canyon behind them. The brothers and Patch scattered for cover. Les and Mark fell off their horses and tried to scoot under the same rock. Fire from the bluff ricocheted off the bottom of the canyon.

Les crawled upstream on his belly. A riderless VO horse came careening, skidding, and ploughing wide-eyed through the running water on the apron of flat rock past Les, and headed home. Les hurried on and found Teddy Briggs moaning and pivoting in circles on his back with an arrow near his heart. He was on sand, so the arrow did not have him pinned to the ground, but it had paralyzed the side where his heart pumped. Teddy could only move himself around the dead space that had been killed by the arrow. A horse lay dead a few feet away with a bullet hole behind his ear.

The sight of the dead horse and the dying Teddy made Les angry. He had not hated Royal's gunsels until that moment. Most of them, including Royal, were so inept they were a joke. The realization of the harm they caused had not occurred to him until the moment he found Teddy and the dead horse. Even the horses were wasted and lost in the war because they were such damned bunglers. They weren't smart enough, brave enough, or mean enough to hurt an enemy in a fight, but their cowardly bungling made them killers even of the horses they rode.

Teddy's Sharp .4570 lay in the rocks on the edge of the wash with its stock broken. Teddy's holster was empty and his pistol gone. Les stood over the boy and glared at him. "Now, look at you, Teddy. You just had to keep after us, didn't you?" If the arrow had struck him one half-inch to the left, it would have bounced off the constable's badge.

Teddy groaned pitifully and Les knelt beside him and pillowed his head on his lap. He felt his back and found that the point of the arrow had not come out, but bulged near the surface of the skin. "Damn it, Teddy. Why did you follow us? Didn't you know we'd find Apaches?"

Teddy babbled something Les could not understand. He leaned close to the boy. "All right, tell me again."

"Shhh . . . shoot m . . . me."

"Aw, Teddy, no."

"P . . . please."

Les thought, Lord knows, I can do that for the kid and at least stop his suffering. He's going to die. Les gently laid his head down. "Look at the tops of the trees, Teddy. See how they wave in the breeze? Watch the clouds swim in the wind. Do that and you'll stop hurting." He wiped Teddy's brow with his fingers and closed his ear with his thumb so he would not hear the pistol cock, then shot him in the temple.

He was immediately sorry. How would he explain this to Lorrie? Lord almighty! His troubles had finally grown big enough to finish him. He could only hope nobody else found out what he'd done. In a daze, he stumbled down the wash toward his brothers. He hoped the snipers on the bluff would put him out of his misery.

The Yawner and four warriors Les had not seen at the meeting were sitting their horses by Ben and Mark. Patch was not there. The Yawner stopped talking when Les appeared. Les stopped by his horse and stood behind his brothers so no one could see his face and that was not lost on the Yawner. His brothers turned and looked closely into his face. He could not hide his shame.

"El Bronco holds back," the Yawner said. "Why? What has he done?"

Ben said, "I don't know. Who did that shooting up there, brother?"

Les only shook his head as if the shot did not matter at a time like this.

"Who's up there?" Ben said.

Les shook his head.

Mark turned his horse slowly, stood up in his stirrups, and looked upstream as though he would investigate. Les mounted his horse and blocked the way. Mark stopped, backed up and said, "What's the *matter* with you?"

Ben was holding Patch's horse and the loose horse that had run down the canyon. "Who was riding this horse?" he said.

Rocks tumbled above them and Patch and four of the Yawner's Apaches climbed down from a direction that made Les positive they had seen him kill Teddy. Every one of them looked him in the eye.

The Yawner spoke to the men with Patch and they hurried away in their quick-legged, busy, shoulder-rolling gait that always reminded Les of javalina. Les's brothers turned away from him and everybody forgot him while they discussed the serious business of the Yawner's recovery of his women and children.

The Yawner looked rested, less troubled than he had been at the meeting. His buckskin shirt was fine and new. The other buckskin trappings on his person and his *cantinas*, saddlebags, and the sharp colors of his blankets showed his pride in his appearance.

The Yawner was back on the prowl. He spoke in a quicker, more vibrant manner than at the previous meeting. His patience with the soldiers was at an end. He wanted his people back so he could go to Mexico for the rest of the winter and he would not allow the soldiers to return to Camp Huachuca until his people were released.

"Tell Jackrabbit that he has no right to hold my people," he said. "I asked him to come and talk and he did not talk. He only grabbed my people. My *gente* must be returned or I will not respect him."

"I'll tell him," Ben said.

"Respect is important. Did I lie to anyone? Why then did the Jackrabbit show me so much disrespect as to loose the town dogs on me? Men must respect each other if they are to trust one another."

"I agree," Ben said.

"Instead of bringing himself and his men, whom I respected, the Jackrabbit brought me townsmen. We could smell the town dog fear on them before they even came in sight. Who sent those townsmen to me?"

"Their leader is the brother of the one you call El Alacrán. The Scorpion is everybody's enemy."

"Get rid of him. He wants to own the earth."

"You said it."

"Chato is as bad as the townsmen, but the townsman who had his pouch was so much a fool he begged to die."

"My brothers and I were happy they settled their differences the way they did."

"How long will it be before we quit this world, Horseman?"

"Sometimes I think we've already lived too long."

"Short or long is all the same, Jinete. The day our bones are dust and the odor of us is gone, the world will not have changed at all. The rocks will be the same, the sky the same. How many pretty summers will pass before we are forgotten? Not even one. How large a basket does a woman need for her *pinole*? How much *pinole* can her family eat, how large a basket does it need?"

"Your people make good baskets, so you should know."

"We make them good, but not big. We only need them to carry water and *pinole*. How big a basket can a woman carry? When it is empty, she can run with it. She can't run with even a small one when it is full."

"Everything you say is true."

"Then listen to this."

"Yes."

"Get rid of the townsmen and others like them who make baskets out of lumber and adobe, rock and mortar. Those cannot be satisfied, even after they are dead. They covet goods, space, ground. They think they will need ground even after they are dead. Get rid of them, Horseman. They want to own the rocks, the sky, and you. If they chase away the humans who have long been part of the earth, don't you think they will chase you away someday, too?"

"I know it."

The Yawner looked at Les. "What is my horse's name?"

"El Tacaño," Les said. "The Codger."

"Like me. A good name for a horse." The Yawner lifted his reins on his fingertips, and to show that he only needed a light touch to handle the horse, reined him slowly in a half circle. "He has a rein. Now he has become a basket, a big store of things I own, and I can't eat him because he was a gift."

The Yawner turned Codger all the way around and rode away with his warriors.

The brothers agreed their only course was to convince Lieutenant Buck to release the Yawner's women and children and try to talk to him another day. Ben, Mark, and Patch started their horses toward Calabasas Canyon, but Les sighed and stayed back. "Wait," he said.

Ben and Mark stopped and turned to him.

"We have to get Teddy Briggs. He's back there dead." Les led them back to Teddy.

"My sweet Lord, what are we gonna do?" Ben said.

Les's bullet had destroyed the boy's head.

"Is that how you found him, Les?" Mark asked.

"No, he was dying from the arrow in his heart when I found him."

"How did he get shot in the head?"

"He was hurting so bad, he asked me to shoot him."

"Lord, Lord, Lord. Don't tell Lorrie," Ben said.

The brothers tied Teddy on his horse and rode back to meet Lieutenant Buck. They asked him to dismount his patrol and stop for a talk. They told him the Yawner wanted his people back and, if the lieutenant did not release them, he would fight for them until everybody was dead.

The lieutenant listened patiently while the brothers gave him the Yawner's message. The Yawner would not run now. He would harass the patrol. The lieutenant would gain nothing by keeping the Yawner's folks. The patrol could not fight him and chase him and keep the captives. Sooner or later the women and children would tire and sit down. The Yawner's message to Lieutenant Buck was, give us our people back and we might return and surrender quietly in the spring.

Les sat away by himself and did not participate in the deliberations with Lieutenant Buck. He was too worried about the grief Lorrie would suffer when she found out her brother was dead. His guilt made him so sick he did not want to live. What he had done would make all the women cry.

Lieutenant Buck ordered Sergeant O'Kane to release the women and children.

Ben said, "Next time I guess we better do what the old savage asks us to do."

"A real solution would be to round up the VO and shoot them all," Lieutenant Buck said. "Then I wouldn't have to explain to my superiors how the Yawner asked me to receive his surrender and I practically chased him away at the point of my saber."

Twenty-five

LORRIE WAS TIRED. Joe Coyle had been keeping her busy night and day with his pain. Even though Paula Mary, Jimmy, and Sergeant Broussard took over the menial chores, the nursing care Joe required took all Lorrie's time and strength. She had been with him constantly, even in his thoughts and fears, for a night and a day.

As she helped Doctor Tucker change the dressings on Joe's legs early the second evening after he had been shot, the smell of blood and the sight of torn flesh and bone finally made her totter on her feet. Doctor Tucker looked at her face and ordered her to go outside and get some air.

Paula Mary and Jimmy were down at the barn looking after Sergeant. They had decided they better protect him. Lately the VO had been showing an inordinate desire to shoot people who guarded the Cowden barn. Sergeant was not used to being shot at by the VO yet.

Lorrie stepped out the back door into complete darkness. The moonlight had not yet touched the bottom of the canyon. Momentarily blind from the last effect of lamplight on her eyes, she groped her way into the orchard. All of a sudden she smelled the musky, campfire odor of an Indian, stepped into a hole that bumped a small cry out of her, and stumbled into a man. He grunted and caught her by the shoulders. She let out such a scream and flailed him so violently with her arms and legs that not even owls could have held her. She whirled to run home, butted into a tree, bounced off, clotheslined herself on a limb, jumped up, and ran screaming back into the kitchen.

Sergeant scared her again when she heard him running through the night toward the house. She was ready with the cleaver when he burst into the kitchen. Doctor Tucker calmly came to the door, wiped his hands on a clean towel, and began rolling down his sleeves.

"There's an Indian in the orchard," Lorrie gasped.

"What's he doing?" the doctor said.

"Well, I don't know. Why does anybody lurk in the dark unless he's a bloodthirsty thug?"

Sergeant lit a lantern and led the way to the orchard. A child was sitting under a peach tree wrapped in a blanket.

"See, I told you somebody was here," Lorrie said.

"But it's such a little bloodthirsty thug," the doctor said. A tall figure glided out of the darkness into the light. "There's the big'un, all right," he added.

Paula Mary and Jimmy had been hiding under the eaves of the house and now they showed themselves. "It's Casimiro," she said. "He's brought Patch's little sister. *Vengase*, Casimiro *a tomar café*. Welcome, Casimiro, come in for coffee."

"*Gracias*," Casimiro said quietly.

Paula Mary tugged on his finger to start him toward the house. He turned back and picked up Casi.

"*Vengase, vengase*," Paula Mary said. "Come on, come on."

Very slowly, Casimiro followed her into the house. "*Gracias*," he whispered again as he passed Lorrie, but he did not look at her.

Inside, he told Paula Mary that Casi could not walk because her feet were sore. Doctor Tucker uncovered and treated them and left Paula Mary a jar of salve for them.

Lorrie left Sergeant to sit with Casimiro and Casi while they ate supper and went with Paula Mary and Jimmy to walk Doctor Tucker to his buggy. The doctor used that time to give Lorrie instructions for the care of Joe's wounds. Only his deep voice sounded in the night. She went ahead to open the barn door. The moon was high enough to illuminate the yard. She swung open the door without looking inside, then Doctor Tucker stopped talking in mid sentence and Paula Mary and Jimmy stopped in their tracks to stare into the blackness of the barn.

The front door was open and the silhouettes of three riders could be seen against the moonlight. The riders remained absolutely still. The hair on the back of Lorrie's neck stood up.

Jimmy cocked his pistol and the sound clearly identified itself. "Who is it?" Paula Mary yelled. "You better speak up, before we shoot right down through the middle of you."

Somebody chuckled in a deep voice. A lamp was lit in the office and A.B. carried it out and illuminated the Cowden brothers sitting their horses.

"We're sorry if we scared you," A.B. said. "We saw the doctor's rig and heard his voice, but we didn't know you were all out there."

Lorrie was so glad to see A.B., she hugged his neck and kissed him. He raised the lamp to keep from burning her. He patted her shoulder so he could step back. Lorrie was so happy, she was on the verge of tears.

Jimmy, Paula Mary, and the doctor came forward and began telling A.B. about the arrest of the Cowden women and the shooting of Joe Coyle. A.B. already knew about it. The Porter brothers had informed him by wire.

The brothers dismounted and Lorrie smiled into Les's face and hugged him. He held back and she tugged at both his sleeves to pull him closer. She could not see his face well because he was standing in the shadow of his horse and his hat brim was down. She thought he was feeling shy, so she moved close against him and gave him a wet kiss on the lips and spiced it with healthy breaths.

Still, he interrupted the kiss. "Lorrie," he said softly. "I've never felt worse about anything in my life, but I have bad news."

Lorrie only moved her head so she could see his face. He pushed up his hat brim, sighed and, as he met her gaze, big tears ran out of his eyes. "Teddy got killed," he said.

Lorrie looked as vulnerable as a little girl whose face had been slapped. Her hands gently fondled his breast, as though she still wanted to love him. Then she cooled and turned away, leaned against his horse and hid her face against the saddle. "Oh no, not Teddy, too," she said softly, and her heart broke.

Lorrie could not have abandoned Les more completely if she had boarded the train and headed east where he would never go. After he told her Teddy was dead, her communication with him might as well have been by telegraph wire, for all its warmth. Ben and Mark kept busy unsaddling horses. Les had hoped they would lie for him and tell Lorrie her brother was killed by an Apache arrow. Nothing ever worked for him when he wanted to lie.

Lorrie pressed her face against the saddle leather and hung on to it as though she might fall if she let go. "How?"

"He took an arrow next to his heart, and . . . a bullet."

"Where?"

"It doesn't matter, darlin'. He was killed."

"Where was he shot?"

"In Pesqueira Canyon yesterday."

"Where was he hit?"

"In the head."

"My folks have to be told."

"We already took Teddy to their house in Patagonia. Papa went with us so we wouldn't have trouble."

"Why did you think they'd give you trouble?"

"Oh, us being Cowdens and all. Ben remembered how they acted when he took Hoozy's body home."

"That kept you from acting like men? You needed the undersheriff for protection? How long would you have waited if you hadn't found your Papa in Patagonia?"

"We wouldn't have waited. We were just lucky Papa was there."

"Yes, I know. He was there protecting his criminal when we needed him here more than any man was ever needed in the world."

"He hated that, but he needed to stay with his prisoner until the train came."

"Well, it doesn't matter anymore. I have to go home now."

"Your papa and brothers are coming for you."

"My papa and the two brothers I have left?"

"Yes. Your two big, tough brothers."

"Aren't you happy? You'll get another chance to beat them up." Lorrie began to weep against the saddle.

Les tried to draw her away, but she would not budge. He hugged her softly and laid his head on her shoulder. "Come on, darlin'. Come on." But her shoulder was hard and tense and she would not move.

Paula Mary came and took her hand and she finally moved away from the horse. As she started toward the house, A.B., Mark, and Ben tried to console her, but she would not look at them, or speak, or let them touch her.

Les wiped Lorrie's tears off his saddle with the palm of his hand, unsaddled his horse, and put him away. He lit more lamps and put them in their places to illuminate the barn and stalls, climbed into the loft and began pitching hay down to the horses. Someone shouted from the road and everybody turned to the sound of a rig and horses.

Indiana, Wash, and Elk Briggs rode horseback into the barn ahead of a buggy driven by Hattie Briggs. A male passenger huddled in an over-coat beside her.

"Get down, everybody," A.B. said. "The boys will take your horses and we'll go to the house for coffee."

"Where's my daughter?" Indiana said.

Lorrie had gone to the house. Paula Mary started after her.

"Tell her to bring everything she owns," Hattie yelled at Paula Mary. "She's moving out."

"Wouldn't that be up to Lorrie and her husband?" A.B. asked.

"Don't worry, my daughter won't stay here after she hears Mr. Cres-well's story," Indiana said.

The brothers saw that the passenger in the buggy was Creswell. His head was protected by a muffler and his hat was pulled down low, but the bandage on his nose was plain to see.

Les said, "What's Creswell's story?" As he climbed down out of the loft, he thought, damn it, Creswell saw me shoot Teddy and Lorrie's going to find out. There had been two horses in Pesqueira Canyon, one loose horse and one dead one. He cussed himself for not looking for the other rider, though he did not know what he would have done with him. He probably would have been within his rights to shoot him. Teddy and Creswell could only have been there to bushwhack the Cowdens.

"He saw you kill our Teddy, you son of a bitch," Hattie Briggs yelled. When Lorrie looked mean, she looked just like Hattie. Lately that had not been all the time, but from now on it probably would.

A.B. turned to Les. "Is that true, son? Did you kill Teddy?"

"Papa, it's not like I murdered the boy."

"You couldn't stand it, could you?" Lorrie said. Les turned and saw she was back. "You caught my little brother out alone where you could blame Apaches and you bastards killed him like you did Hoozy and Whitey, didn't you?"

Lorrie strode toward Les and he looked at her ruined face. A blue bruise marred her forehead and her eyes were still black and swollen to her nose. A great volume of tears was smeared on her cheeks, but cold-blooded mahem was in her eyes. She snatched up a pitchfork that was leaning against the wall, raised it with both hands, and aimed it at Les like a spear.

Les wanted her to end his life for him. He did not want to live anymore. He had not done anything right. Lorrie could do it. She hurried at him with the pitchfork.

Mark caught the handle in both hands and stopped her.

"Let her go," Les said.

Mark said, "Are you going to let her kill you, for God's sake?"

Lorrie let Mark have the pitchfork.

"Don't bother with him anymore, Lorrie," Hattie yelled. "He's pitiful. Get in the buggy. We'll send someone for your clothes."

"Mr. and Mrs. Briggs, Teddy was killed by an Apache arrow," Ben said.

"Did you see the arrow strike my son?" Indiana asked.

"No, sir, but I saw the arrow in his heart."

"Sir, Mr. Creswell was riding beside my son when he was killed," Indiana said. "Mr. Creswell, how did Teddy die?"

"Teddy took an arrow and fell off his horse. Les Cowden came running up the wash with his pistol drawn, and when he saw Teddy was down and wounded, he stood over him and shot him in cold blood."

"Where were you when this happened, Mr. Creswell?"

"My horse was shot out from under me when Teddy took the arrow. I ran upstream for cover. When I looked back for Teddy, I saw Les Cowden kill him."

"That's not the way it was at all," Ben said. "Teddy took an arrow in his breast. You saw it yourselves. He was in agony and begged Les to shoot him."

Indiana stared at Ben, smiled mirthlessly, shook his head. "How could you expect anyone to believe that?"

Paula Mary walked up to Lorrie and took her hand again. Lorrie ignored her, but did not take her hand away. When Indiana ordered Lorrie into the buggy again, Paula Mary tried to hold her back and softly pleaded with her not to go.

Lorrie bowed her head and stepped on the buggy, but Paula Mary made her pause with one foot on the ground. "Please, don't go, Lorrie. You're our sister."

"Let go, Paula Mary." Lorrie took her hand away and climbed into the buggy.

Ben and Mark backed Hattie's team out of the barn and helped her turn it around. The Briggses rode off toward Harshaw. Les tried to look into the faces of his family, but none of them would meet his gaze. A.B. told everybody to come with him to the house and, when Les hung back because he was hurt and ashamed, A.B. made him come on. A.B.'s way was to forget about hurt feelings as soon as possible. He did not abide people making a fuss over the way they felt. Uppermost in his mind was the problem of bringing Viney and the girls home.

A.B. sat his sons down in Joe Coyle's bedroom and told them he had been afraid the VO would break Campana out of jail, or kill him so he would not go to trial and talk about the VO's crimes. A.B. had been forced to stay and keep watch over Campana until the Porters answered his wire and came to help. Five Porters were standing watch at the jail now. Weldon Rutledge, the Tombstone marshal, was taking Campana to his jail for safekeeping by train the next morning as a favor to A.B.

A.B. had used his time in Patagonia to interrogate Campana and he now had an eyewitness to almost every crime the VO had committed in the past eight months. Campana did not know the machinations of Duncan's land fraud and bribery of state and government officials, but he had been witness to murder, theft, beatings, dope smuggling, and illegal traffic of aliens, and his signed confession attested to it.

Joe Coyle told A.B. that Ted Randolph had shot him in the legs. He said Randolph had come to the door with the constables, said hi, how are ya, shot him in cold blood, and left him for dead. Joe was only lucky that neither bullet severed an artery and that Sergeant Broussard had been sleeping in the loft. Sergeant stayed down when he heard the VO at the door. His presence of mind saved both his and Joe's lives, because he was able to stop Joe's bleeding while the VO were at the house arresting the ladies.

Armed with Campana's confession and the atrocity to Joe Coyle, A.B. reminded his sons that they were his deputies. He gave them his plan for retrieving the Cowden women. They filled their pockets with biscuits Lorrie had cooked and went back to the barn to saddle fresh horses and to hitch the landau. All the livestock was turned out to pasture. A.B. was gambling all his resources. If his family did not return to El Durazno, and something happened to Sergeant, at least the stock would not starve in the corrals.

The brothers carried Joe Coyle down to the barn and loaded him in the landau with Paula Mary and Jimmy. A.B. took the lines, his sons mounted their horses, and they headed for town.

At the edge of town, A.B. left the brothers and drove to Vince and Edna Farley's house. Grandfather Porter and eight of his sons and grandsons came out to help him carry Joe into the house to bed.

Ben stood his horse in the shadows at the lower end of Saloon Row. Les and Mark rode up the alley to the rear of the hotel. Mark tied his horse and waited in the alley. Les went in the back of his Uncle Vince Farley's saloon, walked through the rear storehouse with its whiskey barrels and new sawdust smells, and cracked the door that opened onto the dance hall of the hotel bar. The hotel bar was run by Uncle Vince and the storeroom of his saloon also served that bar.

Les could see the whole room from the dance hall door. Creswell and the Briggs brothers were standing at the bar with several VO constables. One of the constables stared over the swinging doors that led to the lobby, then went back to the bar, and shook his head and cussed the Cowdens for the disgraceful way they had beaten Lorrie and marred her beauty.

The Briggses were aloof to Creswell and the others. Packrat came in and announced that A.B. had just driven up to the front of the hotel. Randolph came in and ordered the constables to the lobby.

Everybody left except Creswell, Packrat, and the Briggs brothers.

Packrat had lost favor for throwing his hat under the Cowden ladies' carriage.

The bartender put up his apron and left the bar to look for better cover. The whole town was anticipating another fight between the Cowdens and the VO. Creswell reached across the bar and grabbed a full bottle of whiskey, unstoppered it, saluted the departing bartender, and took a big drink. He offered the bottle to the Briggses. They shook their heads.

"What's the matter with you fellers? I know you feel bad about Teddy, but you ought to be celebrating about everything else," Creswell said.

"We don't see any reason for that," Wash Briggs said.

"You don't? I do."

"What are you celebrating, Creswell?"

"Everything's going good for me, that's what, and it's all because of your little brother. I don't know if you know it, but Teddy was a gutty feller. You know what he was doing when he was killed?"

"No, what was he doing, Creswell?"

"He'd decided to follow the Cowdens until they made contact with the Apaches. Then he was going to shoot an Apache. He figured the Apaches would blame the Cowdens for it. Then he was going to help the Apaches kill the Cowdens. That was the surest way he could think of to get the Cowdens, and he would not have needed to explain to his sister how he killed her husband."

"How come you were with him?"

"Hell, I figured the Cowdens knew the quickest way home. Going with Teddy was better than staying with the soldiers and maybe having to fight Apaches all the way home. Teddy's plan worked out fine for me."

"How is that?"

"Well, I got even with that goddammed Les Cowden. Didn't the son of a bitch shoot off my nose? What I was able to do to him was worse than back-shooting him. Now I can look forward to watching him suffer a while before somebody kills him or he gets so miserable he kills himself. The prettiest girl in the whole country's quit him and his own family probably isn't having anything to do with him."

"Sounds real good, but it ain't good, Crez."

"Why? You think Les Cowden is a happy man right now? Hell no, he's not."

"As his enemy, I'd think you'd rather see him happy. You are his enemy now, you know. Before this you were just another peon in the pack. Did you see what he did to me and Elk when we made him unhappy? If I was you, I'd leave the country on the fastest horse I could buy, beg, borrow, or steal."

"Naw, he's finished. I fixed him good when I left out the part about Teddy asking to be shot."

Wash stopped his whiskey glass halfway to his mouth. Elk straightened to his full height. That was lost on Creswell, because he felt good with the whiskey and the victory over Les. He said, "You know what Royal said to me? He said, 'Nice work, Crez.' "

Elk relaxed with his back against the bar and said, "Teddy asked Les to shoot him?"

"Hell, yes. I'm telling you, Teddy was guttier'n hell. When that arrow whished down past my ear and thunked into his chest, I thought *I* was killed, but he didn't even make a sound. Then my horse dropped in his tracks and I was *sure* I was dead. Then me and Teddy were down in the wash side by side. When he asked *me* to shoot him, I ran up the wash and hid."

"How did you get away from the Apaches?"

"I don't know. The Cowdens talked to them a while and they left. The Cowdens loaded Teddy on his horse and left and I stayed hid until evening. All I had to do was walk around to the other wash and find the soldiers' fire."

"What did you tell the soldiers?"

"I just acted dumb and scared to death and said I'd been hiding from the Apaches that killed Teddy. Hell, the lieutenant hadn't even missed me. The army didn't care what happened to any of the VO out there."

"You acted dumb, but you sure are smart, Crez," Wash said. "The trouble is, you've made enemies for yourself now."

"Hell, I don't give a damn."

"The real trouble is, you made us your enemy, too."

"What?" Creswell laughed. "Why? You joking? You guys're my best friends. I rooted my lungs out for you when you stomped Les Cowden and when you had your fight in the corral. How could you be my enemies?"

"We thought our little sister was set for life. Our mother and father were happy with her marriage. We didn't think we would ever be bothered with her again. She was actually becoming a nice person. Now she's turned mean again. Our mother's turned meaner. Our father's taken dead aim at the Cowdens and feels he has to get even with them again. We more or less got out of trouble with the Cowdens when Les tromped us. Now, we'll have to start another fight with them, and this time with guns. All because you came to our house and lied to us."

"I didn't lie to you. Les did shoot Teddy in the head, you know. He admitted it right in front of your whole family."

"Yes, but you didn't tell us Teddy begged him to shoot him. He must have been hurting a lot. I wouldn't have had the guts to shoot my own brother, but I'm glad Les was there to do it. He must have known his ass wouldn't be worth a peso if Lorrie found out, so he must have done it for Teddy. If he'd wanted to be mean to him, he could have let him suffer."

"So what? I made sure he lost his ass over it. You ought to be happier'n I am."

"Well, we're not, and I just told you the reason." Wash and Elk drank the last of their whiskey.

"Wait a minute, don't leave me now. Let's talk about it. Don't leave mad anyway."

"We're not going to leave mad," Elk said. "You know why?"

"That's good. Why?"

Elk put his 225 pounds of thick, hard-rock miner's muscle behind a sudden punch into Creswell's belly and said, "Because of that."

Creswell bent over with all the air punched out of him.

"And this," Wash Briggs said, and he straightened Creswell with an uppercut to his very sore nose.

Then the Briggses went out to the lobby. That second punch was almost a coup de grace, except that it was so hurtful it did not render Creswell even a trifle unconscious. He had been afraid he would die from the blow to his belly, but he wished he could die after the blow to his nose.

Poor Packrat did not know what to do about Creswell. He could only watch the man weep and flop his bones on the floor. He finally helped him to his feet, but that did not ease his pain.

Then Packrat looked around and saw Les behind him. "Oh, no," he said.

Les smiled. "Packrat, I'm glad to see you."

Surprised, Packrat gave him a limp and frightened hand.

"Is that the hat you used to scare my mother's horses when they ran over the VO?" Les said.

"Yes. Listen, I'm sorry I did that. I was drunk and didn't know what I was doing."

"Don't worry, I'm glad you did it. My mother and sisters were happy to run over those men. I guess I ought to thank you."

"Well, you're welcome, then."

"But I ain't going to thank you, Packrat."

"No, I guess I didn't think you would."

"No, because you didn't mean for it to turn out the way it did."

"Like I said, I didn't know what I was doing. I was drunk. So, if you're going to give me a beating, get started. There's nothing I can do about it."

"Aw, I'm not going to beat you up, Packrat. You're too little. Now, Creswell here. He's another story. What's the matter with him?"

"The Briggs brothers just beat him up."

"Oh, they did? Why? I thought you fellers and the Briggses were comrades."

"Yes, we were, but he said something to them."

"Something about their sister?"

"Yeah, I think it was something like that."

"They beat him up for something he said about my wife?"

"I guess so."

Creswell straightened and looked at Packrat with teary eyes. "Packrat, you trying to get me buried?"

Les said, "Did you say something about my wife that made her brothers mad, Creswell?"

"You're damned right, Cowden. I said plenty about the old bladder. What do you care? She was everybody's woman before she married you and she'll be everybody's woman again."

Les measured three blows to the end of his nose, then stepped back and let him fall.

Twenty-six

LES CRACKED the swinging doors and saw Lorrie sitting in an easy chair in the corner of the lobby. Her mother was leaning forward on the edge of a sofa talking to her, but she was not paying attention to anything in the room.

The room was crowded with VO men and curious townsmen. Royal's young riffraff from Tucson had lost their zeal. The survivors of the Apache rout in the Pajaritos passed small bottles of whiskey among themselves and cast about with hungry eyes for more comforts.

Duncan and Royal Vincent were seated in a circle of easy chairs in the center of the lobby smoking cigars. Von and Randolph were seated to one side, waiting. The other four chairs in the circle were empty, though the lobby was so crowded the men barely found standing room.

Randolph whittled on a foot-long board with a bright-bladed pocketknife. Von rolled a cigarette in brown paper. Les noticed his expensive boots were tiny. He lit the cigarette, then scratched something off the sole of his boot with the matchstick, then inspected the luster of his bootshine carefully by stretching his leg and swiveling the toe in the light. He was real fancy about his feet.

Duncan was so closely, cleanly, and recently shaven that his chin shone. Les wondered how he could always look so rested and in command. His hair seemed whiter at the temples than Les remembered. He wore a big, wide-brimmed, brown hat and it was shoved to the back of his head while he relaxed. When he had first come to the country, he tucked his trousers inside high-topped lace boots. Now he wore a neat, three-piece suit like A.B. and richly polished western boots. He'd learned to dress the part of a cattleman just right.

Duncan's image was now perfect, but Royal's was all wrong. Royal had recovered from his ordeal and the run home from the Pajaritos and his bright hair was combed and brushed on his shoulders and his mustache and chin whiskers were trimmed to military specifications, but the image he wanted to portray was all wrong. The town of Harshaw and his own VO rangers knew that he would never be another George Armstrong Custer.

These two had brought the opposing factions of the war here so they could finally set themselves up as owners of most of southern Arizona's land, cattle, and mining, but this was going to be their Last Stand. They were Custer and the Cowdens were the Sioux. The Cowdens had them bunched. The VO was surrounded and contained. If they could get Viney out of the hotel, the Cowdens would be able to do as they wished with the VO.

A stir of men on the veranda stilled the talking and in another moment the crowd parted and A.B. walked in. The crowd almost closed behind him, but then it got out of the way in a hurry for Grandfather William Porter, Uncle Billy, Jim, and John. All were armed with double barreled shotguns. They walked to the center of the room and faced outwards so they could hit a VO in any direction they fired.

Duncan was the last man in the room to know that A.B. had come in. He finally noticed that someone approached him from behind who was making everybody move out of his way and he turned and looked at A.B. He had expected A.B. to come in and give up his sons for his women, not to come in with four heavily armed Porters, but that did not stop his mouth. "Oh, there you are, er, Cowden. Have you come to help me get to the bottom of this conflict once and for all?"

A.B. stopped behind Duncan so that both Duncan and Royal would have to stand up and turn around so they could see him. Von and Randolph drifted away and stood against the wall on A.B.'s flank.

A.B. told Jim and John Porter to please go upstairs and tell their Aunt Viney it was time to go home.

"Where are your sons, Cowden?" Duncan said. "Your women can't leave until your sons come in and submit to arrest."

A.B. shifted the shotgun comfortably on his arms, almost as though quieting a creature. "The best thing you can do, Mr. Vincent, is shut up. You've insulted and harmed my family so much I feel like unloading both barrels of this gun in your face. That would be a disastrous for everyone, so try to watch what you say until I leave here with my family."

"Now, that's where I enjoy an advantage that your own code bestows, Cowden. I always say, there's not a community on this frontier that won't hang a coward who shoots an unarmed man. As you see, my brother and I are unarmed. I know you don't want to hang. Why don't you just call in your sons, make the exchange for your women, and go home in peace as per our agreement?"

"We have no agreement, Mr. Vincent. I am simply here to take my ladies home and kill any man who stands in my way."

Jim Porter came down the stairs ahead of the Cowden ladies. Viney was in the lead, Eileen the last lady in the file, and John Porter brought up the rear. Jim headed straight for the door, but Viney put her hand on his shoulder and stopped him, then left the file and went across the room to Lorrie. Lorrie raised her head and looked into her face. Viney put her hand on Lorrie's cheek. The place was quiet as a church.

"Please come home with us, daughter," Viney said.

Lorrie shook her head slightly, but did not shift her gaze from Viney's.

"Wait a minute, old girl. She ain't your daughter," Hattie Briggs said.

Viney paid no attention to Hattie.

"Think about what you truly want," Viney said to Lorrie. "You've become part of our family and we love you. Come home with us. No one can stop you."

"Les killed Teddy and that put an end to everything else," Lorrie said. "I'm sorry."

Viney rubbed her cheek. "All right." She turned and walked toward her daughters.

Hattie Briggs said loudly, "Lorrie's *through* with the Cowdens. So don't come around calling her daughter anymore."

She took a breath to say something else, but Viney paused and faced her. Viney was a small woman, but her backbone was as strong as any six-foot soldier's. She fixed a look on Hattie Briggs that killed whatever else Hattie wanted to say, then went out the door with her family.

Ben and a band of Porters took charge of the ladies on the veranda and Jim stopped and posted himself at the door. Les had been so intent on watching his mother that he opened the swinging doors wider than he intended. Before he closed them, he glanced at Lorrie and she was looking straight at him. Her expression said, "See, because of you, our lives are over." Her look was so forlorn, he did not care if he lived another minute.

Duncan turned to Lorrie and said, "That was a very wise and safe decision, young lady. Before this day is over, not a woman in the territory will want to be aligned with the Cowdens and their breed. No man or woman will be safe in their company, either."

A.B. said, "Duncan and Royal Vincent, you are under arrest for murder, cattle theft, and illegal traffic of aliens and drugs."

"What, you think you can arrest *us?*" Duncan said. "You are a crazy man."

A.B. motioned and Jim Porter picked up two sets of manacles and started toward the Vincents. The Vincents backed toward Les's swinging doors.

A.B. stopped Jim Porter when he came abreast of him. "Stand fast, you Vincents. I won't chase you. I'll blow your legs out from under you."

The Vincents stopped. Then Duncan ruined the day for himself and said, "Do you really think you can get those women safely out of town, Cowden? Did you think I would not anticipate your every move? Now, either give up your sons, or the very wrath of God will fall on that carriage full of women outside."

"Go on, Mr. Vincent. Tell us the rest of it," A.B. said.

"I mean they will only stay alive as long as they don't try to leave town. If you hear rifle fire, it will be because they've started their carriage toward home. I have men stationed along the street who will kill any Cowden who tries to leave before I give my permission. Because this has become total war between us, that includes all Cowdens, men and women. It even would have included this poor, unfortunate Lorrie, had she decided to leave with your wife. The order is not rescindable."

Les knew no Cowden would leave Harshaw that day until they were all able to leave together, so he decided the time had come for him to go berserk. He hit the Vincents in the back with the swinging doors and went for their throats. Royal was the quickest to recover and turn to defend himself. Les shoved Duncan aside, took Royal by the hair, and slapped his face fore and aft until his nose bled, then raised his face so he could see the teary eyes and waylaid them with two straight right hands. He dropped Royal and turned to Duncan.

Duncan acted confused, as though he had been addled by the blow of the swinging doors. He wanted to keep his dignity by appearing to be a man who had been stunned and made helpless by something unseen and unexpected. He did not want to let on that he was in danger of being hurt, because anyone dignified as he did not deserve to be hurt. He was trying to look older than he was, as though anyone should be able to see his advanced age should protect him from physical attack.

He must have known that, unless he could fool Les Cowden, he was in awful danger. He did not fool Les. Duncan was not as old as A.B., yet his henchman, Frank Marshall, had given A.B. a terrible beating with a blackjack. Duncan must have known that someday he might be made to pay for that.

Les walked up and stopped in front of him. Duncan straightened and held up his hands without making fists. He did not open them as if to ward off blows, either. He only held them up to show how helpless and unwilling he would be to defend himself. "I won't fight you, young man," he said.

"That's all right, you can still pay. It's time you paid, Mr. Vincent."

Duncan turned his head away and Les slapped him so hard his nose burst open like a melon. Les slapped him against a wall and then kept him standing by slapping him from side to side. By not striking with his fist, he kept Duncan standing and in range. He slapped him with all the strength and meanness of his ability as a fighter, and he exercised all the vengeance in his spirit, unmercifully.

Les did not think he could kill the man by slapping him. Duncan's neck bone was husky enough. But the punishment Les inflicted with a half dozen slaps instantly delivered made John Porter pale. John stepped in to stop his cousin from killing the man and Les laid him on the floor with a hook to the belly. Les returned to his business and whacked his palms against Duncan's face like two green two-by-sixes. Duncan's flogged snout snuffed air and blood like an animal's. His ears and cheeks swelled with hot blood. His jaws and neck bone were heard to crack. The first slap had sloshed open his mouth. Subsequent smackings did not allow it to close or even gap open normally. It only hung open with its slobbers pouring.

"Les!" His brothers stepped in front of him. He stepped back and stopped hitting. Mark embraced Duncan like a referee would cover a beaten boxer to protect him from further punishment. Ben stood his ground in front of Les.

Royal still lay in a swoon. Duncan began to weep in a loud, heartbroken voice. His punishment had been almost as swift as the guillotine and he was relatively unharmed, yet from the sound of him anyone would have thought he had lost his father and mother, the love of his life, all his money, and his life.

The look Les gave Lorrie said, "I agree with you. My nature will always stand between us." He turned away and wept with no expression and no sound. He wept for what he had become, for finding out what he was, but he was relieved that he had given the man what he deserved without killing him. Everybody else in the room was sure that Les had tried to kill Duncan Vincent. They believed, if Ben and Mark had not been there, Les would not have stopped until Duncan Vincent's head came off.

Not one man remained, whether he be a Cowden or a VO, who entertained a desire to continue the war. Randolph did not make a sound when A.B. arrested him for the assault on Joe Coyle. A.B. ordered Ben and Mark to manacle him to Jonas Von for good measure. Von also submitted meekly, even though he was not even being charged with a specific crime.

The war seemed to be over and all the townsmen and VO split away from the crowd and headed home by themselves. Nobody wanted to fight anymore. Nobody even went into the saloons to talk about it. Les and the Porters went out on patrol and found a half dozen armed VO spaced along the street, but none who did not turn and hurry away out

220

of sight as fast as he could when they saw Les coming. Duncan and Royal and their cohorts were locked in the Harshaw jail and the Porters took over the guard.

The rest of the Porters escorted all the Cowdens to the Farleys'. A few said good night and rode home in the dark to tend to their livestock. Pallets of bedding were spread on the floor for the youngsters. The ladies went to the bedrooms to sleep. The men found blankets and laid down to sleep on the floor without conversation.

At dawn, Porters, Cowdens, and Farleys were sprawled in every corner, soft spot, and level surface inside the Farley house. Nobody slept after dawn. The smallest children were fed and turned out of the house first. The men took care of the livestock and prepared for their ride home, then went in to breakfast.

Les ate without a word, excused himself, and went out to the patio to smoke his pipe. Later in the day, he and his brothers would transport the VO to the Patagonia jail and then to Tucson for arraignment.

Les had not left the table because he wanted to be comfortable somewhere else. The family always had a lot of fun when it met for breakfast in these numbers. Family news, reminiscence, and gossip brought on a lot of laughter. Les would rather have stayed, but he was sure no one would have any fun if he did.

No one spoke to him, but that was not because they did not love him. His family might have considered him as bad and mean as Attila the Hun, but they still wanted him alive and well. Lorrie was the one who would have liked to see him pulled apart by wild horses. As far as she was concerned, Les would have been a lot better off if he'd turned away and left Teddy to die a slow death on the arrow.

His family just did not seem able to get over the way he'd manhandled Duncan. As far as his family was concerned, he also might have been ahead if he'd used his fists and beaten Duncan to death. His family would have rallied to him and given him a world of attention if he faced prison or the gallows.

As it was, he'd shocked everybody by the systematic way he unstitched and unraveled Duncan Vincent. His family had been fooled by the helpless way Vincent acted before Les started punishing him. Their memories were short. Duncan was guilty of worse sins against the Cowdens and Porters than slapping their faces.

Well, at least he wasn't in jail. Maybe he could find a way that day to lose his life. Maybe it would be possible for him to just perish. He guessed he couldn't do it on purpose, though, because he did not want to leave another mess for his family to clean up. That kind of mess would only make his family madder.

Paula Mary and Casi were out early playing with Myrtle Farley. Myrtle showed Paula Mary new projects that kept her busy those days. Casi followed them around with a death grip on a ruined little doll Myrtle gave her.

The family was leaving Les alone because it knew he healed quickly that way. He in no way should have felt unloved. His people figured he could not participate in normal family life while he limped so badly. Everybody moved around him more or less as though he was an old post that had long been a family fixture that was used to club enemies. Paula Mary even leaned up against him when she needed to button her shoes to quicken the pace of her play.

Les watched his little sister course in ever-widening circles as she searched for the project that would keep her most entertained.

The head of Harshaw Creek ran by the Farleys' house and the winter rains had livened it. The three girls romped along its banks. Lorrie's house was across the creek and on the other side of an oak and willow thicket. Les could see spots of its plastered adobe sides and shake roof. Lorrie had come there to keep house for Hoozy and Whitey when they first started working in the Harshaw mine. She'd rented the house at first, then started paying on it, and now owned it. She could take care of herself. Smoke was already coming out of her chimney.

The smell of mesquite smoke from Harshaw's morning cooking and warming fires filled the canyon. Paula Mary, Myrtle, and Casi lined out through the thicket toward Lorrie's.

Casimiro came in sight around the corner of the house. He watched Casi follow Paula Mary and Myrtle through the thicket. The girls' footing was soft and spongy and the ground was littered with deadfall. Every once in a while Paula Mary stopped to make sure Casi kept up. Casi would not have had much trouble with that, but she was hampered by the tight hug she kept on her doll.

Casimiro moved over to stand by Les. His blanket was spread over his shoulders and he was smoking tobacco rolled in cornleaf. He said, *"Buenos dias,"* and sat down.

Betty brought Les and Casimiro coffee with hot milk and sugar. Les was Mexican about his coffee. He liked it bleached with hot, rich milk and sweetened with three and a half spoonfuls of sugar.

Betty's bringing coffee and the way she looked at him and patted him on the shoulder made Les appreciate how good she was about being a sister. Paula Mary's leaning on him to button her shoe had warmed his heart at a time when he would have been satisfied for the sun to come up and do it.

Casi went out of sight in the thicket with Paula Mary and Myrtle and Les knew Casimiro would feel better if he could keep her in sight. Les felt the same way. Predators were still rampant in the country and would not stop preying just because Les and Casimiro wanted to have coffee. Any morning early was a good time for them. Les and Casimiro did not speak about their worry, but they swallowed the coffee quickly and headed toward Lorrie's house.

They went straight through the oak thicket, even though the best way to go was on a wide trail that skirted it. Casimiro went that way because he was used to staying on tracks. Les went that way because he did not want Lorrie to see him coming. Les hoped Lorrie's blood had cooled. He wanted to talk to her with nobody else around.

He knew he was probably only a big blight on her life and she would not want to see him, but he could not sit and mope about her when he knew she was home. Her chimney smoke told him her folks had gone home without her and she was trying to make it alone again.

The children were in the woodyard watching Lorrie split a chunk of oak with a maul and wedges. Les offered to take over the chore and she relinquished the maul and took the children inside the house. He was happy to see she'd cooled enough to have that much to do with him, anyway.

He was glad to use his hands and muscles at useful work. He warmed to the job and made the fireplace and stove-size chunks tumble away from his blows. Casimiro carried the wood into the house by the armload and later began stacking it against the wall outside under the eaves.

After a while Lorrie, Myrtle, and Paula Mary came out the front door without Casi. The woodpile was on the side of the house by the trail. The back door was inside an L, out of sight of the woodpile. The back door faced the thicket.

Casimiro straightened from stacking wood against the house, "And Casi?" he asked Paula Mary in Spanish.

"She's playing with her doll by the fire," Paula Mary said. "Her feet are cold."

Casimiro smiled and looked uncertainly at a window.

"Don't worry, *Tio*, Uncle. She and her baby doll are staying warm by the fire with hot *café con leche.*"

"*Ah, gracias.*"

Paula Mary noticed a slingshot wrapped around Casimiro's waist and asked him to show her how to use it. He walked away to the front of the house and began an effortless lofting of rocks over the trees along the creek. When the girls began to try it, he squatted against the front porch, built himself a smoke with his homegrown *macuzi* and cornleaf, and watched them.

Lorrie sat on the porch to watch. Les figured he had split enough wood. He sure did not want to spend the whole morning playing work ox for Lorrie. He laid the maul down and went to the porch.

He sat on the bench beside her, but she would not look at him. The girls were fifty yards away and Casimiro could not understand English, so Les said, "Is there anything I can do to patch up our marriage, such as it is?"

Lorrie acted as though she had not expected him to speak to her. "You're asking me?"

"You're the one I'm supposed to be married to, aren't you?"

Lorrie laughed. "You've never been real sure of that, have you?"

"No, but I was getting a little bit sure."

"That must have been nice."

"Well, weren't you?"

"Never. I don't know how I ever got the notion to marry you. I tried to make it work by joining the women in your family. I don't think you and I could ever be close, not as friends and not as lovers."

"Well, that sure ain't true, we got plenty close as lovers. I know how you feel, though. I'm sorry about everything that's happened. It's a wonder you'll even talk to me."

"I've cooled off. Wash and Elk came by and told me Creswell admitted that Teddy asked you to shoot him."

"I tried to tell you the same thing, but you wouldn't believe me."

"Oh, I believed you. You and your brothers killed three of my brothers, and that's a fact. It's hard for me to live with that. I still don't know what to do about it. You should be able to understand that living with you as your wife has to be last on the list of what I might do. If I stayed with you, I might end up shooting you in the head like you did Teddy. I've always had a spark for you, even when Ben and I were making people think we liked each other. I was even beginning to love you and was starting to believe you might not be to blame for my troubles. Then you killed the boy I loved most in the world. When you told me you shot Teddy, I don't know, you just killed my love for you, too."

"I guess I should have let Teddy die in agony."

Lorrie began to cry. "My three dead brothers were the only friends I ever had before your mother and sisters. Now I don't have any at all, thanks to you."

"Aw, Lorrie, you're so wrong. I didn't kill your brothers. The Apaches killed all three of them."

Lorrie controlled her weeping. "I hate you as much for ending my friendship with your mother and sisters as I do your killing my brothers. When I came to know your mama, I found out what it was like to do right, and I liked it."

"My mama thinks it's right for you to come back to us."

"I don't know if trying to make a life with you is right. You don't seem able to do right unless you've got your family to tell you what to do. You and I are alike that way. I've never in my life felt like behaving so much as I did when I lived with your folks. I shudder to think what would have happened if you and I had gone off as husband and wife by ourselves."

"We could make it because we're alike and we both know how to try. I can handle you and you can handle me. You know what would have been bad? It would have been bad if you'd captured Ben like you did me. You'd have made his life a hell, because he would never understand the way you work. I do. That's the reason we got married the way we did."

"I couldn't have made it with Ben and he's a good man. You're as much a man as Ben, but not good. That's why I wanted you as my man. If I'd made your life a hell, you'd have deserved it and given me hell right back without batting an eye. That's also another reason I don't think we can make it. Les, we're both so mean, we'd probably end up killing each other."

"Aw, Lorrie, just because you think that could happen is no reason to quit. People can try to do right, if they want to."

A chair fell in the house. Lorrie stood up. "I mean it, Les. I think we've lost our chance to stay married. Wait a minute, I want to see how the little one is doing. She's been awful quiet in there."

The sun was shining into the porch. Les leaned back and relaxed. At least Lorrie talked to him. They'd never even talked before.

Someone gave out a surprised murmur inside the house. Les stood up and stretched his sore carcass and opened the front door. A scream chilled him with fear for Lorrie.

He slammed into the front room and saw someone carry a kicking and growling Lorrie toward the back door. Lorrie was holding onto an Apache's hair and ears with both hands and riding his shoulders. The Apache was trying to get away and her weight boosted the speed of his momentum so that he fell, stumbling top-heavy down the corridor, and rammed through the back door. Lorrie kicked and clawed and yowled on his head and gave the Apache the Lorrie treatment.

They fell off the back door landing and down a flight of steep stairs. Les ran after them and saw them land on their heads on frozen, shady ground. Lorrie's pretty bare legs flashed in a somersault, but she did not turn loose of the Indian and she got her bearings sooner than he and caught another solid purchase on his head.

The Indian grunted, mumbled, and hissed Apache words to himself as he floundered to get away. He looked up at Les for aid. He was Chato. A long, wide-bladed, murder knife showed in his hand. Lorrie saw it and turned loose all holds and tried to roll free. Les took a running dive off the landing and drove the top of his head into Chato's jaw.

The side of Chato's head made a groove in the icy ground. Les lifted himself off the ground one limb at a time as he found them able to function. Chato was unconscious, his eyes glazed, his head lying awry on his shoulders.

Les helped Lorrie to her feet. She kept her head down and he bent to see her face. Her lips, nose, and the outer corner of an eye were cut and bleeding. "You're a brave baby," he said.

Lorrie only shook her head, pushed him softly and turned away. Then she screamed again. Chato was three strides away running for the corner of the house. Lorrie pulled a little revolver out of her pocket and tried to shoot him.

Chato sprinted around the corner out of sight. He was fast and quick and ran like a mountain lion. Lorrie ducked her head and started running. She must have thought she would have a much better chance of outrunning him than she ever would of overtaking him with a bullet. Les rounded the corner after them and saw Chato sprinting across the front yard.

Lorrie saw he had gained too much ground to ever be caught, stopped, and commenced firing. Every time her pistol went off, Chato glided closer to cover. He was about to gain the trees on the creek. Nobody would ever overtake him now, and Lorrie had proven time and again that she was the poorest shot in Arizona Territory. Les was unarmed. He pulled up. Lorrie stopped, took dead aim, and sent her last shot into the ground at poor old Casimiro's feet and startled him into a fearful dance.

Chato must have counted the shots, for he straightened and began to coast. He did not need to look back, for he knew he'd made his escape. Then Casimiro's *honda*, slingshot, whipped and popped over his head and a round creek rock the size of a doorknob conked off the side of Chato's head and knocked his eyes in the dirt.

Les and Casimiro tied him hand and foot and dragged him back to the front porch. Lorrie quickly examined Casi and saw that she was unhurt, for Chato had snatched her up to steal her again and Lorrie had caught him and wrenched her free. A quarter of an hour passed before Chato's dirty eyes were able to see again.

Twenty-seven

LIEUTENANT BUCK was waiting in Patagonia to take charge of Chato. A.B. unchained him from the Farleys' corral post, loaded him on the front seat of the spring wagon, and drove to the jail. The Cowden brothers, sporting their deputy's badges on their jackets, escorted him on their saddle horses. A.B. tossed Ben the key and he unlocked the jail's iron door and Les and Mark ushered the Vincent brothers, Von, and Randolph into the daylight.

Duncan directed the basest verbal abuse at the Cowdens. His night in the Harshaw jail had taken away all his poise and most of his reason. For his night of disgrace and dishonor, he blamed the Cowden women, the worthlessness and disloyalty of the Pima County Live Stock Association rangers, and the meanness and unfairness of A. B. Cowden. He warned the Cowdens that he would soon arrange to be set free and then his retaliation would take such a vicious new form, the meanness of the Cowdens would seem to be as only the cooings of doves.

Royal's trousers fly was unbuttoned. His military tunic was soiled and the buttons were fastened in the wrong holes. His hair was tangled and his chin trembled when he tried to talk. Instead of realizing his dream of becoming a great Indian fighter, he was to be tried for murder and mayhem against his neighbors. He was careful to do as he was told and listened to the brothers' quiet instructions for loading in the wagon and even helped them chain him down.

Von and Randolph were cooperative and matter-of-fact about being loaded and chained. Their pay would be the same whether they were taking a wagon and train ride to jail, or shooting an able young man in the knees.

When he saw his enemies again in the light of the new day, Les wanted to punish and humiliate them some more. For Joe Coyle's sake, he would have liked to make Von and Randolph trot "the shuffle" in their leg irons on a tight leash behind the wagon. Seeing the Vincents and the two henchmen riding flat on their butts in the back of the wagon like ordinary sacks of meal did not give Les the taste of victory he wanted. He would have liked to see their legs hurt so much from the shuffle that they cried for mercy. Joe Coyle had not even been given a chance to ask for mercy.

The Cowden brothers did not believe A.B. would be able to keep the Vincents in jail. Duncan would effect their quick release through his pull with the federal and state governments. He owned the county law. A.B. was able to hold his office as undersheriff only because of his friendship with the governor of the state and his popularity with the people of Harshaw.

A.B. tried to save the VO some humiliation by avoiding Saloon Row on his way out of town but they still looked forlorn. Duncan's mouth did not cease its tirade against the world. At first, because he listened only to the words, Les was angered and wondered why A.B. allowed it, but then he realized that even though the words were insulting Duncan's tone was whiney. Anyone who could not understand what he was saying would have thought he was wailing and whining like an old woman at a wake.

Duncan set up a complaint about having to ride on his tailbone with his legs flat on the wagon bed. He could not stop his feet from bouncing. He said that A.B. should at least allow him to ride beside him on the driver's seat as befitted his equal rank as a community leader.

Chato was in that seat. A.B. preferred to ride beside a bloody-handed murderer than his counterpart in the war. He told Duncan he respected him less than Chato. Chato deserved more consideration as a prisoner because he was a murderer by nature and disposition. Duncan ordered all his killing done for him and never dirtied his own hands, not even to defend himself.

Chato was quiet and placid in his chains. Mean as he was, anyone would have thought he should have been caged, but A.B. sat him in the place of honor and did not worry about him. Chato knew enough about the Cowdens to be absolutely sure, if he made a false move, he would be shot dead. A.B. Cowden did not feel an obligation to deliver him to Lieutenant Buck alive and Chato knew it.

Randolph rode with his legs trailing over the tail of the wagon and stared out from under his hat brim at Les. He and Von had not made a sound, because Duncan Vincent's mouth never stopped. Les was aware of Randolph's stare, but did not mind it much. The stare seemed normal for a man on his way to jail. Finally, happily, he stared back.

Randolph folded his arms and said, "Why are you in such a good mood, Cowden?"

Les only looked at him and smiled.

"You ought to do something about your attitude. You're awful high and mighty for a town drunk," Randolph said.

Les raised a forefinger to his lips and said, "Shhh."

Randolph feigned surprise, looked over his shoulder at A.B., then back at Les, his eyes round. "Why? Am I mistaken? Tell me, where's your bottle hid today?"

Les smiled and raised his finger to his lips again.

"I hope you don't think you're rid of me, Cowden. Mr. Vincent'll have us out of jail so fast, we'll probably beat you back to Harshaw. Then I think I'll just come and look you up again and serve that warrant we've been carrying around. After that, I'm going to whip your hide all the way to the Yuma pen."

"Aw, you should have said something yesterday in the hotel. Didn't you have your warrant with you? Hell, I'll tell you what I'll do, have you got it with you? I think I can get A.B. to stop the wagon. I'll unlock your chains myself. I'll even hand you a pistol if you want it that way, and you can try to take custody of my hide."

Randolph's stare darted away from Les's. "Oh, you make a helluva show with old men and prisoners," he said. "I'll wait. I've been chained too long. I'd rather meet you when I'm sound. I want to do a good job on you. I'm not a woman or a dignified old man who would stand still for being slapped."

"I understand. You want to fight me man to man, not like a night-stalking salamander who shoots a man when he answers your knock at the door. When do you think you'll feel like coming out from under your rock to fight, Mr. Salamander?"

"Just as soon as Mr. Vincent gets us out of jail."

Les rode up close to the wagon, smiled, and whispered, "Just you and me, then."

"I can't wait." Randolph laid down on his back on the bumpy wagon bed and pulled his hat over his eyes.

Les wished he was not the Cowden everybody always chose to challenge for open combat, as though he was the one everybody knew liked to sneak around in the dark and attack from the rear. Nobody ever challenged A.B. or his brothers. They were too damned dignified. It was easy for a prisoner to challenge the one with the cauliflower ear. That way the indignity of his chains protected his big mouth.

Dignity did not mean a damned thing to Les. He didn't need it, and he did not respect it in anyone but his own family. Woe to the sonofabitch who tried to do Les or his family wrong, then hide under a cloak of dignity.

Les thought, Lorrie darlin', you're right. I'm not becoming a good man, but I'm learning how to fight a war.

Lieutenant Buck and his troop of soldiers were resting under cottonwoods near the train station in Patagonia. The Porter men that A.B. had deputized were also there. Les saw Patch sitting away by himself with the big bow and its quiver of arrows. A crowd formed at the station and stood by while the Cowdens unloaded their VO prisoners and put them on the railroad car they would ride to Tucson. The train was to leave in an hour. The Cowdens were through with the VO prisoners. Two young Porter deputies would be their guards to Tucson.

Les stayed by the spring wagon and Lieutenant Buck ordered a horse brought for Chato. He was to be taken to Camp Huachuca for a military trial. The troop moved out of the trees toward their mounts. Les unlocked Chato's hobble chain and helped him mount his horse, then helped Sergeant O'Kane connect his feet with the hobble chain under the horse's belly.

For an instant before Chato was joined by the crowd of troopers, he could have made a run for it, but Les took hold of his reins. Chato grinned at Les. Les looked away. He did not like him. The son of a bitch did not have any of the fabled qualities of the noble savage.

From the railroad car, Ben shouted, "No, Patch!" Les turned and saw Patch unleash an arrow toward him. The thing waggled its tail on departure, then lined out and came on with a sound like the drawing of an anxious breath. It struck Chato under the ribs, passed through his abdomen, and sprouted under his other ribs with such force that it lifted him off his seat. He took hold of it and rode it as far as his bound feet allowed him to fall, then hung head down beside his horse and talked to it.

Sergeant O'Kane sighted his pistol at Patch and marched down the street toward him. Les turned Chato's horse loose and blew a raspberry to scare him. The horse took a backward look as blood began to pour. Chato babbled in Apache to explain to himself what had happened. The horse tried to wheel away to escape him, then ran sidling down the hard street toward Sergeant O'Kane with Chato flopping on his side. He was looking at Chato and did not see Sergeant O'Kane. Les shouted a warning, but the horse rammed the Sergeant squarely in the back with his chest and leveled him under his feet.

"*Corre*, Jose! Run!" Les yelled at Patch. Patch only laid down the bow and walked toward him. Ben and Mark ran the horse down and brought him back. Patch drew his knife and cut the string that held the leather pouch on Chato's neck and threw the pouch to Les. "*Para mi hermanita*. For my little sister," he said.

Sergeant O'Kane recovered as though being rolled under the hooves of a panicky horse should not cause pain. He saw Les catch the pouch, but was more concerned about taking the knife from the Indian. Patch handed it, handle first, to the Sergeant. Les pocketed the pouch in his chaps. When Sergeant O'Kane turned to him, Les said, "Did you see the man throw something to me? You didn't, did you?"

"Hell, I don't care if he did," Sergeant O'Kane said.

Chato was long dead. Les and the sergeant unchained his feet and laid him on the ground. His poor, empty innards groaned.

The Cowdens could only stand by and watch while the soldiers put Chato's shackles on Patch. Patch looked into the Cowdens' faces only once and did not look back when he rode away with the troop.

Ben decided he wanted to drink beer while they waited for the train to leave with the VO, so the Cowdens led their horses over to Los Parados, a place that sold beer and mescal under an open ramada. A.B. did not drink beer, so Les bought a large glass of mescal for him.

A.B. made a face before he even tasted it. "I hate this stuff, but I have a use for its spirits." He drank a swallow, made another face, and handed the glass to Les. Les passed it on to Ben without tasting it.

"Don't you want any, brother?" Ben said.

"No, and I dearly hope I never take another drop as long as I live," Les said.

Ben looked at it, lifted the glass, took a swallow, and carried it a few steps to Mark.

A.B. said, "Well, son, I never thought I'd see you turn down a drink of mescal."

"Aw, it'll always be there. No use trying to dam it up and drink it all every time I see it. I just feel like letting some of it run on by for a change."

"That's good."

"It seems so, but who knows? Everything I do usually goes wrong."

"Ah, not everything. You're a good son."

"I wish you'd tell Lorrie that. She told me I wasn't any good. I always knew I was good for nothing, but I didn't know I wasn't any good at all."

"You're a good boy, Leslie. You have to learn to think before you act, that's all."

"I don't seem to be able to do right, no matter how hard I think."

"Son, I'm only saying you ought to try to stop acting on wild impulse to do what *might* be right. Take life a little slower. Be more patient and take it a step at a time."

"It's probably no use. I lost a wife before I got a chance to be a husband."

"You had a chance, son. You didn't take it. You can still make something of that marriage, if you really want to."

"I don't think so, Papa."

"I wish you'd try. I never thought I'd say this, because I don't approve of her people, but I think Lorrie is the perfect wife for you."

"What could I do, Papa?"

"Woo the child. Take her back and pick her up. When she gets down, she gets way down, but nobody's ever been there to help her up. Let her know she's soft on your heart. Let her forget her toughness. She'll give in. I know she will."

"I don't know how to woo anybody, Papa. How does a man do that?"

"Ah, you have to find out for yourself. I'll tell you this, it's not much different than winning the confidence of a young horse. Keep your touch, your voice, and your heart gentle and offer yourself as a gift. Put yourself out."

"I don't think she wants me."

"Oh, I think she does, son. Give her a chance to heal a while, then go see her."

Les had long since decided there was no way he could keep from doing that.

A native of Nogales, Arizona, J.P.S. Brown is a fifth-generation cattleman. He was the middleweight and light heavyweight boxing champion at Notre Dame University in 1951 and 1952.

His first novel was *Jim Kane,* published to critical acclaim in 1965; it became the movie *Pocket Money* with Paul Newman and Lee Marvin in 1971. His second novel, *The Outfit,* is considered a Southwestern classic. In 1974, his third novel, *The Forests of the Night* was published, and 1986 saw the publication of *Steeldust.* In 1989, Bantam Books began publishing his original series, the Arizona Saga. He is also the author of *Keep the Devil Waiting* and a previous Double D Western, *The Cinnamon Colt and Other Stories.*

The author and his wife, Patsy, make their home in Tucson, Arizona.